FOR THE CROWN

MELISSA MITCHELL

Paperback ISBN: 978-0-578-67956-3
Hardcover ISBN: 978-0-578-67956-3
Ebook ASIN: B087NVFTG9

Dragonfire Sea
Port Ice
Shadowkeep
Vestur
The Vestur Gate
Valla Fort
Eagle Lake
Mistport
Redport
Stormy Bay
Fort Squall
Squall's End
The Eigaden Gate
Esterp
Swinston
Weldon
Lormont
Osbourne
The Flat River
Eigaden
The Scattered Islands
Fort Kastali
Kastali Dun
Bay of Bandu
Graymont
Landor
Clayton
White Sholes
Irelia Island

alderland
Ice Mines
Belnesse
Landow
The Kengr Gate
Kengr Hills
Kengr
The Marble Dragon
Fort Edge
Northedge
Pavv
The Gable Forest
Kaljah
The Gable Mountains
Austar
The Austar Gate
Brushbridge
Thornwater
Fort Lin
Lincastle
Beachrest
South Seas

PROLOGUE

KATHERINE GASPED. It was a rattling breath, one that burned hot and cold all at once. "It's coming," she hissed. "The baby is coming." Stabbing pains radiated through her, burning her from the inside out. Her contractions intensified.

"Deep breaths, my lady. In then out. There now." The words were spoken calmly, with encouragement.

Katherine tried to follow orders, squeezing tightly to the hand that held hers. Around her, the darkness was alight with glowing dragon eyes. There were thirty-two of the creatures in the cavern, all humming with excitement. Their voices were penetrating, reverberating throughout her body, but they did nothing to calm her rising fear. Something was wrong.

The Sprite midwife began to sing, weaving her magic through the air. A contraction wracked her body. She pushed —hard. Each time she pushed, she cried out, growing weaker, pained, more desperate. She was hurting.

"This Rider is losing too much blood," the Sprite said

aloud to the dragons. It did not matter. As long as the child was safe. In the end, she would die no matter what.

"*Please,*" Katherine hissed. She begged Asjaa, the Mother. "Please let my baby live."

At first, she could be sure of nothing. Then she felt a kick, and another contraction, and this one felt different than the others. More productive. The Mother had listened. Somehow Katherine knew one thing with certainty: Her child would be strong, a leader, like its father.

The baby freed itself from her body, followed moments later by a shrieking wail. "It is a boy, my lady! A boy! A healthy son!" The Sprite's relief rang in her voice.

"Call him Tristan," Katherine begged, "after my father."

A dragon trumpeted in refusal. Its bugle was too loud for an enclosed space like this and threatened to crumble the rock around them. Then a telepathic thought filled her mind. *"We agreed, my lady. If this child is to be raised by our clan then he will bear a dragon's name. A proper name. And that name will bind him to his deeds…forever."*

She wanted to protest. Dragon magic was different. She hated the idea of imposing a future on a son who was only minutes old. Yet, she could not fight this because she had agreed. "What shall he be called?" she breathed, taking the screaming child into her arms, loving it as only a mother could, even if her time was fleeting.

Her gaze was already dimming, but she could see that he was beautiful, with a tiny tuft of pearlescent white hair. "How unique!" she whispered, caressing it. The pale wisps were soft against her calloused skin. "Please be like your father," she begged, hoping the gods would hear her prayer, for he would never know his father. As her vision faded, she could feel the years of her life, her exhaustion, her sorrow, slamming against her like heavy blows. Death was close.

"We will name him Gallant, my lady." The dragon's voice was tender, soft, easing her into the world beyond this one. *"For your son will be our hope."*

"Gallant," she whispered. It was a good name. An honorable name. Her eyes closed, her breathing stilled. She met Daudagher, the god of death, with open arms.

CHAPTER 1
GUESTS IN THE KEEP

THE CUPBOARDS of Princess Lena's mind were filled with mischief, the drawers with wisdom, and the exposed shelves, composure. Beneath everything was the ever-constant reminder that she simply wasn't good enough. How could she be? Being born a female automatically disqualified her from gaining the throne on her own. Yet it was this disadvantage that made her different, unique, quite unlike those who had come before her.

It wasn't because she enjoyed playing nasty tricks on the patrons at court, like leaving frogs in Lady Hoffman's vanity, or letting goats into Lord Norton's chambers to chew up all his books. They deserved it, after all. Nor was it because she had a knack for sorting out her father's political problems when he needed a creative mind. Hers could conjure up the most elaborate solutions—fixes he'd never considered. They always seemed so obvious once they were out.

No, Princess Lena was unusual because she was the *first* Princess of Dragonwall to reach the age of seventeen. Moreover, she was only the second princess that Dragonwall had ever seen. That made her special. She wouldn't have agreed. Being a princess left her disqualified from the crown unless she could find her male counterpart. That alone was enough to make anyone feel inadequate. Thus, she considered her title of princess awfully close to a curse.

Today that curse had come to fruition. In the lowest courtyard of the Great Keep of Kastali Dun were a number of guests, all waiting for her. These weren't simply *any* guests. These were hopefuls who desired to become Dragonwall's next king. Making them feel welcome was the last thing Princess Lena wanted, so she decided to give them a welcome they would never forget.

She raced through the keep, carrying out her most mischievous plan yet, but she was not unhindered. "Lena!" A breathless shout came from behind her—from her handmaidens. They were chasing after her, begging her to stop. Instead, she ran faster. Her heart hammered in her chest, spurred on by the excitement. Passersby laughed. They were used to her silly antics. "Oh, that's just Princess Lena," they said, "up to more of her tricks."

"Lena, come back here!" Voices continued to echo down the stone corridor. Snickering at their discomfort, she threw herself down another set of stairs, trailing her fingers along the smooth rock wall of the stairwell. "Please Lena! You are already late!"

"Then I must hurry," she cried over her shoulder. She burst into another corridor. The south wing of the castle led into a courtyard with a fountain at its center. She doubled over to catch her breath, placing her hands on her knees. What fun she was having! Too much fun.

The irritated cries of her kenna closed in. Kenna Margaret was too old for this exertion, but that did not deter the woman. "Princess Lena! I insist you cease this at once!" Margaret came to a stop beside her.

"Stop what, Kenna Margaret?" She turned to face her tutor. "As you said, I am already late."

"All...the more reason...to go and...get *dressed*," said Margaret. She took hold of Lena's arm, attempting to pull her away.

Lena pulled her arm free, smiling sweetly. "Oh, Kenna. You are being too serious, just like Mother. See here? I am already clothed."

Kenna Margaret's eyes bulged. "Princess Lena! You cannot greet your guests in *that*! The queen will find out."

"So much the better." Lena stood erect, her shoulders squared. Her three handmaidens caught up. They were breathing harder than Kenna Margaret, with red faces.

"You take this rebellion too far, Princess." Kenna Margaret also squared her shoulders, placing her hands on her hips as she scowled. "Think! Think about what you are doing. You will embarrass us all."

"My dear Kenna. You let me worry about that. In the meantime, I intend to go the rest of this alone. The four of you must wait in my apartment."

Kenna Margaret sighed. "Very well, child. If you wish to dig your own grave. Come along, ladies. You heard the princess." Margaret shooed the others. Then she afforded Lena a final, appraising look before shaking her head. Just as she turned to leave, the corners of her lips twisted into a smile. Her kenna wasn't so bad. The woman was a great lover of fun after all, else Lena would not have put up with her for so long. And despite her growing age, they were good friends, even if Margaret was a bit old-fashioned.

She waited for her kenna to disappear before making her way

through the remaining levels of the keep. All the while, she wore a sly grin on her face. Margaret had every right to be upset with her attire. Each tattered garment was purloined from one man or another—soldiers mostly. It was an immense struggle finding things to fit her slight figure, but a great deal of fun stealing them.

Beige leggings with knee-high leather boots adorned her legs. A red tunic with a black padded doublet covered her chest and arms. A sashed belt wrapped tightly around her waist. And leather bracers were strapped to her forearms, even though she'd never fired a bow. The only thing she was missing were weapons. If only she could have succeeded in stealing a sword, or a bow and set of arrows, or even a knife for her belt. Then she would have truly looked the part.

Her hair was fierce too. It was braided in tight rows along her scalp from her hairline to her crown. The braids were pinned to avoid unraveling, while allowing the remainder of her long brown hair to fan out behind her like a barbarian pirate. How magnificently ridiculous she looked! Princesses were not supposed to dress like peasant mercenaries. Her mother was going to have an absolute fit.

She passed a planter box and stopped short. Ignoring the roses, she looked at the dirt and smiled. Yes, this would do nicely. Bending over, she scooped up a small handful and rubbed it on both hands, savoring the gritty texture. She smeared a bit upon her cheeks and forehead before generously wiping the rest upon her tunic. Then she descended to the final level of the keep and came to a stop in a shadowy corridor just beyond the entrance courtyard.

The Great Keep of Kastali Dun was at the heart of Dragonwall's capital. It was built upon a rocky outcropping that loomed over everything. Its many corridors and courtyards overlooked the Bay of Bandu to the south-east, with its mighty ports and dockyards. And to the west, the setting sun often lit the waters of the Dragonfire Sea aflame with light, offering spectacular views. To the north, the sprawling city of Kastali Dun stretched outward, housing tens of thousands of Dragonwall's inhabitants.

The hopefuls in the entry courtyard stood before the portcullis where they had been advised to wait. They had been told that the Princess of Dragonwall was supposed to welcome them, and Lena had assured her parents that she could handle the responsibility. Her grin widened. She had never promised her parents that she would handle it *well*.

She surveyed her guests from her hiding place. They shifted from foot to foot while they waited, clearly affronted by her lateness. These men were taller than human men ought to be, with strong muscular builds and perfectly shaped faces. By all accounts, they were far too handsome for their own good. This was because these men were not simply men. They were *Drengr*—dragons blessed with humanity— and each of them had come with high hopes.

She marched out into the open. "Greetings, gentlemen!" Her voice rang out, amplified by the towering walls surrounding the courtyard. She placed herself before them, hands on her hips. The group regarded her, observing her attire with looks of confusion. A few expressions twisted into distaste. Who was this untidy woman in men's clothing? What right did she have to address them?

She smirked at their reactions. "Thank you all for coming," she said. "I regret to inform you there has been a change in plans. Your services are no longer needed." She paused, watching as scowls deepened. "You may turn around and go home now."

One of the Drengr hopefuls boldly stepped forward. His eyebrows were tightly drawn together. "Excuse me, *miss,* but who are you to command us? We have traveled across an entire kingdom at the bidding of our monarchs. You have no such authority to turn us away."

"Yes, unfortunate," said Lena, "but I assure you I do have the authority."

A second Drengr stepped forward. "Well, *we* were assured a full fortnight of rest before the ceremony." He had green eyes and loosely cut dark hair, which he swept into a side part. Frustration and disdain appeared to manifest beneath his handsome features, twisting together like black shadows.

"Were you really? Two weeks?" She shook her head, as if feeling sorry for them.

This frustrated the second man even more, and he took a step forward to sneer at her. "Who do you think you are, girl?"

"Oh!" A thrill shot through her. "Do forgive me. I almost forgot to introduce myself. My name is Pr—"

"*Leeeeeenaaaaa!*" A horrifying screech silenced her. She flinched.

From the corridor behind her, her mother's feet could be heard padding against the flagstones, silken skirts rustling about her ankles. "Lena! What are you…?! What in the name of every god—" Her mother's voice echoed through the corridor behind them.

"Oops." Her smile turned into a grimace. "*That,* gentlemen, is my queen mother." They muttered and glanced between them. "Well. That's my cue. I must be going! It was an absolute pleasure, meeting you." She gave them a final, victorious smile then took off like a cat, sprinting away just as the queen came to a halt before their guests. The moment she reached the neighboring corridor, she stopped and clung to it, bursting into hysterical laughter. She had to lean against the wall to breathe. Oh, their faces! Nothing in the world was worth more than their astonishment. She didn't care that they could hear her roars.

What would her mother make of that, eh? She stopped to listen. The queen's profuse apologies drifted to her ears. Queen Amara was doing her best to diffuse the situation by explaining away Lena's love of practical jokes. And then her mother offered to show them to their accommodations. When Lena next glanced out, she saw Queen Amara leading the band of Drengr away.

Her heart leapt in her chest. She needed time to get back to her apartment, and quickly. She took off at a sprint. The sound of her boots against the flagstones followed her.

Several minutes later, she all but tumbled into her apartment's entry chamber. She slammed the door behind her and rushed into the main room. "Quick!" she gasped, looking at her handmaidens. They glanced at each other, uncertain. "Help me with these!"

Avra, Cora, and Theresa rushed forward at last, helping her with the ties of her bracers so that she could slide them off. Kenna Margaret watched on with an amused grin. It was a flurry of orders and activity. "Cora, my gown! Avra, my chemise. Theresa—"

Theresa rushed forward with a wet cloth to clean her face and hands. It was still warm from the pool in her bathing chamber. She exhaled as the last bits of dirt were wiped away.

"Are you going to tell us what happened, Princess?" Kenna Margaret stepped forward, pausing to examine her.

"Not now, Kenna. We must hurry!" It was a struggle to keep the laughter from her voice. She couldn't stop picturing the Drengr's shocked expressions when they realized that the crazy woman before them was the princess they were hoping to discover a bond with.

A trail of what she had been wearing littered the floor

from the entryway to the vanity where Avra threw a chemise over her head. That was followed by Cora with the gown she was supposed to have worn, which had been made for the occasion. It was a deep, royal blue silk brocade. Royal blue was reserved exclusively for the royal family, by pain of death. This gown in particular had been made as a statement piece. Silver embroidery adorned its hem and trimmings. On the left side of her chest was the Drengr monarchy's sigil: a dragon's head. All who served the royal family proudly displayed it.

When she was dressed, Theresa rushed to do her hair, tearing at the braids on her head. Lena winced and closed her eyes against the tears, hating her sensitive scalp. Kenna Margaret stepped closer. "There now, you are looking much better, Princess. Much more as you ought. Now, are you going to tell us what happened, or will we have to guess? What has you in such a frantic state?"

"Oh Kenna!" she snapped, opening her eyes and turning to her. "Just come help with these braids. We haven't a moment to spare. But I can assure you, I gave those Drengr hopefuls quite a surprise." Just thinking about it made her smile again.

Lena's hair frizzed up to twice its usual size once free of the braids. Theresa rapidly replaced the small braids with four large ones, which she then skillfully weaved into a bun.

Shrieks sounded down the corridor, making them all jump. Someone was calling her name. "*Leeenaaaa!*" The noise came closer.

"Oh, Gods! Mother's coming. Hurry!" Lena gasped. Theresa placed the last pin in her hair and Lena nodded, turning to her handmaidens and Kenna Margaret. "You must hide. Quickly. Pretend you are not here."

"Truly, Princess Lena?" Her order was met with knitted

eyebrows and wide eyes. "Pretend...pretend we are not here?"

"Yes, truly! Go, go, go," she said. "Into the bathing room. Do not let my mother see you. Oh, this is great fun, isn't it?!" She laughed darkly, looking at her pristine appearance in the mirror. This was Princess Lena as everyone *wanted* her to be, as she was expected to be. She stepped away from her vanity, bracing herself for what was to come.

Kenna Margaret whispered in the background, ushering her handmaidens away to her bathing chamber. The paneled door clicked shut behind Margaret just as the door to Lena's apartment burst open. In strode Queen Amara, radiating frustration and disbelief. The queen's patience had come to an end.

CHAPTER 2
ACCEPTING THE HOPEFULS

Queen Amara swept into Lena's room and bade her to sit before pulling up an additional chair beside Lena's vanity. Her round face was stony as her honey-colored eyes roved over Lena's blue gown, finished hair, and clean face. When she next spoke, she kept her voice calm and controlled, honed from years of practice. "That was a very irresponsible thing you just did, Lena. You have not behaved the way a princess ought to behave."

Lena crossed her arms. "I'm not sure what you're talking about, Mother."

"*Do not play dumb with me,* young lady." Amara's eyes narrowed and her voice lost a measure of its control. "Your games have gone *too* far. Do you think this is a joke?"

"I'll tell you a joke, Mother, a wonderful joke." Lena's face flushed. "That I cannot rule because I am a woman—that I cannot step into my birthright because of my sex? That is a joke. The funniest joke in all the world."

Amara's chest deflated. The queen had a slight build, similar to her daughter's. "We've been through this *so many* times. What you say is not true. Your father and I are not withholding your right to rule."

"Then why can't I become queen on my own?" Lena sat up straighter.

"You know the answer, but still you ask." Amara shook her head. The deep blue gems in her hairnet glittered as they caught the light. "You are a human, Lena. *Human.*"

"You mean, I'm not good enough," said Lena. No matter how many times her parents told her that, no matter how many times they made it painfully clear, hearing it never got any easier. Dragonwall was meant to be ruled by the Drengr, with the crown passing from father to son. Lena had broken the line, but even then, there was still a chance for it to continue. That's why the Drengr hopefuls were here.

"Lena, you're intelligent, strong, clever..." Her heart constricted upon hearing her mother's praise, rarely given. "Even if you are a little *too* stubborn. You can still be queen. You can still rule."

"Only with a mate, Mother. Only with a Drengr king as my figurehead." The nails of her fingers were biting into her skin, but she kept her fists clenched and her arms crossed.

"All the more reason to take this ceremony seriously," said Amara. "Frightening away your guests is *not* a good start."

"Ugh!" Lena threw up her hands, slumping back in her chair. "I don't *want* a mate, Mother! Perhaps someday, when I'm ready, but not now. It is unfair—you know it is. You know that if I were a male, this ceremony business wouldn't be required."

"If you were a male, Lena, you'd fledge into a dragon. If you were a male, you'd have hundreds of years to live. But you're not and you don't. Your eighteenth name day is right around the corner. You understand what is at stake here. Why must you be so difficult?!" Amara sighed in an attempt to regain her composure. Little lines had appeared around her eyebrows where they were drawn together. "You know the words as well as I. In the rare event that a female is born unto the Drengr monarchy, she has until her—"

"Eighteenth name day to find a mate, else she must give up her right to rule. I know what the Charter says, Mother." She had read it over and over, trying to find a loophole. Late nights spent with a candle in hand, haunting the library, poring over the document in hopes of finding a way out. None existed.

"Then why must you fight your father and I? We did not make the rules." Amara leaned back in her chair, finally abandoning her good posture. These arguments of theirs had become increasingly frequent.

"I'm fighting you, Mother, because it is absolutely ridiculous—absolutely unfair."

"Be that as it may, it is tradition, and you will abide by it."

"How can this be tradition if it has never happened before?" She already knew her mother's answer. She could have ended the argument here, but instead she pushed. "In six thousand years, I am the *first* female born unto the royal family. The *first*! How can it be tradition, if it has *never* been done before?"

"Princess Irelia was the first, Lena. We all know that."

"Yes, sure, but she died before she reached seventeen."

Red blotches of frustration appeared on Amara's face. "Yes, Irelia died. That changes nothing. Just because you dislike the rules does not mean you can throw them out." Amara placed her hands on the armrests of the chair. "Look, Lena, I thought you would take this seriously. Perhaps I was wrong. You have a choice to face." She hesitated, letting her words sink in. "It is not too late. I can send the Drengr hopefuls home tonight. We can end this here and now. You can give up your right to rule. Is that what you want?"

Lena remained silent. Her mother was offering her a way out. Should she take it? The idea of tying herself to another squeezed the very breath from her chest. It left her feeling trapped. She had her whole life ahead—years and years and years to find someone.

An uglier thought nagged at her. It wasn't the first time she had considered it, either. She frowned, trying to push it away, but couldn't. "Mother, what if there is no Drengr mate for me? What then?" She dreaded failure more than she dreaded being trapped.

"We both know the answer, Lena." This time, her mother's voice was softer. "In the event that no bond exists, the Tournament for the Crown will be scheduled. The winner will become the crowned prince. When your father and I finally pass from this life, that Crowned Prince will become Dragonwall's next king, whether he has a mate or not."

The rules were cruel. "So...you really want me to cooperate in this ceremony thing?"

"Your father and I would appreciate it, yes. You becoming the next queen means keeping our bloodline alive. It would mean a great deal to us if you cooperated."

She considered her lessons, her training in politics, the things her mother and father had taught her. Her whole life had been spent preparing to become the next ruling monarch. She didn't know anything else. At last she sighed, beaten. "The ceremony should continue. I don't have a choice. But... maybe we can make a deal—you, me, and Father?"

"A deal? I do not think you are in a position to bargain." Still, her mother looked relieved.

Lena held up her hand. "Just hear me out, *Mama*." She often used *mama* when she wanted something. "If I agree to cooperate—to participate in this ceremony and behave over the next two weeks—will you and father finally allow me to take archery lessons?" All Riders were taught to use a bow as part of their training regimen. She was not a Rider—not yet, anyway.

"*Archery* lessons?" Her mother placed a hand over her chest. "That is what you are bargaining for?"

"Well—yes. Every time I ask, you say no. You both know how badly I want to learn now, not later. And I promise that I will not let it interfere with my tutoring from Kenna Margaret, nor my afternoons with Father. What does Father think?"

She knew her father was listening to every word of this conversation. Her mother and father were mates—a Drengr and Rider pair. They shared their minds. And like all pairs, they were capable of having only one child. When the great Queen Isabella blessed dragons with humanity, allowing them to take on a human form, she imposed a cruel price upon them. Drengr-Rider pairs always cherished their children more because of this. Perhaps that's why Lena tried to get away with so much.

"Your father has agreed," Amara announced almost instantly. That's how paired minds worked. "If you promise to behave yourself, meaning no more childish tricks, you may begin your training with the bow."

"Yes!" Lena screeched, jumping to her feet. She ran to her mother and locked her arms around Amara's neck, giving her a big hug and a kiss on the forehead. "Thank you, Mama, thank you. I promise I will do my best to behave."

Her mother's smile was slow, but soft. "I know, dear heart." She affectionately nuzzled her nose against Lena's cheek before pushing her away. Then she stood and walked over to Lena's bathing chamber, as if there were an important task to complete. She hesitated just a moment before pulling the door open. Four women toppled out. Lena's hand-maidens must have been leaning against it, listening to the entire conversation. They brought the queen down with them into a pile of billowing gowns. Everyone burst into a fit of hysterical laughter. Oh, to see a queen buried and laughing!

Lena grinned as she watched the spectacle. "I suppose I should have mentioned that they were listening in," she said.

"Oh, I already knew," said Amara, getting to her feet. She brushed herself off and collected her golden crown, which had rolled across the floor. "Now"—she looked around Lena's room—"get rid of all these *rags*. I don't want to see them ever again." She pointed at the leftover clothes upon the floor. Only then did Lena realize she'd forgotten to clean up her mess before her mother's arrival. No wonder she'd been so transparent.

"At once, Mama."

Her mother nodded, satisfied. "And when you finish with that, you are to see your father." She swept from the room leaving Lena to do as she was told.

THE KING'S Tower was located on the south side of the Great Keep, just down the hall from Lena's apartment. She made her way to her father, walking slowly. Along the way, she studied the six paintings that adorned the walls. They were taller than she was, taking up a great span from floor to ceil-ing. It was called the *Hall of Kings,* as if the queens were an afterthought, or no thought at all. Each pair of rulers, begin-ning with King Eymar and Queen Isabella, had their own painting.

She stopped before the one of her parents, admiring the

vivid colors and gilded gold frame. Her queen mother stood proudly beside her father's hulking turquoise dragon form. She was dressed as a Rider and held a beautiful bow in her left hand with a quiver of arrows strapped across her back. They both gazed back at Lena with uncanny likeness. She knew this painting so well that she could picture it in her mind's eye with her eyes closed.

The Hall of Kings was simply another example of unfairness. She snorted and moved farther down, her mood threatening to unravel. A queen could not rule without a Drengr king by her side, but a Drengr king could easily rule alone. No one understood why females born to pairs never fledged. Like many aspects of the Drengr race, it was a question without an answer. Queen Isabella had left the world with many of these mysteries.

Lena placed herself before the tower guards and smiled. Being a tower guard was a prestigious position and these guards took their role very seriously. They saluted her when she appeared. "Good afternoon, Thomas, Renly," she said.

"Princess Lena." They did not uncross their spears. "We heard you gave our new guests quite a show."

"Did you now?" She arched an eyebrow. "Word travels quickly."

"Your mother was furious, I'll bet?" Thomas smirked.

"You can say that." She grinned, knowing they had heard the yelling. "Now, are you going to let me by? I have business with my father."

"Of course, Princess." Their spears uncrossed. Thomas opened the door for her and then closed it once she was through.

The King's Tower was enormous—larger than any house in the city. Its cylindrical shape jutted from the side of the keep's southern wing, overlooking the sea with a spectacular view from all directions. There were multiple levels to the tower, but only a single entrance. This allowed the royal family some privacy.

Lena stood within the tower's entryway, greeting the two male servants that stood like statues in their gold and white livery. The entry led directly into a round, formal sitting area. Behind that was the largest balcony in the keep, large enough to fit a dragon. Today was a nice day, so all the doors were thrown open to allow the sea breeze entry. Along the inner sides of the sitting room were a number of interior doors leading to multiple stairways—some up, some down—that wound around the inner wall of the circular façade. Her father's study was through a door to her left, then down a stairway to the floor below.

She found the king poring over documents, hunched over his mahogany desk, his nose nearly kissing the parchment. His study also had a balcony and the doors were likewise thrown open. Cream-colored curtains rustled softly in the breeze. She greeted her father from behind, leaning around his high-backed chair to plant a kiss on his cheek, then went to stand before the open doors, parting the curtains to gaze out at the Southern Sea. She never tired of the view.

When her father finished with his task, he cleared his throat. "And how did our honored guests react when you presented yourself in that ridiculous costume?"

She giggled and turned to face him. For someone slightly over six hundred years old, he didn't look much older than a mortal fifty.

She and her father shared the same chestnut brown hair and eyes, though his face was more oblong than hers. She had her mother to thank for that. And like all the Drengr, King Cornan was handsome, especially with a crown atop his brow. He set his quill down. "I can only imagine what a fright you must have given them. I'm surprised they aren't already fleeing."

"Oh, Father, I wish you had been there." She failed to keep the laughter from her voice. "I don't think they've ever seen *anything* like me. And when they discovered that I was the princess, they were speechless." Cornan's mouth turned up in a half smile. "I am sorry, though," said Lena. "I suppose I should have taken it more seriously. You entrusted me with a responsibility that I was not ready to confront."

King Cornan leaned forward, folding his hands together. "And are you ready now?"

"Oh *Papa!*" She sighed and plopped into the chair across from him—her favorite chair. "You know how I feel about this. For years you trained me, taught me everything I needed to know about ruling a kingdom, but there was one thing you missed." Her chest crumpled in on itself whenever she thought of it. "You did not prepare me for the realization that I may never become queen."

She had been cheated, and no one could possibly understand what that felt like. She'd spent the early years of her life believing that she would become queen. When she discovered it was conditional, she was devastated. Now everyone expected her to find her mate, but even if such a mate existed, finding him was entirely out of her control. It wasn't a thing of choice. Fate alone was responsible for the pairing. To her, it seemed like trying to find a one-of-a-kind starfish at the bottom of an ocean without knowing where to look.

"Darling Lena, you act as though you have already failed." Her father's voice pulled her from her reverie. "At this very moment, there are twenty-seven unmated Drengr living in our kingdom and every single one of them is in this castle."

"And that guarantees me success?"

He shrugged. "Females born unto Drengr-Rider pairs—females like you, Lena—are incredibly rare. They almost always become Riders."

"Almost, Father. Not always."

"Almost, is enough reason to take this seriously. With a Drengr mate you will live a long life—a happy life—and you will be queen." He tossed her a letter. "What do you make of this?"

She frowned before turning to the letter, skimming its contents. "Another pirate raid?" Her stomach tensed. "Norshore can't afford it. How will they recover?" She skimmed further down. "Seventy dead? One hundred missing?"

"Slave-trade. I'm certain of it."

"It's disgusting! How can they…?"

He agreed. "What do you reckon we should do? What would you do, were you Dragonwall's ruler?"

She recognized this. It was a test. Her father liked to present her with questions like these. Challenges. At least that was a good sign. After her stunt today, he hadn't given up on her.

She considered her words carefully. "This is the fourth coastal attack in three months. The first two were nearly two months apart. They are coming more frequently now. If I were ruling, I would first determine if there is any pattern to it. I would try to anticipate their next strike. Meanwhile, I would fortify the surrounding towns and villages. All four were under-defended, making them ideal targets. That must change. We must fight back. Cut off the head of a snake and the body will wither."

Her father smiled. "And the Drengr? How would you use your mightiest of warriors?"

"The Drengr can mobilize more quickly. I would increase the frequency and number of coastal patrols, but I would not permanently station them among any of the towns and villages, as the writer of this letter suggests."

"Why not?"

"It's too dangerous—spreading them thin. That's how we lost so many before."

Nearly fifty years ago, the kingdom had seen similar raids. The Drengr attempted to stop them, and many lives were lost.

"And what of the pirate weapons?" asked her father. "Spear-ships are dangerous. The dragonlances on a single ship can take out an entire fighting wing, twenty strong."

Lena sighed. Human strategies were easy. Drengr strategies? Not so much. "There are always losses in battle, Papa. Our Drengr must be stronger, smarter, and faster. If we do not use them in battle, then what good are they?" She paused for a moment to think. "The magic of the pirate ships might make them immune to fire, but what about weight? Dragons can lift massive objects." She fell quiet. "What if…what if we drop giant boulders on them or something, crushing their ships?"

"Ha!" Her father roared with laughter until tears dripped from his eyes. She couldn't help but smile too. When he calmed down, his eyes were twinkling. "My dearest Lena, it is easy to see why you are so good at practical jokes. Your head is ever full of ideas! If the ships cannot be burned, you simply find another way to destroy them. We Drengr can lift immense weights, after all."

"Why do you think I suggested it?" She beamed back at him, basking in his praise. "Do you actually think it's a good idea?"

"I think it ought to be considered, amongst other options. Now, where do you recommend that we find these huge boulders heavy enough to break ships in half?"

She allowed a giggle to slip from her lips. "I suppose it does sound rather outlandish when you word it *that* way. But—" She shrugged. "At least it is better than doing nothing."

"And *that* is why you would make a grand queen. Only foolish rulers sit back and do nothing. The best rulers are those who use what they can and make the most of it." Her father had a way of making her feel big and important. "Now, this business of our guests—"

She groaned loudly, sinking down in her chair.

His eyes went unfocused. He paused before adding, "Your mother wishes to tell you that you are not being ladylike when you groan and complain like that."

"Well, you can tell *Mother*, that I do not wish to *be* a lady." He did not answer. "I suppose this is the part where you lay out all rules I must follow?"

"Aye. I am a great layer of rules." His eyes twinkled.

"Don't I know it!"

King Cornan's tone turned professional again. "I asked each of our forts to send every mateless Drengr they have. It turns out there are twenty-seven and they have all come."

"Of course they have. Who would pass up the opportunity to be king?"

"Lena! Why must you take it so negatively? Finding his mate is a young Drengr's chief desire." She snorted but he ignored it. "Over the next two weeks, I expect you to learn all of their names."

"What?! *Papa*, you know how bad I am with names."

"Be that as it may, I expect it. And that's not all. Over the next two weeks, you will schedule time with all twenty-seven."

"What?" she choked. "No! Father, that's hardly fair! What am I supposed to do with them? Sit and talk about the weather?"

"Gods, Lena! You've got a creative mind. Can you think of nothing?" She opened her mouth but he kept going. "Go horseback riding. Take a trip to the market. Have a walk. Visit the dockyards. Enjoy a picnic. Ask one of them to give you an archery lesson. Must I spell it out?"

"Wait—" Her brow furrowed. "Did you say archery lesson? You mean…I don't have to wait until the two weeks are up?"

"Not if it constitutes quality time spent with your guests."

"Oh…" Perhaps this wouldn't be so bad. "So I must be a gracious host, learn their names, and spend all of my time with them? Anything else?"

He shrugged. "The rest is up to you."

She nodded before falling silent. "What's the point of all this anyway? Seems a bit excessive. Why not get straight to the ceremony part? Everyone knows that the existence of a bond is entirely up to fate."

"Fate or not, we will be gracious hosts. These Drengr have come all this way for you, Lena. Show them that you appreciate the effort they are making. Perhaps you might grow fond of one of them, or perhaps one of them might grow fond of you. Maybe fate will see that."

She doubted that very much. "All right, Father, we will see."

"I am being serious, Lena. You have a chance here. Give this an honest effort."

"You really think one of them is meant for me? What if I don't like the one fate chooses?"

"I know with certainty that if a bond exists, you will forget your hatred over the mate idea. Your heart will rejoice. Ask your mother."

"What do you mean? Is that what happened to Mama?"

His eyes unfocused. "Your mother said she would rather tell you the story from *her* perspective—that I'll get it wrong."

"Yeah, right! You're in each other's heads all the time."

He smirked. "That's exactly what I told her. Now, our welcoming feast will begin at sunset. Your mother took great pride in having a slew of gowns made for you." He paused, his eyes going unfocused again. "Twenty, my dear? I do hope you did not drain the coffers." He said this aloud for Lena's benefit before turning back to her. "Now, run along and make your mother happy."

"Yes, Father." She stood and gave him a quick peck on the forehead before rushing off. Something about his confidence bolstered hers. He was a man to be trusted, after all. And if he was right, if she had a chance at influencing fate and finding a mate, perhaps she could indeed become queen. That meant she had better look her best tonight, and she certainly intended to.

CHAPTER 3

LEARNING NAMES

LENA SPENT the remainder of her afternoon with her hand-maidens, preparing for the welcoming feast. The twenty new gowns her mother had commissioned to earn her cooperation were spectacular beyond words. They had been laid out as a surprise when she returned from the king's tower. Six were meant for daywear, while the other fourteen were specifically for their evening meals. The evening meal was considered a nightly formal affair, and the nobles who dined in the great hall took every opportunity to dress impressively.

For tonight, her mother had a special gown set aside. It was the most stunning of the bunch, with layers of sweeping silken skirts that fanned out behind her. "I can hardly breathe in this, let alone move," she complained whilst dressing. "Does she expect me to be a statue all night?" Avra, Cora, and Theresa chuckled but said nothing as they continued to tighten the strings of her corset.

The gown's fabric was made from silver and royal blue silks. The entire neckline was embellished with tiny, multifaceted glass beads that sparkled as she moved. And while it was breathtaking, both literally and figuratively, the front was cut a little low for her tastes. "I look like a harlot," she muttered when she studied her reflection.

"You are nearly eighteen, Lena," said Margaret, who watched her handmaidens work. "There is nothing wrong with allowing the opposite sex a small peek at your bosom." Margaret winked.

Lena's jaw dropped in mock surprise. "Kenna! You of all people should be appalled."

The corner of Margaret's mouth turned up. "You would never see me in something like that, dear. But I am not young. Nor am I the princess. Flaunt it while you can."

"Kenna!" What had gotten into her? Margaret merely smiled and watched on, fanning herself every so often as she sipped from her goblet of wine.

While Lena sat for her face and hair, her handmaidens fluttered about, trying to get everything perfect. As they worked, they gossiped about each of the Drengr hopefuls, asking for detailed descriptions of their appearance. Lena hadn't much to give, other than a few snippets about the ones she liked the *least*. Specifically about those who had spoken down to her.

"Perhaps they were just tired," said Cora, twisting one of Lena's braids tightly into a band of hair that wrapped around her head. Cora had insisted on being the one to do her hair for the evening. Both Cora and Theresa were magicians when it came to hair, while Avra was better with face makeup and fashion. "Besides," Cora added, "perhaps they won't be so bad once you get to know them."

"I doubt it," Lena snorted, pinning Cora's reflection with her gaze in the vanity's mirror. "Either way, I will need help tonight when I make my introductions."

"Whatever for?" Cora asked.

"To learn their names, of course. I cannot manage it all on my own. You ought to know *that*." As a rule, handmaidens went everywhere with the mistresses they served. At feasts and parties, they were not quite so clingy. "Tonight, I want you by my side."

Just before the evening was to begin, Queen Amara dropped by Lena's apartment with a final surprise, presenting her with a new tiara. After fussing over it, her handmaidens finished up with her hair and placed it upon her head.

"How beautiful you look," said Kenna Margaret, stepping closer for a good look. "It was meant for you."

Lena's mother stepped forward and adjusted it slightly, gently caressing Lena's cheek. "It suits you well, my dear."

The tiara was a comfortable fit, made simply of woven silvery substance that gleamed like starlight. The front came to a point over her forehead and held three small diamonds. "It was made by the Sprites," said the queen, "commissioned by Queen Isabella for Princess Irelia."

Lena gasped, looking at her mother with wide eyes. "Truly?!" Queen Isabella was something of a legend to the people of Dragonwall.

"Truly." Her mother beamed back at her.

"But...that makes it six thousand years old! How...how do you have it?"

"The same way I have all the jewelry worn by former royalty." Lena knew all about her mother's jewel closet closely guarded in the king's tower. "I found it tucked away in a special box with Princess Irelia's name and a little note that said it had never been worn."

"Never? Not even by the princess?" Lena fell quiet, stunned. She turned her head to the side and studied her reflection, noticing the way the diamonds glittered with the slightest movement. It was so very different from her typical tiaras. And with the way her hair had been pinned up, she looked exotic.

"The note said that the tiara was commissioned shortly before the princess died. I strongly felt that you should have it."

"Oh, Mama!" Lena jumped from her vanity stool and threw her arms about her mother's neck, kissing her before the queen departed. Then it was time for the evening meal.

The dining hall within the Great Keep was the third most impressive architectural feat of the kingdom. Lena considered the second to be the King's Court, where his throne was located. She considered the first to be the keep's secret passageway system. Its vast number of hidden doors, halls, and underground tunnels had offered her years of possibilities, years of mischief and fun. What was even better, few knew of its existence.

The keep's dining hall had vaulted ceilings with high windows that let in plenty of light throughout the day. For the evening meal, the hanging chandlers were filled with hundreds of candles that had been lit by magic, no doubt a single word that made the task easy. Lena didn't know much about magic for she hadn't been blessed with it as some rare female Drengr offspring tended to be.

This hall seated some three hundred patrons at rows of long trestle tables, already full. They were arranged perpendicularly to the head table, which was elevated upon a dais. Aside from the royal family consisting of her father, her mother, and herself, only six were permitted to sit at the head table. These six sat three to the king's right, and three to the princess's left, with the queen framed in the middle. The king's six *Drengr Fairtheoir* were his royal bodyguards, his brothers in all but blood, Shields sworn to protect the royal family.

As per her mother's advice, Lena had arrived later than everyone else. The doors had not yet closed—she still had a few minutes to prepare. As a rule, the evening meal awaited no one, and once the doors were closed, none were permitted entry. The rule had been set by Queen Isabella after too many dinner disruptions and was still observed to this day.

Lena stood with her handmaidens outside the entryway, just hidden from view. Her kenna had already gone inside some time ago. "Just take a deep breath," Theresa whispered, brushing a stray strand of hair from Lena's face. "Everything will be all right." Lena nodded, swallowing against her dry throat before taking several deep breaths. Her heart hammered against her chest.

"And make sure you stand up straight." Cora grabbed hold of Lena's shoulders, forcing them back. "You know how you forget about your posture when you're nervous. It's unbecoming of a lady." Lena nodded again, still trying to take deep breaths.

"Oh, leave her alone!" Avra swatted the other two away before taking Lena's hand in her own. "You'll do just fine. The room will be so shocked to see how beautiful you look, it won't matter what you do, will it?" She kissed the back of Lena's hand before dropping it. "Besides, you only have to walk to the end of the aisle." Then she winked.

Lena smiled. "I suppose you're right, and the hopefuls will be so surprised to see me."

"Exactly!" Avra smiled widely, leaving Lena feeling more confident than she'd first felt. She loved her handmaidens. They were but a few years older than she, and made for great friends. Sometimes she pretended they were sisters, for she dearly wished she had sisters.

"Well, here we go." She placed herself within the entryway. Her handmaidens assembled in formation behind her.

It took a moment or two, but as soon as her mother and father spotted her, they stood. On cue, everyone else did the same. Every gaze in the hall settled upon her. There were gasps of surprise that left her cheeks burning from the attention. She enjoyed pranks done in secret. But this? It was almost too much.

"Go on, Princess." Cora prodded her, spurring her forward. She moved down the center aisle, her ladies following in her wake. Whispers followed them. "Look at her *gown*!" And, "I need one like it."

She kept her eyes focused upon her beaming parents, ignoring everything around her. *Keep breathing*, she told herself. *Just keep breathing*. Each time she placed her feet, she was careful to keep from stepping on the hem of her gown. Imagine if she tumbled in front of everyone! It would not do.

The Drengr hopefuls were seated together nearest to the head table. She let her guard down and glanced at them in passing. How could she not? She was rewarded with wide eyes and open mouths. Who was this polished woman parading before them? Surely not the barbarian pirate who greeted them earlier?! A smile tugged at the corner of her mouth, threatening to break free. Yes, they were surprised. Oh, how she loved her wicked trick. It was definitely the best so far.

When she reached the head table, she gave her mother a reassuring smile. Her father winked at her—a job well done. Each of the Drengr Fairtheoir greeted her with bowed heads. Ramar was her favorite. Tonight he, along with the other five, wore livery of gold and green. His velvet tunic clung to his muscular build, accentuating his strength.

He stepped away from the others and around the table,

taking her arm to escort her up the stairs of the dais. "I think you owe me a good story," he whispered before pushing her chair in. Her face remained emotionless except for her flaring nostrils.

Ramar returned to his seat while her handmaidens went to stand with the queen's ladies in waiting. Then the queen took her seat and the entire hall followed. Only her father remained standing—he was going to give a speech. Lena's breath quickened in anticipation. King Cornan loved speeches. "Good evening to all." His deep voice filled the hall. "Our princess is nearing her eighteenth name day—an occasion to be celebrated."

A cacophony of clapping and cheers broke the silence. Shouts of, "Congratulations!" and, "About time!" followed.

Her father smiled and nodded before continuing. "Our governing Charter written by the races of Dragonwall clearly states that the princess has until her eighteenth name day to find her mate. That mate will rule by her side. Together they will continue the bloodline of the Drengr monarchy. Therefore, I have invited every unmated Drengr to our keep!"

The crowd released more cheers. Some clanked their cups against the tables. Lena glanced over at the Drengr hopefuls. They looked especially smug in light of the crowd's attention. A frown pulled at her lips. She was reminded of what she had to do over the next two weeks.

Briv sat to her immediate left. She leaned over and whispered, "Anyone promising? If you ask me, they all look like greedy little urchins."

His gaze followed hers, flicking from Drengr to Drengr. A smile twitched at the corners of his mouth. "What makes you say that, Princess?" His lips barely moved.

Her father continued speaking. "Over the next two weeks, our princess will get to know each of our guests." Lena groaned, tempted to sink lower in her seat. Instead, she kept her posture rigid. "At the finale, we will host a ceremony in the arena. Princess Lena will touch the scales of each hopeful. If a bond exists, it will be discovered!" Deafening cheers marked the end of the king's speech.

He took his seat and the procession of food began. In the meantime, the royal musicians silently waiting in the corner of the hall began playing. Everyone was free to talk amongst one another, and the noise levels grew.

It was a succulent feast, albeit awkward. Every time she looked up to assess her new guests, she found more than one pair of eyes upon her. She did her best to ignore them, distracting herself instead with her own tablemates.

The three Shields to her left were eager to hear about her wicked trick that afternoon. It was Ramar who spoke first. "Is it true, Lena, that you pulled a sword upon them, demanding they leave at once else you would gut them?" His eyes sparkled as he leaned around the others to get a good look at her. He knew she didn't have a sword.

"Is that what the gossips are saying?" She feigned surprise. "Gods! The rumors sound better than the actual story." Even still, she gave them the details of all that had happened, including the part about changing back into her formal gown before Queen Amara's arrival. That alone had them in fits.

"Perhaps," said Briv, wiping his eyes, "you should have removed the clothing littering the floor *before* Amara arrived."

Lena laughed too and shrugged. "Even still, I think it was my best prank yet."

When the formal portion of the feast was over, desserts were brought out. Everyone began abandoning their seats to mingle among friends, moving from table to table in good conversation. Some nobles made their way over to the Drengr guests for introductions. Others came up to the royal family to pay their respects.

Before long, the hall was a chaotic mess of conversationalists. Some patrons had become so drunk that they took up the hands of various ladies to dance in the empty aisles. This was when Lena's father turned to her with eyebrows raised. "Lena?" he said, prompting her. "It is time. Perhaps have some more wine so that you might soften that expression of yours."

"Yes, Father," she mumbled. Maybe he was correct. She presented her goblet to the cupbearer who topped it off. Then she drank deeply. The effects did not take long, for she was not fond of the stuff and rarely drank. Maybe it was time to change that. Gods only knew she was going to need a bit of liquid courage throughout the next two weeks.

"Wish me luck," she muttered to Briv and the others. He jumped up to pull out her chair. As she descended the dais, her handmaidens jumped into action, taking up their positions just behind her. Many of the Drengr hopefuls also noticed and took the opportunity to place themselves confidently before her. It seemed that each intended to be the first to greet her.

She thought more highly of those who stood back, displaying patience instead of a desperate need to be first. It came as no surprise that the two who had spoken out earlier were amongst the eager ones. The first was the one she particularly disliked, with the dark hair and green eyes. He closed in on her immediately. "Good evening, Princess. Please allow me to formally introduce myself. My name is Raff." He bowed deeply.

She curtsied, though she would have preferred to stomp on his foot and disappear. "What a *pleasure* it is, Raff." It was hard to keep sarcasm from seeping into her voice.

He nodded. "I hope, Princess, that you will excuse my behavior earlier. I was tired from my long journey and surprised to be turned away. The way I treated you was not respectful." As he said this, she felt Cora pinch her arm as if to say, "Told you so."

Lena smiled sweetly, though it did not reach her eyes. "It is forgiven. If you had known my true identity, I am confident that you wouldn't have responded as you did."

"Aye. Had I known..."

"Allow me to introduce my handmaidens." As she gave him their names, she wondered how he treated his inferiors. It was unfortunate that she had promised to give each Drengr hopeful a fighting chance. If she had it her way, she would have dismissed him immediately.

He greeted Avra, Cora, and Theresa with cordiality, though she was sure it was all for show. And when they finished with that, she filled the awkward silence by asking about his journey and the fort he hailed from.

"You are very kind to inquire, Princess." He bowed his head before continuing. "My journey was uneventful, though tiring. I hail from Fort Edge."

"Ah! A northerner," she said, pretending to be interested. "Is it true there are giants in those parts?"

"None that I have seen, Princess Lena. But there are tales of them, great ice giants that come from the north beyond the range."

"Amazing! Perhaps some other time you can tell me about them. For now, I must continue on to the others." She nodded to her handmaidens, preparing to move away.

"Begging your pardon, Princess, but before you go I wished to ask, might we take a walk tomorrow through the royal garden? I am told it is spectacular. Moreover, I promise to be an open book about northern giants and such."

She considered his question, desperate for an excuse—any excuse—to turn him down. Perhaps it was better to get the worst of it over quickly. "How kind of you to ask. Very well. I am available after tomorrow's midday meal."

His eyes sparkled with smug satisfaction and she hated him all the more for it. He fancied himself a great success, winning time with her before any of the others. "Excellent! Most excellent. I will meet you at the garden's entrance tomorrow then."

Saying nothing more, she curtsied before moving away. A sudden idea came to mind that left her smiling. These Drengr needed nicknames to make matters more bearable. She could already think of one rather fitting for Raff. Raff the Ruthless, for he had no concern for others besides himself. He meant to have the crown if he could. Thank the gods that fate was the decision maker.

Civoi was the other Drengr who had spoken to her that afternoon. He made it a point to introduce himself next. She disliked him too, but not as much. At least he had not called her '*girl*' with such an insulting tone as Raff had.

Civoi was too bold and entitled for her tastes. He too insisted upon carving out time together so they might become better acquainted with one another. "I was hoping you would share a private meal with me, Princess. Perhaps breakfast?"

She stifled a groan at his offer. She was quickly realizing that with twenty-seven hopefuls, she would hardly get a moment to herself. "Breakfast sounds lovely," she said as she struggled to muster feeling in her voice. Her words came out monotone. "Unfortunately, tomorrow morning I have several duties requiring my attention." It was a lie, but she couldn't bear the idea of seeing any hopefuls as soon as tomorrow morning.

"I see." Civoi stroked the stubble on his chin. "The day following, perhaps?"

"Yes, the day following."

Pleased, he dismissed himself and moved away displaying better sense than Raff had. The other introductions were not as painful. The Drengr hopefuls were polite, though she wasn't sure if it was feigned. Those from Fort Squall and Fort Kastali she liked the best. But there were a few from Fort Lin who were also easier to bear. It seemed that those she cared for the least were from Fort Edge in the north.

She did her best to learn each of their names that night, hoping that where she failed, her handmaidens would succeed. It was a true struggle, and sometimes she found herself thinking up nasty pranks to play on the ones she didn't like, only to remind herself that she had promised to behave. Fortunately, there were a few favorites among the bunch. She discovered that she liked Daryn the most, and not simply because of his mop of curly brown hair, dreamy dark eyes, rosy cheeks, or fine straight nose. He was gracious and attentive. Moreover, his suggestion of how they might spend their time together was more favorable than anyone's. "I thought perhaps we might go sailing," he offered.

"Sailing?" She was momentarily caught off guard as her stomach fluttered.

"Why, yes. Have you ever been?"

"I have!" She answered all too quickly, forgetting her reservation. "My mother and father take me occasionally around the bay. Sailing is grand."

"Wonderful!" He clapped his hands together. "In Stormy Bay, I often sail when the day is calm. It's a great way to clear my mind. I hope it will be a good opportunity for us to better acquaint ourselves." She eagerly agreed and set aside her third afternoon for the occasion.

Once she acquainted herself with all twenty-seven hopefuls, she quietly excused herself from the hall. As they walked back to her apartment in the south wing, her handmaidens were full of gossip. They talked of nothing else for the remainder of the night as they got her undressed, arguing over which of the Drengr were the most handsome, which had better manners, and which would make good mates. By bedtime, her head pounded from the wine and exertion.

When she closed her bed curtains and crawled under her covers, the darkness seemed to swallow her up. A sense of foreboding settled about her, twisting her stomach. Her mind ran away with itself. Merely thinking about all the activities scheduled made her feel sick. The next two weeks weren't going to be easy…far from it. Worse still, tomorrow was probably going to be the hardest day of them all.

CHAPTER 4
TESTING RAFF

THE MORNING after the welcome feast Lena made a list. She sat with her handmaidens and Kenna Margaret at the small table in her apartment over breakfast, and together they recorded the names of all twenty-seven Drengr hopefuls. She only remembered half of them, but with help, she managed to include everyone.

"Now," she said, scanning her register. "I have already scheduled time with the following." She ticked off several names with her quill, writing subscripts about each activity. "But it seems a handful of them never bothered to request time with me." She sighed, though she wasn't offended by it. "I suppose I'll need to call upon them at some point this week. As if I don't already have enough to do."

"What do you have in mind, Princess?" Cora's blue eyes sparkled with eager curiosity.

"Well…" she paused. "Father offered me suggestions. The time I spend with each hopeful can be as simple as a walk." She thought about the one scheduled for later that day with Raff and shuddered. "Or it can be as complicated as I desire.

47

But, if I must do this, then I would like to get something out of it for myself."

"Lena!" Kenna Margaret scolded, slapping her arm. "I should have known you would have a trick or two up your sleeve. Let me guess, archery lessons?"

Lena offered her a smug grin. "That...among other things." She looked down at her list again, glancing through the names and circling several of them. "The following hopefuls are still unscheduled. I think I remember this one. Ivrir. Do you remember him?" She looked up at her handmaidens.

"Oh yes!" Avra eagerly nodded before turning deep red. "He's the one with sandy blonde hair and blue eyes, From Fort Squall. Ivrir Ironborn."

"Ah, yes. That's right. Ironborn, like myself." She added a note next to his name. "I think I will recruit him for lessons after my walk with Raff."

"How do you think it will go?" Theresa gazed at her.

"What? My asking Ivrir for archery lessons?"

"No!" said Theresa. "Your walk with Raff."

"Oh! Terribly, I'm sure. I would rather do anything else in the world. I almost regret that I promised Father to take this seriously."

"Perhaps it won't be so bad," said Cora.

Lena groaned. "If only..."

For the remainder of the morning, she worked with her handmaidens on the list she'd drafted, making little notes next to each of the names. With guidance, she documented which Drengr came from which forts, descriptions about their appearance, information about any scheduled activities, and details about the conversations they'd had the night before. By midday, the list was extensive. She folded it and tucked it away, profusely thanking her helpers. Without them, she would already be floundering.

Too nervous for her impending walk, she ate very little during the midday meal. Today it was served in her room, though she usually took her meals in the dining hall. With all the hopefuls who would surely be there, she preferred to spend what little time she could in hiding.

When it was time, she made her way to the royal gardens, followed by Avra, Cora, and Theresa. On the second level of the keep, she spotted Ramar, lurking as if he'd been waiting for her. He leaned against the corridor, one leg propped against the wall, as if he hadn't a care in the world. "Ramar? I didn't expect to see *you* this afternoon."

"Ah." He moved away from the wall and bowed politely, though it was unnecessary. They were such good friends as it was. "I am to escort you during each of your *activities* with the hopefuls."

"To ensure I behave myself?" She arched an eyebrow at him, suspicious of his intentions. He was sure to relay everything to her father, including whether she behaved herself or not. "Well? Am I right?" His eyes sparkled, but he said nothing more. "Fine then. Keep your secrets if you must, but I have somewhere to be. Shall we?"

"Ha! Yes, we shall." He offered up his arm and she took it. They continued down to the lowest level of the keep, passing other keep patrons meandering through the corridors. "Lovely gown, by the way," said Ramar. "One of your mother's commissions?"

"How do you know about that?" She glanced up at him.

"How could I not?" He smirked. "It suits you well, by the way...the color especially." She had donned a dusty blue brocade with muted gold silken trim and white sleeves. The neckline formed a sweeping V that left the tops of her shoulders exposed. Cora had picked out her necklace so that her chest didn't feel so bare—a simple diamond pendant from her mother.

Lena pinched Ramar's arm. "You're not trying to tease me, are you?"

"Upon my honor, Princess!" He gazed down at her, his eyes trained upon hers. "Why would I do such a thing? Can you not take a compliment?" He paused. "I can retract it if you wish."

She blushed under his scrutiny. "No, no. Thank you. I appreciate your kindness." Ramar was a fine gentleman and a finer Drengr. If only some of her Drengr guests were more like him.

They found Raff the Ruthless waiting just outside the garden's entrance, arms crossed. Ramar dropped her arm and her entourage slowed their pace, giving her the illusion of privacy.

Raff stepped forward. "Good afternoon, Princess. You look…lovely." He bowed deeply.

Her stomach convulsed. The last thing she wanted was to be considered lovely by someone like Raff. She forced a smile. "Thank you, Raff. You are too kind." Then she curtsied and quickly clasped her hands behind her back.

Raff did not acknowledge the off-putting gesture, but he also did not offer up his arm on account of it. Instead he swept his arm outward. "After you, Princess."

"Yes, thank you." She stepped forward under the stone archway and he fell into step beside her.

The royal gardens were spectacular by the highest standards, initially constructed by Queen Isabella when she built the great keep. Sprites were lovers of nature—it was a part of them. It was even rumored that their love of the forest did not allow them to stray far for too long, else their magic would dry up and they would die. Perhaps that was why they remained hidden from the rest of Dragonwall.

Lena and Raff made their way down the main path walking at a meandering pace. The garden was a maze of flower beds, shrubberies, and giant trees, all housed within the keep on its lowest level. One could spend hours wandering within and still find new things to gawk at.

Raff was the first to speak. "I always wondered what it might be like walking through this garden. My father told me stories. 'Trees bigger than some in the Gable Forest,' said he. Now I believe him."

"Did he?" She momentarily forgot about being snide. "And who is your father?"

"Why, he's Lord Azrith."

"Lord Azrith?" She faltered. "The leader of Fort Edge?"

"Unless you know another Lord Azrith?"

"I…obviously not."

"He came here when he was a youngster," said Raff. "I believe he and your father are good friends."

"They are." She had not expected this. "My father told me stories about their younger days."

"Is that so?" Raff was interested.

She recalled one tale in particular, relaying it to him. When Gobelins had invaded the east—as they were wont to do from time to time—many Drengr fought them along the outskirts of Pavv. Azrith and her father, still a prince at the time, were among them. One day, her father and Azrith grew bored with slaughtering Gobelins. It was too easy. For a bit of fun, they abandoned their Drengr forms in favor of their human forms, fighting alongside the kingdom's soldiers.

"I heard much the same from my own father," said Raff. "I am told they killed over four hundred Gobelins that day with nothing more than their Sveraks."

Sveraks were great battle swords carried by each of the Drengr, to protect them while in human form. They received these weapons from their fathers when they fledged, as a coming of age gift.

"It is a feat to be proud of," Lena mused. They fell quiet as they rounded a bend in the path, coming across a bed of purple roses. Lena paused and bent forward to smell them, sighing with delight.

Raff copied her actions. When he straightened, he glanced about. "I am afraid my father's descriptions hardly did this garden justice."

Lena nodded. "Indeed, it is unparalleled by any other garden I have seen." That wasn't saying much, for she had never been allowed out of the capital. But she wasn't going to tell *him* that.

They continued their walk and she kept her hands behind her, fidgeting with her fingers. "Tell me, Raff," she said after some thought, "since your father is a fort leader, surely he trained you in politics?"

"Of course, Princess Lena. He drills me relentlessly."

"I see." Hers had too, but she was certain the measure of drilling was not the same. "I am glad to hear it. I was hoping you might help me to solve a problem."

"It would be my pleasure," he said, his chin jutting out. "After all, these things can be difficult for the fairer sex, especially without the correct training."

A faint chuckle from Ramar prompted Lena to glance over her shoulder. The look on his face was priceless. She turned back to Raff. "You are quite correct regarding my training," she lied. Conceding made her want to vomit. "I often find myself struggling, especially when my father enlists my help. He recently asked that I settle matters regarding the Dragon-doms. With twenty, it can be difficult to manage them all."

Raff whirled to face her, his eyes cold. "He enlists your help in such matters?"

"But of course. My father takes my advice seriously." Once more she glanced over her shoulder and found Ramar's intent expression.

"I see," said Raff, thrusting his chest forward. "All the more reason to request my assistance. How can I be of aid?"

They rounded another corner in the garden that took them directly into a grove of trees. The winding path took them past various pines and poplars. It was a small forest, tucked away within a huge city. She often escaped here when she wished to be alone. Now it would be forever tainted with memories of Raff the Ruthless.

Without further hesitation, she told him of her challenge. "It has come to my attention that there have been several uprisings in Celenore, along its northern coast. Celenore, as you may know, is a Dragondom in—"

"In Eigaden—I know."

She gritted her teeth at the interruption. Were Raff a smart man, he would know better. Instead, he was a very stupid man trying his hardest to appear intelligent. "Yes. Right."

"I had not realized that there were uprisings," Raff mused. His gaze was calculating.

"Yes, unfortunate business. We have decided to keep everything quiet for now." The truth was, her father had already settled the matter with the utmost discretion. Raff didn't need to know that. She planned to test him the same way her father tested her. "Shall I give you the details? Then perhaps we might discuss a solution?"

"Of course, Princess. As I said, I would be honored."

"Excellent!" She launched into the particulars, telling him about the instigators, how they were unhappy with their circumstances, how they encouraged others to rebel alongside them. She talked about the deaths that resulted from the riots. The only thing she left out was how her father had fixed the matter.

"Rotten usurpers!" Raff growled. "The law states that disturbers of the peace must be punished. Those who rebel against the king's laws are traitors. Death is the only way to deal with these types. I have seen it before."

"Have you?" she feigned interest. A faint grunt sounded behind her. Ramar was enjoying this conversation.

"Of course, Princess, I have dealt with these same issues. The people in the north can be unruly."

"Is that so? And based on your *experience* with the people in the north, how would you deal with this particular issue? You would put the usurpers to death, as you have said?"

"Indeed. I stand by my beliefs. Death is the only way to deal with those who would resist the king's law. Treason is treason. Set an example for others and eliminate further rebellion."

She took a deep breath, leashing her temper. "The law is important, I agree, as is eliminating further rebellions. But what about the laws themselves? Might you wonder what prompted the behavior? And should there be any action taken to evaluate the current state of politics regarding the underlying reasons?"

"The law is the law, Princess. You of all people should understand this."

"Indeed. Without the law there would be chaos. But who wrote these laws? Can we be certain that the authors were all-knowing? Can we be assured that their experience and solutions for matters of justice were correct? After all, times change." Although she was addressing the uprisings, she was ultimately thinking about the law that restricted her from ruling without a mate. Could it be changed if she wasn't meant for any of the twenty-seven hopefuls? If she failed?

"Rest assured that the laws are legitimate, Princess. The authors of the Charter knew what they were doing. To argue otherwise would be treason."

"Right. You're correct." And he was, but that did not make his answers any better.

"Then the matter is settled. Execute the traitors and be done with it." He paused. "See? Thank the gods you have me to guide you."

"Thank the gods indeed," she muttered as her mood turned sour. The worst rulers followed the law with unyielding rigidity. The best used the law as a guide but still offered a measure of flexibility. If a king's only purpose was to enforce rules, he would be little more than an executioner. Regardless of this, Raff had failed her test.

They walked a short while longer, discussing matters of less importance. Just as promised, Raff told her what he knew about the Kalds—ice giants from Kalderland. There was little he knew beyond her own knowledge, though she had hoped that with his northern experience, he might know more. All in all, Raff the Ruthless seemed nothing more than a catastrophic disappointment.

When the time came to bid him farewell, she was nearly weeping with joy to be rid of him. He offered her a deep bow and a smug farewell. His face was easy to read; he believed that the afternoon had gone well. Let him believe what he wanted. He would be the one duped in the end.

There were still a few hours left before the evening meal, and Lena had one further errand before she could prepare for it. Ramar insisted on accompanying her to Ivrir's accommodations, her arm draped through his, while her handmaidens trailed behind, whispering. "That was very bold of you," he said, "to talk politics with Raff. I am impressed that you did."

"Impressed? And why is that?"

"Because we learned a great deal about him, didn't we?" Ramar grinned. "After all, we both know how your father dealt with the uprisings."

"We certainly do, you more than anyone." She paused. "Our king is wise, and when he isn't, he has you." She nudged his arm and smiled up at him.

Dragonwall's king had first sought to determine the reasons for the uprisings and why the rebels moved against the law. In so doing, he discovered a great many flaws in the governing of Celenore. These were failings of the lord governor himself. The people could not be at fault for wanting better living conditions.

"You will make an excellent queen someday, Lena."

"You really think so?" She lifted her chin a little higher.

"I know so."

They arrived at Ivrir's door where Ramar bid her and her handmaidens farewell. Avra, Cora, and Theresa hung back in the shadows. She knocked, hoping Ivrir would be within.

The door opened a measure and Ivrir popped his head out. His eyes widened. "Princess Lena!" he gasped, opening the door wide enough to bow. "I...I was not expecting you." His hesitance was a favorable contrast to Raff's egotistical flamboyance.

"Might I come in and speak to you for a moment?" It was very forward to request something like this—time alone in his quarters, even if just for a few minutes—but she had a job to do and had no qualms about taking matters into her own hands.

"Of...of course, Princess. Please, come in." Ivrir Ironborn

stepped aside. With a single expression, she signaled to her ladies to wait outside.

When he shut the door behind her, she walked into the middle of the room, pretending to study it. "Tell me, Ivrir. Are you skilled with a bow?"

His brow furrowed. "Of course I am, Princess. Like all Drengr, I have mastered the basic weapons for killing."

"Good!" A slow smile came to her face. "I was hoping so. How would you feel about spending time at the target range tomorrow? Perhaps after breakfast?" She was scheduled to spend her morning meal with Civoi. This would give her something to look forward to afterward. "I have several hours free between then and the midday meal."

He quickly hid his surprise. "It would be an honor, Princess. I only hope that I might display as much skill as you undoubtedly possess."

A nervous laugh slipped from her lips. "Of course. I'm sure you'll do great." Since her parents had refused her lessons, she had no skill whatsoever. For a moment, she considered telling Ivrir this. He deserved to know she was using their quality time together for her own personal goals, but at last she decided tomorrow would have to do. "Until tomorrow then," she said, bidding him goodbye. Then she slipped from his room and told her handmaidens exactly what had happened.

CHAPTER 5
ARCHERY LESSONS

LENA'S BREAKFAST with Civoi was uneventful—painfully so. She nicknamed him Civoi the Bore. They dined in the king's tower, at the table in the formal sitting area. For the entirety of the meal, they were waited on by a slew of servants. Her own ladies hung back, no doubt bored to tears like herself.

Civoi was nearly as unpleasant as Raff, though in a different way. She did not bother drilling him on politics because he was simply too dull to listen to. Her mind was already taken up with daydreams of archery. So they talked of small things instead, his life at Fort Edge, what it was like living in Raff's shadow, how much he disliked the isolation of the North. In fact, the entire conversation was about him.

"I consider myself lucky to see the South," she found him saying. There was something nasally about the way he spoke. His nose was slightly crooked too, as if it had been broken, but she knew as well as most that the Drengr had unique healing abilities, making them nearly immortal. "Yes, I'm quite lucky to witness Kastali Dun in all its splendor—for myself."

"I can understand why." She stifled a yawn, hoping the conversation would be over soon. Their plates had been taken away long ago—or so it felt.

Civoi glanced about the room and sighed. His eyes lingered over the golden vases against the wall, over the chandeliers and lavish furniture. "If only I might make this my home someday. I think I'd be happy in the South. Yes, happy indeed." His eyes fell upon her. "After all, one never knows..."

Her muscles tensed and she sat up straighter. Were all young Drengr this unpleasant? Perhaps she had simply been spoiled all her life. The only Drengr she regularly interacted with were her father's six. The rest lived tucked away in Dragonwall's forts.

Yes, she decided as she watched Civoi drone on. Her father's six were the perfect examples of what the Drengr ought to be. They were also hundreds of years older than the hopefuls here in the keep. Most of the hopefuls hadn't reached their thirtieth name day.

"Anyway," Civoi was saying, "when you consider how long it took to build the keep's walls alone, it's easy to understand why."

Understand...what? She blinked several times. Civoi had just paused to take a sip of juice. She seized the silence. "Well, goodness, I'm stuffed." Before he could say another word, she jumped to her feet, allowing her chair to obnoxiously scrape against the floor. "If only we could spend the whole day like this." She glanced at the door. "Alas, I have obligations and must be going."

Civoi stood, both surprised and displeased. "Go—going? Right. Of course." He nodded. "The obligations must be numerous." Bowing deeply, he added, "Thank you, Princess, for your company."

She curtsied and swept from the room. Her handmaidens, lingering in the main sitting area, jumped into action and fell into step behind her. Together they strode through the tower's entryway and through the main door. She was free at last.

"The worst of it is behind me," Lena said to Kenna Margaret when they returned to her apartments. "The others can't *possibly* be as bad as Raff or Civoi." Her nose crinkled.

Kenna Margaret had been waiting patiently, embroidering one of Lena's gowns beside the fire, but looked up to smile at her. "Do not celebrate just yet, Princess. You are required to meet with each hopeful at least twice over the course of this fortnight." Her face turned stern. "And before you protest, just remember that your father gave you the next two weeks off from your *other* duties."

Lena groaned, throwing herself upon the sofa. "Must you remind me?" She put her arm over her eyes and savored the darkness. "At least I can put *those* two off until next week."

"Civoi was not as bad as Raff," Cora said to Margaret. "Though, he talked about himself excessively. We heard him all the way in the other room."

Lena snorted. "I thought he'd never shut up. Boring, useless facts about a Drengr I could never stomach as a mate. Ugh." The very thought of spending her life—and a long life it would be—with Civoi, listening to him drone on about himself, would be torture. Better that she live a human life and have it be her own...But, the other's weren't *all* bad. A couple hopefuls held promise. "How long do I have before meeting Ivrir?" She lifted her arm from her face to look at Cora.

"We ought to go now. Come, we will get you ready."

"Good! I need some excitement." Lena's heart felt lighter. She rushed to her feet. Her handmaidens outfitted her with a new pair of bracers, a surprise gift from Avra who'd commissioned the leather tanner to make them especially for her. Then they made their way to the practice grounds located on the far side of the keep's second level. The grounds offered a spectacular view of the city in one direction, and the Dragonfire Sea in the other.

When they arrived, they found Ramar waiting with a smug look, and he wasn't alone. Briv and Ferand stood beside him. Briv walked over, grinning widely as he handed Lena a bow and quiver of arrows. "Let's start you off with the *training* bow, Princess. This one ought to do."

"Come to laugh at me, have you?" The king's Shields were like brothers to her. They took every opportunity to tease her when they could, and she got them back whenever she had the chance. "Ramar can stay, the rest of you have better things to do."

"Oh no!" said Briv. "Ferand and I are staying. This'll be too good."

At that moment, Ivrir arrived. "Good morning! Forgive my surprise. I did not expect any others besides Princess Lena."

"Come now, do not let our presence make you uneasy." Ferand slapped Ivrir on the back. "Always a pleasure to meet a fellow Ironborn."

Ivrir smiled and his shoulders relaxed a measure. "*Jarnin eflai verus sterk,*" he replied in greeting.

"Iron makes us stronger." Lena remembered the translation of the Iron Clan's motto. All the clans had a motto and the Drengr took satisfaction in using them even though they no longer belonged to clans. The wild dragons were nearly gone from the world.

"Good morning, Princess Lena." Ivrir added, bowing

gracefully. "Shall we leave these gawkers to their gawking and get started?"

A smile came to her face. "Yes, let's!" She glared at her father's Shields one last time before turning away. Then she slipped her arm through Ivrir's and he escorted her to the target range.

As they walked, he kept the conversation light, inquiring about her morning. "Oh, it was rather dull, but fine otherwise," she said, settling for vagueness. If only she could complain to him, tell him how much she disliked Civoi, then things might have been even better. It was unbecoming of a lady to complain, especially to someone she hardly knew.

Ivrir was handsome in a unique way. Like the others of his race, he possessed a rugged beauty—his otherworldly eyes of blue and gold, his dominant brow, and the perfect smile that dimpled his cheeks. But it was his reserved nature that lent the most attractiveness to his being.

"This looks like a good place." He stopped and set his things down. They stood at the middle-most range, staring down a target on the opposite end. Lena studied it apprehensively. It seemed a bit far.

She glanced over her shoulder. Her entourage had assembled at the edge of the field. Her father's Shields appeared at ease, hands clasped behind their backs, watching the event unfold. Her handmaidens whispered and fidgeted.

Lena turned back to the matter at hand, taking a deep, steadying breath. "You may go first, Ivrir." Her eyes remained fixed on his every movement.

He nodded and took his position. His quiver was strapped to his side for quick reach. She made a mental note to do the same with hers. With ease, he produced an arrow. Then he nocked it smoothly before releasing. Her brow furrowed, trying to follow. He repeated the motion, moving rapidly. Again, she was at a loss. Both arrows struck true, just outside the central black dot.

"Not *terribly* bad," he muttered, more to himself than anything. "I suppose I need to warm up before expecting perfection." He turned to her with a shy smile.

"Your modesty impresses me," she said. "I assure you, I will not perform half as well."

His eyes sparkled. "Surely you will, Princess. Go ahead. Your turn. Show me how it's done."

Heat flooded her face. She opened her mouth but closed it before anything came out. Then she glanced at the target and swallowed against her dry throat.

"Is something the matter, Princess?"

Somewhere behind her, Briv, Ferand, and Ramar burst into laughter. She paid them a look of disgust before turning back to Ivrir. "Can I be perfectly honest with you?"

"Perfectly. What is it? Are you feeling unwell?"

She shook her head. "Quite the contrary. I feel wonderful. It's just...well, I haven't fired an arrow before." A silence stretched out before her. "Actually," she added, "I was hoping you might teach me."

His gaze widened. "Me? Truly?"

"Truly." If he had been Raff or Civoi, she'd have glared at him, but since he wasn't, she did not mind displaying a measure of hesitation.

"Well! I find myself entirely honored. You could have singled anyone out, but you have chosen me. I promise to teach you everything I know."

She smiled with glee. "In that case, I hope to be a worthy pupil." With that, they got straight to it. All pretenses were off, so she had no reservations about looking silly no matter how many snickers sounded from behind her.

"Just ignore them, Princess. Focus on the target."

Ivrir was patient beyond imagining, guiding her through the act of drawing an arrow, nocking the bow, and firing. She enjoyed watching him, noticing little things like the way his chest puffed up before he fired, and how his face frowned in concentration. She did her best to memorize every movement.

"There now. It's your turn." He turned to her with eagerness. She nodded and began to imitate what he'd shown her. As she moved, he offered detailed critiques regarding the proper grip and how to take aim. "Make sure you keep your right hand like this," he clarified, stepping close to her to correct her posture.

His right hand closed over hers, around the bow. Her breath caught in her chest. She blinked several times. Ivrir's skin was warm against hers. He moved her arm upwards, positioning it properly. Then his left hand reached around her shoulders until it rested gently over her drawing hand. Again, her breathing hitched.

"The fingers on your left hand ought to be positioned like so," he advised. She could feel his breath on her ear as he spoke. For a moment she forgot they were merely having an archery lesson. "There now, keep them delicate. Much better. And keep your wrist straight when you pull back. Stop when your fingers reach the area between your ear and jawbone. Right there. Good." She narrowed her gaze at the target, trying not to allow the proximity of his body to distract her. "There. Now release."

She followed his command and the arrow sped from the bow. It shot through the air and landed in the grass beside the target. She groaned. "Must it be so difficult to land it where I want it?"

Ivrir grinned. "Like all things, Princess, this takes practice." He stepped away, putting space between them. She almost wished he hadn't moved, then inwardly scolded herself for thinking it.

Better equipped after going through the mechanics of it, she tried again. And again. And again. Each time Ivrir offered advice regarding her stance, breathing, and technique. Hours sailed by effortlessly. By midday, they were both laughing in frustration.

"I promise, Princess, after a few lessons you will be better than I."

She sighed. "I hope you are right. Besides, I do not mind that you are better than me, so long as I manage to hit the target *eventually*."

They put their things away and returned to the keep, walking side by side, joking about her silly mistakes. When they entered the dining hall for the meal, she felt everyone's gazes glued to her.

She bid Ivrir farewell and proceeded to the head table. Briv, Ferand, and Ramar were close on her heels and followed her up the dais. After that, her father questioned her about the entire lesson. "Am I to understand that it was a success?" His sly grin left her unsettled.

"Father!" She glared at him, then smiled. "I admit, I do like him, better than all the others."

"Ah-ha. I knew it just by the way you are smiling. Well, try not to decide *too* soon. You still have the remaining hopefuls to meet." She sighed. He was right—too many hopefuls. "Besides," said the king, a wicked smile pulling at his lips, "I am certain you will enjoy sailing tomorrow."

The reminder left her giddy. "You know, I think you're right." Sailing would be fun, maybe as enjoyable as her archery lesson with Ivrir. Still, her mind jumped back to the moment when he moved in close. She could practically feel the proximity of his body, the comfort of his hands against hers. Her face burned and she glanced over at him. His focus was intent upon his food. She breathed a sigh of relief.

SHE FOUND her mother later that evening relaxing in her private parlor. "My darling girl!" Queen Amara's voice was warm and inviting. "Come, sit by the fire." She patted the seat beside her before turning to her cupbearer. "Clifford, my daughter requires wine. Give her a mild option, please."

"At once, Your Majesty." Clifford bowed and rushed away.

"You know how I hate the stuff, Mama." She curled up on the couch beside the queen, close enough that her tucked legs rested against her mother's.

"I used to say that too, once upon a time." Amara chuckled, patting Lena's thigh. She took a sip of wine. Clifford rushed over carrying a goblet and handed it to Lena. "There now," said her mother. "Drink up."

Following orders, she took several sips, sighing as she relaxed into the couch. For a time, they were both quiet. It had been an overwhelmingly long day. She had met with two additional hopefuls after her midday meal. It was enough to make her head spin with exhaustion. Her mother's company paired with the crackling fire was the exact remedy she needed. When she felt a little better, she said, "I met with Caden this evening, after dinner."

"For dessert?" Her mother turned to her, eyebrows raised.

Lena nodded, gazing into the fire, watching the cracking logs as they sparked.

"I see. Was he more favorable than Aldis?" Lena snorted— a very unladylike sound to make in her mother's company.

Aldis had been her afternoon entertainment, and she'd told her mother all about him during the evening meal.

Their time together consisted of a walk through the city's market. Aldis wasn't necessarily rude or self-centered. Instead, he was overly concerned with her welfare. He spent most of their conversation tied up on repetitive questions. "Are you sure you're okay, Princess? The market is rather loud." And, "It's terribly chilly today, Princess, won't you allow me to buy you a shawl? I hate to think of you catching a cold." At one point, she nearly yelled at him to shut up. Aldis the Annoying, she had decided to call him.

"Compared to Aldis, Mother, Caden was a great deal better, and I do not simply claim that because we met over dessert." Everyone knew she preferred sweets. Sugar made life worth living. "In fact, I find Caden to be quite funny." As she said it, she recalled a few of his jokes and smiled. Caden the Comic seemed fitting. But he was not Ivrir—for whom she had not yet thought up a fitting nickname. The ones she *really* liked seemed harder to make fun of.

"Funny is good, darling Lena. Laughing is good too. But —" Her mother paused. "I get the impression you are still caught up on Ivrir?"

Lena's eyes narrowed. "Is it that obvious?" Judging by her mother's smirk, it was. "I suppose it is. I just...he...I..."

"He makes you feel different."

"Yes," she breathed. Some believed that mates could sense a bond before discovering its existence. Was she already feeling invisible strings that tied them together? Hope flared up within her. "Do you think—?"

"It's probably too soon to tell, darling."

Her chest deflated. "How was it for you and father? He said you wanted to tell me the story from your point of view."

The queen chuckled. Her gaze took on a faraway look. "What your father and I felt was very different to what you feel with Ivrir. In fact, I couldn't *stand* your father."

"What?!" The shocking revelation left rocks rolling around in the pit of her stomach. "Really?" She couldn't stand Raff or Civoi. Did that mean...No, she could not afford to entertain the idea, not without wanting to vomit. "How did it happen —for you and Papa?"

Her mother smiled. "Clifford, I think we'll both need a refill for this." Then she launched into her tale. "I was twenty-four when it happened, with no intention to marry."

"Not...ever?"

Her mother shrugged. "Why did I need a man to be happy? My own mother and father were furious about it, of course. My mother insisted on parading me in front of every available bachelor in town."

Lena smirked. "And here I wondered where I got it from."

"Our circumstances were different than yours, Lena."

"Right, but you cannot blame me for hating the mates idea when you yourself never wanted to marry."

Giving up, her mother sighed. "I suppose...Anyway, when the news spread through the kingdom that the young Prince Cornan was looking for his mate, every single woman in Dragonwall must have flocked to the capital. Even a few of my friends made plans to journey to Kastali Dun."

"But not you, right? You did not care for such things."

Her mother laughed. "No, indeed. I did not plan for it so I did not go. I am told six-hundred did, though."

Lena's jaw dropped. "*Six-hundred?*" She pictured that many women banging down her father's door.

"To be sure! An impressive number." Her mother's laugh was triumphant. "As you can imagine, the prince did not find his mate. He sat in his dragon form as one woman after another proceeded forward from the line that stretched all the way into the city. They each touched his scales and left disappointed."

"I...I never realized..."

Her mother nodded. "When he failed, he refused to give up. He insisted that he knew his mate was out there, somewhere. That he could feel her. That she was alive and waiting."

"You!" she whispered. "He knew you were waiting for him."

"Gods above, Lena!" Her mother feigned shock. "I was hardly waiting."

"Did you know, though? Did you know you were meant to be a Rider—his queen?"

"Ha! Hardly. I had every intention of dying an old spinster." Amara giggled, which turned into several hiccups. "One day, it reached my mother's ears that the prince had decided to travel—to get away from the capital. There were plenty of rumors as to why, but everyone realized the true reason."

"He was searching for his mate," she answered. "For *you*." Her mother nodded. "So, he came looking for you?"

"Yes, and by some miracle, he found our small town."

"I would not call that a miracle Mama, I would call that fate."

Amara grinned, placing a hand over her chest, over her heart. "Perhaps you are correct. Fate. Regardless, no one knew who he was. No one in our little slice of the kingdom had ever *seen* the prince. He had left his entourage behind, so it could not be guessed. When he arrived, he was dressed as a commoner—a rather pushy and overbearing commoner, if you ask me. He sought me out almost immediately. But of course, he did not tell me who he was, not at first anyway. He merely wanted to get to know me. He suspected it then, but I did not. Even when he told me the truth, I disbelieved him. Moreover, I boldly insisted that I was no Drengr's mate, nor would I ever be."

"No!"

"When he informed me of his true identity, when he told me that he was not simply a *Drengr*, but Prince Cornan, I laughed."

"You...you *laughed*?"

"But of course. I did not believe him. I found him rather annoying. I hated his cockiness, his insistence, that he was so sure of everything, that he had manipulated me, played me. I told him to leave—to go back to the spoiled world he'd come from. I had no intention of marrying, especially not a stuffy prince. I was not about to tie myself to another man. I wanted nothing to do with him."

She listened with rapt attention. "So, what happened? Did he...did he go back?"

Her mother's eyes took on the familiar, faraway look. "Well, Cornan transformed into a beast of a dragon, then placed himself before me, blocking my path. When I still refused to touch his scales, because secretly I feared that he might be right, he snatched me up into his claws and forced me."

"No! He...he forced you? But..."

"Come now, it is not as bad as it sounds. He did not hurt me. He was not violent. Rather, he was quite gentle. But the moment my skin touched his scales, our minds merged. It was..." Her mother trailed off.

She sat up straighter. "It was *what*?"

"*Wonderful...*"

"That's—that's all? That's all you will give me, Mama? *Wonderful*?"

"It is an experience you should discover for yourself. My telling you would not do the moment justice. Besides, the surprise of it is worth waiting for."

She slumped back against the sofa. "Really helpful, Mother. *Really.* So what am I to make of this conversation? How does this help me with Ivrir?"

Her mother was laughing outright now and had to set down her goblet to keep from sloshing wine everywhere. "Well, I suppose my point is, you never truly know if a Drengr is your mate until you touch his scales."

"Ugh." Lena gritted her teeth in growing frustration, set her wine upon the end table, and crossed her arms to scowl at her mother.

"Listen, Lena. What you are feeling towards Ivrir is very normal. This is the first time you've put yourself in this situation. You are always so closed off. You've never allowed yourself to get close to anyone intimately. Gods only know, I don't think you've ever considered opening your heart to another *boy* until now."

"There is nothing wrong with being closed off, Mother."

"That is not what I'm saying, *young lady.*" Her mother grew stern.

"Then what *are* you saying?"

"For the first time, you are allowing yourself to feel things that are very natural, very normal. They feel unique because you've never experienced them before, not necessarily because Ivrir is your mate."

She jumped to her feet, too emotionally overwhelmed to sit still for another minute. The weight of an entire day was crashing down upon her. "So, you're trying to tell me that he's *not* my mate?"

"No, dear, that is not—"

"You know what, Mother? Forget it. I have had enough of

this ridiculous mate business." Enough to last a lifetime. "I'm done for the night. I'm going to bed." With that, she stormed from the room, but she couldn't escape the lesson, the idea that her mother had hated her father the same way she hated Raff and Civoi. It followed her all the way back to her apartment and all the way to bed. All she could do was hope and pray that her mother's experience would not be her own.

CHAPTER 6
DUTY ISN'T EASY

Tʜᴇ ᴍᴏʀɴɪɴɢ after her argument with her mother, Lena went to see her father. She found him with his Shields for company, preparing for court. "My darling! This is a pleasant surprise." He greeted her through his reflection. "What can I help you with?"

She threw herself into the nearest chair to watch him. "Father, I have met with less than half the hopefuls and already I want it to be over."

"Dear girl, welcome to *responsibility*." Her father's manservant handed him his large Sverak, which he strapped to his belt. A Drengr's Sverak was his most prized possession. When a male fledged, he threw away his practice sword and took up a new one, gifted to him by his father. Each Sverak was made with a rare material called Ice Metal, mined in the mountains of the Northern Barrier Range, which was then combined with steel. All Sveraks were uniquely decorated to reflect the Drengr's color. Her father's Sverak was adorned with turquoise gemstones.

"Tell me, Papa, can we not move the ceremony forward? Can we not schedule it for tomorrow and be done?"

He shook his head, giving his appearance a final check before walking over to her. He took her head in his hands, planted a swift kiss upon her nose, and then smiled. "I know you can do this, Lena. If not for us, then for yourself. Prove to yourself that you can handle duty when it calls, even when you hate what you are doing. Ruling is hardly ever easy, and it is rarely enjoyable." With that, he walked from the room. His six Shields winked and waved goodbye before following him out.

She sat several minutes longer to consider his words, then she returned to her apartment. There was little time to lounge around. She had two meetings before her afternoon sailing excursion with Daryn. Rhold was scheduled to have breakfast with her, and Thos the midday meal. She rushed through both appointments absentmindedly, determined to get them over with. By the end, she had nicknames for both Drengr: Thos the Smug and Rhold the Bold. She managed to forget the majority of their conversations. Boring interactions were easy to forget, interesting ones, not so much. Her time with Ivrir was still heavy on her mind.

Maybe her mother was right. Perhaps she merely felt drawn to Ivrir because she wasn't used to being touched by another. He never touched her intimately, just for the purpose of instruction, but it still set her mind spinning with excitement, with possibility. What frustrated her the most was the lack of time she had to figure it out for herself.

By the time she reached the Port of Kastali to go sailing with Daryn, she was tired of conversations, fed up with maintaining pretenses, and weary of politeness. It was exhausting, having to be a princess all the time for twenty-seven Drengr. That was partly why she enjoyed misbehaving and pulling pranks. Such behavior allowed her to step out of her everyday shoes. A deeper worry plagued her. This strict lifestyle would become the norm if she became queen. Was that really what she wanted?

She shook her head. All she wanted right now was an escape, some peace and quiet, tranquility to manage her burdensome thoughts. It was almost a shame because she wanted to like Daryn. She wanted to enjoy their afternoon. Out of all the hopefuls, he'd invented the most creative way of spending time with her.

She walked through a maze of docks, accompanied by Ramar and her three handmaidens. Some of the walkways were anchored deep in the sand beneath the waves. Others, such as those connecting the larger docks, acted as floating bridges. Her ladies giggled and gasped, clinging to one another for balance as they walked over each. They were not used to the swaying. She loved the floating feeling, and couldn't hide the sudden smile it brought to her lips. Perhaps she might enjoy herself after all.

Smaller boats were permitted to dock. The larger ships were required to anchor out in the bay. Sometimes she sat at her balcony, gazing out at the large vessels, playing games with her handmaidens as they guessed what each ship might be bringing to port, or taking away to a faraway land.

"I think this is ours." Ramar stopped their party in front of a medium-sized, finely built cog. It had a single mast and looked strangely familiar. She glanced up and saw her father's flag flying high. This wasn't just *any* ship. This beauty belonged to Dragonwall's king.

"Princess Lena!" Daryn greeted her, excitement coloring his voice. His head popped into view just before he jumped from the rear deck. He landed gracefully beside her. Only a Drengr was capable of the agility he displayed. His dark brown curls were long enough to cover his ears. The cool breeze left him looking windswept, with rosy cheeks and a red nose. That only added to his attractive appearance as he gazed at her with dark eyes.

"Good afternoon, Daryn." She curtsied politely before asking, "How did you manage this?"

"Ah. Your father was kind enough to lend us his most prized sailing vessel."

"I can see that." She hid her smirk. "My father must really like you. He is not often so generous." In truth, her father was very generous when he wanted to be. But for someone he hardly knew, that generosity was more difficult to come by. She suspected that her father had made an exception, in hopes of affording them quality time together.

Daryn beckoned. "Come aboard! All of you!" He looked at the others in her party, inviting them forward. "You must see how spectacular she is. *The Selena.* I wonder what inspired such a beautiful name?" His eyes twinkled as he spoke, making her lips twitch. "May I?" he asked, turning to her with an offered hand. Just like that, he had won her over.

Together they climbed aboard. A small crew was already preparing the cog for departure. Daryn led her to the stern's deck, which was elevated slightly above everything else. After seeing her comfortably seated upon a padded bench, he set about helping the crew. From her vantage point she watched him work, grateful for the silence it afforded.

Daryn wore black pants, knee-high boots, and a baggy white tunic that had a deep V. His Sverak was proudly belted to his waist, not that he would need it for such an activity. Shamelessly, his shirt billowed and flapped whenever the wind struck it, outlining his chest all too generously. She caught her mind wandering a little too far and had to look away.

Meanwhile, Ramar escorted her handmaidens to a bench opposite her while chatting about the mechanics of sailing. Her ladies nodded with wide eyes. They were nervous but pretended otherwise. Ignoring them, she listened to the sounds of the port. Gulls cawed overhead, shouts rang out as deckhands unloaded their cargos, bells tolled, announcing the approach and departure of ships. It was chaotic yet calming.

"Shall we depart, Princess Lena?" Daryn shouted up to her, hands cupped around his mouth.

"Yes!" she cried, clapping her hands together with sudden excitement. "Let us depart!"

Daryn turned to the crew and began calling out orders. They jumped into action, removing the lines that held the cog in place. The sail was unfurled and secured. The moment it caught the wind, she felt the ship lurch.

Cora cried out in alarm, clinging to Ramar. Avra and Theresa clung to each other, dealing with their fear silently. She glanced over at them, trying not to laugh. "I can assure you, it is quite all right," she called. "You need not be afraid."

Ramar had been against their coming for this exact reason. "Perhaps you ought to have excluded them today, Lena."

"Nonsense," she yelled over the wind. "I would not deny them the opportunity to go sailing. You only live once, Ramar. At least now they can say they have experienced it." Fortunately, the waters in the bay were mild. She would never dream of taking her ladies out on open ocean. Watching them wretch overboard was not her idea of an enjoyable afternoon.

The cog moved away from the docks and before she knew it, they were sailing around the immediate bay. Voices called out to them as they passed, bidding them a good day and safe voyage. She waved to many of them. Everyone was excited to see Dragonwall's princess aboard.

After a time, Daryn beckoned her over. "You should steer," he prompted, removing his hold from the helm.

"Really?" She came up beside him and took over. Her father occasionally afforded her the privilege. It was always exhilarating.

"You need not apply *too* much force when you turn the wheel," he said, placing his hands over hers. "Just enough. See? Feel her respond?" Her heart pounded as the ship answered.

She nodded, concentrating on the task at hand. Her eyes scanned their current path, then glanced about, looking over the various possibilities. "Can we go towards the rocky formation there?"

"Which direction?"

"Starboard," she answered, glad to have remembered some of the sailing terms. He guided her hands appropriately, and *The Selena* responded. When he was happy with her steering, he removed his own hands and clasped them behind his back to watch. His penetrating gaze made her slightly anxious. What was he thinking? She could feel his eyes upon her face when he ought to be watching their progress.

"Tell me, Your Highness, why does no one use your *full* name?"

She exhaled, relaxing her shoulders. "I never liked Selena. It's too formal. I'm a jokester, as you know." She kept her gaze focused. "My parents always called me Lena when I was a child. When I learned it was only a nickname, I insisted otherwise."

He chuckled. "Selena is not a bad name."

"Correct. In fact, it is a beautiful name. I merely prefer Lena."

They spent an hour navigating *The Selena* through the bay before dropping anchor. Several platters were brought forth bearing fruits and cheeses. She snatched a handful of berries and curled up upon the bench beside Daryn, tucking her bare feet and her skirts comfortably beneath her.

"How are you finding the others?" he prompted, catching her off guard with his question. "Entertaining us all day must be exhausting."

She sighed. "You're right. Time has hardly afforded me a moment of rest. Though, I have greatly enjoyed sailing, watching you work, feeling the breeze in my hair. It has allowed me to be quiet. Life is far more peaceful on the water than it is in the city." Despite their distance from land, many of the city's sounds still reached her ears.

"I can understand that," Daryn agreed. "Perhaps it would be wise to limit my conversation with you. I ought to allow you more quiet time. I want this to be relaxing and rejuvenating, not stressful."

Her smile was slow, hesitant. "You seem to understand more about my responsibilities than my other guests."

"Why? Are your other guests particularly frustrating?" The corner of his lips twitched.

"I should keep quiet."

"Come now, Princess. We are friends, are we not?" His teasing was playful. "But go on then. Have your secrets. I for one have already found many of them unbearable."

"Have you?!" Her heart leapt.

"Indeed! Shall I name names? Let's see…" He paused to watch a passing seagull. "There's the worst of them—that would be Raff. He and Civoi never shut up about how superior they are. I suppose Raff having a father as a fort leader automatically makes him better than everyone else."

She feigned a surprised gasp. "Now, now! No one's father is higher in rank than my own. I hope I have refrained from acting the way he does."

Daryn roared with laughter. "Aye, Princess. I would take your company over his any day."

"That's good to hear." Already she felt her mood lifted, so they continued to talk about the other hopefuls. Daryn had a great deal of inside information and he offered it freely, so she took advantage, finding out as much as she could, especially regarding some of the guests she had not yet spent time with. It was such fun, discussing the personality traits of the others while avoiding their own.

When the sun began its descent towards the horizon, Daryn excused himself. "I have already taken up enough of your time, Princess Lena. The crew and I will prepare *The Selena* for her trip back to the docks. Please, take these moments for yourself. Enjoy the tranquility while you can."

There was something in his eyes, a deep understanding for her need, for the way sailing might fulfill it. It was strange, but she got the impression that he preferred spending his time on water rather than in the sky. She spent the remainder of their slow voyage back to consider it. When they docked, she asked him about it.

"If you give me a moment to spruce things up, I would be happy to escort you to the keep. We can discuss it while we walk."

She happily agreed. The others waited with her until he was finished, then he took her arm in his and led her away. As they made their way through the city, her entourage trailed behind.

"There is a reason I love the water so much," Daryn said. "Can you guess why?"

"Because it's peaceful?"

He chuckled. "That it is, but it's also more than that. I am descended from the Sea Clan."

Her eyes widened. "Ah-ha! Now I understand." She recalled the words of his clan. *"Ealar efla verus vinnai."*

He nodded. "Spoken with a perfect accent. Salt makes us conquerors."

"Now I get it," she whispered, considering it. That each of the Drengr should have an affinity, a love of things related to their clan's heritage made sense.

"Indeed. I have always felt more peaceful on the sea, breathing the salty air, feeling the water beneath me. I sail when I can—when I get the time. My own ship is a lot like your father's."

Her heart fluttered. She should have realized that he had his own vessel. "She must be a true beauty. What have you named her?"

"Storm's Maiden, for she has battled every storm that Stormy Bay has seen during her lifetime, and she has done so with honor." There was pride in his voice. He loved sailing, and she admired him for sharing his passion so openly with her. Much to her surprise, she found herself longing to return to the sea, and more so, to see the *Storm's Maiden* in action. She yearned for it even after they said their goodbyes.

The next several days were spent with the remainder of her guests. Daryn's valuable knowledge allowed her to craft fitting activities for each of the hopefuls: card games with Elliar because he enjoyed gambling; painting views of the sea with Neziss because he was an artist; a private performance from her father's minstrels with Braeon because he loved music. She did her best with each hopeful, even if it meant gritting her teeth. It wasn't so much the activities she minded, but rather, the company.

After a time, she came to agree with her father's advice. As a ruler, she would be required to do many unenjoyable things, making this a relevant test to her endurance. Once she understood that, she pushed herself to complete her responsibilities with minimal complaints. And whenever she felt particularly unamused, disgruntled, or frustrated, she allowed her mind to drift back to her archery lessons with Ivrir, or to sailing with Daryn. In that way, she was able to pass an entire week.

CHAPTER 7
MAKING MISCHIEF

THE IMPENDING CEREMONY LOOMED CLOSER. As it did, unease settled in Lena's stomach turning her into an unfamiliar version of herself. She picked at her food, grew irritated over the simplest things, and lay awake at night imagining terrible outcomes. Because she was required to meet with all twenty-seven hopefuls at least once more, she worked diligently to craft a timetable for her second week. She planned to meet with each hopeful in the same order as before, with Raff the Ruthless first, followed by Civoi the Bore. The only exception was, she intended to see Daryn and Ivrir more than the others.

Unfortunately, there was no good way to spend time with Raff. Seeing him would be torture no matter the occupation. She had hoped horseback riding would be favorable, but quickly learned she was wrong.

"You may not know it, Princess, but we Drengr are not fond of riding." Raff's voice had a tendency to make her cringe. This time was no different. "We have other, superior means of transportation, if you get my meaning." She rolled

83

her eyes, glad that he could not see it. "I suppose there's naught to do about it now," he grumbled, spurring his steed forward to keep up with her fast pace.

"No indeed, Raff," she called over her shoulder. "My father always says, 'When life gives you a bad situation, it is your choice to make the most of it.' Some people make the correct choice and others don't."

"You don't say." He was quiet a moment, then, "So tell me, Princess, how do you usually spend your days when you're not riding off into the sunset?"

She took a deep breath, letting the air out slowly, reminding herself to be patient. "In the morning, I work with my kenna. We study poetry, languages, and literature." She could tell that he was automatically bored. Good. If she could bore him to death, the world would be a better place. "In the afternoons, however, I work with my father. I help him with his affairs. It is important that I learn how to rule before I become queen." At this, Raff snorted. "Is there a problem with your nose?" she asked.

They were just outside the city walls now, guiding their horses through the grass fields. Several of the keep's guards trailed behind them. The king's Shields were busy today, so Ramar was not present.

Raff shook his head. "No, no. Your Highness. I was merely holding in a sneeze."

"Right. Clearly you disagree with me, else you would not have sneezed in the first place. Let us have it then? What do you see so wrong with my afternoon activities?"

He had caught up to her now, and they rode side by side. Raff waved a hand in dismissal, holding the reigns with the other. "Nothing at all, Your Highness. The way you spend your time is up to you. I just found it amusing that you expect to be queen with so much uncertainty surrounding your future…at present."

She gritted her teeth, bit her tongue, clenched her fists, but nothing could keep her anger at bay. "You speak as if you know the future, Raff. The law may keep me from ruling on my own, but there is a good possibility I will find my mate. What then?"

"I certainly hope you do, Princess." His voice was threatening. "For everyone's sake, I hope it is me. This kingdom is in desperate need of strong leadership, now more than ever. But if you fail, if the fates decide otherwise, you can be sure I will return for the Tournament."

"Gods above!" She rounded on him. Her body was shaking with cold fury. "Could you be any more awful? Any more insufferable? I hope to the gods that you are not my mate. You disgust me!"

With that, she kicked her heels into Sir Chomper's sides, desperate to get away. Her noble steed responded, galloping off towards the city's gates. Raff called out after her, and very likely tried to catch up, but he failed. The guards failed too. Sir Chomper was a champion horse, the fastest in Dragonwall. He'd never lost a race, nor would he now.

As Sir Chomper's hooves clambered through the cobblestone streets taking her to the keep, she struggled to suppress her rage, her revulsion. Raff had inadvertently insulted her father, alluding to a lack of strength in Dragonwall's ruling. It was treasonous!

After seeing Sir Chomper fed and watered and brushed, she stalked out of the stables, still angry. "Princess Lena!" A familiar voice called out to her. It was Ivrir. He rushed over. "Is everything all right? You look unwell."

With no intention of worrying him, she faked a smile. "Everything is fine, Ivrir. Thank you for your concern. I have just stabled Sir Chomper. Perhaps you might escort me back to my apartment?" She could desperately use his company. If anyone might tame her angry thoughts, it was Ivrir the Gentle. Yes, that was a good name for him.

"Of course, Princess. It would be my supreme pleasure. What shall we discuss together?"

"Anything." She shrugged. "So long as it is of good merit."

He smiled. "How about Sir Chomper? That is your horse's name, isn't it?"

She giggled. "Yes. I suppose you think it's a ridiculous name."

"Indeed! I was going to keep that to myself, but since you say so." They burst into laughter as they walked along the corridor of the third level, working their way towards the south wing of the castle.

She slowed her pace to prolong their conversation. "I'll have you know, I've a very good reason for naming him Sir Chomper." She was teasing now, already in better spirits than before.

"Is that so?" He was genuinely interested. Yet, his mouth continued to twitch.

"It is so. My father got him as a gift when I was tall enough to ride. I remember trying to think of a name for him, but my inspiration was dry." They rounded a corner. Several nobles stopped to bow. She nodded her head in acknowledgement as they passed.

"One day, I came to find one of the stable boys harassing him. I had just walked in and saw him at the end of the hallway." She giggled, recalling the memory. "Sir Chomper—before he was named that—was very unruly, and many hadn't the patience to handle him. I've tamed his attitude a great deal. Anyway, the stable boy, who has since been turned away, was trying to convince Sir Chomper to leave his stall for a bath, pulling at his bridle. Sir Chomper didn't like baths at the time. I had to explain that it's because he likes warm water, not cold water, but that was after all of this." They reached a staircase and began to climb. "Anyway, the stable hand was getting rough, yelling and slapping poor Sir's sides. Well, Sir didn't like it one bit. He was nearly full grown by then. He'd had enough. The moment the stable boy turned his back to grab another rope from the ground, exposing his behind to the world, Sir leaned forward and took a nice chomp out of his arse. You should have seen how he stood up and howled, grasping his buttock as he ran from the stable."

Ivrir's roar of laughter could be heard echoing down the corridor as they came off the stairs. Lena couldn't help the tears leaking from her eyes. "So, you named him Sir Chomper?" Ivrir said once he regained his voice. "Now that I know the story, I admit it is a splendid name, a name that makes me smile with happiness. And he's earned it too—a true hero."

"You think so?" she asked. Ivrir nodded. The name was one she was very fond of, just as she was fond of the horse. "And tell me, Ivrir. How do you find horses in general? Do you dislike horseback riding?"

"Of course not! Granted, I have little need to travel that way now, but they are very convenient for getting around when one cannot take up dragon form. Why do you ask?"

She sighed. "Raff told me that you Drengr do not like horses."

"Nonsense!" Ivrir rolled his eyes. He grew serious. "Your father has a horse, does he not? And your mother?"

"Well...yes."

"They do not think horses are silly or useless. Nor do I." His voice was soft, almost sad. He looked pensive, which left her curious. Then he cleared his throat and the look was gone.

"Take little stock in what Raff tells you, Your Highness. He gets beneath the skin of everyone here. I can only imagine how he would be as a ruler."

"Thank the gods I'm not the only one frustrated with him," she muttered. Not only did Raff get beneath her skin, he burrowed straight down to her bones.

They reached the Hall of Kings. Instead of continuing to her apartments, Ivrir stopped before the first painting, turning to gaze upon it. King Eymar stood proudly in his dragon form. His scales were a deep emerald green that faded to black on his underbelly. Queen Isabella stood beside him, dressed as a Rider rather than a Sprite. But her Sprite markings peeped from beneath her light armor and snaked around her neck, kissing her cheeks. Her golden hair was caught in the breeze, fanning out behind her.

"I had a horse once." Ivrir broke the silence, immediately satisfying her curiosity. "Isabella, she was named, after her." He pointed to Queen Isabella.

"You? You had a horse?"

Ivrir chuckled and turned to her, his eyes bright. "I did. Before I fledged, my father got her for me to get around the city of Squall's End. I was twelve. She is long gone now…"

"Oh! I did not realize." Her chest constricted. She disliked thinking of death. Sir Chomper was dear to her. She couldn't imagine life without him.

"I had Isabella for nearly fifteen years," Ivrir explained. "Once I fledged, I did not ride her as often as I should have, but I still enjoyed spending time with her. Sometimes I took her out into the wilderness and let her run free, flying high above her." His face radiated happiness. "She loved running free, roaming through the grasslands outside of Squall's End." He shook his head. "When she grew old, I took her out to that same wilderness, to the place she loved so much, and allowed her to pass under the open sky. I think she liked that..." His voice constricted. When she glanced up at him, his eyes were wet.

"I'm sure it meant a lot to her," she managed to say. "Others would not have been so kind."

"I think you're right." He turned away. Perhaps he was embarrassed to show emotion. Slowly, he proceeded towards her apartment door. She followed, giving him distance.

"Well, Princess, this is where I leave you. Are we still on for archery lessons tomorrow?" He was back to his professional, polite self.

She gazed up at him then placed her hand gently upon his arm. His muscles flexed beneath his tunic. "Thank you, Ivrir, for sharing your sweet memory with me." A smile pulled at the corner of her mouth. "I feel I understand you a little better now. I'll see you tomorrow at the practice field." Then she slipped into her apartment to tell her handmaidens exactly what had happened.

The weather was beautiful the following day. It was perfectly pleasant for an archery lesson. There wasn't any touching or close proximity this time, though she almost wished for it. But she and Ivrir shared many laughs together, and by the end, she'd made progress. "I've managed to strike the edge of the target a grand total of once!" This she loudly proclaimed for her entourage to hear. She heard Ramar's snicker behind her.

Ivrir turned to her. "If we squeeze in another lesson, Your Highness, perhaps two, I suspect you'll hit the target every time."

Her heart quickened. "I think we can manage another," she whispered. "What about the day after tomorrow before breakfast? I know it's early but..."

"Done!" His confirmation took no thought on his part, and that left her feeling warm.

TWO EVENINGS FOLLOWING her terrible adventure with Raff, a servant boy by the name of Bartlett arrived at Lena's door. He couldn't have been older than twelve, though she never asked for his age. Dinner had just started but she was absent, claiming to be unwell. Her handmaidens were sent on without her, so she was very much alone.

Bartlett was a chimney sweep responsible for cleaning the castle's flues. The Great Keep had a vast number of them, so he was most frequently sooty, and more often than not, unnoticed by all. When he wasn't working, he was a street urchin with a gang of boys, who he led into all manners of mischief. More than once, she had to secretly bail him out of trouble, and because he was so small for his age, he made a wonderful accomplice.

"Good evening, Bartlett." She greeted the lad with a kiss to the forehead. Although they had quite different stations in life, she considered him a friend. Moreover, she was terribly fond of him, and not having the luxury of a little brother he had filled that void. Together, she was the brains and he the brawns behind almost all of their tricks. "Have you got the pinching bugs I requested?"

She had promised her father to behave herself. Truth was, she had tried very, very hard, but Raff the Ruthless made it impossible. Besides, after what he'd said to her on their ride together, she couldn't resist paying him back.

Bartlett came in and quietly shut the door. "Of course, Princess Lena! Wait till you see these beau'ies." He tiptoed across the floor and set the large box upon her table.

They lifted the lid and peeped in. "Oh Bartlett," she gasped. "You little fiend, you! You have outdone yourself this time."

Pinching bugs were rather nasty. These were the size of her thumb and scurried around inside the dark box, their littler critter legs scritching and scratching at the walls. At the front of their faces they had sharp pincers and enjoyed biting and sucking blood. One always knew when a bite occurred, for it felt like a painful pinch, and there was always a welt left as evidence. Better still, pinching bugs attacked in groups, timing their bits to be simultaneous.

"These are a feisty bunch, Princess Lena. When you told me yesterday, I went straight to the docks. Got 'em off a questionable merchant crew, I did, from across the Dragonfire Sea." Bartlett looked rather proud of himself.

"They're perfect!" She clapped her hands together in glee.

"Can I come with you this time? Oh please! Please, Lena. You know I be good for it." There was a well of desire in his eyes. He loved mischief even more than she did, and that was saying something. Most times, she did not allow him to participate in the final step of her plans for fear that he'd get into trouble, but sometimes she did.

"Well..." She dragged out his suspense. "Hm..."

"I'll be good, I swear!"

She smiled. "I suppose I could use a small lad like you. Especially because the man in question will undoubtedly recognize my scent." Bartlett's face lit up like a thousand suns. He thought the world of her and would undoubtedly do anything she asked of him. "But," she warned, "you will have to make yourself scarce afterward. I do not want you in the vicinity of the keep for at least two days. The Drengr have a very keen sense of smell."

"Oh, Lena! I dare him to catch me even if he tries."

She chuckled. "I know you're fast, but you know what I mean. You must hide yourself away. Can you do that?" He nodded eagerly. "Very well. Then you may come. We will leave at once." The grin that followed did not leave his face. She gathered a torch, lit it in the fireplace, then gave it to him to hold.

Pulling back a wall-sized tapestry near her fireplace, she revealed a secret door. Bartlett had seen it before. Touching the correct stone on the wall opposite the door, she activated it. They watched it slide back and slip into the dark shadows. Together, they stepped into the passageway. The torchlight lit the narrow space, casting dancing shadows. Then she traded him and gave him the box to carry so that she might light their path.

They continued through the castle, twisting and turning. There were few who remembered the old passages. Her mother had once shown her the one that led from the King's Tower to her own room. At the age of eight, she found herself exploring every stone in the castle in search of secret doors. Now, she knew more of them than her parents.

"This is it," she whispered, stopping before what appeared to be a blank wall. There was a tiny crack in the wall. She peered in. The room was dark. "Okay, do you know what to do? When I open the door, you will go and empty the bugs beneath his mattress." The little critters would wait until their tasty meal slept, then they would coordinate and bite him all at once. Smart little things, they were.

"You got it, Princess." Bartlett kept his voice to a whisper.

"Make sure you do not touch anything besides the mattress. Very carefully now." Raff's ruthlessness would be especially bad if he found out who was behind this trick. Pushing on the hidden stone in the wall, the secret door slid to the side. The scent of Raff's aftershave met her nose and it crinkled. Gods, how she hated him.

Bartlett was quick. He scurried in soundlessly. She heard only the faint noise of a mattress falling back into place before he came back with an empty box. Giggling, they crept away. When they reemerged in her room, she paid him handsomely. "You know it ain't necessary, Princess." His eyes were wide as he gazed at the five gold dragons she placed in his palm. It would be enough to feed his family for months.

"Come now, I doubt those pinching bugs were cheap on such short notice."

"True," he said, grinning wickedly, "But not as expensive as you think."

She shrugged. "It's yours. Now, off with you. And toss that box into the sea. Remember what I said." She gave him a kiss to the forehead which left his cheeks red. Then he departed.

She climbed into bed just in time. Her handmaidens returned shortly thereafter to fuss over her. "Sure you are not hungry, Princess?" Cora began feeling her forehead with the back of her hand. "You do not feel feverish. That is a blessing."

"It is nothing more than a headache now." She tried to sound unhappy. It was difficult to fake illness when inside, she was jumping with joy. What a fun night Raff would have! "I suppose my tummy is a little hungry, now that you mention it, Cora."

Cora turned to Theresa, "Get her some soup and bread from the cookery."

It was fortunate that she had her ladies with her and that they believed she stayed in bed the whole time. It was a good alibi if she needed one, not that anyone would believe it. Those closest to her knew what she was. In fact, more often than not, misfortunes in the keep were blamed on her even if she wasn't responsible.

After eating, she sent her ladies away and stayed in bed reading by candlelight. It was difficult to focus on the words. Her mind kept drifting to Raff. Oh, how she wished she could see his reaction. That night, she fell asleep happier than she had been in a while.

IT TOOK LESS than a day for word to reach her: Raff had requested—in a most put-out manner—for a new accommodation in the keep. Rumor was, his skin was covered in welts. And when she saw him that night at dinner, she confirmed the news. It took mighty control to keep from laughing.

Did he suspect her? If so, he made no show of it. But others did. "Dearest Lena," Briv whispered as they ate. "What have you done now? Eh?"

"Whatever could you be speaking of?" she innocently replied, throwing a furtive glance in Raff's direction.

"Your feigned ignorance is unconvincing. I thought you promised your father? You agreed to behave while they were here. Look at him. Come now, what could possibly warrant such a mean trick?"

The great thing about pinching bugs was, their venom was potent as it was poisonous. Unfortunately, poor Raff was unable to self-heal as Drengr did with most wounds. These would have to heal on their own.

For a moment she considered denying it. Then she merely shrugged. "You know, I think it improves his appearance, don't you?"

"Lena!" Briv's attempt to sound appalled failed.

"All right, okay. If you must know, he insulted Father,

your king, the man you're sworn to protect. So, he got what he deserved."

"You lie." Briv's skepticism was obvious.

"I do not."

"Very well then," he said. "What did Raff say?"

"You really want to know?"

"I do." She was happy to divulge Raff's words. In so doing, she grew upset all over again. "You're sure he meant it that way?"

"Briv, come now. I'm not stupid. I know exactly how he meant it."

Briv narrowed his gaze and turned it to Raff. "Very well then. He deserves every painful bite and then some." There was admiration in Briv's tone.

"Everything I do, Briv, every trick I play, has a purpose. You ought to know that by now."

Briv smiled. "Indeed, Lena. I was wrong to doubt you. When your father next asks, I will make sure he knows that you are not at fault." She had an ally.

"Thank you."

Briv's eyes went unfocused. She was certain that he was relaying everything to her father. When she glanced at King Cornan, he smiled and winked at her. She breathed a sigh of relief. She was safe—for now.

A few days later she spotted Bartlett from afar. He must have spent some of his earnings because he looked sharp in a new tunic and pants, though his clothing already had sooty smudges upon it. He carried a bucket and his brush, which he propped over his shoulder as he walked. There was a group of sweeps with him, otherwise she might have bid him a quiet hello. Instead, they passed in silence. When their eyes locked across the corridor, they shared a wicked grin that left her heart swelling with happiness.

Her trick had helped to take her mind off the impending ceremony, and had even lifted her spirits, but only for a short while. She knew that with each passing day, as it grew closer, her fate would be made clear for the world to see. She only hoped it would be a worthy one.

CHAPTER 8

THE LAW IS THE LAW

Lena did not feel selfish for carving out extra time with her favorites. Just as she'd done with Ivrir, she also did with Daryn, slipping in an additional meeting with him before the end of the second week. This was how she found herself touring the dockyard with him, arm in arm, admiring the ships at anchor beneath the cloudless sky.

Daryn was a great conversationalist. He enjoyed talking about more than just ships, though their discussions often went back to the topic of sailing. The more they talked the more he opened up, allowing her to discover hidden facets, simple things like his favorite foods, complicated things like the difficulties he faced during Drengr training, and even his accomplishments. She was delighted to find that he'd recently been promoted to *wing second*. "Isn't that a prestigious position for one so young?"

"Indeed!" He grinned, glancing down at her before turning his attention to a pair of dockhands hauling crates. "I'm rather proud of it, you know. And surprised. If I continue to perform well, I may take over my wing someday."

"You would make an excellent wing leader," she mused. Daryn did not count on becoming her mate. So many other hopefuls did. They avoided any mention of their future, afraid to consider the possibility of failing. A sly smile came to her lips. "What if you *do* become king?"

He chuckled. "I would have more than a wing to lead, wouldn't I?"

"You'd have an entire kingdom." She pinched his arm, teasing. They continued on for several minutes in silence before she spoke again. "Daryn? Can I ask you something?"

"Of course, Princess." They were on their third round of the dockyard as they dodged the hustle and bustle of busy bodies. "Ask away."

She carefully considered her words. "You know that I cannot be queen unless there is a Drengr mate for which I am destined."

"Yes. The rule is well known. That is why we are here— why I am here."

She nodded. "When I discovered this conditionality, I was devastated. If I had been born a male, the need wouldn't be immediate."

"What are you trying to say?" He appeared thoughtful.

She took a deep breath. "Well, if I had been born a male, I would not be forced to find a mate at such a young age. As it stands I'm only seventeen—soon to be eighteen."

"Us males are given decades to search for our intended mate. We live long lives. Some take centuries to find the one they are destined for."

"Exactly!" She exhaled her pent up breath. "For the Drengr, time is hardly a concern." Several passersby bowed and curtsied in passing. "Me? My time is measured in days. If

I fail, my entire birthright is gone, fleeting, like dust scattered to the wind."

"Ah. I see now what you mean." He rubbed the stubble upon his chin.

She sighed. "The law is the law. Was I wrong to be upset?"

He fell quiet, but she remained patient, allowing him time to think. A smart man considered all options. "Well," he said at last, "I think it is safe to say that you have been dealt an unfair hand."

She glanced up at him. "You mean that? You're not just saying it to make me happy?"

He stopped and turned to her, dropping her arm. His face was all seriousness. "Princess Lena, while you are Dragonwall's princess, and technically heir to the throne, I am not afraid of offending you. I would not say something simply to *please* you. You asked for my honest opinion and I have given it. It is not fair that Isabella did not extend the same abilities to females that she afforded us males." He grunted. "Were Isabella still alive, I would give her a piece of my mind, and not simply for your sake, but for the sake of each rare female borne unto a Drengr line."

She smiled, filled with joy, as if watching a sunrise for the first time. "It means a lot to hear you say that. Each time I complain about how unfair my lot is, others tell me to recover my senses." She screwed up her face to impersonate her mother. "This is the way things are, Lena. Accept it!" Then she shook her head. "What if I don't *want* to accept it? I'm tired of feeling like I'm not good enough simply because of being born."

He frowned, but his eyes were warm. "If I could do something to help you, something to change it, I would."

"That's the worst part," she said at last. "There's nothing we *can* do. I won't live past sixty, if I am lucky, even with the medicines that exist today. No one wants a short-lived ruler. But..." She shook her head, growing more frustrated by the moment.

"You're allowed to be mad, Princess. I know everyone around you says otherwise. They aren't living with your burdens." He paused. "If I have learned anything during my time with you, it is that you are more capable of running a kingdom than half the hopefuls at court."

"You...you mean that?"

"Of course I do." he said. She smiled, relieved. "Princess, I pray that fate selects someone worth your while. Someone worthy of your quick mind." He shrugged. "Perhaps it will be me, perhaps not. It is not for me to decide. But know this, I truly believe that you will make a great queen. Gods! Even if the law allowed it and you ruled independently, I would pledge my allegiance to you." Her heart skipped a beat. "If I could rewrite the Charter, I would. Unfortunately..."

"Unfortunately you are not king, so you do not have the authority to," she said, seeing the irony in it. "And if you *did* become my king, rewriting the law wouldn't be necessary because I'd be queen beside you. Though..." She turned thoughtful. "New laws might benefit the next princess to come along."

"That is very selfless of you, Princess." He paid her a sidelong glance. "And would you? Would you rewrite the law if you could?"

She faltered. "I... No, I would not, as much as I hate it, as much as I *despise* it. This law makes sense regardless of how unfair it is." They had come full circle. "Dragonwall was formed by the Drengr monarchy, meant to be ruled by a single ruler for periods of a thousand years or more. Changing that would be akin to reforming the entire political system. I am ambitious, but not *that* ambitious. There is too much else I want to do."

"Oh?" His head tilted to the side. "Like what?"

She sighed. Her voice took on a dreamy tone. "I want to travel, to see the world, to see what else is out there. That is why I like sailing so much. The possibility of exploring distant lands, discovering new people, new cultures, new ideas. Instead, my world is so small." She spread her arms wide. "This is my world—Kastali Dun." Then she shook her head. "I wish it was bigger."

"Rulers don't travel much. How often does your father?"

She snorted. "Good point. Hardly ever. He's too busy, too bogged down with his duties. He has people who do it for him, emissaries and such." She shook her head. "Maybe I'm going about this all wrong. Maybe becoming queen isn't what I should aspire to. Maybe I should become an explorer, or a cartographer, or…I don't know. Someone who sees the world. I want to see the Northern Barrier Range. I want to see the Vallahurst Forest. Mistport. The Scattered Islands…" She sighed. "As it is, I fear I'll never get much further than Kastali Dun's city wall."

"Never say never, Princess. You've got your entire life ahead of you."

A mischievous grin took her. "You know what? You're right." She squeezed his arm, happy to have such a companion by her side. They continued the remainder of their walk in comfortable silence.

It wasn't until they turned from the docks and began making their way through the city to its keep that the silence became too much. The ceremony was scheduled for the following day, and she tried not to think about it, but the challenge was immense. She could feel the frown pulling at her lips, the pounding of her heart, the heat of anxiety that burned her skin.

"You look tense." Daryn broke the silence. "Are you worried about tomorrow? Do you want to talk about it?"

Her eyebrows pulled together. "Is it that obvious?"

His jaw was set. "It shows plainly on your face." He glanced away from her, his eyes alert, then smiled. "Here, I know what will help you feel better." Without another word, he pulled her in the direction of her favorite sweets shop. "You told me you liked this place, did you not? Let's go inside." The little store front was located in the Merchant District, just outside the keep's walls.

She felt better as soon as she set foot in the small sugar heaven. Sugar was an expensive commodity in Dragonwall, most of which was imported and taxed heavily. This particular shop was the only one in the city. Its brightly colored delights were a treat under *any* circumstances.

She and Daryn managed a bag of sweets each, his treat, and left in good spirits. She snacked on the surgery bits of toffee as they walked, considering Daryn's question from earlier. He was willing to listen if she was ready to talk. But was she?

As Dragonwall's princess, she was used to being closed off, tight lipped, keeping her feelings, emotions, and opinions restricted to a select group of people. Opening up terrified her. It required her to cross a canyon that seemed vast. But Daryn had offered, and she had to hope that he would not chastise her or belittle her for how she felt. A leap of faith was supposed to be intimidating. That's why it was a leap and not a step or a hop. So she ran and then jumped, throwing herself as far as she could. "Daryn?"

"Yes, Your Highness?"

"Is it...is it normal for me to be nervous about tomorrow?"

He gave her a deadpan look. "Of course it is. Absolutely normal on all accounts. If you were not, I would be concerned." He handed her a round blue candy. "Here, try this one." She popped it into her mouth and its fruity flavor exploded upon her tongue.

"Mmm. I love it." She enjoyed it for a few moments before asking, "Why would you be concerned over my lack of nerves?"

"Nerves imply that you care, Princess Lena. If you did not care about tomorrow's outcome, you would not be the woman I believe you to be."

"Oh..." There were so many reasons she cared. Finding a mate was important, certainly. But it was the idea of failure that terrified her the most. "Sometimes I feel so small. The law makes me feel as though I am not good enough as is—as myself." Her brow furrowed. "I've let this feeling eat into me, day after day. Some mornings I feel sick to my stomach. I've struggled to keep food down." She shook her head. Whatever this was—it didn't feel healthy.

They had reached the keep now, and the portcullis loomed before them. Beyond that, the royal garden was just out of view. Daryn pulled her into the keep towards the garden's entrance.

She allowed him to guide her as she continued speaking. "What's even worse, is that I want so desperately to please my parents. I want so badly for them to be proud of me. I'm terrified of disappointing my father, who is already disappointed in me."

Her words stopped Daryn in his tracks. He grabbed her arm and turned her to face him. "Why would your father be disappointed in you, Lena?" Abandoning pretenses, he failed to use her title. "Has he said this?"

She faltered, surprised by his shock. "Well…no. But I know he is. If my parents could've had a son, they would have. And why not? I can hardly blame them. With me, there is no guarantee that their bloodline will continue."

"Gods above, Lena!" He led her to a bench beside a planter of roses and sat down beside her. "I promise that your parents are happy to have such an impressive daughter."

"You…you think I'm impressive?" Her voice was hesitant.

"Of course I do!" He sighed. "Lena, listen, there is more to life than ruling. And there are far more important things than *bloodlines*." He rubbed the back of his neck. "I always wondered what went on in that sharp mind of yours and now I understand. You have made your demons known."

She exhaled, allowing her chest to fall. It felt good—*really good*—opening up to someone. "It's so hard," she whispered at last. "Some days, I want to run away from everything. The pressure…" She shook her head, falling silent.

"Is that why you're such a trickster?" He held his mouth firm, but she saw the corners of his lips twitch as she searched his face. "After your little incident with the pinching bugs last week, I asked around. It turns out you have quite a reputation for tricks. Some of them aren't necessarily nice, either. Cockroaches in a certain noble's bed? Rats in the steward's apartments? Confetti? Rooms emptied of all their furniture? I have heard a great deal of stories."

She offered him a weak smile. "Do you hate me for it?"

"Hardly! I don't necessarily agree with all you've done, but at least you make a little more sense now."

She folded her hands in her lap and turned her regard upon a bed of peonies that had attracted several butterflies. They sat in silence for a time, but a wormy thought continued to nag at her. "What will happen tomorrow if I touch every Drengr's scales and no bond exists? What will happen if I'm not meant for any of them? If I fail?"

Daryn was silent, thoughtful, before speaking. "If fate is cruel, Lena—if no bond exists—then you will go on living as Dragonwall's princess. Your parents will still be king and queen. You will wake up the following day when the sun rises. You will put on your tiara like you always do. You will keep living. And you know what? The world will keep turning. The baker will wake early and prepare his bread, same as he always does. The ships will enter the bay with their wares, ready for the market. Your mother and father will go on loving you just as much as they *always* have. The important thing is, you will *still* be Lena."

A tear escaped to slide down her cheek. She quickly wiped it away, turning her face from him. "You make it sound so easy—so normal. But it won't be. I'll be crushed."

"You're strong, Lena. I know you are."

She wanted to argue—to tell him that she wasn't. She didn't *feel* strong, not at all. Instead she said, "What about you? Will you go back home?"

"Aye." He exhaled. "I will return to Fort Squall. But I won't be away too long."

"You will come back and visit me? Perhaps bring your *Storm's Maiden* along?" That hopeful thought left her chest warm. Maybe things would carry on in a manageable way, after all.

"I will bring her. Yes."

A sudden thought came to mind. "What about the Tournament for the Crown? If I fail, the tournament will take place. Will you compete for the crown?"

"No." He took no time whatsoever delivering his answer.

"No? But—"

"I am not like the others, Lena. I did not come here for the crown. I came here in hopes of finding my mate. I have looked for two decades now. I believe she's out there, somewhere…perhaps right here." The way he looked at her, his eyes fierce, left her stomach fluttering.

"How—how old are you?"

"Nearing forty." He shifted uncomfortably, as if his age would bother her. He didn't look a day past twenty.

She hesitated. "Daryn, I want you to come back. I want you to compete."

"Why?"

"Because…because I'll be damned if I hand my crown over to Raff the Ruthless. And I know you feel the same way. If I fail tomorrow, he will be back for it. We both know he is a dirty fighter with a good chance of winning. I cannot let that happen. Nor can you."

"I don't know, Lena…"

She placed her hand in his and covered their hands with the other. His skin was warm. The bold move left her heart racing, but the gesture felt *too* right. This wasn't the first time their hands had touched. When he helped her steer *The Selena*, they had made contact. This time, his fingers curled around hers.

"Promise me," she whispered. "Promise me that if I fail tomorrow, you will come back and compete, that you will do everything you can to keep him from getting the crown. I'll *die* if he wins."

Daryn's brow furrowed. It left her heart sinking to see his lack of eagerness. But his words did not disappoint. "You truly wish this of me? Even though I'd rather not?"

"Yes." She put everything in to that single word.

He held her gaze a moment longer before answering. "Very well. Then on my honor, if you fail tomorrow, I will return to compete in the Tournament for the Crown, but only because you have asked it of me."

She sighed. Some of the tension fled her shoulders. "You promise?"

He nodded. "I promise." Suddenly, her world looked a little brighter.

CHAPTER 9

THE TOUCHING CEREMONY

THE DREADED CEREMONY arrived at last, and it was just as diffi-cult to bear as she had expected. She took a slow, deep breath, filling her lungs as much as her corset allowed. Then she squeezed her eyes shut and began to count. One, two, three… Deafening cries from the gathered crowd roared through the arena.

Four, five, six…She remained hidden from view, just outside of the arched entryway. It led directly to the floor of the arena where twenty-seven Drengr hopefuls were taking their form, one at a time, as a show for the crowd. Each would be a different color, with magnificent scales that glit-tered in the sunlight.

Seven, eight, nine…With each transformation, she could hear the people going crazy. Only when the hopefuls were in dragon form was she permitted to emerge. This was *their* time to shine.

Ten, eleven, twelve…Keeping her eyes shut and her breath trapped, she waited. She tried to block everything out. She tried to keep calm.

Thirteen, fourteen, fifteen…More screams of excitement. Her heart thudded in her ears, roaring as loud as the audience. She reached for the heavy skirts of her gown, clenching the fabric in handfuls.

Sixteen, seventeen, eighteen…Her lungs were screaming now. She wanted to cry out, to bid them to hurry. But she couldn't release her breath—not yet.

Nineteen, twenty, twenty-one…The beading and sequins on her dress pressed painfully into her palms. She squeezed tighter, letting the sting cut through her doubt, letting it ground her.

Twenty-two, twenty-three, twenty-four…Just a few more, then she could get this ceremony over with. The outcome of her entire life was minutes from revelation. Her mind flashed to Ivrir, to Daryn. She prayed to the gods—to Asjaa the Mother—the most merciful of them all. Let it be Daryn or Ivrir.

Twenty-five, twenty-six, twenty-seven. There! The breath fled her chest. She gasped loudly, fruitlessly pulling against her corset, sucking in air to replenish herself. Little stars popped in front of her eyes. It was time.

She looked down at her gown once more. Even in the darkness, the fabric sparkled. Every inch of the white tulle was covered. The queen had insisted that she wear it. "This ceremony will change your life forever, Lena. You must look the part—Dragonwall's future queen." But she hated it. She hated the way it screamed, *look at me!*

A jarring noise broke the quiet anticipation of the audience. A shaft of golden light sprang into her hiding place. She gasped. The giant, arched doors swung inward, giving way to the arena. The silence was profound, as if even the arena façade held its breath.

From where she stood, she surveyed the scene before her.

Scattered across the arena's floor were twenty-seven massive Drengr. Sunlight glistened off their scales. Varying shades of blues, greens, reds, oranges, golds, and even a silver were assembled, all waiting for the princess to reveal herself.

The pressure was immense, smothering, absolutely *unbearable*. Terror seized her, slowing her world to a stop. Everything tipped on end. Her life became a freshly-turned hourglass, the grains of sand were fragments of her soul trickling into a chamber, combining into what she was meant to be, slowly reminding her of who she was.

She was Princess Selena of Dragonwall and she did *not* want to do this. She never had. The ceremony was something her parents wanted, a tradition her kingdom expected, a chance to find her mate. But she wasn't ready to permanently bind herself to another. This seemed cheap, like she was signing herself away simply to have the crown.

Frightened, she took a step back, deeper into the shadows. One of the dragons heard her movement and curiously swung his head around. She knew this one—she knew them all. His eyes were familiar, warm, encouraging. She closed her own, unable to bear the gaze. It was Ivrir.

The way behind her was clear and she was alone. Without her usual entourage, she could flee without restraint. She knew the outcome if she did: The right to rule would pass through her fingertips like the sand falling through the neck of her hourglass. She would be free, much to the disappointment of those who loved her. Her parents would train a crowned prince instead.

But if she stepped forward into the light, if somewhere in the arena her mate waited, she would gain what was otherwise lost. She would please her parents; she would live a long life; she would become queen someday; and finally, she would find her purpose.

Why wasn't the solution clear-cut? Shouldn't the correct path be obvious? Easy? It didn't seem easy. It seemed like the hardest thing she had ever done. But she had to make a decision once and for all and stick with it.

"You have to do this," she whispered, trying to find courage in her voice. "If you do not, you will regret it forever." The darkness of her hiding place was all the answer she received. Taking a final deep breath, she stepped forward, out into the light.

Tens of thousands of screams split the arena asunder. Even the stands rumbled with excitement as countless feet stamped and pounded. Everyone in Kastali Dun had come to see the event, from the lowest beggar to the richest noble. She gazed up in wonder, blinking back tears from the glaring sunlight. Her parents were in the middle of the stands, sitting beneath a shaded awning. They clapped, bright smiles upon their faces. Accompanying them were their six guards, the king's Drengr Fairtheoir. She saw Ramar—he was beaming with pride.

She brought her gaze downward. Taking another step forward, and then another, she forced herself to move. Ivrir was the closest. His orange scales gleamed like the horizon at sunset. He had two massive horns upon his head, just above his eye ridges. These curled like a ram's. There were smaller spikes beneath them and along his spine. His tail was forked, and each fork had numerous lethal barbs. It was enough to scare even the bravest soul.

She could be brave. She had to be. She was Princess Selena of Dragonwall.

Keeping her gaze locked upon his, she proceeded to his side. As she went, she prayed again to Asjaa, begging the goddess. Let it be Ivrir. Let this end here. Beside his hulking form, her head came a third of the way up his belly. She was short for a woman, making his dragon form look all the larger.

Reaching out with her hand, she hovered over his scales. Closing her eyes, she placed her palm against him. Fiery heat erupted upon her skin, nearly burning her. That was all that happened. In the silence around her, she realized that their minds didn't touch.

"No!" she breathed as a deep sense of disappointment crushed her chest. She opened her eyes, careful to keep her shoulders straight. Ivrir's intense gaze was upon her, displaying large orbs of sadness. Why? Why hadn't it worked? Her heart tightened. Giving him an apologetic look, one that spoke of how sorry she was, of how much she wished it could be him, she moved away.

The next dragon had scales of deep blue like the sea. His underbelly was a lighter shade of violet. She proceeded to him. This was Caden the Comic. She did not mind him so much. If he was the one the fates intended, so be it. There were worse things in life, worse like Raff.

Placing her hand upon his scales, she felt the familiar warmth, the same heat Ivrir possessed, the same heat all dragons radiated with. She waited the length of two breaths but nothing more. Shaking her head to acknowledge her failure, she set her jaw firmly and went on to the next.

The mighty Thos regarded her with eager hope. She placed her hand upon his grass-green scales. She never really cared for him, so it was no surprise she wanted to fail. And she did. When it was clear they were not intended, he gave an irate snort, blowing plumes of dust around them.

"Thanks for that," she muttered, sputtering and coughing as she emerged from the cloud.

Next was Rhold the Bold, then Elliar the Gambler, Civoi the Bore, Aldis the Annoying, Neziss the Artist, and a number of other hopefuls she never particularly enjoyed spending time with. She was working her way in a circular direction around the arena, leaving Raff for last with the intention that she would never need to touch him.

One after another, she went to the Drengr hopefuls, touching skin to scale. With each failed attempt, her feeble confidence cracked little by little. By the time she reached Daryn, so many fragments had fallen away that she was trembling. She tried to give him a reassuring smile, but it was weak, unsure. Unlike so many others, Daryn was merely here to find his mate. He cared little for the crown. That kind of desire awoke something inside her.

Daryn's saucer-sized eyes regarded her with certainty. Did he know something she did not? Perhaps he had every right to be so self-assured. After all, besides Daryn, there was only Raff who remained.

She covered the remaining distance between him, stopping at arm's length to regard his appearance. His scales were dark red, nearly the color of blood. His monstrous head boasted four horns and these did not curl. They stuck straight out, ominously challenging any who might oppose him. And like all dragons from the Sea Clan, his tail was clubbed.

It had to be Daryn! It simply had to be. She lifted a trembling hand, reaching forward. Before it came to rest against his scales, she paused. A fearful realization doused her, freezing her in place. If she failed—if Daryn was not intended by fate—then she'd be left with only one other choice. That choice was the worst possible option available. Her stomach churned just thinking about it.

Sensing her tension, the crowd was silent. They too were waiting for the moment of triumph, holding their breaths in anticipation. This was a big deal for everyone.

She felt a warm breath upon her skin. Looking up with

her hand still posed, she met Daryn's gaze. His head hovered just above her, his neck craned around so that he could see her better. His regard was gentle, encouraging. It was all the reassurance she needed.

Squaring her shoulders, she brought her palm down upon Daryn's scales. Time stopped as she waited for something to happen, for their minds to merge, for her life to change. Nothing happened—nothing at all! Was this a cruel trick? Her brow furrowed in disbelief.

Refusing to accept it, she stood in utter shock, allowing the heat from Daryn's scales to burn into her skin until it felt raw. Maybe if she waited long enough, fate would change its mind. When Daryn nudged her with his head, she realized the implication. Her stomach dropped, and she looked up at him, blinking several times. *You are not the one*, his gaze said. *You are not my intended.*

But if that was true, who was?

Turning, she faced the silver dragon. Raff waited with pompous superiority. No! It couldn't be! She would die a thousand deaths before becoming his mate.

Shaking her head in refusal, she stepped back two steps. Again, Daryn's head nudged her away. She threw him a panicked look. Didn't he know? Didn't he realize how much she was against this? He rose from his belly and backed away from her. She had no choice but to carry on. She felt very alone.

Like a puppet, her legs began to move forward without permission. She felt tears of helplessness pooling up in her eyes. Her body trembled frightfully. This was a curse—a *cruel* curse. Fate was condemning her.

She had to end this misery. She had to end it now. She marched straight up to Raff and slammed her palm forcefully against his scaly arm. At the same instant, the crowd prematurely cheered, expecting the last Drengr to be the one. She heard their ear-splitting yells all around her. But why? All she felt was the same familiar heat, burning into her already raw hand.

She waited several agonizing moments before pressing her lips together. Then she began looking around in confusion. Had there been a mistake? Pulling her hand away, she took several steps backwards. Raff was not her mate. Nothing had happened when skin touched scale.

Seeing her strange reaction, the excitement of the crowd died. Their cheers were replaced by shocked whispers. Thousands of remarks, and they were directed entirely at her. That kind of pressure was more than she could bear.

She didn't know how to feel. Stunned? Upset? Relieved? Was she supposed to be happy that she was free of a monster like Raff? Or should she be crushed by the disappointment of failure? Still, the comments poured forth like water, filling the arena, threatening to drown her. She began gasping for air, desperate to get away, to escape, to hide from her shame! She did the only thing she could. Hiking up her heavy skirts, she fled the arena.

CHAPTER 10
SEARCHING FOR PURPOSE

THE ROOFTOP GARDEN of the king's tower was a private place, isolated from the rest of the world, just as Lena felt. Many aspects made it uniquely beautiful, like the way it towered above the great keep, the fragrance of flowers and herbs in their planter boxes, and the sea breeze. No one would see these qualities, nor would they experience any of its other secrets, like the night flowers taken from the Gable Forest and planted by Queen Isabella. These rarities relished in the darkness, opening to emit a blue glow. Their glory along with everything which made the garden so special was to remain hidden from view—a thing whispered about by those who knew nothing of the garden's true mysteries.

Lena felt safe here, not simply because she could rely on its privacy, but because the garden knew exactly how she was feeling. She sat curled up, arms tightly wrapped around her knees, gazing quietly at the horizon. Her face was tear stained and swollen. Her body ached with hurt. Her heart was crushed.

A clicking sound pulled her from her reverie. The trap

door was flung open. She turned as a tray of food materialized, clamoring upon the stones of the tower rooftop. This was followed by Ramar's face.

Her eyes narrowed. "You aren't allowed up here." Technically no one was, other than Queen Amara.

Ramar walked over and set the tray at her feet. "I can leave if you wish."

She looked down at the pile of fruit, cheese, and bottles of wine. "You can stay," she decided. He nodded and took a seat beside her. "How did you know I was here?" she asked.

Ramar shrugged. "When you disappeared, your parents searched the castle. This was the likely guess." His eyes were dull.

Not wanting to meet his gaze, she reached for a chunk of cheese, turning away to eat. "Here—" He poured her a generous cup of wine before taking several sips directly from the bottle. "Drink. You'll feel better." She did as he said.

For a time, they ate and drank in silence. She'd already been up here for hours. The sun was racing towards the horizon, bathing the garden in a soft glow. Birds took advantage of the late afternoon to flutter about, foraging for bits and pieces of sticks and leaves they might use in their nests. "I'm glad you came," she said at last, surprised to admit that his company had improved her mood. Or was it the wine?

"I am always here for you, Princess. My oath is for life. I serve none but the king and his family through the good times *and* the bad."

"Even the really, really bad?" She glanced at him, searching his face.

"The worst of the worst." He smiled, but it didn't reach his eyes.

She sighed. "I'm sorry Ramar—about all of this."

His expression turned into a scowl. "Sorry for what?"

"For failing—for failing you, my parents, everyone. I have failed an entire kingdom." It felt different saying it out loud. She had considered it plenty, but verbalizing her pain was something else.

Ramar took a hearty swig from the bottle. "You're wrong, Lena. You did not fail anyone. Fate failed you." She opened her mouth to speak, then closed it, crossing her arms instead. "What?" He eyed her. "Don't believe me?"

"It's just…if I didn't fail, why does it hurt so much?" The familiar sting of tears returned.

"Disappointment always hurts, my dearest Lena."

She wiped her eyes on the back of her sleeves. "What do you mean? How can I be disappointed if I didn't want anything to do with this stupid ceremony? I never wanted them to come here. I never wanted a mate!"

Ramar set his hand upon her shoulder. "Lena…I think you wanted it more than you care to admit."

She scowled, brushing his hand away. "You're wrong. I wanted nothing to do with it." Her words came out louder than intended. "I put myself out there, Ramar. I let myself open up. To Ivrir. To Daryn." She rubbed her temples, trying to massage away her growing headache.

"Opening up is good. You did all that you could. For once in your life, you allowed your heart a measure of freedom, freedom to care for someone beyond yourself, freedom to love."

She snorted. "Love?! Is that what you think? Right!"

"Oh come now. I have seen you with Dar—"

"Ugh!" She rounded on him. "You're not helping at all! Why are you here, anyway? To make me feel worse?"

His face turned to stone. "I am here, *Princess* Lena, because I am sworn to protect the royal family—to protect *you*."

She grunted. "There is nothing dangerous up here, *Lord* Ramar. You can go."

"I am afraid you're wrong. In this case, I am here to protect you from yourself, to protect you from taking a road that is not yours to take, a road that might hurt you irrevocably." He reached over and refilled her emptied cup. The wine was making her bold, more so than usual, and it was too easy to take her frustrations out on someone like Ramar, someone who would easily allow her to walk all over him if she tried. Thinking it made her feel more miserable.

She put her head in her arms to hide her face. "I'm just so *upset*," she said at last.

"I know…" He fell quiet. "There are times when bad things happen—unfair things, hurtful things—and we try to forget about them. We lock them away, tossing them into the void of our being. We hope the void is deep enough, that those things might never resurface. Sometimes they don't. Sometimes they stay hidden forever. But other times? Other times they sit in their dark place and fester and rot. They rot so much that their contamination spreads into our soul, eating away at it. All that is left is madness."

Her face screwed up in disgust. "Are you telling me I'm going to start rotting from this experience?" It was intended as a joke.

"No, Lena. What I'm saying is, if you don't confront your feelings, they might get the better of you."

"You could have just said that." She took several sips of her wine, mulling the liquid over in her mouth, letting it roll across her tongue before swallowing. "What happened to the hopefuls?" she asked, changing the subject. "What did they do when I left?"

"Your parents sent them away."

Her brow furrowed. "Away? Do you mean they're gone from the capital?"

"Aye. Your father felt it would be better that way. Your parents do not want you to suffer more than necessary. Seeing them is not a reminder you need."

She wished she could have said goodbye to Ivrir and Daryn. She would miss them—their company. But what did it matter? They were not meant to be hers. Any relationship beyond friendship would result in hurt. She exhaled loudly. "Perhaps it is better this way. I cannot bear to see what Ivrir and Daryn might think of me now."

"Lena, no one thinks anything bad about you."

"You don't know that!" She spoke through her teeth. "How could you possibly know what an entire kingdom is thinking? You don't even know what *I'm* thinking!"

"Try me." His voice was calm—too calm.

"Fine! Here's something to think about while you're sitting there all composed like nothing is wrong. Everyone—you included—knows what comes next for me. If the princess fails to find her mate by her eighteenth birthday, then she loses the crown." How many times had she recited this law? To herself? To everyone else? Too many to count. "My name day is today in case you've forgotten. Don't you get it, Ramar? I've lost the crown! Worse still, I have no mate! Now I will grow old and die like every other human out there. I was counting on the magic from a Drengr to give me a long life, so that I might have time to do some good in this world." Her fists were clenched. Her breath was coming in great gasps. "My parents will be forced to watch me grow old in the blink of an eye. They will go on living without me. My birth into the royal family was pointless. I've brought nothing to the table. Where is Dragonwall now? Hmm? No heir if my father dies. I'm useless!" Bitterness oozed into her voice as she allowed the realization to sink in. "I'm useless..."

"Lena!" Ramar's face lost its color. "You will never be useless! Not to me. Not to your family. Not to those who love you. Certainly not to the kingdom."

She shook her head. She wanted to believe him, but how could she? "It hurts so much," she breathed, taking great gasps of air. Her body began to shake. "Make it stop, please. Aren't you supposed to protect me from stuff like this? Make it stop!"

Ramar pulled her into his arms, cradling her against his chest, tucking her head under his chin. He cooed for a little while, attempting to calm her. When her body stopped shaking, he continued to hold her.

She knew that he loved her. He was the brother she never had, and she, the sister. The thought of everyone she ever loved living for hundreds of years, having to watch her grow old and die, was difficult to bear.

When she was calmer, he spoke, "There is plenty of time left for you to make a difference in this world, Lena. Your father will continue to seek your help in matters of politics, and I will continue to benefit from your never-ending mischief. As insignificant as you may feel right now, you should know that you are loved. You will always be loved and needed, so long as you live."

"Thank you," she whispered, mumbling into his chest as she buried herself deeper. She hadn't been held like this since childhood. It felt good, safe. She wished they could stay like this forever. She tried not to, but it was hard to avoid thoughts of the future. "What should I do now? How will I find new purpose?"

"Perhaps it is time to find a new path for yourself," he mused.

A dark laugh escaped her lips. "I don't even know where to start."

"Well…" He shifted her in his arms. "What do you enjoy —besides pulling pranks? Surely there is something you wouldn't mind spending your time doing?"

She considered his words. There were a great many hobbies she enjoyed: painting, music, taking Sir Chomper out, and most recently, sailing. But there was one thing she wanted above all else. "I have always wanted to travel, but I don't know how that would give me purpose beyond simply seeing the world."

"Hmm…" He fell silent. "What if you found a way to merge your strengths with your desire to travel?"

"How do you mean?"

"The king is always in need of emissaries, people to travel on his behalf." His words left her stomach fluttering. "As Dragonwall's princess, you have been trained in politics. The lord governors would respect you more than anyone. You could visit each of their Dragondoms on behalf of your father, broker deals, ensure that they have kept the peace, see that their people are happy, report things back to your father."

She jumped to her feet, heart racing. "Ramar! You're a genius! Why didn't I think of that?!" She began pacing back and forth, thinking. "But of course, who better than me to travel on behalf of my father? Do…" She chewed on her bottom lip. "Do you think he would allow something like that?"

He shrugged. "I don't see why not. As long as you have appropriate protection on your journeys. It wouldn't hurt to ask."

"Do you think if he's hesitant, you could convince him? You are his Drengr Fairtheoir, one of his most trusted advisors."

"Humph! He trusts you just as much. But yes, I would be happy to put in a good word if he hesitates. However, it should be proposed as your idea. He will respect the fact that you haven't given up on life, that you care enough about the monarchy to find a way to use your talents for good."

"It's brilliant," she whispered. "Absolutely brilliant." The clouds hovering over her mind had cleared and the sun reemerged. Having a purpose muted the feelings of failure.

It was well past dark when they left the queen's garden. Lena opened the trap door while Ramar carried their emptied wine bottles balanced on the tray. He muttered something unintelligible and an orb of light appeared, allowing them to see their way down the narrow ladder.

The wine made her clumsy, so he abandoned the tray at the bottom and guided her back to her room. Her ladies had already retired. Of that, she was glad. Only Kenna Margaret and her mother sat awake in her apartment, waiting. They jumped up and rushed to her, taking her into their arms one at a time, muttering loving remarks into her ears.

Ramar silently excused himself and when she next turned, he was gone. With the help of her mother and Kenna Margaret, she was able to get out of her heavy gown and into bed. As she lay there, trying to avoid thoughts about the day's outcome, Daryn's words from the day before replayed in her mind.

'If fate is cruel, if no bond exists, then you will go on living as the princess...' She smiled because he was right. Ramar's suggestion had created something within her, something she never thought she would find: hope. What better way to go on living as Dragonwall's princess than aiding her father in a different way, as his emissary? She could travel, see the world, work with the kingdom's people in an effort to do good. There in the darkness, her spirits lifted higher than

they'd been in weeks. Perhaps all of this was a blessing in disguise, as if fate had intended for it all along. So instead of thinking about all the ways things had gone wrong, she rehearsed her request to her father over and over in her mind until she fell asleep with a heart as light as a feather.

CHAPTER 11
NEW RESPONSIBILITIES

THE FOLLOWING DAY, Lena approached her father while he prepared for court. Briv and Ramar were with him, lounging on a nearby sofa when she entered his dressing area. "Papa, might we talk for a few minutes?"

"Lena, my dear." He had not seen her since watching her in the arena, so he took the opportunity to pull her into an embrace. "How are you holding up? I'm glad to see you haven't shut yourself away."

"I…I'm holding up." She pulled away, glancing over at Ramar before speaking again. "Papa, there is something I wish to ask you."

"Oh?" He stroked his chin. "Is it archery lessons? If so, my answer is yes. You behaved admirably over the last two weeks and I couldn't be prouder."

She shook her head. "It's not that. Although I would still like lessons."

"Then do tell! You have my full attention." He gazed down at her, unblinking.

"I've done a lot of thinking since yesterday. About my purpose. About what I should do now…now that I won't be queen." She tried not to flinch as she said it. "I think I have come up with an idea—something that would make me happy." She paused, letting her words sink in. "I would like to become an emissary for the crown." Her statement was followed by silence. Her stomach tumbled. "Before you say no, let me explain. In all that I do, I would be acting on your behalf. I am well trained in politics, perhaps better than anyone because you have trained me. Not only that, I have always wanted to travel. There is a great need for reform throughout the Dragondoms, especially for those farther north—Warsile, Kadworth, Murton, Tarnworth. And given what has happened along the southern coast, the people need us now more than ever. I know it could be dangerous, but if we allow danger to hold us back from doing what is right, we would never get anywhere. I hope that you will at least consider my request—think it over."

When she finished speaking, her father was beaming. "You never cease to impress me, Lena."

She studied him, taken aback. "Does that mean you agree?"

He chuckled. "While I am hesitant to put your life in danger traveling, neither can I keep you caged. Who am I to deny you the desires of your heart?"

"Oh, Papa!" She jumped forward and hugged him again. "You have no idea how happy I am."

A satisfied growl reverberated within his chest. "Now, I *will* expect you to travel with plenty of protection. The road can be a dangerous place for a lady."

Ramar stepped forward, shoulders squared. "My king, I would be honored to accompany Princess Lena and her entourage through whatever travels her business takes her."

King Cornan smiled. "Of course. And I would be glad of it. Nothing would put me more at ease."

"Oh, thank you, Papa! Thank you." A smile plastered itself to her face.

"I only wish for you to be happy, dear one." He hesitated. "As soon as I return, you and I will discuss your first journey. I do have need of your services—as does the kingdom."

"Return?" She tilted her head. "But where are you going?"

King Cornan sighed. "There have been two more attacks along the coast. Your mother and I have called an emergency meeting in Fort Lin. We leave for Lincastle tomorrow."

"*Two*?! No…" Her chest tightened. "How bad?"

The color drained from the king's face. He glanced at Ramar and Briv before answering. "Bad. Beachrest was hit the hardest. At least one hundred and fifty men dead. Numerous women and children missing. Thornwater suffered similar casualties."

Her breakfast turned sour in her stomach. She moved over to the sofa and took a seat. "When will it end?" she whispered. "How can they keep doing this to us?"

Her father shook his head. "Your mother and I are doing all that we can. But we need you to rule in our stead while we are away." He eyed her. "It will be up to you to hold court, meet with the lower council, and keep things in order."

"You want *me*? To rule?" Her heart quickened. He had never asked something so monumental of her.

"I do. You are the highest in rank. Besides, you think I want the steward running things in my absence? Hmph!" He moved over to the mirror where his manservant fitted his doublet with sleeves before crowning him for court. In the process, he studied her in the mirror's reflection. "Don't worry, Lena. I see it in your face. You'll do a splendid job."

She nodded, swallowing against her dry throat. She had

not expected this much responsibility so soon after her failure in the arena. Yet, she welcomed it. This would be her chance, her opportunity to prove that she was capable. "I will do what I can. You can count on me, Papa."

He nodded. "Good. I expect nothing less."

KING CORNAN and Queen Amara departed leaving Briv, Ferand, and Ramar behind to watch over her. They intended to be gone two weeks. In that time, she did what was asked of her. Court was especially trying. Each morning at nine, the double doors opened to the throne room and patrons piled in. Announcements were given first, when warranted. This was followed by important cases—if any. Grievances were aired. She was expected to hear each problem and rule fairly.

By her fourth day, she was altogether exhausted and couldn't wait for her father's return. It had been silly of her to want such a responsibility as queen. What had she been thinking? Perhaps she might have fared better had the king's steward been favorable. He crossed her at every turn. The man saw each opportunity as an attempt to unravel her, to prove she was unfit to rule, not that it mattered anymore. Despite his attempts, she did what she could to best him.

It so happened that she was sitting in court on the fourth day, listening to the grievances from her subjects, when a poor peasant was thrown before her. After hearing a few details of his case, she sought to let the man off with minimal punishment. "Princess Lena." The steward rushed forward, his gravelly voice interrupting the proceeding. "If we do not punish *thieves*, more will follow in their footsteps." His dark eyes glittered with contempt.

She looked from him to the frightened man at the steps of the dais, attempting to hide her frustration. "Tell me, Steward, do you question my father as you question me?" Her voice echoed through the quiet hall. Patrons watched the exchange with bated breath.

"I do not question your authority, Princess," replied the steward. "I merely wish to make a point."

She gave him a curt nod. "Your point is noted. Now tell me, *sire*, why has this man been brought forth in the first place? Surely there are laws in place to address thievery?"

"He has requested it, Your Highness. When a punishment is given, and the culprit requests a higher order—"

"Then the matter is to be addressed at court. Yes, I may be young, but I know the law." She waved her hand to silence him from further protests before looking upon the thief. "Tell me, sir, what was the reason for your theft?"

The man stood up a little straighter. "Please, Your Highness. I only tried to feed my family. We be humble folk. The work I get at the docks don't pay enough for all the food."

"So you broke into a butcher's shop in the Pauper's District. They say you stole an *entire* pig?"

The man flinched, shrank in size, then fell to his knees. "They were starving, Your Highness. My wife, she needed something more to be feeding the children, the baby."

She sighed. His case was all too common, and it broke her heart. "What is the punishment for stealing food?" she asked, eyeing him. Though she already knew the answer, she wanted to know if he did too.

The steward rushed forward instead. "Repayment in full, Your Highness. As well as twenty lashes and a month in the cells."

A strangled cry escaped the thief's lips. "Please! I asked to come before ye in hopes of finding mercy. If I go into the cells, my family will starve. Without my wages, I cannot hope to feed them. They will die!"

"Then they ought to die," hissed the steward, sneering.

"Sire Robert Waymore! Leash your tongue or I'll have it cut out!" She wasn't sure she had such authority but made the threat anyway. "Such comments, *sire*, are unnecessary." She glared at him before turning back to the thief. "Tell me, how many children do you have and how old are they?"

He blinked up at her, opening and closing his mouth before answering. "T-three, Your Highness. The youngest is but a month old, the others are seven and nine."

"Boys, girls?" A plan was brewing in her mind.

"All boys, Your Highness. All boys."

She nodded but hid her smile. "And do your two eldest currently work?"

He bobbed his head. "'Course, Your Highness, when they be finding it. Odd and end jobs, really."

"Good." She clasped her hands together. "We recently acquired six new horses in the royal stable. Our stable hands are overworked and in need of assistance. So it appears that I shall solve *two* problems today." She glanced at the steward, rather proud of her wit, before turning back to her subject. "You will send your two eldest to our stables beginning tomorrow morning at dawn until sunset. They are to report to the stable master, Micah Mallock. There, your boys will work off your debt. In exchange, the royal coffers will directly reimburse the butcher for his pig." She paused for a moment to think. "Six weeks of labor are sufficient to pay for the pig and the damages." Another idea came to mind. "If your boys prove themselves to be honest workers, Master Micah Mallock will keep them on permanently. This way you will be permitted to postpone your jail time until your boys can earn enough to feed your wife and growing baby."

The thief's face turned radiant. "Truly, Your Highness? Truly?"

"*Truly.*" She afforded him a kind smile. "However, you will still receive twenty lashes. Is this repayment acceptable? You may take it or revert to the default."

He fell to his knees, ringing his cap and looking at the floor. "I will take it! I will take it o'course! Thank you, Your Highness. Thank you! Praise Asjaa! Let none say that you are incapable of fair and honest rule!"

At those words, she beamed. If his boys were kept on, their family's circumstances would vastly improve. Work within the Great Keep paid much better than elsewhere. For those lucky enough to get in while it was available, such positions were life-altering. Bartlett was a perfect example of that.

The steward looked as though he smelled something rotten. Nothing brought her more joy than to see his displeasure. Regardless of his disagreement, he instructed the chronicler to take note of the situation. The thief was led away and the next culprits brought forth. Thus, she began her game anew, battling the steward for fair punishments and besting him in each circumstance. When the morning ended, she left court immensely satisfied but entirely exhausted.

During the midday meal, she told Briv, Ferand, and Ramar how tempted she was to put a sleeping drought in the steward's drink. If she were less determined to prove her worth, she might have done it. Still, it was fun to speculate. "Can you imagine the look on his face if he were to wake up in the middle of the Eigaden Plains?" They all burst into laughter.

Ferand was the first to recover. "I can imagine a hungry grazer slobbering all over him with its wet tongue. Imagine waking up to that! How shall we transport him? Once he is asleep, Briv can procure a net and we can carry him into the middle of nowhere."

She burst into a fit of giggles, laughing until tears seeped from her eyes. "Gods! How I wish we could! If only…At least the pranks I've pulled on him in the past were warranted."

"Oh yes," said Briv, "I think the rats were my favorite."

At that, she snorted, spilling juice from her lips before she could quickly wipe it away.

"And anyway," Briv added, "I don't know about you all but I would pay *anything* to rid the world of that infuriating man." He wasn't the only one who felt that way. The steward was not well tolerated by most. But he did his job well enough to please her father. Because the line of succession for stewards went from father to son, King Cornan was reluctant to upset the norm. Fortunately for all, the kingdom's stewards were only human. A king might have anywhere from two to seven in his lifetime.

Ramar grumbled. "I'm also at my wits' end with him. Can you believe he has taken to pestering me about plans for the tournament?" Ramar pinched the bridge of his nose. "Like I care about fabric colors for the competitors' bedchambers."

Lena's jaw dropped. "Wait…he's been dumping that on *you*? But…that should be *my* responsibility. I told Father before he left that I wanted to assist in the tournament's organization."

"Humph." Ramar rolled his eyes. "One would think he would go to you, but clearly not." He took a swig of wine before screwing up his face. "*Lord Ramar*, there aren't enough apartments with adequate views of the sea. *Lord Ramar*, there are not enough pillows for each competitor's room. *Lord Ramar*, do you think they will appreciate running out of candle sticks? *Lord Ramar*, might you wipe my ass while you are at it?"

They all burst into laughter, roaring loud enough to attract many gazes to the head table. "Gods! You sound just like him." Lena had to calm herself.

"Trust me, Lena, if you can handle his remonstrations then by all means, please do. The man is driving me mad."

She sighed. "Not that I *want* to, but I shall be glad to take him off your hands." She had every intention of deeply involving herself in the upcoming tournament, even if it meant postponing her new emissary duties. Of course, it was under the pretense that she merely wanted to help. But there were more selfish reasons involved. A number of young Drengr were unfit to rule. She was particularly dead set against Raff and would do everything possible—even if it required sabotage—to keep him from his goal.

From that day forward, all matters regarding the tournament were brought to her. The rigor of the responsibility kept her busy. Moreover, it did a great deal to heal her, though she often found herself thinking of Ivrir and Daryn. She missed their company and even considered writing to them. Worse still, she often found herself daydreaming of what could have been, especially with Daryn.

When at last King Cornan and Queen Amara returned, they found her in excellent spirits. She was overjoyed to have them back. She eagerly relinquished the privilege of court. But it was the discussion about becoming the kingdom's emissary that she most anticipated.

"Have you given any thought to your first assignment?" her father asked as they sat in his study, enjoying the breeze that snuck past the curtains. "There is great need of your services in the south. There is great need everywhere, but I think a shorter journey will do best for now." He paused to shuffle through a few leaves of parchment on his desk, withdrawing one. "How about Eryas? Their Dragondom has suffered most from these attacks. It could be good for the people to see you and know that they are valued, that their losses are on our hearts and minds." He glanced down at the parchment. "This is from Lord Kanton. He says that a visit made by me and your mother would be most welcome. Might I suggest you instead? There is just over a week until the tournament, but if we sail you there, you would be there and back again before the start. Everyone expects you to be here for it. Tradition dictates such."

She was filled with longing. "I intend to be here for it, yes. But I also understand Lord Kanton's need. You really think I could get there and back in time?"

"I'm sure of it. If you leave at dawn tomorrow, you could be in Graymont in two days, perhaps sooner. Lord Kanton's manor is just across the bay. I would suggest spending three days in his company, touring his city and visiting with his nobles."

"Then I must go," she whispered, already thinking about what she would do once she was there. "Graymont's people will appreciate me being there, and they will be most eager to hear about the preparations for the tournament. I have heard that there is a deep sense of fear settled upon them, so it might give them some distraction."

"Aye, they fear the pirates will strike them next, but I doubt it. The city is much larger than the previous targets."

"Still, I think it would be worthwhile. Very well. I'll do it."

King Cornan beamed. "Excellent! I shall have *The Selena* readied for your departure. Ramar will accompany you, and your handmaidens and Kenna Margaret if she can be spared. Best that you get to packing and travel light. There won't be time to send a letter to Lord Kanton, so your visit will be a pleasant surprise, but I expect he will be a most gracious host."

"Thank you, Papa." A nervous thrill shot through her. She stood and made her way round his desk, kissing his forehead. "I will not disappoint you." Then she hurried away to pack and prepare her ladies for departure.

CHAPTER 12
A MUCH NEEDED JOURNEY

"GRAYMONT!? GODS ABOVE, LENA." Kenna Margaret placed her hand over her heart. "When were you planning to tell us of your change in duties?"

"Uhm…now?"

"A little warning might have been nice for my poor nerves."

"I'm sorry, Kenna." She gave Margaret her best pout. "Things have been rushed and it was only just decided." She hesitated. "Will you come?"

Margaret glanced at Lena's handmaidens, busy chatting and packing Lena's things in a trunk. "I think I must. I cannot trust any of you alone on your first journey." She fanned her face. "I would never forgive myself."

"Good!" Lena couldn't help her smile. "You'd best go and pack."

"Hmph! I should think so." Margaret squared her shoulders and disappeared.

It was a rushed effort, so Lena helped her handmaidens with the remainder of her things, discussing the journey with excitement. None of them had traveled outside of the capital.

"I only wish we might travel by carriage rather than over sea," Cora mused.

"Come now, Cora, there isn't enough time. Besides, it's only two days on the water," said Lena. "And the bay's waters are calmer than open sea. You'll get used to it. I promise."

The following morning dawned gray and overcast, and a light breeze blew from the north. Ramar had a carriage waiting to take them down to the docks. Lena's parents came to see her off, full of smiles and well wishes. "Take care of yourself, darling." Her mother held her tight. "It's dreadful that I must remain behind. I will worry whilst you are away, but you will make us proud. Ramar will keep us abreast of all that transpires, won't you, Ramar?"

Ramar stepped forward, his fist over his chest. "Upon my honor, Amara. I will take the best care of her."

Because he was a Drengr, it would be easy for Ramar to keep her parents updated on all that happened. Their telepathic abilities meant they could send thoughts in an instant. It became more difficult with distance, but they weren't going too far. Eryas' peninsula was just on the other side of the bay.

The carriage carried them through the city. Ramar chose to transform into his hulking red dragon form and fly overhead. Before she knew it, she found herself on board *The Selena*, settling in. "Let me know if you need anything at all, Your Highness," said Marcos, the ship's captain, as he bowed.

Once her things were stowed in the royal cabin, she made her way to the upper deck—the same place she had occupied when Daryn took her sailing. It was difficult to keep him from her mind. She found herself picturing his muscled chest covered in a billowing white tunic, calling orders to the deck hands. The very thought left her stomach fluttering. She sighed, shaking her head. "I miss him more than I care to admit."

"Who, Princess?" Cora sat beside her.

"Daryn. That day he took us sailing."

Cora smiled. "He was a handsome sight to behold, was he not?"

Lena felt her cheeks burn but she said nothing more. There was naught to do about it now. Best that she consider the journey ahead rather than what lay behind.

By midday, both Cora and Theresa were forced below deck with seasickness. Lena found them in her cabin with pale faces, their arms wrapped around a bucket each, swaying. She and Avra got them some water and a little something to eat before encouraging them to come above deck. "The fresh breeze is better than stale air," she advised. At last they agreed to follow her up.

The day passed quickly and her exhilaration grew. As the coast sailed by, its shores tiny in the distance with miniature sandy beaches, she couldn't help but feel the deep effects of adventure in her breast, calling to her. She imagined that she was a sailor, sailing off to a distant land far over the Dragonfire Sea—Oshea perhaps. Deep down, she knew that she had made the right choice—this was to be her future—and she rejoiced.

Being on board *The Selena* was a direct opposite to the stuffy capital where everything was on top of everything else. Here the open space stretched far and wide, embracing her like a daughter. The sounds were muted and the quietness calming. She understood why Daryn liked sailing so much, though she tried not to think of him *too* often. It was hard when she knew he would be returning to Kastali Dun for the tournament. Harder still when she realized he would never be hers. Weeks prior, having any of the hopefuls was an appalling thought, but perhaps knowing she couldn't have him made her want him more.

"Being out here certainly gives one time to think, doesn't it?" Ramar took a seat beside her. The afternoon sun caught his face, making him glow. She squinted at it. It's yellow orb was like the drop of a yolk falling towards the horizon beyond Kastali Dun's peninsula, small enough to hold in the palm of her hand. "How are you liking your first trip so far?" Ramar asked.

She turned her attention away from the west and smiled at him. "It's splendid. Getting away from the capital seems the perfect medicine—as if I have left my worries and cares upon the shore. I hadn't realized how welcome this would be."

Ramar chuckled. "I'm glad to hear it. Enjoy it while you can. The tournament will take up much of your time after we return."

"Yes." She sighed. Ramar's words were like the tide, washing things up she would rather not think of. "I suppose. I just hope that whoever wins is a worthy candidate."

His expression turned to mock surprise. "You mean Raff isn't worthy of the crown? Who would have guessed?"

She let out a sound of disgust. "I will do everything in my power to ensure he doesn't win."

His eyebrows lifted. "Careful, Lena. Meddling could result in consequences."

She shrugged. "Let's hope I don't need to. He's got plenty of other candidates to contend with. Perhaps one of them will pick him off. It isn't as if he made friends while he was here."

"True." Ramar sounded thoughtful. "But still, just be careful. Your father wouldn't take too kindly to meddling in something like this."

"Yes, I suppose so." They fell quiet. She watched the seagulls that swooped and dipped about the bay, looking for fish. *The Selena* wasn't the only ship out today. The route to Graymont was a busy one, with carracks and galleys passing fully loaded, sitting deep in the water. Each ship's crew shouted and waved as they sailed by.

CORA AND THERESA were much improved by nightfall. Things became more cheerful. They ate a modest dinner on the floor of the deck, sitting in a circle under the open sky as Ramar watched on, sharing stories and speculating over what they might find in Graymont. The crew and guards ate together too, near the front of the ship. They were a rowdy bunch, laughing and joking.

"What do you think will happen once we arrive in Graymont?" Theresa asked.

Lena shrugged. "I suspect Lord Kanton will introduce me to everyone he can—though I hope he will spare some time to discuss the pirate attacks. I am not a silly woman to be paraded about. Business comes first."

"He will want to throw a party, I am sure." Cora's eyes sparkled. "All great lords enjoy throwing parties."

"You will *all* behave yourselves," Margaret warned, as if reading their minds.

"Of course, Kenna. Isn't that why you have come?" Lena tried to hide the laughter in her voice. "Oh, don't look at me like that. There is nothing to worry about." For the first time in her life, she had a measure of freedom that she was unused to. The prospects were tempting. But she was determined to put her work first.

That was easier said than done when they arrived at Graymont's port the following evening. The moment they set foot on the dock, Ramar informed the dock master of their arrival and a messenger was dispatched. They had no sooner unloaded their belongings when a number of carriages raced along the shoreline in their direction. In the darkness, Graymont sparkled with hundreds of golden lights and they could see the lanterns swaying on each carriage.

As the four carriages clattered to a halt at the dockyard's entrance, the door to the first was thrown open and a finely dressed man emerged. He was followed moments later by a woman in a large, ostentatious gown. "Gods above," Lena muttered. "Were they expecting us? Or do they always dress so extravagantly?"

"Your father did not have time to send word," said Ramar. "Lord Kanton is rather showy—his wife more so."

Lena snorted. "I should say so! She's dressed louder than I am and I'm the princess."

"Welcome! Welcome!" Lord Kanton spread his arms wide as he made his way over. Upon closer inspection, he appeared to be in his thirties, with a smooth face and closely trimmed black beard. "I am honored! Absolutely honored, Princess, Lord Ramar. A most unexpected surprise!" He and Lady Kanton bowed deeply. His lady had a pinched face, with dark hair that had been braided and pinned elaborately. She took her superiority seriously.

Lena curtsied. "Thank you for such a timely welcome, Lord and Lady Kanton. Let none say that you lack hospitality."

Lord Kanton waved a hand in dismissal. "Think nothing of it, Princess! And please, Gerald will do. This is my wife, Mira."

"Pleasure to meet you." Lena curtsied again. "I am here on behalf of my father. It has been a long two days, Gerald.

My ladies and my guards are tired. I hope that we might stay three days but will impinge upon you no longer than that."

Gerald's face split into a smile. "Of course! The tournament, eh? We receive a great deal of news being so close to the capital." He rubbed his hands together. "No matter! I have brought my carriages. Let me show you to Gray Castle where we might rest and dine and be merry!"

She bowed her head. "Thank you, Gerald. That would be much appreciated."

She instructed the others and they loaded themselves into the carriages. Ramar preferred to fly overhead for some fresh air. She and Margaret rode with Lord and Lady Kanton, who took the opportunity to point out everything along their journey, from the blacksmith to the bakery, and many storehouses filled with surplus from a bountiful harvest the year prior.

"There you'll see the oldest building in Graymont," added Lord Kanton. "Some say Lord Bain built it himself when he was exploring the shores. It's owned by the Belchers now."

"Lord Bain?" Her eyes narrowed. "As in King Eymar's first Drengr Fairtheoir?"

"The very same!" Lord Kanton's face lit up. "And that building over there was burned down a century ago and rebuilt. We use it as a bower now—some of the finest weapons..."

"Forgive me, Lord Kanton, but I hope that tomorrow morning we might meet—you and I—to discuss the pirate attacks along the eastern shores of Eryas." While Eryas wasn't the only Dragondom to be hit, it had suffered two attacks.

"Oh..." Lord Kanton's face fell at the reminder. "But I had hoped to introduce you to a number of my nobles. It's not every day a princess comes to town. Perhaps we might meet over such matters the following morning? Sir Milstead will be most disappointed if he is delayed a meeting with you. Trust me when I say he will speak of nothing else otherwise."

Lena sighed. "Very well. The following morning will do."

SHE HAD BEEN correct in her assumptions. Their first morning began with introductions. Sir Milstead was first. He was a talkative man in his sixties in possession of a great wealth of land. He and his mistress insisted on showing Lena and her ladies about, with Lord and Lady Kanton in tow. After that, the day was filled with more names than she could follow as they were paraded throughout Graymont. There was Sir Drake Belmore and his wife, and the Trants, and the Warrens…

Most offered their sincere regrets that she had not found a mate, which made things rather awkward. Everyone was particularly interested in details about the upcoming tournament. The only talk they avoided was mention of the attacks along the eastern shore of Eryas and other Dragondoms farther down.

"It seems they would rather avoid mentioning the pirates," Lena said to Margaret that evening. Her handmaidens were busy fixing up her hair in the modest apartment Lord and Lady Kanton had provided. As suspected, a lavish party was to follow.

"Many find it better to avoid frightening thoughts," Margaret mused. She sat on a nearby sofa, fanning herself. "I certainly wouldn't want to concern myself with such melancholy thoughts while a princess was in town."

"I suppose so. And my father is probably right. They need not fear an attack here. Graymont is too big. But what of their neighboring villages? Surely many have family along the coast?"

"Oh, let's not think of such worries tonight. Lord Kanton's party ought to be a merry occasion." Avra had nearly finished with her hair.

Lena sighed. "Yes, I suppose it will. I just don't find such diversions to my liking these days."

That night, Lena found that her handmaidens were adjusting quite well. There were plenty of unmarried men to be introduced, and much dancing to be had. While she was happy looking on, she could not deny Lord Kanton and Sir Milstead two dances each when they requested it. Appearances were important in a place like this and what would be said if the princess closed herself off and appeared unfriendly? So she did her civic duty with as much enthusiasm as she could muster.

THE FOLLOWING morning she found herself in Lord Kanton's study. A tray of food had been delivered for the two of them so that they might dine while they discussed the matter at hand. "I have mobilized my local militia as your father advised," said Lord Kanton. "Many have been summoned from throughout Eryas. They will take posts in the smaller settlements lining the shore. I hope that might act as a future deterrent."

"I am glad to hear that," she found herself saying. "I am sure the villagers will feel safer this way." She paused. "And what about the larger cities? Redding and Wythers? Is there any fear of attacks there?"

Lord Kanton rubbed his beard. "I should hope not. Perhaps just as likely as an attack here—if they grow bolder."

"It is a possibility. One we should consider." They continued to discuss these matters even after the tray was emptied. "And what of the survivors in Landor and Clayton? My father said that their losses were great."

Lord Kanton's face turned red, but otherwise he maintained composure. "They have retreated. After the loss of their villages, they were forced to make a new home."

She tilted her head to the side. "Have you spoken with any? Gone to see them?" His face turned a deeper shade of red. "Lord Kanton," she said, trying to keep the scolding tone from her voice, "you are their lord governor. You cannot abandon your people during times of need. They have suffered a great loss. You should have taken a carriage out to assess the damage yourself."

At this he sputtered. "Have you any idea how many days that would take? I will not abandon my city. What if we suffer a direct attack while I am away? What then, eh? Then I am abandoning my own people in their greatest time of need."

"They are *all* your people, Lord Kanton. And that is a risk you should be willing to take. The likelihood of an attack here, where your city is already well-protected, is slim. Better that your people—those who are suffering—should be cared for. They will think you unfeeling." She sighed. "Have they been offered any compensation?"

Lord Kanton scowled. "For what?"

"For the loss of their homes. Gods, man!" Short of insulting him, she held her tongue.

"Oh. And where would this compensation come from?"

"Your coffers, Lord Kanton. Those storehouses you showed me along the shore laden with surplus. Or you could have written to my father requesting aid for them. Gods only know Kastali Dun's coffers are large, and we have coin set aside for times of need. If ever there was one, I would say this was it."

"Oh. Right. Very well then, I shall see what I can do."

"Yes." She lifted her chin. "See to it that you do."

After she left his study, she made a mental note to speak with her father. All those who had lost their homes would have nothing but the clothes upon their backs, perhaps a little more if they were lucky. They would need assistance. It was the lord governor's duty as their caretaker to handle such matters. But if the lord governors of each affected Dragondom did not speak to her father over such matters, how was he to know of any mistreatment?

"It would seem that my coming here was more necessary than I first believed," she said that night when her ladies were preparing her for bed. Then they discussed all that had transpired during that morning's meeting and all that she intended to do now that she better understood Eryas' circumstances.

"Your new calling has already made a difference," said Margaret, agreeing.

"I only hope so. Assuming I can make the matter clear to my father, I will insist he check with each lord governor and ensure that those affected by the raids are properly cared for. We cannot expect them to start anew in life with nothing. Even if it means setting up a fund to care for them, something to get them started."

"I think that sounds splendid," said Theresa.

The following morning she had Ramar relay as much as was necessary of her meeting with Lord Kanton to her father. Then she spent the remainder of her time in the city's market, buying what she could with the spending money she had brought. Her handmaidens did the same, following her through the stalls. Their guards kept a safe distance, ensuring that no trouble found them—not that anyone was brave enough to try anything with a king's Drengr Fairtheoir present.

The best way to help the economy in Eryas was to pour money back into it. While her purchases wouldn't directly help those who had been displaced in other villages, she hoped that the benefits would reach them eventually. As the day wore on, she found Graymont's people to be a friendly, easygoing sort. Children were out in abundance, and those brave enough to approach her were rewarded with meat and berry pies. Simply seeing their faces light up with excitement was fulfilling. And when all her money was spent, she returned to Lord Kanton's castle.

Dinner that night was a rowdy affair. Her handmaidens were often invited to take part in impromptu dances that arose throughout the evening. She enjoyed watching them have fun, especially given the amount of work they put in day by day keeping her appearance tidy. But she couldn't help wishing Daryn was here to ask her for a dance.

THEIR TIME in Graymont came to an end. On the fourth morning they found themselves tucked away in Lord Kanton's carriages, making their way back to *The Selena*. Lord and Lady Kanton did not accompany them this time, at Lena's insistence that they remain behind. They had been gracious enough, she assured them, though it was really because she was eager for peace and quiet.

After they found themselves on board and settled, Ramar made his way to Lena's side. She stood at the bow, watching their departure, rubbing a small worry stone she had found on the dock. "What are your thoughts now,

Princess? Still think you don't have any purpose in Dragonwall?"

She turned and smiled. "Quite the contrary. And I have *you* to thank." She bumped her shoulder against his. "Venturing outside of the capital has opened my eyes in a way I did not imagine. This trip was liberating."

"It has done you some good I think."

She nodded. "I never imagined that one person could make much difference. I have but to cast a single stone." She tossed her worry stone into the water below. "And hope that the ripple effect will be enough." The ship lurched and her stomach jolted.

"You will never know unless you try," Ramar said, smiling down at her. He was right and she intended to do exactly that.

THE *SELENA* REACHED Kastali Dun mere days before the start of the Tournament for the Crown. Lena was greeted in the lowest courtyard of the keep. Nobles and servants alike had assembled in honor of her arrival. With success swelling in her breast and a crowd of people to welcome her, she felt more important than ever—more useful—and her purpose was growing clear. But there was little time to relish in her accomplishments.

Competitors were already arriving in Kastali Dun. The competition was open to all—both mated and unmated Drengr. Quite a few were expected to participate, all hoping for the right to win the title of crowned prince. While there were a number of new faces, there were many familiar ones too, hopefuls that had previously come to see if a bond existed with her.

Out of everyone, Lena only cared about seeing two: Ivrir and Daryn. She hoped that Daryn would hold true to the promise he had made to compete. And with each passing day, she found herself longing to see him, growing more nervous that he might change his mind.

Two days before the tournament was set to begin, she found herself in the cookery with the master cook finalizing the menu for the opening feast. The cookery was already bustling as its staff rushed back and forth making preparations. She scanned through the master cook's handwritten list of food, chewing on the skin of her bottom lip. Every so often she glanced up at him to make a comment. "Hm...I should think four roast pigs would be sufficient if you plan to have chicken as well. And no need to have sweet potatoes if you're planning to have white potatoes. Save those for another occasion."

"Very well, Princess. We will save that for later." The master cook was a patient man, rosy cheeked with a gray beard trimmed neatly to his face. He smiled a lot and was often found humming as he went about his duties.

"And what of dessert?" she asked. "Apple pies, I hope?"

"But of course! As those are your favorite, I have already planned on making nearly one hundred, along with chocolate covered strawberries." He led her to a storeroom piled with hundreds of green apples. She couldn't help her smile. "You know me too well, Master Fenn. My mouth is already watering. Your pies are the best in the kingdom."

"Why thank you, Princess. You honor me. Now, as you can see, we are quite ready to—"

Cries of dismay brought their conversation to a halt. Ramar burst into the storeroom. He was breathing hard and carried a spyglass. "There you are!" He grabbed her hand. "Come with me."

"What? Ramar!" She tried to resist.

"Just come!"

She threw the master cook an apologetic look and handed back his list as Ramar pulled her away. He led her all the way to the king's tower, up the tower's ladder, and out into the queen's garden without another word, smiling all the while as if he shared a private joke. She followed him to the tower's parapet. It was waist-high and offered a spectacular view of the Bay of Bandu. Taking the spyglass, Ramar looked out over the water.

"There," he pointed. She squinted into the distance, shielding her gaze with her hand. "Have a look at that ship entering the bay." Ramar handed her the spyglass.

She put her eye to it, scanning until she found the mouth of the bay. Then she moved her gaze to the ship Ramar had mentioned, adjusting the spyglass for better focus. She saw a cog that looked nearly identical to her father's. "Sorry, but what should I be excited about?" she asked, studying it.

"Have a look at its *name*."

She squinted into the glass and gasped. "*Storm's Maiden*!" She looked up at Ramar before returning her gaze to the ship. Her heart leapt in her chest. Daryn had come! Just as he'd promised, he'd come to compete in the tournament! And even better, he'd brought the *Storm's Maiden*. A cry sprang from her lips. She thrust the spyglass into Ramar's hands before racing away. She had a guest to greet, and this time, she had no intention of playing dress up before racing to meet him.

CHAPTER 13

A DAY SPENT SAILING

WITH HER FATHER'S PERMISSION, Lena abandoned her duties the day before the tournament to go sailing with Daryn. Since his arrival, she had not stopped smiling. And after his invitation, she couldn't resist.

The *Storm's Maiden* maneuvered beautifully around the bay, cutting through the water with ease. Her modest crew of ten manned the ship so that she and Daryn were free to relax in each other's company. She couldn't help but steal frequent glances at him when he wasn't looking, admiring his muscled chest, the dimples in his cheeks when he smiled, and the way his brown curls rustled in the sea breeze.

Daryn sighed, content beside her. "I couldn't have asked for a better day to take you out, Lena. The wind at our back. The clouds above. A sturdy ship to carry us. This is the life, isn't it?"

She inhaled deeply, tasting the salt in the air. "It's marvelous. I can see why you're so fond of your *Storm's Maiden* and sailing," she said. "I too have found joy on the water." With a blanket spread beneath them, she told him about her trip to Graymont. As they talked, they lay upon the deck watching the clouds, pointing out familiar shapes.

"I'm relieved that you've found renewed purpose," he said at last. There was glad enthusiasm in his voice. "When your parents sent us away, I wanted to bid you farewell but we were not given the opportunity."

She turned to look at him, offering him a slow smile by way of apology. "It was a heavy blow for me."

"Understandably." His gaze was warm, reassuring. "The ceremony placed a great deal of pressure upon you—more pressure than any one person should bear. Yet you handled it with dignity."

She snorted and rolled her eyes, turning her face skyward. "Right up until I fled the arena like a coward."

"Come now. You mustn't be so hard on yourself. I probably would have done the same with a crowd of thousands watching." He got up on one elbow to better study her. "May I be truthful about something?"

"Of course," she whispered, her throat growing dry.

He hesitated. "There were many times I imagined feeling those little strings that tie two people together. I wanted so badly for there to be a bond between us, Lena."

Guilt seeped into her gut. She had hoped for a bond too, but not for honest reasons. Daryn had attended the ceremony in hopes of finding his mate. She? In hopes of winning the crown. Her motives were no better than those hopefuls she'd selfishly judged on their first night.

Daryn continued, his eyebrows drawn tight. "Each day we were together, I hoped you would fall for me. That we might influence fate. It does not seem that fate pitied me, does it?" He ran a finger down her cheek, leaving her skin flushed. "Say something."

"Daryn, I…" She exhaled, keeping her gaze upon the sky to avoid looking at him. "I never wanted the ceremony. Not one bit of it. Not as it was intended, anyway." It felt good getting the truth off her chest. "I hated the idea of finding a mate simply to earn something that should have already been mine. Before—" She cleared her throat but her voice came out as little more than a whisper. "Before the ceremony, I nearly fled. I was terrified of what it would mean to lose my individuality. To me, that was an unfair trade." When she glanced at him, she could see the little flecks of gold in his eyes. She blinked, trying to regain her focus. "I finally worked up the courage to step out into the arena, promising myself that if it got me the crown, it would be worth it." Then she shook her head, ashamed. "All that courage. Look where it got me."

He watched her for a long time, his eyes roving over her face, as if trying to find the answer to a hidden question. Would he hate her? Call her selfish? "So you had no interest whatsoever in finding your mate?"

She shook her head and closed her eyes before speaking. "No…not really."

"And what of our time together? What of the extra attention you paid me? Was that simply for the crown?"

Her eyes flew open. "No! No of course not! I enjoyed every moment we spent together."

"Then why? Why wasn't it enough? Why wasn't I enough?"

"Daryn…You are not being fair!"

"*Fair*? Was I merely a diversion to pass the time until the ceremony? It certainly seems so."

She sat up, scowling. "We knew each other for two weeks. *Two weeks*, Daryn! In that time, I was supposed to hand over my life and be eager about it?" Her voice rose to a new height and she threw up her hands. "Gods! I've never even kissed a man. I've never experienced the things every woman should —love, affection, heartbreak. That's what I call unfair."

He sat up too. A frown pulled at his lips. "You…you've never…" He ran a hand through his hair. "Lena, truly?"

Heat flooded her skin. "Why is it such a surprise?! I'm the princess! I don't go out finding men to…to…well…it would be *unladylike*," she sputtered.

The corner of his mouth twitched into a lopsided smile. She gawked at him. "You think this is *funny*?"

"Gods, Lena! Yes. I had no idea that you were so innocent!"

Her jaw dropped and she could think of nothing to say. Before thinking better of it, she picked up her slippers and threw them at his face with all the force she could muster. They smacked him, hard. He froze for a moment, then roared, doubling over with laughter.

She stood and sulked barefooted to the back of the ship.

"Lena!" he called after her. "Come on!"

She offered him a scowl over her shoulder then turned to watch the waves, doing her best to ignore him. Much to her dismay, he came up beside her. "What do you want *now*? Come to further judge me?"

He wore a smirk. "No, *Princess*, I have come to remedy your kiss."

Her eyes widened. She was about to protest when he grabbed her arm and pulled her against him, planting his mouth over hers. She wanted to pull away—her mind screamed for her to do it. But the warmth of his touch seeped through her. She responded, letting the softness of his lips capture her breath. The feel of his mouth was gentle, inviting, as if no length of time would ever be enough.

When at last he pulled away, her eyes remained closed,

unwilling to relinquish the moment. "So that's what I've been missing?" she said at last.

He chuckled. "Say goodbye to your innocence."

When she opened her eyes, his smug expression burned itself into her mind.

They returned to the blanket and continued to watch the clouds. Was she glad to be rid of his lips? Hardly. His remedy had done nothing more than fix the experience permanently in her mind. And while she wanted to be cross with him for such a brazen action, she couldn't find it in her.

For the remainder of their time, they talked about the tournament, speculating over various competitors, and who might best who in each competition. She told him of how she'd kept busy with the preparations, helping to prepare the competitors' accommodations, organize each of the events, and select the menus for the feasts and parties. "We've had so many competitors arrive in the past few days that the keep is bursting at the seams."

"Well, you won't need to worry about me. I plan to sleep here on my ship." He patted the planks of the deck and grinned.

Her chest fell. "Are...are you sure?" She failed to keep the disappointment from her voice. "I prepared our best available room for you."

"I'm positive. The *Storm's Maiden* is favorable for me. I hate cities. Too smothering. Castles, even more so." As much as she wanted to, she couldn't disagree with him. "Besides, it will be good for me to get away at night—clear my head and all that."

"But..." She frowned. "What if I need to speak with you? What if something urgent arises?" No circumstances came to mind, but one never knew the future.

Daryn offered her a toothy grin that dimpled his cheeks. "Well, *dear* Princess, I have a solution for that." His voice lowered to a husky whisper. "If ever you have need of me, place a torch out upon your balcony. I have a direct view from where I plan to anchor."

A thrill shot through her. "If I do that, will you come?"

"I'll fly right up. And the best part is"—his eyes gleamed—"no one will see me pass through the keep."

Her stomach fluttered. What was he implying? That they might engage in a secret rendezvous? She thought of his lips again, of how soft they were against hers. "What if you don't see my torch?"

"If I don't see it, someone in my crew will. It will be superior to passing a note to a servant and creating rumors."

"Oh…" She hadn't thought of that. "I reckon you're right."

"Hmm…" He hesitated. "Since we're on the subject, you have me curious. What could possibly warrant your need of my services beyond daylight hours?" He scooted ever-so-slightly closer. Her heart quickened.

Before letting her true feelings be known, she offered him a sly smile. "For my *scheming,* naturally. I cannot let Raff the Ruthless win and you know it. I will do anything and everything to ensure it does not happen."

"Princess Lena! For shame! You ought to behave yourself. Be honorable in this tournament." It was difficult to tell if he was teasing or scolding—she decided to take it as teasing. "Count me out of your diabolical plans. I promised you I would compete. I cannot partake in actions beyond that."

"Then you won't come to my room if I put the torch out?"

The corner of his mouth twitched. "Oh, I will come. You need not doubt that." At this, they both began laughing, then returned to watching the clouds.

Their journey back to the docks did not take long. After disembarking the *Storm's Maiden*, Daryn kissed her hand while maintaining eye contact with her. She would have preferred another kiss on the lips, but too many eyes were watching.

That night at dinner, she couldn't help stealing glances in his direction. Nor could she stop her mind from replaying their kiss over and again. As covertly as possible, she studied him, noting how well he looked in his burgundy tunic, Sverak strapped to his side, easy smile upon his handsome face. His hair was still ruffled from their excursion. She liked that.

"It seems a certain *Drengr* has captured your eye," her mother whispered, leaning over.

"What? Of course not, Mama."

"Come now, Lena. Don't play games with me. You snuck away to spend time with him—*alone*. That was very reckless." Her mother's scolding was half-hearted.

"I did not *sneak* away," she said. "Father gave me permission. You know that. Nor were we alone."

"Oh? And which of your father's six went along? Ramar?"

She pushed some food around her plate, understanding her mother's meaning. "Well, none of them. But there were ten crew members aboard the *Storm's Maiden*, Mother, so we were not alone."

Queen Amara sighed, resigned to avoid an argument. "I know you are a woman grown, Lena. I only hope you will be *careful*. Falling in love with a man who is intended for another is a dangerous path."

She swallowed her mouthful of potatoes. Her mother simply meant that if she and Daryn fell in love, and Daryn happened to find his mate, his affections would shift and she would be left heartbroken. "I know, Mama. Believe me, I've considered it plenty. And I promise to guard my heart." She only half meant it. What was life without a little fun?

Her mother nodded and returned to her father's attention. Freed, she allowed her eyes to glance once more in Daryn's direction before circling the hall. There were many Drengr competitors present, most of whom she recognized as the returning hopefuls. However, since the tournament was open to both mated *and* mateless Drengr—as long as they were younger than three hundred—many other young mated Drengr were present to try their luck.

Raff was not. Nor Ivrir. But there was still time to arrive. Competitors had until midday the following day to present themselves. She couldn't help but wish something terrible had befallen Raff. It was a long journey across Dragonwall, after all. The thought left her grinning as she imagined what sorts of trouble might have befallen him.

"What has you looking so mischievous?" Briv asked, bumping his shoulder into hers. Ferand and Ramar leaned towards them, interested.

"Oh, nothing." She winked at Ramar.

"It hardly appears that way," said Briv.

"Well, if you must know, I'm merely considering my master plans. You know, all the best ways to ensure Raff loses in the tournament. I was wondering if there was a way to turn him into a donkey. Hee-haw." They chuckled.

"That's our Lena," Briv said, winking at her.

"Now that you know, I trust you won't get in my way." It was difficult to tell whether they believed and supported her. They knew her well enough to understand her capabilities.

Ferand smiled. "So long as you get the steward again while you're at it, you will find no complaints from us."

"Very well," she said. After all, each knew how much the

steward *hated* being left out. The remainder of her evening was spent fantasizing fresh tricks that might come in handy. By dinner's end, she had thought up quite a few.

CHAPTER 14
A MYSTERIOUS COMPETITOR

LENA'S HANDMAIDENS dressed her with care the morning of
the tournament's initiation. The undertaking was in her
honor, and she was charged with overseeing it. Today especially she played a key role.

Most of her gown was spun gold with the exception of
her bodice, which was cream. Its cream sleeves were tightly
fitted against her upper arm and flared out at her elbows.
The layers of the skirt were so long that they dragged behind
her. Most eye-catching was the delicate bronze embroidery
that covered nearly every measure of the gown's fabric. And
like many others that covered enough of her chest, the
Drengr monarchy's sigil was positioned just above her left
breast.

Her handmaidens speculated while they worked on her
hair, weaving small bits of gold cord into her braid. She
absentmindedly watched them in the reflection of the looking
glass as they discussed which champion was most likely to
win the tournament. She tried to follow, but her mind was too
befuddled.

"I think it will be Thos," said Avra. "He's one of the largest."

Theresa snorted. "*Size* doesn't ensure victory." She paid Avra a look that matched her disagreement. "Besides, most of the competitions will be in their human form."

"So?" Theresa shrugged. "Bigger means more powerful in any form I would think."

"What about Rhold?" Cora asked. "He seems like a fighter."

"Cora?" Lena interrupted. "What was your first kiss with Thomas like?"

"My...? Oh." Cora turned a deep shade of red. "A bit wet. But...wonderful." She fell quiet as if recalling the memory.

"Is that all? Surely there's more." Lena hesitated. "I will tell you about mine if you tell me about yours."

They gasped. "You? Your Highness?"

"Well yes, just yesterday..." She touched her fingers to her lips.

Cora's eyes widened. "You and Daryn?"

It was hard to hide her smirk. "Only if you promise not to tell Mother." Thank the gods Kenna Margaret was occupied elsewhere.

"Very well, Princess." Cora bowed her head. "I promise not to say a word." Cora aimed a look at Theresa and Avra; they agreed too.

"But you must tell me about yours first," Lena prompted. They all knew that Thomas had been courting Cora in secret for some months. Theresa and Avra had not yet admitted to any secret relationships, but she was confident they would if any arose. Besides, just because they weren't in a declared relationship did not mean they hadn't kissed.

It was good fun until Kenna Margaret swept into the room. "The carriage is ready for us, Princess Lena." She stopped in her tracks. "My! Don't you look pretty today. You are positively glowing."

Was she? She touched her cheeks with her hands. They burned at the thought of exposing her happiness. "And here I thought you would hate this tournament," said Margaret. Truthfully, she should have hated it. For weeks, the mere thought of it left her stomach boiling. Giving up her crown to its winner was no small matter.

"Come now, girls," said Margaret. "Finish her up. There you go. Get her tiara in place. We must be away or we'll be late. And we don't want to miss the entrance!" Her kenna ushered the women about, speeding them along. Then they made their way to the bottom level of the keep where the carriage awaited. It took them through the city to its west side where the arena was.

With her mind occupied by thoughts of Daryn, her kenna did most of the talking. "Your mother and father will fly in," said Margaret, but she hardly listened. "Your father has a table set up in the royal box where the chronicler will be taking count of the competitors. Once everyone has arrived, you'll be able to begin."

She already knew all of this, so she allowed her mind to wander over thoughts of Daryn, imagining a scenario where his shirt was torn to shreds during a fight such that she might see his bare chest. Her stomach began to flutter. She placed her hand over it.

"Are you unwell, dear girl?" Her kenna's brow furrowed. "You're hardly listening to a word I say."

"Fine, Kenna, and quite well, thank you." She shared a knowing look with Cora before turning to the window. "Besides, I know what to do. My father and I went over the particulars yesterday. You need not worry." The arena loomed up before them.

"Very well." Her kenna sniffed.

Their carriage took them to the back of the arena, to it's private entrance where they were let out. They proceeded to the royal box. It provided the best views in the stands. As expected, she found the chronicler and steward sitting before a table that had been erected, scratching over parchment as they took note of names. Small stacks of coins were piled at the table's edge. She moved over to examine them. Each coin had a twin, and each set of twins a unique symbol like trees, fish, boats, and the like. These would be used to determine the fighting pairs.

While no fighting would take place today, the initial pairs would be decided. Following this, a six-hour feast would commence. She had organized the entire affair. There would be twelve courses, all manner of entertainment, perhaps some dancing, and plenty of drinking. Tomorrow the real fighting would begin.

She glanced down at the floor of the arena. Many Drengr warriors had already gathered. They moved about, conversing with one another. Those with mates brought them along to stand beside them for this important moment. At midday the bell would toll, and the final competitor count would be taken. After that the tournament would officially commence, and a matching number of coins would be placed into a bag to be passed around.

She watched her father's lazy descent into the arena. His turquoise dragon form drew whispers of excitement from the crowd as they pointed at their king and queen. When he landed, her mother dismounted with absolute grace, keeping the skirts of her gown intact. Then her father transformed into the king everyone knew and loved. Together they ascended the stairs to the box.

"Lena!" Her mother took her in her arms. "You look positively divine!"

She kissed both her mother and father before the three of them took their seats. Then—along with the rest of the crowd—they waited for the competitors to assemble. Those who had yet to arrive, circled their way into the arena. If they were alone, they transformed gracefully landing on two feet. If they carried a Rider, they waited for their Rider to dismount as her father had, before taking up a human form. Each competitor announced themselves loudly to the crowd and their name was taken down.

At last, she spotted Daryn's blood-red scales above, glittering as they caught the sun. Her chest fluttered as her gaze fixed itself to him. He was coming in quick, unlike the others who'd taken their time. Nosediving from high above, he plummeted towards the arena's floor. As he gathered speed, the audience gasped. With an impressive show of agility, he pulled up from his dive, back-winged, then transformed. When his boots hit the ground, plumes of dust rose into the air. The audience applauded, delighted, as he walked over to the line of competitors to take his place. She joined in, clapping and smiling.

After this, many others took note, making their own entrances before announcing themselves. Some circled around the arena before landing, others did barrel rolls with their wings tucked tight. When she spotted Raff the Ruthless's silver form, her stomach turned and a familiar hatred returned, burning hot within her. He did three rolls, wings tucked tightly to his body. It should have made him dizzy and she wished it had. How wonderful it would be to see him smack into the arena's wall. She stifled a giggle.

As the sun reached its zenith, the anticipation in the arena rose to an all-time high. She knew the bell would toll any moment. The competitors had arrived. They stood waiting, shifting from foot to foot. She did not see Ivrir among them. Perhaps it was better this way. She was preoccupied with Daryn, after all. Though it would be nice to have her archery teacher back. She'd been practicing diligently and couldn't wait to show him her progress.

The crowd had fallen silent, listening, waiting. Restlessness left her shifting in her seat. She could hear the chronicler muttering to himself as he prematurely counted the competitors and began adding coins to the sack. They clinked when they tumbled in.

A loud roar echoed through the arena, shaking its stands. She jumped. "What in the name of all the gods?!" she whispered as her hand covered her breast. A second followed, which left her frowning and looking about. Others did the same, whispering. While she was well acquainted with the roars made by the Drengr, these were deeper, more guttural, harsher. A third roar sent goose pimples along her flesh.

From the east, three dragon shapes approached.

The crowd began shifting for a better look. As the Drengr neared, she noticed two of them were much larger than the other. They flew in a V-formation, with the smallest at their point, though he was still monstrously large by Drengr standards. His scales were pearlescent white, unlike anything she had seen. As the sun fell upon him, he glistened with shades of pastel colors. The other two were blues. Something about them was…different.

The newcomers took two passes around the arena. Then the white Drengr split away. Without losing any altitude, he shifted into his human form. The crowd gasped. His body plummeted towards the ground and people began to shriek and cover their faces. A human body falling from this distance would surely break…but not a Drengr's. His feet slammed into the ground. When the dust cleared, he was crouched upon one knee, with his fist upon the ground and his head bowed. "He bows to his king and queen," she whispered, eyes wide. The crowd erupted, standing, clapping, whistling. She too stood because she could not resist. She wanted a better look.

The Drengr's escorts perched themselves upon the arena's walls. The audience was too busy with the spectacle to notice these beasts, but she noticed immediately. "Dragons!" she whispered, leaning over the railing to get a better look. "Real wild dragons!"

Her father noticed too. He muttered something to her mother. Both of them gazed at the two sentinels.

At last, her father called to her and she took her seat. The crowd hushed. "Rise, young Drengr." Her father's voice boomed through the arena. The Drengr stood, looking up at them. He was tall and powerfully built like all Drengr, with unusual hair that matched his scales. Their eyes met, leaving her skin flushed. Who was he? Where was his Rider?

"I do not recognize you," said King Cornan. "What is your name?"

The young Drengr stood as if he were a soldier, feet together, fist over his heart. "You may call me Tristan Forestborn, Your Majesty."

King Cornan nodded. "Will your guests transform and join us in the stands?"

Tristan threw a glance upward before shaking his head. "These are no mere *Drengr*, Your Majesty. These are wild dragons. They cannot transform, and they prefer to remain where they are." The stands erupted into speculative whispers.

King Cornan glanced upward once more then nodded. Did the dragons make him nervous? "Very well, Tristan Forestborn. You may go and join the other competitors."

He bowed and walked away, joining the others. The bell tolled. This was her cue.

Taking a deep breath, she stood. The line of competitors fell to one knee. "Good luck, darling," her mother whispered.

She moved forward to the edge of the box and cleared her throat. "Greetings Drengr warriors." Her voice was not as powerful as her father's, but comparable. "You have come here in hopes of claiming my crown." She paused to take a breath. "Dragonwall's next king must be strong, powerful, wise, charismatic"—she looked from face to face as she spoke, lingering over Daryn's for far too long—"but above all, our next king must possess a good heart!" She turned to the crowd. "What say you, people of the kingdom? Do you agree?"

The crowd erupted into applause and shouts of agreement. Allowing them a minute of rowdiness, she lifted her hand when she was ready to speak again. "The laws of the Charter state the following: the winner of the Tournament for the Crown will become the Crowned Prince of Dragonwall. He will train side by side with the king in all matters of ruling. He will become the heir to the throne."

Again, more cheers. She looked back at the competitors, her gaze falling upon Tristan. Who was he?! When silence fell once more, she finished her speech. "Only one will be worthy. Only one can be crowned." Again, she took a deep breath. "In just a moment, I will come down and present each of you with a bag of coins. From it you will pull one. You will find the coin's twin among your competitors. This determines who you will fight tomorrow. The winners will continue on to the next round of the tournament, the losers may go home or choose to remain behind and take part in the remainder of all the tournament has to offer—parties, events, and of course, the ball." With that, she curtsied to the crowd and turned to the chronicler. "Have you added another coin for Tristan Forestborn?"

"Aye." He handed her a velvet drawstring bag. "Thirty-nine competitors. One lucky Drengr will not participate in the first round of fights. A single coin has been placed without its twin."

She nodded before proceeding to the arena's floor. The dusty ground was hot beneath her slippers. With great care and grace, she moved slowly to each competitor, allowing each to reach into the bag and remove a coin. Some were quick. Others took their time, fishing around, hoping to find the one that called to them.

When she reached Daryn, he winked at her while he removed his coin. Her flesh remembered things it should not have. She couldn't help her smile, nor the way her stomach fluttered beneath his gaze. "Good luck," she whispered before moving away from him. Down the line she went until she reached the final Drengr.

Tristan's gaze was impassive. Before she offered him the bag, she asked, "Where is your mate, sir?"

"My mate?" There was a measure of confusion in his answer.

"Surely you have a mate, else you would have come to the capital last month for my ceremony."

"Ah," he answered. "I do not have a mate. I merely had no desire to attend the ceremony." With that, he held out his hand. "My coin, please?"

She blinked back at him, looking for answers in his green eyes. No mate? No desire to attend the ceremony for a chance to become king? She was too surprised to make a retort. And affronted. All she could do was produce the bag. He reached in and took the remaining coin, then closed his fist around it. The crowd erupted.

CHAPTER 15
COMPETITION DAY

TRISTAN FORESTBORN'S name was on everyone's lips for the remainder of the day. Lena feigned disinterest, but she couldn't help her growing curiosity, especially as it began to outweigh thoughts of Daryn. "I suspect," said Cora with a sly gleam in her eyes, "Tristan was raised by wild dragons, deep in seclusion. That's why no one knows him." As her hand-maidens helped her tidy up for the feast, they couldn't help but discuss the matter further.

"How can you be certain?" said Avra. "Tristan might have been raised by a humble serf. Or perhaps he grew up in a small village. He could be the son of a merchant, or a butcher, adopted at birth, mistaken for a human." She placed Lena's favored jewel about her neck, a single teardrop emerald on a silver chain.

"Bah!" Cora's nose crinkled. "That's unrealistic. Can you imagine the reaction of his adopted parents upon seeing him fledge? Besides, you saw the dragons that accompanied him."

It was common knowledge that those of the Drengr race fledged during puberty. For the young lads, even though they expected it, the change was often surprising, taking them unawares. One moment the young Drengr might be seemingly human, and the next, morphing into a young dragon. Their Drengr-Rider parents always prepared them for these moments, but if Avra was correct, if Tristan was mistaken for a human and abandoned by his parents, such a lecture may have never come.

"What if his parents died when he was young?" said Theresa. "Why else would dragons accompany him?"

Lena sighed. "Everyone is *so* caught up with him. Mysterious Tristian. Am I the only one slighted by his actions?"

Her handmaidens exchanged confused glances in the mirror's reflection. "Why should you be slighted, Your Highness?" Theresa asked.

"Isn't it obvious?" She looked at their faces and realized they'd failed to make the connection. "Tristan is *unmated*. Everyone has overlooked the fact that my father summoned all unmated Drengr to the capital last month."

"And that angers you?" Cora frowned.

She let out a sound of disgust. "Of course it does! Tristan disobeyed a direct order from the king, Cora. It's treason. Oh, come now! Don't balk!" Her handmaiden's shock only further annoyed her.

"Can you not forgive him?" Avra's voice was dreamy. "He's just so…"

Lena's jaw dropped. "I might have pardoned ignorance, had he not known about the summons. But he did know! He blatantly chose not to come."

"Gods above, Princess!" Cora's surprise was evident in her voice. "How can you be so certain? Has he told you of this?"

"He told me directly…as if it were nothing." Her words

had the desired effect. A gasp slipped from Theresa's mouth. "Indeed, Theresa. It is shocking."

"But, what did he say?" Cora fussed with a few stray strands of Lena's hair, tucking them back into place. Her massaging fingers were calming.

"Nothing particularly...offensive." In truth, his words held no insult. But his bluntness, his lack of consideration towards his delivery, irked her to no end. "He told me that he had no desire of attending the ceremony."

"Why, that's not as bad as you made it sound," said Avra.

She exhaled. "I suppose not. I should not be offended. Yet I am." Why did his words bother her so much? She never wanted a mate. Admittedly, she was beginning to wonder what it might be like to have Daryn for one. Unfortunately, that impossibility made him all the more enticing.

"There now, Princess." Cora rubbed her shoulders. "You're correct. He was inconsiderate. You have every right to be upset." Her ladies said and did whatever was necessary to please her. Sometimes the pretense was too much. She turned from the mirror. She could do little about it now. "Shall we go, Princess?" Avra asked.

She squared her shoulders. "Yes, we had better."

They left her apartment in a hurry. She was already running late—unintentionally of course—for an event she herself had planned. Fortunately, the doors had not yet closed. As she entered, the dining hall came to its feet. She proceeded down the center aisle, not nearly as nervous as she had been when the hopefuls had first arrived. As she passed Daryn, she afforded him a furtive glance. The corner of his mouth twitched when their eyes met. Her mind jumped back to their kiss, longing to feel his lips again.

When she was seated, the hall followed suit. The first course was brought forth, followed by each thereafter. The entertainment consisted of multiple diversions. First jugglers, then the court jester, then a choral group singing popular ballads. These included *A Bond Unveiled*, which left her feeling awkward. She was reminded of her failure to find a mate, and while it didn't bother her as much these days as it had when it first happened, the reminder was not welcome. The night ended with music from her father's minstrels and a few impromptu dances in between the aisles of tables.

By dessert she was stuffed, but since it was apple pie, she had a modest slice. The six-hour feast had every possibility of continuing late into the night. But one by one, the champions excused themselves. She too snuck away through a side door just behind the head table, leaving her handmaidens to continue their fun. Ramar followed her out and escorted her to her chambers, taking her arm and looping it through his. She always appreciated his company.

"Excited for the fighting tomorrow?" he asked. "I hear Raff is paired with Thos."

"Well, I dislike them both so I suppose it hardly matters." Then after a brief pause she added, "Too bad they both can't lose."

"Ha! If only." His smile widened.

"And what do you make of this Tristan fellow?" She was curious if Ramar knew more than she.

"Well, it would seem that the rumors are true."

"What rumors?" She faltered. They had reached the Hall of Kings.

"Tristan was indeed raised by the dragons of the Forest Clan." He pulled her along until they stood before her door. "Surprising, since we haven't seen any for the last fifty years."

"That's...all?" She had hoped for much more.

"Tsk-tsk, Lena. So demanding." He shrugged. "If I hear more dear Princess, you will be the first to know."

She grinned. "See to it that you find out everything you can, and report directly to me when you do."

"You sound like your father already." He smirked. "No matter. Your wish is my command." With that, he gave her a sweeping and most unnecessary bow before departing.

That night, she dreamt of dragons flying into battle. Tristan's handsome face swam in and out of her dreams. At times, she glimpsed vast numbers of ships throwing dragonlances at the flying creatures. She awoke in a cold sweat at dawn. It was merely a dream, and by the time she supped on a breakfast of leftover apple pie, she didn't remember anything.

Today she decided upon a simple gown. It was rich red like Daryn's scales. There were no frilly skirts, no fancy corsets, no sweeping sleeves. It did have the Drengr monarchy sigil embroidered in gold upon her left breast. She paired the gown with her emerald teardrop necklace and a diamond and emerald encrusted tiara.

During the carriage ride, she and her handmaidens chatted while Kenna Margaret looked on. They speculated over the fights, taking bets on the winners. By now, most of the dueling pairs were common knowledge. She only cared about Daryn. He was fighting a mated Drengr by the name of Raylor.

When she arrived at the royal box, a list had been posted with the order of the competing pairs. She took a moment to scan it before sitting down. It was still early, but a crowd was already gathered. She heard calls from the peddlers as they sold their wares up and down the grandstands.

"Meatballs on a stick," one voice penetrated the crowd nearby. "Get 'em while they're hot! Six steelys each."

Steelys were their lowest form of currency. Ten steelys made a silver, and twenty silvers a gold dragon. The gown she was currently wearing had cost six gold dragons. That was merely a fraction of the cost of her welcoming gown worn the night before, which came in at an incredible thirty-two gold dragons. No one truly knew how large the king's coffers were, not even she.

Her mouth watered as the scent of meat drifted towards her. She sent Cora away to fetch them snacks while the royal cupbearer stepped forward to pour them wine. It was going to be a long day and they would need plenty of refreshment.

"Are you ready, Princess?" The steward's gravelly voice made her flinch. She looked behind her for confirmation from Ramar. He sat with Briv. The other four of her father's guards were off assisting her father and mother with crown business in response to a new pirate raid that had occurred far to the east in Zaikar's Dragondom. They would not attend this portion of the tournament. The increasing pirate attacks meant her father had his hands tied, and often.

She stood. Those on the arena floor fell to one knee. "Good day to all!" She opened her arms wide. "Today we begin with our pairs. Each competitor will be permitted *two* weapons of choice." She paused briefly. "Now, I imagine their Sveraks will be their first choice. But the other options available to them will be spears, knives, bows, axes, and a plethora of other dangerous options." A grating noise attracted the crowd's attention as a rack of weapons was rolled out onto the arena's floor.

"I will call each competitor's name as they come. The rules are as follows: All non-lethal blows are most welcome. Blood is welcome and we hope there will be plenty. The first Drengr to submit loses." She took a deep breath, turning to the arena master down on the floor. "Let the games begin!"

Cheers erupted all around her. All thirty-nine warriors rose and moved down into the waiting area, out of sight. The blue dragons from the Forest Clan had returned, taking up their perch atop the stands, well above the spectators.

The competitors were given fifteen minutes to prepare themselves. A trumpet signaled when their time was up. She stood once more. The steward handed her a scroll, which she unfurled. Lifting her voice, she called out the first names. "Ellair and Civoi—you may now proceed." The crowd applauded politely before a hush fell.

Both competitors entered the arena, plucking up an additional weapon of choice near the entrance. The vast floor of the arena was empty otherwise, except for the arena master who would act as referee. When everything was set up, she nodded to the arena master. Then she took her seat.

The two competitors grasped forearms politely before moving away from each other and taking up their favored stance. The arena master's arm lifted high. He paused, increasing the suspense. Then his arm came down. "Begin!" The crowd clapped and cheered with excitement, then fell quiet.

Ellair and Civoi circled each other. She never particularly liked Civoi the Bore. Ellair was all right. Between the two, she hoped he would be victorious.

Their legs moved fluidly in crouched positions. The tension in the arena increased. Ellair was the first to move. He jumped into the air, bringing his Sverak down upon Civoi's. The reverberating clang of metal cut through the tense silence and everyone began stamping their feet with excitement. After that, it was difficult to follow their quick movements. Every blow Ellair imparted, Civoi parried. They moved back and forth, one gaining the upper ground, and then the other. Then Ellair found Civoi's side unprotected and sank his

Sverak into Civoi's flesh. She flinched and the crowd gasped. The blow was enough to bring a human to his knees...but they weren't human. A mature Drengr healed in a matter of minutes, so long as they weren't weakened and the blow wasn't fatal, they would be fine.

Ellair backed away, giving Civoi a chance to heal or surrender. She knew better than most that Civoi would not surrender. Especially now that he was healing.

There were several ways to win. The rules did not permit beheading or lethal blows, such as a sword through the heart. However, accidents were inevitable. If a fatal blow was delivered and she deemed it an accident, the Drengr would be pardoned. Everything else was fair game. The victor had to win by a surrender, death, or a blade to the throat. As it stood, killing a Drengr in Dragonwall was the highest form of treason unless it was during a tournament like this. She hoped no one would die, especially since she would feel responsible for it.

The match lasted little more than fifteen minutes. By some miracle, Ellair managed to bring his sword to Civoi's throat. Civoi the Bore was defeated. He sulked from the arena, a clear show of the personality in him that she disliked so much. The arena master moved forward and took Ellair's arm, lifting it high in the air. The crowd cheered and trumpets blasted.

She announced the next pair and a new match began. Each took about fifteen minutes. With nearly twenty fights to get through, the day began to stretch on. She was eager to watch Daryn and unfortunately, he was last.

When Raff the Ruthless took his turn, she was annoyed by his superb fighting. The rumors were correct. He was both a good fighter and a dirty one at that. Her stomach rolled over as she watched him. The way he jumped through the air with perfect form was impressive. He was strong, which meant he had a good shot at winning.

For this fight, he chose to use his Sverak paired with a knife. This he threw just before closing in on his victim. Poor Thos didn't stand a chance. Distracted by the knife, he did not see Raff's blade approach his throat until it was too late. The match ended. She couldn't help but clench her teeth in annoyance.

Several fights later, the mysterious Tristan entered the arena paired with Caden the Comic. She liked Caden. He'd been kind and funny, making her laugh on numerous occasions. She decided to root for him.

The fight began like all the others, with Caden and Tristan circling each other. "He didn't take a second weapon," she realized, whispering to herself. "How silly of him!" Instead, he pulled his sword from its scabbard. Her eyes widened and she glanced over her shoulder at Ramar. "No Sverak? I thought all Drengr carried Sveraks?"

He leaned forward to whisper in her ear. "They usually do. Do you know what kind of blade that is, Princess?" He paused. "I have discovered something more and as promised, you will be the first to know."

Her heart quickened. "Tell me!"

"It's a Spriten blade. See the blue markings that glow along its metal?"

Her gaze narrowed as she focused on it. Sure enough, marks swirled along the length of the blade, glowing vibrantly. Her jaw dropped. Caden looked surprised too. In fact, seeing this caught him off guard. He was already uneasy because Tristan did not opt for a second weapon.

"Show off," she muttered. Ramar's chuckle sounded behind her. How had Tristan obtained a Spriten blade? He was no forest Sprite. They were a reserved people who never ventured from the depths of their trees. She made it her next mission to find out.

The match was hardly a fight. Caden and Tristan never had the chance to pair their blades. Tristan moved too quickly, feigning a blow at Caden's side before tripping Caden and pulling him up by his hair to place his blade over his throat. A look of anguish passed over Caden's face when he realized he'd been defeated so quickly. Tristan was the only competitor thus far to win in such a way.

Caden stalked off, clearly as disgruntled as she was. Tristan was awarded victory. The arena master lifted his arm high. This time the dragons roared with approval along with the audience. Once the crowd settled down, Tristan turned. Instead of leaving immediately, he faced her, pinning her with his green gaze. Then he bowed deeply, sweeping one arm down and tucking the other behind his back. A universal sigh went up around the stadium and her cheeks warmed.

Ramar chuckled from behind her. "Now *that's* what I call respect."

"Shut up, Ramar," she whispered back. None of the other victors had done this. She was taken aback. After the longest bow she'd witnessed, he stood and walked out of the arena. The onlookers cheered after him. It was obvious that in this gesture alone, he had become their favorite.

It was well into the afternoon when Daryn finally proceeded to the arena floor. Her heart fluttered, threatening to jump from her chest. She begged the gods for a win, hoping they would grant her request. She needed him to face Raff if there was any hope of eliminating the ruthless Drengr.

Daryn and Raylor grasped forearms. This mated Drengr was unknown to her. She hoped he wasn't as skilled as Daryn. When she stole a look at his beloved mate, sitting near the royal box, she noticed that her eyes were glued to Raylor.

As soon as Lena gave her permission, the arena master lifted his arm in the air, then brought it down. "Begin!" Thank the gods this was the last time she'd hear it today.

The two competitors began to circle, Sveraks drawn as they crouched low. Like Tristan, Daryn did not choose a second weapon. Tristan had started a trend by the show of confidence. Daryn was up for the challenge. She liked him all the more for it.

After several tense minutes, Raylor launched himself forward. With effortless movements, Daryn lifted his Sverak. The two blades met midair, reverberating in response. Again and again, the swords clashed as their masters lunged and swiped. Quick feet stepped back and forth moving like dancers to a silent rhythm only heard within their minds. For a time, Daryn and Raylor seemed equal. She could hardly breathe as each sword blow was blocked and returned.

Then their Sveraks met especially forcefully, sending a teeth-grating clang through the stands, and Raylor remembered his second weapon. The spear he held in his non-dominant hand thrust forward, sinking into Daryn's side. She screamed. Her hands flew to her cheeks. The crowd also cried out, drowning her voice with theirs. Daryn staggered back, putting distance between himself and his attacker. She forced her shaking hands into her lap and clasped them tightly together. Daryn winced and pulled the spear from his side, tossing it away. She winced too when she considered his pain. His face did not show it. Yet, he finally looked vulnerable to her. Her chest tightened with desire. She needed him to win more than anything in the world. "Come on, Daryn!" she whispered. "You can do this!"

As if hearing her, Daryn lunged forward. New fury took form in his movements. He struck Raylor's blade with so much force, Raylor staggered back. This was his moment!

Utilizing Raylor's surprise, he twisted around and brought his sword to Raylor's neck. The crowd went *wild*. Raylor gazed into Daryn's eyes for a full minute, chest heaving with each breath, before dropping his Sverak in defeat.

When Daryn's arm was lifted as victor, she jumped to her feet applauding. The audience did the same. She was not supposed to pick favorites, but one could argue that the fight was worth the extra attention. In her opinion, it was the best match of them all.

Like Tristan, Daryn turned and bowed to her in the same respectful manner. Even from her elevated position, she saw something fierce in his gaze. It left her hungry for more than food. She wasn't used to feeling this way. Their kiss flashed through her mind and her stomach jolted. She craved another —wanting it more than she had wanted anything else in a long time.

In that moment, she hated being Dragonwall's princess. Were she anyone else, she might have rushed down to Daryn and claimed that kiss. But she couldn't. That kind of behavior was untoward, especially for someone in her position. She was forced to enjoy his victory from afar. As he departed the arena, she hatched a mischievous idea that involved darkness and torchlight. She had only to wait for nightfall to carry it out.

CHAPTER 16
KISSES AND TEA

DINNER after the first round of matches took an eternity. Lena could hardly contain the anxious fluttering of her heart. She tried restricting her eyes to her dinner plate. Still, they continued to flick in Daryn's direction. She needed a distraction.

It was a small mercy when Ramar brought up Tristan's sword. "Do you think it was a gift?" he asked Ferand. She perked up.

So too did her father, who leaned over to answer. "The Sprites dislike dragons and Drengr alike. Tristan must have impressed them to receive such a mighty gift."

"Why doesn't he have a Sverak?" she asked. Her voice sounded far too eager.

Pedrus, her father's Shield sitting to his right, answered. "The Sverak is a gift from father to son, Lena, as you well know. If Tristan never knew his father, he wouldn't have one." Then Pedrus turned to her father. "Personally, I find it interesting that Tristan has such a human name."

She bit her lower lip. That was something she hadn't

thought of. "Why haven't you spoken with him, Papa? We know so little about him. If anyone might learn something, it is you."

"I plan to do exactly that." He lifted his goblet to drink before speaking again. "I invited him to my study tomorrow." Her eyes widened. "For tea. Like you, my darling girl, I am eager as ever for answers."

"What a nice gesture," said her mother, finally joining in.

"Would you like us at the meeting, Your Grace?" Pedrus failed to hide his eagerness.

"I would like to come too," she said.

Her father shook his head. "No, this will be a private meeting between myself and Tristan. No others." He lifted his goblet again, and it was clear the conversation was at an end.

Her mind quickly returned to its original pursuit—Daryn. For the remainder of dinner she picked at her food, too nervous to eat. She thought of what she would say to him when she called him. Each scenario she imagined brought heat to her face.

After dinner, her handmaidens escorted her to her chambers to prepare her for bed. Once in her nightgown, Cora began unpinning her hair and brushing it out while Avra and Theresa put away her gown and jewels. "Whatever has gotten into you?" asked Cora. "You're fidgeting."

"Oh. I...Do you think I'm in love?"

"Love?" Cora's head tilted to the side as she regarded Lena's reflection.

Lena lifted her hands to regard them, as if they were suddenly strange to her. "My fingers tingle when I think of him. I feel so...so strangely about him. The more I try to forget him, the more my mind conjures up our kiss. My heart flutters something terrible! Oh, tell me I am being silly!"

"You are not his mate, Princess. He will never be yours—not entirely. Even the best of us want what we cannot have."

"So what I'm feeling is infatuation?"

"Let us hope." Cora hesitated, holding her hairbrush mid-stroke. "What exactly happened today that set your heart aflutter?"

"Well, just the match. I…" She shook her head. Perhaps it was stupid. "I don't know. I just wanted him more than ever before, especially when I watched him fight. And my nerves…"

"We were all nervous, Princess," said Avra, coming over to join them.

"But, what does *love* feel like?"

"Love is different for everyone. For me, it is consuming. I cannot stop thinking about Thomas even when we are together. Being around him makes my heart soar. And if anything should ever happen to him, I think I might die."

"That sounds more like infatuation than love, Cora." Avra gave them one of her famous all-knowing looks.

In the end, they were no help at all. When they finished settling her in for bed, she sent them away and pretended to go to sleep. Once they were gone, she waited a little while longer, counting each breath as if it lasted a lifetime. At last, she could take it no longer. She rose and removed the torch she had hidden away. Her heart hammered with each movement. Thrusting it into the fireplace, it blazed into life. What could be more romantic than summoning a man with flames?

Out on the balcony, the night air was cool against her face. Winter was approaching. She loved the cold, though it never got cold enough to freeze the ground—not in the south. Perhaps on her emissary travels she might someday see snow. She had only ever read stories of it.

She inhaled and exhaled, letting the cold sting her nose,

while she stared out over the sea. As she stood—one hand clasping her robe shut and the other holding the torch—she realized how stupid she looked. "I must look like a desperate harlot!" she muttered, frowning. Why, if Daryn cared for her so much, did she need to summon him?

Doubt snaked into her belly. Was this the right thing to do? It was shameful, calling to him for the sake of having a kiss. Her mind filled with second thoughts—she needed to rethink this. Only a few minutes had passed. Surely the *Storm's Maiden* had not yet noticed her.

She was about to dart back into her apartment when she saw a flicker of torchlight out upon the dark water where she thought his ship to be anchored. Maybe she was wrong. Maybe they had already spotted her. She sighed. Why were her feelings so difficult? So frustrating? One moment she felt completely in control, the next, all rational thought evaporated.

A draft of air attacked the flames of her torch. They flickered and crackled. Dragon wings. A man dropped out of the sky and landed before her, crouching low to absorb the force of his body striking the flagstones of the balcony. Daryn straightened before sweeping into a low bow. "You called, Your Highness?"

In that instant, she realized she had nothing to say. All the conversations she'd imagined were forgotten. She simply stood there, looking like a silly girl in a night robe. Inwardly, she balked at her stupidity.

Daryn regarded her for the length of several long seconds. His eyes danced with amusement. Or was that a trick of the torchlight? "What's the matter, Princess Lena? Nothing to say? No congratulations?"

Her eyes widened. "But of course! Congratulations, *sir*. You fought bravely today. I find myself impressed."

"Do you?" he moved a step closer and her breathing hitched. She scolded herself. He was an arm's length away and she couldn't manage to contain her ridiculous emotion. How childish was she?!

"Well—yes." She cleared her throat. "I was impressed. I admit, when you were wounded, I thought I might faint." She cringed at her choice of words.

"Is that so?" He took another step closer—just one.

She nodded. "Yes." Her voice was little more than a whisper.

"You looked very beautiful tonight at dinner. And last night too."

Warmth spread through her body, making her fingertips tingle. She opened her mouth to thank him, but somehow, she'd lost the ability to form coherent words. Another step. He was less than an arm's length away now. She looked at his lips.

He must have noticed. "So, is that why you have summoned me? And here I believed you merely wished to make me an accomplice in some new *diabolical* plan of yours."

"No," she squeaked. "No plan." And that was the literal truth. There was no plan at all. She had no idea what she was doing. She only knew one thing: she badly wanted to kiss him.

"I see. Well then, I should not keep you. It is late, after all. And ladies, especially *princesses*, need their beauty rest." At this, he took a single step back.

Her brow furrowed in disappointment. Was he leaving already? Frustration welled up inside her. She stepped forward, just a single, hesitant step. That was all she could manage. "What about..." The words died on her lips.

"Yes?" he arched an eyebrow. She watched the torchlight dance upon his skin, highlighting the shadows beneath his cheekbones, his dominant brow, and the gold flecks within his eyes.

"Before you go, perhaps…" Again she tried and failed. She was a princess. Didn't that mean she could have whatever she wanted? She merely needed to ask for it. She tried again. "Perhaps a goodnight kiss for…for your princess?" Inwardly, she groaned. She knew it was wrong before the words were out. But she could not take them back.

The corner of his mouth curved upward. "Accomplice in a masterplan? Unlikely. But a kiss? Now that I can manage." Without another word, he covered the distance between them.

His arm went about her waist as he pulled her against him. Then he brought his mouth down upon hers. Her heart jolted, pounding against her chest. His lips moved over hers. She tried to gasp for air, but the moment she opened her mouth wider, his tongue began exploring hers. She gasped and pulled away.

"Too soon?" He opened his eyes and smiled knowingly.

"No!" she whispered. She hadn't meant to show her surprise or her innocence. She put her free hand against his neck, inviting him once more. This time, she gave in to his tongue's petition. He responded, squeezing her more tightly against him. At some point, he must have grabbed the torch from her hand and tossed it over the wall into the sea below.

She didn't want the moment to end, not ever. He pulled away. "That was far more than a goodnight kiss, Lena." She loved the way he said her name, drawing out the syllables in a sensual way. "But alas, I must be going." Giving her a final kiss upon her forehead, he stepped away. "Until tomorrow, fairest of them all." With that, he jumped from the balcony and transformed midair. She could hardly see his form in the darkness.

She must have stood there an hour, motionless, watching the little lights on the bay as they came and went from the city. It took a long time for the heat to leave her cheeks. After that, she was overtaken with exhaustion and went to bed with thoughts of Daryn playing through her mind.

Her dreams retraced a familiar path. Foreign ships entered the Bay of Bandu, fighting against dragons and Drengr alike. Tristan was there pleading with her. He asked her something. But what? The ships were firing spears into the air, shooting the dragons out of the sky. Drengr-Rider pairs were falling into the ocean. The city was under attack. Large projectiles were lobbed at the walls, crumbling them. Smoke lifted into the sky from the Pauper's District. "I cannot do this alone, Lena!" Tristan shouted at her, holding out his hand.

Her eyes flew open. It was a dream. Only a dream. She lay back panting against her pillows, sweating. "Only a dream," she repeated. Sleep took her once more.

When she awoke the next morning, her memories had room for just one. What she felt for Daryn was dangerous. Her mother was right. He would never be her mate. Fate made that perfectly clear. A bond wouldn't magically appear. It was either there, or it wasn't—she understood that now. Knowing this cut her to the quick. And when she really thought about it, clouds of disappointment rolled in, subjecting her to a light rainfall that began to build and build, burying her beneath water.

Ramar dropped by her apartment for breakfast. He accidently let slip that a certain meeting for tea was to take place just before the midday meal, lifting her spirits and offering a partial distraction from Daryn. "I can neither confirm nor deny this," he added, winking. "But if you were hoping to perhaps…eavesdrop, then this would be the time to do it."

"Gods above, Ramar!" She couldn't help her smile. "Are you implying what I think you are?"

He laughed. The low rumble sounded more preternatural than human. "You mean, that you might sneak out onto the king's balcony and hide yourself from view, effectively overhearing the entire conversation?" He gasped in shock. "I would never assume such a thing, Princess."

"Sometimes your ability to predict my behavior is frightening." She smirked. He affectionately ruffled her hair before departing.

"Thanks for that," she groaned, smoothing her curls back into place. His laugh drifted to her ears just as the door shut behind him.

WHEN IT WAS TIME, she sent her handmaidens away on a fool's errand and snuck away to the King's Tower. "I need to get something from my old room," she argued when Thomas refused to let her pass.

"The king has an important meeting this morning. He is not to be disturbed."

"Oh, leave off, Thomas. Let me pass. Otherwise, I'll tell Cora you were being difficult."

Thomas turned a dark shade of red before nodding to his comrade. He and his guard-mate separated their spears. She moved through the main living area and out to the main floor balcony which wrapped around the tower at various levels, connected by flights of stairs. Ever so quietly, she crept down to the balcony outsider her father's study. Then she sat on the lowest step.

Everything was quiet. Tristan had not yet arrived. All she had left to do was sit and wait.

When Tristan arrived, her father was cordial in greeting him. He congratulated him on his win in the arena. "I hear you bested your opponent in record time. It's unfortunate I was not present to witness it."

"I am flattered, Your Grace. There were many impressive competitors yesterday, each worthy of such praise."

From her hiding place, she clenched her teeth. Not only was Tristan an efficient warrior, he was too modest.

"Come. Sit. Join me for tea."

There was the sound of chairs sliding across the floor, tea being poured, and cutlery clinking against dish ware. For several minutes, they did not talk. She waited, her impatience growing.

It was Tristan who broke the silence. "I admit, Your Grace, I was surprised when you invited me to your tower. I suspect your invitation was singular. Is there something I might assist you with?"

Tristan was direct. Her mind flashed back to their shared words on the arena floor.

"You are quite perceptive, Tristan." King Cornan chuckled. "Very well then, I *too* shall be direct. I would like to know more about you. You show up here to compete. No one knows who you are, *where* you come from."

She wiped her sweaty palms upon her skirt, desperate to know Tristan's secrets. Perhaps more desperate than anyone else.

"Ah. Of course."

"Forgive me for delving into your personal life but—"

"It is very much your business, Your Grace." Her jaw dropped. "I apologize for interrupting. You are Dragonwall's king. You have every right to inquire into my personal life. If I were king, I would be curious about a young *nobody* appearing on my doorstep, too. Especially a young nobody fighting for my daughter's crown."

At the mention of her crown, her heart raced.

"I am glad we understand one another, Tristan."

"The truth is, Your Grace, there is not much to know about me. I was raised in unusual circumstances—quite untraditionally. I did not grow up in a fort surrounded by my own kind."

She scooted closer until she could reach out and touch the curtains that fluttered in and out of the doorway. It was a welcome breeze. She'd grown sticky with suspense.

Tristan continued. "Perhaps my untraditional upbringing places me at a disadvantage. But know this, Your Grace, I have every intention of winning this tournament." Her eyes widened. "It is bold of me to say so. But why else would I be here if I believed otherwise?"

"I admire a man who fights for what he wants," her father said.

"Thank you, Your Grace."

"The two dragons outside our gates—did they raise you?"

Tristan hesitated. She began to count her inhales and exhales. How much was he was truly hiding? "I suppose you could say that. It might interest you to know that they are dragons of the Forest Clan." She caught his quick subject change.

"Ah, yes. The Forest Clan. And how fares that clan?" Her father had fallen for the bait. She stifled a groan.

"Truthfully, not so well. They are a dying race. They lost many in the attack on Lincastle."

Her eyebrows knitted together. What attack?

"Yes, but that attack was over fifty years ago." Her father's words triggered her memory. They were talking about the pirate attack that had occurred long before her birth. After nearly fifty years of quiet, the pirates were back.

"The Forest Clan's numbers continue to dwindle as years go by. They can no longer afford to fight Dragonwall's battles for fear of losing their entire race. This is why they have gone entirely into hiding."

"I see. They must do what is best for their race. I admire that. Let me guess, you have come to petition for them?"

"Something like that." It was another vague answer. For someone so direct, Tristan was a master at partial truths.

"Admirable of you," said the king. "And how many are left? With the dragons in hiding, I find it difficult to track their numbers."

"The Forest Clan is the largest, with thirty-two. The Mountain Clan, twenty-five. We have lost contact with the Iron Clan. I believe the Sea Clan boasts eighteen. All others? Who can say? If they are still alive, then they have chosen to hide from us."

This information was quite unexpected. She hadn't realized their numbers were so few. That they'd gone into hiding was common knowledge. Though most never bothered to spare so much as a thought for the dragons. They were so far removed from today's society—a thing of the past.

Over time, dragons faded from everyone's memory. Six thousand years was a long time for humans, albeit not so long for dragons. Still, with the Ice Clan having been banished, and many of their supporters either killed, or blessed with humanity, it was easy to see why the numbers had dwindled.

"That is fewer than I expected," said her father. "I will do what I can to help."

"Thank you, Your Majesty. Your offer is greatly appreciated." The sound of more dishes clattering meant they were pouring more tea. She heard the trickle of liquid. She was tempted to peek around the corner, but refrained.

"Tell me Tristan, why were you absent last month when I summoned all unmated Drengr to the capital? Did your unusual upbringing shield you from outside news?"

She swallowed incorrectly and choked. Her eyes watered as she held her breath to keep from coughing.

"I wondered if you might ask." Tristan paused. She sat frozen, waiting for his answer. "Forgive me. While I did know of the ceremony, I chose not to come. I hope you are not offended."

"Offended? I am. I take my daughter's well-being seriously." Pride flared up in her chest like fire.

"Please forgive me, Your Grace. At the time, I believed it wholly unfair to come. My lack of desire to find my mate kept me away. I am simply not ready to tie myself to another."

"You sound exactly like my Lena." She stifled a snort.

"Princess Lena did not wish to find her mate?" Tristan sounded confused. "Why then did you bother with a ceremony?"

A long silence followed. "She is very headstrong, my daughter. She wishes to rule, you see. To do so requires a Drengr mate by her side—long life and all that comes with it. Unlike *you*, she does not have the privilege of fighting for the crown."

She grinned. Her father was snide when he wanted to be. She had him to thank for her sharp wits.

"Unfortunate indeed, Your Grace. That females were not blessed with the same privileges as us males is entirely unfair." She hated the sincerity in his voice. She wanted to believe he was merely pretending.

"Yes, unfortunate indeed." Her father sighed. "Because you have been raised under unique circumstances, I will forgive the offense, Tristan. You should take note for future instances. When a king issues a summons, it is to be answered. Failure to appear is considered treason."

"You are quite right, Your Grace. I do hope that in time, you might forgive me."

They fell silent for several minutes before she heard a knock at her father's door. "You may enter," he called.

"Forgive me, Your Majesty. A letter from Fort Lin."

There was some shuffling, chair scraping, clattering of cutlery. Tristan spoke, "I ought to leave you, Your Grace. I have taken up enough of your time already."

"Certainly. Thank you for coming."

The door opened and closed. All fell silent. She waited, motionless for several long minutes. When she was sure her father was occupied with his letter, she stood to leave. "You may come out of hiding now, Lena." She froze. Her father poked his head through the curtains, looking around until he found her lurking against the wall on the bottom-most stair.

"How…how did you know I was out here?"

"Dearest daughter, I am a Drengr, remember? I smelled you the instant you took up your post."

"But…you knew? You knew I was out here and you didn't insist I leave before Tristan arrived?"

He shrugged. Then he gave her a hug and kiss on the forehead before walking away. "Where would the fun in that be?" he called over his shoulder. She followed him back into his study.

"Do you think Tristan also knew I was hiding?"

He sat down at his desk. "Doubtful. He is not familiar with your scent."

She exhaled, slumping into the chair she usually occupied. "That's a small mercy." She would have been mortified otherwise. "What did you think of Tristan's answers?"

"I think he is hiding something. Nothing dangerous. I have no reason to worry."

She sighed. "I wish you would have pressed him for more answers. You're the king."

"King or not, it is not my place to use my title against people when unnecessary. If I truly saw him as a threat, I might have considered it. He is genuine. Would you not agree?"

"He is genuine," she admitted. "Still, I cannot help but be offended. He didn't come when summoned. "

"Even the best of us make mistakes, Lena. Even you. Would you deny it?"

"No. I suppose I cannot." She had not yet eaten her midday meal, but still she asked, "Shall we get started on our afternoon duties?" His servants could call for a plate of food easily enough.

He smiled wide. "I worried you might never ask." She gave him a smile in return and they set about their duties.

Each afternoon they worked together, answering letters, often in the form of grievances, dealing with matters that did not make it to court, and solving the occasional political issues that arose as a result of unruly subjects. With the string of pirate attacks, there were plenty of matters to set straight.

She made herself comfortable in the chair opposite him before grabbing a stack of folded parchment from the growing pile. Then she took up a quill and bottle of ink. She set about answering each of the kingdom's inquiries with newfound pride, knowing full well that these opportunities with her father were fleeting. A day would come when she would be too old to help, when her hands would shake, and her mind would weaken. But that day was not *this* day, and until then, she would go on doing exactly what she knew how to do.

CHAPTER 17
AN UNEXPECTED GIFT

AFTER FINISHING an afternoon of work with her father, Lena had just enough time to prepare for dinner. Her handmaidens helped her dress in an emerald and gold gown, one of the twenty her mother had commissioned before the hopefuls had first arrived. This gown had a rigid bodice that laced up the back and was rather uncomfortable—most evening gowns were.

She studied her reflection. "I think a braid down the back will do."

"Of course, Your Highness." Cora lifted a cloth from her vanity, revealing what lay beneath. "I collected these flowers from your mother this morning. We can weave the stems into your braid."

"How divine!" She bent forward and inhaled, smiling. Her mind went to Daryn. She would surely catch his eye.

They had just finished when there was a knock at the door. Her heart fluttered and she exchanged a curious look with her handmaidens. "Daryn, perhaps?" He was the only person she wished to see.

"Maybe he has come to escort you to dinner?" Avra stood to answer the door. Lena heard muffled voices as she strained to listen. Avra closed the door and returned. "There is someone here to see you. Might I invite him in? I think you will be happy to see him."

"Daryn?" Avra shook her head but continued smiling. "I would have preferred Daryn," she sighed. "But all right." Avra nodded and went back to the door.

Her guest swept into the room. Lena lost all dignity as she jumped from her vanity and rushed over. "Ivrir!" In her excitement, she nearly hugged him before settling into a formal curtsy.

His face glowed. "It's wonderful to see you, Princess!" He too offered a formal bow.

"You look...well! I thought you had forgotten me. But never mind that. You're here. What has kept you away so long? And what brings you here now?" Words were falling from her mouth before she could censor them.

His eyes crinkled as he laughed. "Slow down, Princess. Slow down."

"Here!" She eagerly took his arm, leading him to the living area. "Come and sit."

Her handmaidens bustled about, looking busy and giving them distance as she and Ivrir exchanged pleasantries. She inquired about his journey and time spent over the last month, and he about her trip to Graymont and the preparations for the tournament. "Why didn't you enter?" she asked. "I thought for certain you would compete."

Ivrir shrugged. "I'm not so interested in becoming king. Perhaps with you by my side I would have braved it. Truthfully, I like my life as it is." His honesty spoke volumes to his character.

"I understand." She smoothed a few wrinkles out of her skirt.

"Good!" He smiled. "You know, I'm glad to see you in such high spirits. Oh! That reminds me. I almost forgot." He turned to her handmaidens. "Ladies, if you wouldn't mind, I have a gift for our princess."

Lena's eyes widened. "A gift?! For me?"

"Indeed. I left it just outside the door. Cora, would you be so kind?"

"Of course, Ivrir." Cora curtsied and then rushed to retrieve it.

"You shouldn't have, Ivrir. I can't believe…But, what could it be?" She was bursting with excitement. Surprises like this always struck the right cord with her.

"You'll have to wait and find out. I would have come sooner, but, well, it took some time to have it made…your gift." He shifted, leaning back against the couch with his arm propped up along the adjacent cushion.

Cora entered with a large box and set it upon the table. It had a pretty green ribbon tied around it. "You remembered my favorite color!"

"Indeed. Now, that brings us to the reason I have come." She sat up straighter. "Your father wrote recently. It seems he intended for you to take archery lessons?" She nodded, her eyes wide. "I was told you do not yet have a suitable train-er?" She nodded again. "Good. He requested my presence in the capital for such a purpose."

"To be…my archery tutor?" Her pulse quickened.

"Aye. He also informed me that you've been sneaking out at dawn to practice." Her cheeks burned. Her father paid more attention than she realized. "I suppose the king must have noticed what a great teacher I am," he added. The side of his mouth twitched.

"But you are! You're the greatest teacher I've ever had."

He threw his head back and roared with laughter. "The greatest and only." While it was true, it did not diminish his skill in tutoring her. "Well then, go on. Go open it."

She jumped from the sofa and raced to the table. The box was long and narrow, hinting at its contents. Based on their conversation and his purpose, she already knew what she would find, but it did little to diminish her eagerness. Pulling the ribbon away, she lifted the lid. A little gasp escaped her lips.

"I had it made especially for you," he said from the sofa. "With your height and skill level in mind. Carved by hand from a bow maker in Squall's End."

Sitting in the box was a delicate bow made of lightly colored wood. She lifted it from the box to admire it. The bow's wooden limbs were carved with tiny leaves of different shapes connected by scrolling vines. She hardly breathed as she studied it. "It's...wow! It's stunning! And it's mine to keep?" She turned to him, failing to hide her grin.

"All yours. Have a look at the bottom, just where the bowstring attaches." She did. The letters P and L were carved there.

"Princess Lena?" she asked.

"So that everyone knows it's yours. And there is more, lift the tissue to see what's underneath." Following his instruction, she turned back to the box. There she found a quiver filled with goose feather arrows.

"You had the fletching dyed green?"

"Do you like them?"

"Oh yes!" She turned to him, holding both the bow and quiver of arrows. "Can we go try it out? We must. I can hardly wait." Her chest heaved. Her fingers itched to nock an arrow.

He chuckled. "I believe it is time for the evening meal and nearly dark, Princess. But how about we begin our first lesson at dawn? We shall practice each morning for an hour. Is that favorable?"

She nodded, bobbing her head. With great reluctance, she placed the bow and quiver of arrows gently back into the box. "I love it," she whispered, mostly to herself.

"It is a grand gift," said Cora. Her ladies watched with interest. "Shall we go to dinner now?" Cora added. "Ivrir, I *do* hope you will escort us?"

"It would be my pleasure!" He stood and held out his arm for Lena. Together, they walked to the dining hall.

As they walked, she told him all about the first event that had eliminated half of the competitors. Tomorrow would be the next. "You should sit with us in the royal box," she said. "There are twenty competitors left. Ten matches. It's great fun!" She thought about Daryn. Who would he fight against this time? The drawing of the coins would occur right before the match. She hoped it would be Raff.

"That does sound like fun," said Ivrir. "I would be honored to join you. Shall we all ride over together?" He looked at her ladies as he asked. They giggled. "I'll take that as a yes."

Having Ivrir back lifted her spirits. While he did not leave her heart fluttering the way Daryn did, he was becoming a dear friend, and she was glad to have his company once more. Better still, he would be around for a while. She couldn't wait to show him how much she'd improved all on her own.

When they arrived, the dining hall was already full. They'd taken too long to admire her new gift. She could hear her mother now, "Do not make this lateness a habit, young lady."

The hall rose to greet her as Ivrir led her down the aisle. As they went, she searched the crowd for Daryn's face. When she caught his eye, she noticed his look of surprise. She turned away to stifle a smile. Let him wonder! Perhaps he might even be a little jealous. Maybe then she wouldn't have to *ask* for kisses.

Ivrir bid her goodbye at the stairs leading to the head table. She noticed her father's smug smile. This was his doing after all, his gift, and he probably knew all about her new bow. Nodding briefly to him and her mother, she went to her seat. Briv stood and politely pulled it out for her.

When dinner began, she stole a glance at Daryn. He was watching her openly, a look of curiosity upon his face. She afforded him a smile before returning to her food.

"Princess Lena." Briv pulled her from her thoughts. "I hear you are to begin archery lessons."

"It's true. I have a new bow, too. No more training bow." She crinkled her nose. He was the one to poke fun at her inexperience on her first day.

"I am glad to hear it."

Ramar leaned forward to better see her. "When can we see this finely crafted weapon?"

"Why, when I feel like *showing* you. Perhaps·I shall wear it to the tourney tomorrow." She pictured herself with it. "Just like Queen Isabella." The picture from the Hall of Kings came to mind. The queen's bow was strapped over her shoulder as she posed beside her king.

Dinner was a pleasant affair. Once Briv, Ferand, and Ramar finished drilling her about her father's meeting with Tristan, they began taking bets on who would be victorious in tomorrow's events.

"My bet is on Daryn," she wagered. "He has exactly what it takes to win this tournament."

"Of course he does," came Ramar's snide reply.

"And what is *that* supposed to mean?" She glanced over at Daryn as she said this. He was still watching her. It left her cheeks burning.

"Oh, nothing at all, Princess. Pay us no mind. We are merely guards, after all, charged with watching over your life."

"Does that include my private time with Daryn?"

"We watch out for that too." Ferand chuckled, sipping his wine.

She rolled her eyes and turned away from them. So what if they silently judged her? She was a young woman after all. Her pursuits were her own business.

"Lena?" Her father captured her attention.

"Yes, Papa?" She turned to him.

"Your mother and I will attend the tournament tomorrow. Now that it is underway, our support will be more significant."

"You can afford to step away from your work? What about court in the morning?" Both her parents were overworked. Perhaps this would be good for them.

"Court can wait. Your mother and I will meet you there."

"Perfect." She smiled. With dinner finished, she snuck away to prepare for the day ahead.

Shortly after her ladies were dismissed, she'd just leaned over to blow out her candle when something made her freeze. She heard a quiet tap on the glass doors leading out to her balcony. Her heart jolted.

Tap—tap—tap. There it was again! Picking up her candle, she tiptoed to the doors and parted the curtains. Standing before her was Daryn. He had his arms at his hips. She was shocked for several moments. She should have ignored him, replaced the curtains, and gone off to bed.

Her mind was too filled with irrational daydreaming. She bit at the skin of her lips, contemplating. Should she? He gave her a stern look that said, "Don't you dare walk away." She couldn't just leave him. So she unlocked and opened the door.

"I do not recall lighting a torch for you," she said. He chuckled, closing the distance between them. Then he took her face in his hands, and planted a sweet kiss upon her lips. She was left gasping.

"Dearest Lena." His voice was low and husky. "Set that candle down so that you might kiss me properly."

"*Properly*?" She looked at him with a stern expression. "You should not be here. I have not called upon you."

"Lena!" he mock-scolded. "You do not wish to bid me good luck for tomorrow's event?" His reminder brought her back to reality. "How am I to perform adequately if I do not know that your love goes with me."

She took several playful steps backward until she stood once more in the darkness of her room. The glow of the candle made the shadows dance. When she did not set it down, he took it from her and set it on a little table nearby.

"If a kiss will ensure that you win tomorrow," she said, "then I will gladly provide you with several."

He chuckled, taking her in his arms so that they might do exactly that. His tongue was warm against hers, coaxing, claiming. When he pulled away, she was breathless. "I cannot stay long," he said, "but I had hoped that I might have a token from you, something for good luck. Ladies always offer their knights something special, perhaps your handkerchief? Or a ring? Whatever it is, it must be dear to your heart." He held her in his arms as he spoke. Could he feel her racing heart against him?

She arched away to see his face, studying his expression. "I think I know the perfect item."

"Then I beg that you allow me to borrow it for safe-keeping."

She pulled free of him and went to her jewelry box where she retrieved her delicate emerald on its silver chain. "It was a gift from my father. I wear it often."

"It is your favorite?" he asked.

"Above all else, yes." She placed it in his palm. As their skin touched, her breath hitched. Perceiving the effect, he pulled her into his arms and kissed her once more.

"Now I must leave you, dearest. Until tomorrow." With that, he backed away to the shadowy balcony and leapt from it. She watched his transformation in the air, and admired the moonlight as it glittered off his red scales. She watched him until the dark swallowed him up. Then she sighed and retreated to her bed where she dreamt once more about pirates and Tristan.

CHAPTER 18
A BLADE THAT SINGS

ARMED WITH HER NEW BOW, Lena met Ivrir at dawn. The sun was just peeping over the horizon, bathing everything in soft, golden light. The clouds echoed their greeting, taking on hues of pink and orange. The sea fog was on its way out, rolling away like horse-drawn chariots, climbing over the cliffs to speed across the water.

With her bowstring attached, she nocked her first arrow. Once more, she admired the deep green feathers and the details on the bow's wood. Positioning her arrow so that the notch was caught against the string, she pulled back. There she stood for several breaths with perfect form, remembering everything Ivrir had taught her. She'd done this every morning since the ceremony. Keeping her body side-face and her head turned towards the target, she let the arrow fly.

It sailed through the air, whizzing. *Thud*. It landed a hand's span from the bullseye. She nearly whooped with excitement. "Well done, Princess!" Ivrir clapped. "Your improvement is impressive. I can see how hard you've been working." His praise left her beaming.

"It functions beautifully," she said, holding the bow at arm's length. She flexed the bowstring several times then prepared another arrow.

Ivrir interrupted this time. "If I might add, now that you are comfortable with the motions, avoid hesitating *too* long once you draw."

"But why?" She relaxed her bow arm and turned to him. If she didn't spend time lining up her target, she'd miss her mark.

"You hesitate too long. Your arms will get tired and sloppy. You must now focus on both speed and accuracy." He removed an arrow from his quiver, nocked it, pulled, and fired. Then he repeated the action three times in the span of a single inhale.

"Show off," she muttered. The corner of his mouth twitched before he slung the bow over his shoulder. Doing her best to follow his actions, she tried firing the next arrow with similar speed. This time, it sailed through the air and landed at least ten steps from the target.

She clenched her teeth. "See? I'll never hit the target if I don't take the time to aim."

"Keep trying," was all he said.

They spent the remainder of the morning working on fluid movements. Draw and fire. She wasn't supposed to pause. Unfortunately, when she pulled and fired without taking her time, she missed. "You will get better," he said as they walked back to the keep for breakfast. "Soon your aim will follow your gaze." She hoped he was right.

The remainder of the morning was a rush. She hurried through breakfast to get to the arena on time. Her mind dwelled on Daryn, his kiss, the feel of his arms wrapped about her waist. She was especially anxious for the drawing of coins. Who would Daryn battle today?

She decided upon a sliver gown with a square bodice cut straight across her abdomen. The neckline was also square, and trimmed with black beading. The sleeves were long. They flared out at the elbows then swept all the way to the floor. She'd worn this one many times. It remained a favorite.

"It brings out your eyes," said Avra.

"I think I'll wear my hair down today."

"Are...are you certain?" Cora's hesitance was unsurprising. Ladies usually wore their hair piled atop their heads, or in fancy braids.

"Quite certain. What fun are unspoken rules if they aren't occasionally broken. Besides, if I do it today, every lady in the capital will show up at dinner with her hair let out." She paused, studying her appearance. "Perhaps a braid over the top to hold my tiara in place?"

When they finished, she admired their work. Her long hair fell just beneath the base of her back, and when she moved her head, it rustled like a waterfall of brown over her silver gown. Ever since Daryn's kisses had started, she found herself more often than not, worried about her appearance. She wanted to look her very best at all times, just in case she caught his eye.

She and her ladies met Ivrir and the five of them proceeded to the carriage. "You know, you could just fly there." She didn't mind his company. Nor did she intend to sound ungrateful for it. It was only that if she had the ability to fly, she'd do it regularly, on every possible occasion.

"I certainly could fly there. However, I would much rather ride with you." So they rode over together, chatting.

The day's event began with her. Upon arrival, she went to the chronicler and received the bag of twenty coins. Two of each were embossed with matched symbols. Once the competitors were stationed on the arena floor, she descended to greet them. At that moment, the crowd hushed. She went to each Drengr, allowing them to reach into the bag and procure a coin. She was greeted politely each time.

When she stood before Daryn, she offered him a shy smile, which he returned with a hearty grin. However, it was Tristan's intense gaze that caught her off guard. His eyes followed her as if she were a canary and he, a cat. Once the coins were distributed, she pushed the interaction from her mind.

She ascended the stands to the royal box, greeting her parents before she addressed the crowd. "Greetings to everyone! Welcome to the second round of events!" Everyone cheered and clapped. The arena was multiple levels and towered high above her. At the top were Tristan's guards. They were posed upon hind legs with their wings open, flapping for balance. Like sentinels.

She returned her gaze to the competitors. "The order of today's fights will depend on your coin's symbol. When your symbol is called forth, you will proceed into the arena with your fighting partner. Today the rules have changed. This time, you are permitted only your Sverak—" She paused to look at Tristan. "Or any sword of your choice." He continued to watch her with a furrowed brow. She cleared her throat. "Well then. Good luck to all!" With that, she turned and went back to her seat under the shaded awning.

The day began as each set of fighters was called forth. The first two fights were uneventful. She looked on, clapping politely with the audience.

Third to compete was Raff and his opponent Borin. Borin was a hopeful she wasn't particularly fond of. They faced each other and grasped forearms. She was certain neither wished the other well, though that was the purpose of the gesture. They got into position.

"Begin!" The arena master brought his arm down between them, signaling the start of the fight. Both of their faces were screwed up in fierce concentration. They crouched, their swords drawn, circling. Each waited for the other to make the first move. Even from her position in the stands, she could see Raff's eyes glittering with ruthlessness. He would be the first to strike.

Just as she thought it, he lunged forward, slashing outwards. Borin leapt back, unscathed. Raff struck again. He brought his Sverak down from above. Borin was forced to plant his feet and meet the blow, gripping his Sverak with both hands. The clang echoed around the arena. Borin muscled against Raff's strength. For a moment, the two were motionless. Then Raff slid his weapon back and began imparting blow after blow. Borin managed to parry each, just barely lifting his blade in time. Soon, both were snarling at each other. The tension mounted.

Raff was a dirty fighter. She already knew it from his previous match. He did not display his brutality immediately, but it would come. He dealt Borin a harsh blow, slicing his blade across his Borin's side. It was enough to send Borin to the ground. He cried out and twitched. She flinched, closing her eyes momentarily.

Honorable fighters waited several breaths for a wounded opponent to heal or surrender. Raff did no such thing. He took advantage of his opponent's momentary weakness, kicking Borin in the face.

She cried out in disgust, covering her mouth as Borin's nose broke, spraying blood everywhere. The crowd was screaming in delight. They knew nothing about Raff. To them, this was simply another match—entertainment to enjoy. To her, it was a chance for Raff to exhibit his quality.

Again and again he kicked, pulverizing Borin's face,

turning it red with blood and smashed bone. The ground was stained. At last, Borin scrambled away. Just as he did this, his side was exposed. Raff seized the opportunity, plunging his Sverak deep into Borin's flesh. The Drengr's piercing scream of rage echoed from the stands.

She cringed and turned away, hiding her face. Borin submitted, giving the signal for his surrender. Raff roared into the stands like a heathen. She turned to her father to find his expression unyielding, like that of stone.

The disgust she felt manifested deep in the pit of her stomach. Ramar leaned forward, whispering into her ear. "Got any more of your famous tricks, Princess? I would dearly love to witness another."

"I've never seen a Drengr fight with so little honor." King Cornan spoke through gritted teeth as he gazed down at Raff, arm lifted high in the air.

"Raff has no honor." Ivrir's expression mirrored theirs.

She glanced at Ramar over her shoulder. "If you have any suggestions for something particularly nasty, feel free to chime in." Unfortunately, no matter what she did to Raff—short of killing him—nothing would be enough to keep him from fighting. Still, she had to try *something*.

Two more matches followed. Her mind was still spinning with anger when Daryn proceeded out onto the arena floor. He was set against Rhold the Bold. She clapped with gusto when the two of them grasped forearms. Her mind drifted to the emerald necklace he carried somewhere on his person. She prayed to the gods that it would bring him the luck he needed.

"Begin!" cried the arena master. She cheered loudly with the crowd. The match was a complete opposite to Raff's. Both Daryn and Rhold were *too* honorable. Probably because outside of the arena, they were friends. Daryn made the first move, coming down upon Rhold with a blow intended to cleave his head in two. Rhold evaded the blow before lifting his voice for all to hear. "You'll have to try harder than that, old friend!" Daryn laughed. They stepped away from each other before falling into another sequence of movements.

For minutes on end, they appeared to be equally matched, dealing blow after blow as their swords met with harsh clangs. She watched each movement without blinking. There were times when Rhold would push Daryn back, and then he would do the same, regaining the ground he had lost. Twice Rhold swept his foot out to trip Daryn, while Daryn managed to drag his Sverak across Rhold's side, spilling blood. It was great fun to watch, and far less distressing.

She was beginning to wonder if the match would end in a stalemate when Daryn made his final move. He avoided a swipe from Rhold's blade by dropping to the ground. Just as he did, he swept his legs around knocking Rhold off his feet. With surprising speed, he jumped up and placed his sword point to Rhold's neck. It was over. Daryn had won!

She screamed with excitement, clapping her hands until they hurt.

"Your favoritism is *quite* clear, Princess Lena." Ramar's quiet whisper left her cheeks burning. She did her best to ignore it. Of course she cheered more for Daryn than the others. That was merely because he was a better fighter and deserved more praise.

Daryn and Rhold shook hands before Rhold clapped him on the back in congratulations. Then they both bowed to her, which had become popular since Tristan had first done it. After that, the two strode laughing from the arena. She admired Daryn all the more and made a mental note to tell him so.

Another fight passed before Tristan came into the arena.

He was matched against a mated Drengr by the name of Telgar. Aside from Daryn, she took a keen interest in Tristan because of his mysterious sword and a strong desire to know more about him.

He and his partner grasped forearms politely and wished each other luck before getting into position. The stands fell quiet. Everyone held their breath, waiting for that one special word. She too sat motionless.

"Begin!"

Challenging roars split the arena asunder. The voice of the crowd blended with that of the dragons. She looked up at Tristan's guards, filled with wonder. Then she brought her gaze down. Telgar wasted no time. He jumped through the air, his Sverak posed and ready to strike. A war cry burst from his lips just as he came down upon Tristan. Tristan's Sprite blade met the Sverak. A pure note filled the air, long and drawn out. She shivered at the sound—unreal and unlike anything she had ever heard.

While Sveraks were made of hearty Ice Metal blended with steel, she knew nothing about the Spriten blade. Telgar did not pause to question the noise. He brought his Sverak down again and again, imparting blow after blow. Tristan met every one with ease. Each chime of his blade was music to her ears and she found herself entranced. The sound was not harsh like those of other swords. No, it was a death song, both beautiful and ethereal, almost more seductively lethal than the blade itself.

Tristan played a defensive role. Each attempt made by Telgar was met with perfect precision. She dared not blink for fear of missing a single instant.

Tristan's cat-like agility separated him from the others. He moved with grace, ducking low, or jumping high from the ground. It seemed impossible to get a weapon anywhere *near* him. Were he not putting up such a good show of talent, she might have argued that it was magic. Where had he learned to fight so strangely? So beautifully?

Telgar's frustration began to show in his tense, jolted movements. His face screwed up in fierce concentration as each strategy ended in failure. Perhaps that was Tristan's plan, to exhaust him.

At last, Telgar backed away to regroup. Tristan saw his moment. He jumped through the air, performing an aerial twist, keeping his body straight, while flipping himself over and around. With sheer grace, he landed facing Telgar's back.

Telgar's eyes widened but he did not have enough time. Tristan's sword plunged into his back. He screamed but no one heard him. A sound much louder split the air. The Sprite blade sang in triumph as it buried itself into bone and sinew. Telgar fell to his hands and knees.

Tristan had no intention of allowing the fight to continue. It had already gone on too long. Before Telgar could recover, he removed his bloodthirsty blade and placed it against the back of Telgar's neck. The fight was over.

The dragons trumpeted their approval. She smiled and clapped along with the crowd. Not only had Tristan's fight lasted far longer than the others, his skill was unlike anything she'd witnessed. Arguably, it was even better than Daryn's.

Her father was awed too. His jaw hung open well after the winner was declared. Even his Shields whispered openly to each other.

As Tristan and Telgar marched out of the arena, Lena considered Tristan's match a few days prior. He had been smart, utilizing speed in the first fight, bringing it to a quick end. No one had seen his true talent or heard his blade. Telgar had no idea what to expect until it was too late. A strategy even *she* could admire.

She turned to her father. "Papa, you should have asked him where he learned to fight." They continued clapping until the two were out of sight. As Tristan's match was the last, the excitement for the afternoon was finished.

Later that evening, the remaining ten competitors were treated to a special dinner party in the king's tower. This was their opportunity to mingle with the royal family and certain nobles. She'd planned everything to perfection. There were banners with the finalist names strung up around the room. Confetti was sprinkled upon all the surfaces. Servants paraded around in gold livery and white gloves with heaping platters of fine appetizers. Drinks were served in excess.

She and her handmaidens traversed the large room, making polite conversation with each of the guests. No matter where she stood, she kept Daryn in her sights. She was eager to capture his attention.

"Good evening, Princess Lena," Raff's unpleasant voice brought her to a grinding halt. "I apologize for not coming to you sooner with my deepest apologies regarding the ceremony. I can only imagine what a difficult time it has been for you. Giving up the crown must be a heavy blow to your heart."

Clenching her jaw and her fists, she turned to face him. Though it was difficult, she held her tongue, reminding herself that she was Dragonwall's princess. Otherwise there were a number of comments she would have liked to say. "Thank you for your concern, Raff. Truthfully, I am dealing with the aftermath rather well." That was an outright lie. While she had accepted her future and was glad of the new path it would take, she was hardly happy with defeat.

"Raff, Princess Lena." Tristan came up beside them, interrupting. She sighed with relief. After he bowed to her, he turned to Raff and gripped the Drengr's forearm. It was a tense greeting.

Tristan had white pearlescent hair eerily similar to the color of his scales. He appeared to be the same age as she, but where a Drengr's age was concerned, looks were deceiving. His eyes were pools of dark green with little flecks of gold, capable of capturing anyone's attention. As he gazed at Raff with clear contempt, she noticed that his sharp jawbones flexed. "Raff, I must congratulate you on your win." There was mock approval in his voice.

"Thank you, Tristan." Raff gave him a single nod.

"Your method isn't the way I would have gone about winning. But then again, I was trained very differently than most Drengr, especially those from the north."

Her eyes widened. She silently exalted in his snide remark.

"The north is a harsh place, Tristan. We cannot all be fortunate enough to grow up in the south."

Seeing this as her exit, she quickly excused herself. They hardly appeared to notice.

She made her way towards Daryn, tracking around the perimeter of the room until she reached him. "Congratulations, sir," she said, curtsying.

They shared a silent exchange with their eyes before he followed suit, bowing deeply. "I thank you."

"It seems my lucky charm worked well for you. I am overjoyed by your win. Such an honorable fight."

"Indeed it was. I am pleased with my performance."

"You ought to be."

"Might I hold on to your charm a little longer? The tournament will only become more difficult." His words brought whispers from her handmaidens.

She couldn't help her smile. "It is yours for as long as you need it."

"Excellent!" He offered up his arm. She took it. They proceeded to walk slowly about the room, dodging couches and mingling groups. This allowed them more privacy.

"How are you today, Lena?" He kept his voice quiet.

"Quite well, now that I am in *your* company. It seems Tristan and Raff are still at each other's throats." She glanced in their direction. Her eyes lingered longer than necessary over Tristan. What was wrong with her? She had everything she wanted right beside her.

Daryn chuckled. "I imagine Raff is getting an earful. Tristan was appalled to see a Drengr fight in such a way." He paused. "I can't help but think that he's been far too sheltered."

"Sheltered? How so? What do you know about him?"

"Not much. I know that he was raised by dragons in the forests south of The Gable. Beyond that, he remains a mystery."

She blinked several times, clearing her mind of him. "Tell me, Daryn, will I see you tonight? I had hoped to congratulate you *properly*."

His long pause was unexpected. "I think it will be best if I remain on my ship tonight, Lena. That fight drained me. I need my rest."

Her blood turned cold. How could a short kiss take time away from his rest? She wasn't asking for an entire night, merely a few minutes. Rejection stung her deeply. But she didn't want to look silly. She recovered from her shock by agreeing with him. Rest *was* important, especially in competitions like this one. "I cannot have you taking any risks. Not when so much is at stake. Get as much rest as you need."

"Of course, Princess." Daryn bid her farewell.

Her stomach churned uneasily as he walked away. It seemed very unlike him to turn her down. Had she done something wrong? Perhaps she was simply reading too much into the matter. She continued to mingle, congratulating each of the other ten finalists.

Much to her surprise, Tristan found her again. "Forgive me, Princess Lena, for that slight argument between Raff and myself."

"Don't give it a second thought. You saved me from a most unpleasant conversation."

"Even still, I had not intended to scare you away."

"It was Raff who scared me, not you."

He smiled a knowing smile. "I see. Regardless, I had hoped to get your attention. I have a request to make of you." He held out his arm, so she took it. They began their walk about the room.

"You have my full attention."

"Tomorrow is a day off. I thought perhaps you might join me for a morning walk in the royal garden."

"Oh."

"Oh?"

She cleared her throat. "I find your request unexpected. But yes, I'd be delighted."

He looked pleased. "Excellent. I will meet you after breakfast. Is that favorable?"

"Favorable enough. See you then."

He bowed and left her standing alone. How strange. First Daryn refused to visit her, and now Tristan requested her company? The evening was turning into an odd one.

Daryn's rejection left her feeling unwell. Her stomach churned with worry. Was he having second thoughts? That would be the smart thing for him to do. They could never possibly work. This thing they shared, it was only temporary.

She knew she was making a poor decision, allowing it to continue. No matter, she could hardly think about consequences at the moment. Her mind was too upset. So instead, she quickly excused herself from the party and snuck away to be alone. She'd had enough for one day.

CHAPTER 19
AN UNEXPECTED APOLOGY

LENA SENT her handmaidens away early after the dinner party. She was too distraught. Daryn's dismissal played over and again in her mind. He had said he needed rest, but she didn't believe it. Why didn't he want to see her? She couldn't help but run through every single one of her actions towards him, trying to pick out the point where she might have gone wrong. It was consuming—exhausting.

"Well this won't do! Perhaps I simply need a diversion," she decided, thinking about how much she hated Raff. It was time to plan her next bout of mischief. Heating a small pot of wax, she poured it onto a scrap of parchment and imprinted it with her royal seal—the head of a dragon. Then she slipped it into her pocket and went to the servant's wing.

When she reached Evan's room—a young servant who helped in the cookery—she quietly tapped at his door. "Princess Lena!" He feigned surprise when he greeted her. This wasn't their first encounter, nor would it be the last. He knew to keep his voice to a whisper.

"I need you to deliver this message within the hour."

Along with the scrap of parchment, she passed him five silvers. No further instruction was necessary. He knew the unspoken details. He also knew he'd get the other half of his payment upon receipt. Evan nodded before shutting the door.

She went back to her room to pass the time. Bartlett, along with other low-ranking servants, lived outside the keep's walls. With large families to feed, many resided within the Pauper's District. Bartlett was one of those. He had three sisters and two brothers. His father had passed away, so his mother, siblings, and two grandparents all shared the same tiny, rundown townhome. Although he made good money from their endeavors, she was certain it went to his mother. He had such a giving heart. That left her to admire him all the more.

At last, when she could hardly keep her eyes open and her jaws hurt from yawning, she cloaked herself in dark gray velvet and snuck from her room. She used the secret passage behind her wall-covering to descend into the keep. It deposited her just inside the cookery walls. By now, the servants were asleep, except those few who worked late into the night preparing breads for the next morning. She tiptoed through the servants' dining room and into the back garden. The cookery had its own private herb garden.

At the back of the garden, unbeknownst to most, was a hidden door. It led directly out of the castle to a quiet cobble-stoned street in the Merchant District. This door was disguised by great boughs of leafy ivy. She stood beside it until she heard a faint tap.

She tapped back. She and Bartlett had a specific code to identify each other. She unlocked the door and Bartlett stepped through. He bowed so low, she was sure his nose touched the ground. "Oh thou art magnificent. How the moon sparkles upon thine hair." His quote came from one of her favorite poems: The Maiden and the Dragon. Although Bartlett couldn't read well despite her trying to teach him, he was a great lover of poetry. Surprising for a boy his age.

"And lilies adorn thine bosom with everlasting beauty," she said, quoting the next line. She tried not to laugh since he was a boy with no womanly endowments. He snorted. Then they both burst into giggles.

At last he calmed himself and spoke, "What kind of mischief will we be makin' tonight, Lena? I've got a fresh order of burg flies if you be interested? Or perhaps some mice, eh? I got ones bigger than the size of a man's head! Wait 'till you see 'em."

She chuckled. "I can imagine already. But what I need is serious."

"Oh?"

"Have you heard of Dragon's Bane?" She was certain that he had.

"'Course, Princess." There was a little too much certainty in his voice. She narrowed her gaze accusingly. He merely shrugged. Their relationship was simple. It was a no questions and no answers kind of simple. She did not pry.

"Can you get me a vial? Will it be difficult?"

He shrugged. "Easy 'nuff I suppose for the right price." He was too good.

"I would be happy to pay whatever it takes." From her pocket, she procured a small sack of money. She plopped it into his outstretched hand. "You may keep the rest for yourself, perhaps that will motivate you to strike a good bargain."

"Right sure it will." With that, he snuck back through the door and disappeared into the night. Her plan was set into motion.

THE FOLLOWING MORNING, she found herself in brighter spirits, consumed by details of her new plan. She attended her archery lessons with Ivrir at dawn. Once again, she performed poorly using the kind of speed he encouraged. It was even more difficult with her wandering mind.

Dragon's Bane had the power to weaken her enemy. A small amount would merely slow Raff's movements and dull his senses, a larger amount would make it impossible for him to use magic, and an even greater amount would kill him. However, she was no killer.

Unbeknownst to the champions, when their number reached five, a race was to take place. A flight from Irelia Island to the arena. The winner would be granted immunity from the next round of fights. She planned to do everything in her power to ensure Raff would not come in first place during that race.

"You are distracted today, Lena. Concentrate." Not a single arrow had found its target.

Much to her surprise, she was glad to shoulder her bow when breakfast time arrived.

"I promise to do better tomorrow." She hoped her assurance would mitigate her poor performance. Ivrir would certainly hold her to it.

As she ate her porridge, her mind turned down a new direction. She stole several glances at Tristan. Why did he wish to meet with her? She imagined several reasons, but none seemed likely.

Much to her disappointment, Daryn was not present today. He generally took both breakfast and the midday meal on his ship. Still, she'd hoped to see him, especially after his strange behavior.

Just as she finished eating, a pleasant voice pulled her from her thoughts of Daryn. "Good morning, Princess Lena."

Tristan stood before her in front of the head table, his arms clasped behind his back. He appeared at ease. She however was anything but. "Shall we have our walk now?" His green eyes glittered strangely.

She looked over at her parents. They exchanged a look but said nothing. She swallowed. "Of course, Tristan. Let's." Several ill-disguised snickers from her father's Shields forced her to glare at Ramar before leaving the table. Questioning gazes followed her from the hall.

Her handmaidens kept a healthy distance as they walked. For a time, she enjoyed their silence, allowing Tristan to lead the way down the winding paths of the royal garden. Every so often, she stopped before her favorite flowers to admire their growth.

At last, she could suffer her curiosity no longer. "I admit, Tristan, I was surprised by your invitation." They turned a corner and passed several patrons. Tristan remained quiet until their passing.

"I'm surprised too."

Her brow furrowed. "You? But…"

"After battling my conscience on the matter, Princess, it became necessary to pull you aside in confidence. I believe that I have unintentionally wronged you, offended you deeply. For that, I am sorry."

Her eyes widened. She set her jaw. Was he teasing her? Was this about his conversation with her father?

"I admit to my confusion, Tristan. Why might I be offended?"

"Your father summoned all unmated Drengr to the capital to attend to you. I failed to uphold his summons." His face reflected his disapproval. His apology was entirely genuine. "A summons from a king must never go unanswered. I admit to my fault, to my failure." She opened her mouth but struggled to form a response. "This was not my only shortcoming. I never considered what my absence might do to you."

"Me? Why should you worry about me? We have only just met."

"Yes...perhaps you are correct. Perhaps I should not worry. For reasons most confusing, I suddenly care what you think of me." He paused and then shook his head. "I care deeply."

She stopped and turned to face him. "I admit, I am flattered. But truly you—"

"No, please let me finish. The ceremony was a monumental time in your life—your opportunity to find your mate if a mate existed. My absence was selfish. I see that now. I see the error in my ways."

Once more, she was speechless. His apology was full of feeling. He held nothing back. "Princess Lena, the future of this kingdom is far more important than my own. I ought to have considered that. Instead..." His jaw flexed but he said no more. Something was bothering him. She could see the conflict in his green eyes.

Without warning, he began walking again. She was left standing in confusion before she quickened her pace and caught up. "Thank you for your concern and for your apology, Tristan." Apologies were never easy, she knew that well enough. "The ceremony was a big event, certainly. But..." She chewed on the skin of her bottom lip. "Can you keep a secret?"

Tristan's eyes widened a measure before he recaptured control of his face. "Of course, Princess. Upon my honor."

She nodded. "Then I will tell you truthfully. I *am* offended that you did not come to the ceremony, but not in the way you might believe."

"Oh?" He already knew—based on his conversation with

her father—what she was going to say next. That did not mean it should go unsaid.

"I hope you will not think less of me when I tell you that I was not eager to find my mate—if one existed. The idea of bonding myself to another did not suit me. I am very independent, you see."

He exhaled. A smile crept to his lips. "I understand your reservation entirely. The life of a Drengr is a long one. And the bond can only be broken by death."

"My thoughts exactly!" She breathed easier. "The ceremony was a final desperate effort for me to secure the crown. You were not the only one with selfish intentions. I was no better." She shook her head. Admitting her selfishness was unintentional, but the words were out before she could stop them.

"I admire your confession. Admitting to one's faults is never easy."

"Likewise, it takes a great deal of courage to admit to a mistake. I admire you for seeking me out to clear your conscience."

"Yes…There is a very strong possibility that I will win this tournament—"

She snorted. "You lack reserve, Tristan."

"If I win," he continued, taking her statement to heart, "I wish to start off on good terms with you. I cannot bear any ill thoughts from you."

"Admirable," she said. His intentions seemed well enough. "If you are intent on strengthening our relationship, perhaps you might let me in on a few secrets of your own?"

"Secrets?" His head tilted. "Which secrets would those be?"

"Ha! Surely you can guess?"

"Hardly, Princess. Please enlighten me." By this time, they

had made a full circuit of the garden and began anew. Never mind that too much attention might spark rumors from those patrons who had already passed them more than once.

"Well, we can start with your superb skills in the arena. I struggle to believe that someone raised by *dragons*, could be so skilled."

"Is that so?"

"Who trained you?"

He chuckled. "My, my, you are direct today."

"And you *aren't*?"

"Point taken. My training is not common knowledge. Forgive me if I do not readily discuss it." He fell into silent consideration before speaking again. "I suppose a secret is a secret for a reason."

"I promise not to relay the information to anyone else."

The corner of his mouth twitched. "I see. Well then, since you are sworn into secrecy, I will tell you." The gold flecks in his green eyes danced. He was enjoying himself. "Unbeknownst to anyone here, I was trained in combat by the Sprites."

She gasped. "I...I should have known!"

"The dragons raised me, yes, along with a Sprite midwife who gave fifteen years of her life to my rearing. When the time came, my clan sent me to Esterpine."

"But...but..." She was struggling to understand. It made no sense.

"*But, Tristan!*" he said, screwing up his face in a playful impersonation of her. "Don't the Sprites *hate* the dragons and Drengr?"

She burst into laughter, clutching her stomach. "That's exactly what I was going to say. And remind me next time I need a stand in. You would make a great Princess Lena double for all those times I wish to skirt my responsibilities.

My gowns might be a little tight, but I'm sure we can figure something out." Tristan's smug smile made him all the handsomer. She felt her cheeks burn and looked away before he might notice. "I find myself surprised," she said at last. "I would have guessed it impossible."

"I cannot say what prompted their agreement. But in some ways, I am better for it."

"Some? I would say all. Have you seen the way you wield a blade?" Her hand flew to her mouth. What was wrong with her? She was supposed to be Daryn's biggest fan. Suddenly she was praising Tristan? A horrible, sinking feeling came upon her. Guilt left her skin on fire. Tristan said nothing. She struggled to regain composure and steer the conversation away from her stupid remark. "So aside from your secret about the Sprites, is there anything else hiding behind that edifice of yours?"

He shrugged. "To me, my life is normal. I cannot claim to know what you might find amusing."

"Fair enough," she said, even though she read between the lines of his statement. If she wanted to know anything else, she would have to ask outright. "I suppose nothing further comes to mind yet. If I think of anything else, might I ask it?"

"At any time. Of course." They had reached the entrance to the garden after their second turn. "I shall leave you for today." He stepped away. "Thank you again for your company, Princess Lena, and for agreeing to meet with me."

"My pleasure, Tristan." She gave him a curtsy then turned and left, careful not to afford him a backward glance. For some reason, she so desperately wanted to.

CHAPTER 20
DRAGON'S BANE

Tʜᴇ ɴᴇxᴛ ʀᴏᴜɴᴅ of the tournament saw five competitors victorious. It was no surprise that Daryn, Tristan, and Raff were among them. At the start, when Lena gave Daryn the velvet bag to draw his coin, she tried to glean some hint about him, about why he'd distanced himself. Alas, she was disappointed. He merely smiled and winked. She was forced to move on.

As she watched each match, she wrestled with the idea of lighting a torch for him that night. He'd promised, after all, that he would come if she did. After thinking on it for some time, she decided against it. She was a princess and he, a Drengr. If he was interested in her, he would pursue her.

Seated in her chair under the shaded awning of the arena's royal box, her mind jumped back to their time on the water. What had happened to the man on the *Storm's Maiden*? What happened to the man who took a kiss without her asking? Where was *that* man? If he expected her to crawl after him, he would be sorely mistaken, even if her heart wanted to.

Tristan's fight came last that day. His impressive technique swept everything from her mind. It was welcome after her frustration over Daryn. Once more she watched him with awe, fists clenched, waiting for that special moment when his blade would sing its glory for the spectators. Now that she knew more about his background, she couldn't help but notice his Spriten movements, not that she knew how Sprites moved. She could only guess.

Every reflex was graceful. His aggression was performed with deep intent. He always remained several steps ahead of his opponent, who could hardly keep pace. As she watched, a calm confidence settled upon her. Such a thing had never happened, not even with Daryn. She knew Tristan would win his match. And he did.

Her mind drifted back to his conversation over tea with her father. He had claimed that he would win the tournament, for why else had he come? She had disliked his show of confidence. Perhaps it wasn't brazen after all. He alone understood his abilities better than anyone.

When the afternoon ended, the five remaining competitors paraded around the arena floor. Dragons trumpeted their approval for Tristan. The crowd screamed and chanted for their favorites. She couldn't help but clap. The only person she disapproved of was Raff, and if all went well, soon enough he would no longer be a threat.

THAT NIGHT DURING DINNER, she kept her ears open, listening to the various conversations that took place between her father's Shields. It was delightful to hear Briv, Ferand, and Ramar speculate over Tristan's moves—knowing where he had learned them. "Did you see the way he leapt through the air when he turned the tides on Ragul? What grace! Ragul didn't stand a chance." She smiled but said nothing. It was obvious that her father's six admired him.

Before a week ago, no one in the capital knew Tristan's name. Now, even the king's Shields couldn't refrain from saying it. Her father sang his praises too, but her reaction was different hearing it come from him. "I have been quite impressed with Tristan's performance," he said. "I can see him winning this tournament. Out of everyone, he will make a most worthy Crowned Prince."

His praise left a pit in her stomach. She wanted to remain indifferent, but how could she? Tristan appeared perfect. He was everything a king might dream of in a son. Her father had always wanted a son. Instead, he was stuck with a daughter—a daughter who could never be queen.

"Perhaps we ought to plan for his winning," her father went on. "Perhaps begin his training early."

Her stomach dropped even lower. She had known this day would come for weeks now, but it was no easier. Pedrus squared his shoulders, answering her father. "I would be happy to spar with the young Drengr. Tomorrow will be a perfect opportunity to train with him."

"I imagine that he will benefit from the extra practice," said King Cornan.

It was too much. She returned her gaze to the plate before her and rushed to finish her meal. Not long after, she excused herself. Even though Tristan was Daryn's competition, she liked him, especially after their walk together. He may have won her over, but it was difficult listening to her father speak of him as the son he never had. Whether or not the king realized his actions, they cut her like a knife, creating a hole for hopelessness to dwell.

She hurried from the dining hall as soon as she could, her

handmaidens following in her wake. She had almost reached her apartment when she heard a whisper. *"Pssst."* She stopped and found Evan, the servant boy messenger, peeping out from behind a stone statue of Kenna Sophia, Princess Irelia's kenna.

"Evan," she whispered, motioning him forward. Her handmaidens stood back, watching with curiosity. Evan handed her a small bit of parchment before scurrying off. She waited until she was back in her apartments to look at it. Bartlett sent her a single sketched image of an ash bucket and a chimney brush, delicately done in black ink. She smiled.

"I would like to retire early tonight," she said. Cora helped her out of her gown, Avra brushed her hair before putting it into a single braid down her back, and Theresa brought forth a warm cloth to wash her face and hands. Then they retired.

Once alone, she dressed in her cloak and waited for midnight. When the time came, she made her way through the passageways out to the cookery's garden. There she met Bartlett at the secret door.

He stepped through looking rather smug. "Perhaps, Princess, it is you who ought be bowin' to me tonight."

She laughed and kissed him on the forehead. "Why is that, my little mischief monger?"

"Right difficult time I had procuring this here vial of Dragon's Bane." He popped the cork and wafted it under his nose, crinkling it as he took in the scent. "Potent too, if I might say so myself." He held it forward. "Want a sniff?"

She backed away and shook her head. "I think not. I trust you. Besides, the smell of the stuff gives me headaches." She had only encountered it twice, but she well remembered. Bartlett shrugged, replaced the stopper, and handed it over.

She hesitated before saying, "I will need you tomorrow night, my room, dinner time."

"I get to join you again?" He perked up, his face splitting into a grin.

"Absolutely!" Her invitation left him thrilled. When he departed, she gave him another affectionate kiss upon the forehead and warned him to stay out of trouble.

The next day dragged on forever. Aside from her archery lessons in the morning, and work with her father in the afternoon, she stayed in her apartment. Her handmaidens were a bit peeved, having hoped to go for a walk. At last, when dinner arrived, she claimed to have an upset stomach and bid Avra, Cora, and Theresa to go without her.

Not long after they departed, a soft knock sounded at her door. Bartlett entered and they set about their mischief. Through the secret passageways they went, until they arrived at the hidden door leading into Raff's room. She peered through the tiny crack in the wall, making sure that no light met her eye. The chamber was dark.

When she opened the door, she sent Bartlett through with the vial. He took the torch with him and moved soundlessly. The only thing she heard was the vial's contents being poured into Raff's pitcher of water. There were a number of ways Dragon's Bane could be administered. Since it was tasteless, the best way was mixing its contents with something edible. Once it mixed with liquid as in this case, its awful scent was impossible to discern.

"There we go, Princess. All finished." Bartlett climbed back through the small door, handing her the empty vial. "Not enough to kill him, just enough to slow him down. I bet he'll be right confused to why he ain't flying any faster!"

When they returned to her chambers, she passed him a gold dragon for his assistance in Raff's room then gave him the same advice as before. He was not to enter the keep for the next several days. She could not afford for Raff's keen Drengr nose to notice the lad's scent in passing. Too much was at risk.

Later that night, much to her own disapproval, she lit her torch. She couldn't say why she did it, only that her infatuation with Daryn drove her to irrational thoughts. Within minutes, he was beside her on the balcony. He bowed deeply—a little too formally for her tastes. "Princess Lena, I do hope all is well? I did not see you at dinner."

She nodded. "My stomach was upset, but it is better now, now that you are here." She went to him, wrapping her fingers into his soft hair and pulling his head to hers. Her stomach clenched as their lips met. Too soon however, he pulled away.

She felt her brow crinkle. "What's the matter?" Once more, she was surprised by his strange behavior.

"Truthfully? I cannot say. I have been feeling strangely these past few days."

Suspicion forced her eyes to narrow. Her mind rushed back to the Dragon's Bane. "You haven't been poisoned, have you?"

He laughed. "I don't think so, else my reflexes would have shown it. I am quick as a mouse, clever as a cat, large as a dragon." He shook his head in earnest. "No, whatever it is, I cannot place it."

"And whatever it is has stolen your desire for my kisses?"

He sighed and rubbed the back of his neck. At last, he offered her a rueful smile and pulled her back towards him. "Perhaps it is nothing," he mumbled against her lips. Her mouth met his again and they locked in a long embrace. She felt every curve of his body against hers.

When he set her back upon her feet, she regained her

ability to speak. "The next task will be a race. At dawn, all five of you will fly with my father to Irelia Island."

"Truly?" He frowned.

"You will race from Irelia Island to the arena. The winner will be granted immunity. The four losers will draw coins."

"I see. And the other four—do they know?"

She shook her head, blushing under his scolding gaze. "I am not a *child*, Daryn, you need not look at me in such a way."

"Lena, remember when I told you that I wanted nothing to do with your scheming? I meant it. If I win this tournament, it should be fairly earned."

Her eyebrows drew together. "You knowing this little secret does not put you at an unfair advantage."

His frown deepened. "Perhaps it is best if I take my leave tonight. You are still unwell."

Her heart dropped. "Fine, go!" She turned on her heel and retreated into her apartment, forgoing a goodnight kiss as she slammed the door to her balcony hard enough to rattle it, then yanked the curtains into place, shielding him from view.

When she climbed into bed, sleep did not come. Instead, she lay in a pool of her own tears. The worst feeling of all was her own shame. She'd brought this upon herself. This was her fault. She'd been too eager towards him, too forward, too *desperate*.

A storm found its way to the castle, pelting the walls with rain, perfectly reflecting her dismal mood. Her mother was right. Involving herself with a Drengr was dangerous, especially when she would never have him, and he would never love her the way she wanted. The best thing to do was end it. Could she find the courage for it?

The next morning was gray and depressing. Her mind was torn in two. She poured her frustration into her arrows as they sailed, one after another, towards the target. When she finally struck it, she hardly noticed. It wasn't until Ivrir whooped and grabbed ahold of her arm to shake her. "At last!" he gasped between laughter and excitement. "At last you strike the target without a single measure of hesitance."

She afforded him a smile and looked at the arrow. It rested just on the edge of the bullseye. Unhappy with its distance from the bullseye, she pulled another and another, until emptying her quiver. Some struck the target's edge, while others sailed right past.

"You are improving," Ivrir said as they walked to breakfast. Under any other circumstances, she might have relished his praise, but not today.

The first thing she noticed upon their entry into the dining hall were the five missing competitors. Her three companions, Briv, Ferand, and Ramar, shared hushed whispers until she sat down. After that, they were silent.

"What has you three so worked up?" she asked.

"Nothing concerning you, Princess." Briv glanced at her before returning to his food.

Her mind went to Raff. Until now, she'd forgotten about her escapade with Bartlett, too caught up with her internal struggle over Daryn.

"Ramar?" She looked over at him and failed to miss the twitch of his lips. "Come now, Ramar, since when do we keep secrets?"

"I had wondered the same thing, *Lena*." She watched him for several long moments, glaring at him as best she could, until he finally spoke. "Very well then. We were discussing Raff's unruly attitude this morning."

"Oh? Unruly? You don't say…"

"He was quite unhappy about the race your father had planned. Claimed he was out of sorts." A pleased smile threatened her lips. She pursed them together to keep it hidden. It was a gamble with the Dragon's Bane, knowing there was a chance Raff might never drink the water at his bedside table. But clearly he had!

"*And*?" She raised her eyebrows. "What did my father say?"

"He said, 'You are a Drengr, Raff. It is time you acted like one.'" Ramar quoted her father perfectly. She spat her juice from her mouth back into its cup in a very *un-lady-like* manner so as not to choke from her laughter.

"Lena!" her mother scolded.

"Sorry, Mama, I choked." Then she turned to Ramar. "He makes a good point. It's time Raff starts acting like a true Drengr." Knowing she had succeeded, she felt lighter inside. And hopeful.

She and her handmaidens, with Kenna Margaret in tow, arrived at the arena just after the midday meal. There she informed the spectators of the race, explaining the rules. "Any minute now our competitors will come flying in. The winner of today's race will be granted immunity from today's matches!"

At this, the crowd went wild. Even the dragons trumpeted. It wasn't until she looked up and followed the dragons' gaze, that she realized the reason for their excessive jubilance. There, a white speck against the sky, was Tristan.

CHAPTER 21
DARYN'S BEATING

Tristan was granted immunity for his win. Lena was left to descend the stairs into the arena for the drawing of the coins. The audience hadn't stopped cheering to take in breath. Their cries of elation paired with the cries of the dragons were overwhelming. Her own excitement and happiness surprised her. Hadn't she wanted *Daryn* to win? Was that not the reason for telling him about the race?

She thought of his reaction, of the way he treated her in response. Her chest tightened and her lips pressed into a thin line. She took each step with growing anger until she was gripping the velvet bag with a clenched fist.

Grinding her teeth together, she stepped out onto the dirt floor of the arena and made her way towards the four competitors. The crowd continued their cries, stamping their feet and ringing bells. The sand was hot under the soles of her slippers, but no warmer than the heat in her skin brought about by her anger.

If Daryn's behavior was all she faced, she might have grappled with the matter successfully. But there was another problem that unsettled her. She glanced over at Tristan, mysterious Tristan, standing victorious as he waved to the crowd, basking in his victory.

"Princess Lena," Daryn greeted her as she stepped before the remaining competitors. He opened his mouth to say more, then abruptly closed it. She looked away from him, holding her hands up to calm the crowd. "And there you have it! Our four competitors will draw coins to determine who fights who." She did her best to avoid eye contact with Daryn. "As promised, Tristan has been granted immunity." Loud cheers resumed; he was a clear favorite. She held up her hands again. "Once coins are drawn, our Drengr competitors will have one hour to rest before their matches. In that time, I have organized some entertainment for you." This unexpected announcement left the audience shouting in eager excitement. She smiled.

Holding the bag out for each Drengr, she allowed them to collect their coins. There were only two pairs, so this time they announced their results. Vergoth, one of the two remaining mated Drengr, revealed his first, holding it high. "A mountain!" he cried. Everyone politely clapped. Beside him, Adra held his aloft. "A mountain!" he also cried. It took a moment for the results to sink in. Just then, Raff, who looked thoroughly inconvenienced, cried out, "A star!" Again, the audience clapped. Then finally, "A star!" Daryn's voice echoed in her ears. Daryn would be fighting Raff. It was everything she had ever wanted.

Taking a deep breath, she stomped away, leading them from the arena to the staging area, doing her best to stay well ahead of them. "Lena," she heard Daryn call after her as they walked. She pretended ignorance. "Princess Lena!" he called again. "I'm sorry for last night." Still, she ignored him.

Another voice sounded over Daryn's. "Princess Lena, I am

too unwell to fight today." Had she known Raff would be fighting Daryn, she'd have requested *two* vials of Dragon's Bane instead of one. "Princess Lena," he repeated. "I demand we postpone the matches. I have expressed this to your father." She continued walking without so much as a backwards glance. Her lack of acknowledgement only spurred him on. "Princess Lena, isn't it *strange* that I should be *sick*? Might you know anything about that?"

The accusation in his voice forced her to glance over her shoulder. "The tournament goes on as planned, Raff." Her biting tone silenced his protest. She was not in the mood to deal with him.

"Come now, Raff," baited Daryn. "Afraid I might *best* you?"

"Hardly," Raff hissed.

Ignoring their baiting, she came to a stop before the staging area and spun around. "Good luck, gentlemen." Without waiting for them to file in, she turned on her heel and departed, eyes fixed on Tristan. Seeing him chased away some of her negative thoughts. He stood alone, off to the side of the arena, patiently waiting. "Follow me," she barked without meaning to sound impolite.

His eyes widened but he didn't protest. He took off at a slight jog to catch up. "You're upset?"

"No. Of course not." She hated the sarcasm, but neither could she stop it. It's not as if this was his fault. "I've had about *enough* of those Drengr." She pointed a thumb over her shoulder in Daryn's direction. They had reached the stairs leading to the stands. She sighed. "I'm sorry. My attitude is dismal. I should be congratulating you, not taking out my frustrations on you. If I'm being truthful, I'm glad it was you and not any of them who won. I think you shall sit beside me today." While she hadn't planned for it, the offer left her stomach somersaulting. She had every reason to dislike Tristan. There was a very high chance he would win this tournament and take her crown. Moreover, her father was growing to adore him. Both reasons left her jealous. She couldn't decide whether to love him or hate him.

"Are you sure I'm welcome in the royal box, Princess? I would sooner sit in the stands beside the defeated champions." His offer was half-hearted.

"Nonsense. You shall sit beside me as my *honored* guest. You are today's immunity champion."

A chair was placed beside hers and the entertainment began. Long before the tournament, she'd hired a group of traveling acrobats who claimed their fame by climbing atop each other to create human ladders. Admittance into the tournament was free, and expensive entertainment was rare for the poor. She was most excited for them to enjoy the show. Her mind went to Bartlett. She hoped he had brought his family and smiled at the thought.

When the troop began their act the crowd hardly knew what to expect. By the end of their first trick they drove the audience wild with surprise and admiration. She vigorously clapped along with everyone else. "Wonderful *choice*, darling." Her mother's approval left her beaming. Her father's eyes sparkled. He too laughed and clapped at each feat the acrobats accomplished. As they began to throw each other in the air, higher and higher, she couldn't help but gasp.

"Impressive, are they not?" she asked Tristan, glancing at him. He smiled and clapped along. "I am told they are the best in Dragonwall."

"Is that so?" His eyebrows raised.

She smiled. "Do you have any friends from where you're from, Tristan?"

He chuckled, affording her a quick glance before returning

his gaze to the performance. "Everyone has friends, Princess. Life is rather lonely without them."

"What are they like? Your friends?"

"If you must know"—he kept his face forward as he spoke—"they are rather honorable, sometimes too honorable, if you know what I mean. Their age makes them boring at times. Most often, they are too wise for their own good."

He was referring to the Sprites who had trained him, though he could not say it aloud since it was their little secret. What she truly wished to know was if he had any *female* friends. It wasn't exactly a question she could ask with her parents sitting beside her. She returned her gaze to the acrobats, biting her tongue for the remainder of their stunts.

All too quickly the show was over. The audience sighed with disappointment as the performers bowed not once, not twice, but three times before they exited the arena. A hush fell as large racks of weapons were carted into the arena. Some looked positively barbaric. Axes, spiked balls on chains, hammers, fancy daggers, spears, and all manner of shields were arranged like artwork. From the corner of her eye, she saw Tristan scowl.

"Is that disappointment I see?" she asked. "Look at the excitement you're missing." A sly smile spread across her features. "Today I am raising the stakes."

The crowd picked up on this new change. Their whispers grew into mutters before the volume increased to full-blown speculation. When everything was set, she stood.

"Yes, yes," she cried, lifting her hands for silence. "As you can guess, today is full of fun!" She glanced over her shoulder at Tristan. His face was impossible to read. Turning back to the crowd she continued. "First, let us give another round of applause for our performers! Weren't they wonderful?" At this, the stands erupted. She took several deep breaths before silencing them. "We have two matches. Our competitors will be allowed any weapons they choose with no restrictions. First, we will see Adra and Vergoth. They will be followed by Daryn and Raff." She swallowed, pushing away her unease. "By tonight, only *three* competitors will remain!" She allowed the crowd more time to cheer before calling the first two competitors forward. Then she took her seat.

Adra and Vergoth took their positions on the arena floor. "Begin!" came the shout of the arena master. The fight started slowly. Both Adra and Vergoth had their Sveraks drawn, and neither felt the need to acquire additional weapons, not immediately. However, as they made attempts against each other, swiping and jabbing, jumping and lunging, their progress brought them closer to the racks.

In truth, she hardly saw what took place. She spent the majority of the fight stealing furtive glances at Tristan from the edge of her gaze. She gleaned each notable moment when she noticed Tristan's miniscule flinching. There was a point when Vergoth plunged a spear into Adra's thigh and the crowd gasped. She only knew to turn her attention to the fight because she saw Tristan's eyes widen a measure.

At last, Vergoth succeeded in forcing Adra to the ground. She returned her full attention to the arena in time to see Vergoth encircle Adra's head in his arm before placing the blade of his Sverak against the Drengr's neck in victory. She politely clapped as the crowd cheered.

Standing, she motioned for silence. "Congratulations, Vergoth!" she cried, though not very enthusiastically. "Bring forth the next competitors!" As Adra—who looked rather upset by his loss—and Vergoth left the arena, helping hands rushed forth to reassemble the weapons and tidy things up.

She watched Raff stalk into the arena, quickly followed by Daryn. Her heart skipped a beat in nervousness. Her frustration evaporated. Daryn never wanted this. He was here because of her. She'd made him promise to come back. She needed him to do everything in his power to keep Raff from winning the crown. Now, it was up to Daryn to eliminate Raff. She could hardly stand the idea of Raff in the final three. The thought made her sick. But she was also worried for Daryn, for what Raff might do to him.

The two took their positions, Sveraks drawn, bodies crouched low to the ground, motionless like statues. The arena master moved towards them. Her breath caught in her chest. She could not expel it for fear that breathing might bring about an unfortunate end.

The arena master lifted his arm, paused briefly, then brought it down in a sweeping motion. "Begin!"

She loudly exhaled, earning an interested stare from Tristan. This time, she kept her focus on the fight instead of stealing glances. Too much was at stake.

Daryn and Raff began circling. She followed Raff's movements. They appeared normal and she inwardly cursed herself. The Dragon's Bane was too diluted in a full pitcher of water. Its effects were already wearing off! The look of pure ruthlessness upon Raff's face left her heart racing. His lips were curled baring his teeth, and his eyes were narrowed. The expression alone made her shudder. The world was quiet as the two opponents sized each other up, looking for weaknesses, searching for that perfect moment to lunge.

It wasn't until her mother put a hand upon her arm that she realized her fists were clenched. Her nails were biting into her skin. She exhaled loudly once more, loosening her fingers, trying to relax her tense muscles. Still, Daryn and Raff circled.

Daryn's face was composed and emotionless. She could see that his eyes were calculating, flicking back and forth, looking for a way to break through Raff's defenses. Then he found it. His gaze settled briefly on Raff's left foot. She knew him too well; she anticipated his intent before the rest of the world. He lunged forward. Raff fell for the bait. Attempting to defend his torso against Daryn's Sverak, he failed to see Daryn's leg as it swept his left foot off balance. Raff stumbled.

For an instant, she thought Daryn had him. Raff immediately regained his balance and struck back. The clang of their blades, strike after strike, echoed through the arena. Every time Daryn tried to bring his blade down upon Raff, Raff met it with his own. They danced back and forth, shuffling their feet closer to the weapons racks.

When they grabbed additional weapons, she utilized the opportunity to take several deep breaths. Tristan was intent on the fight too. He sat motionless. Were it not for his darting eyes, she would have thought he was a statue. But she knew exactly what he was doing. He was memorizing their fighting styles. Smart move on his part.

Weapons in hand, they began circling back towards each other. Daryn possessed a spear, shield, and his Sverak tucked in its scabbard. Raff had several daggers, an axe, and his Sverak also tucked away. Raff did not wait more than the length of a breath to pull a dagger from his belt. It sank deeply into Daryn's shield with a thud.

This was just a taste. Several more daggers flew from his hand so quickly, she hadn't the time to blink. Daryn moved just as rapidly, orienting his shield to take the blows. Raff seized this opportunity.

He darted forward and swiped his blade across Daryn's right leg. She winced as the painful cry echoed into the arena. Blood spilled down his trousers from the deep gash. He stumbled backwards, regaining his footing just in time. Raff came down upon him with his axe. It ruined Daryn's shield, causing it to splinter and fly apart in pieces. His hand was left with nothing but the handle.

"Come on!" she screamed at Daryn, losing all composure. She watched Daryn stumble against Raff's strength. Just then, Daryn's spear sank into Raff's side. "Yes!" she hissed.

Raff hardly flinched. Instead, he swung his axe around before Daryn could release his hold on the spear or drop the shield's broken handle. With a bone crunching sound, the axe imbedded itself into Daryn's side. She screamed, and her hands flew to her face.

Daryn sank to his knees. "No!" she cried in fear. "No! *Get up!*" Daryn's legs had already healed, but the deep hack in his side would take much longer.

Lunging again without allowing Daryn time to rise or heal, Raff the Ruthless removed his Sverak from its scabbard and slashed it across Daryn's arms, then again across his abdomen. "He's not allowing him the opportunity to heal!" she moaned, looking helplessly from Tristan to her father. Shouldn't they do something? Tristan's hard expression was easy to read, but he said nothing.

She returned her gaze to the harrowing fight in time to see Raff lunge again. This time, Daryn was ready. He rolled away, dodging the blow. She exhaled but her muscles remained clenched. Raff's Sverak would have cleaved Daryn's head in two, had he not avoided the blow. At that moment, she was certain of one thing: Raff did not care if he killed Daryn so long as he won.

She looked between Daryn and her father, hoping King Cornan would come up with some solution to stop the brutal beating. Raff continued to slash and hack at Daryn, who only managed to dodge half of the attempts on his life. He was finally too weak to heal properly. Large amounts of blood leaked from his gashes. His only hope was to give the signal of defeat. She clawed her nails against her face. Which was better, Daryn maintaining the fight, or Raff winning? If he died, his death would be her fault. She never should have dragged him into this.

A new thought struck her just as Raff's fist crunched against Daryn's jawbone, sending Daryn flat on his back. What if Daryn was only hanging on because of his promise to her? What if he felt poorly for how he'd treated her, and to make up for it, he was willing to risk his life to keep Raff from winning. She jumped to her feet, moving forward so that she leaned against the railing. There she watched in horror as Raff continued his onslaught. It appeared now that Daryn was unconscious. His eyes were closed, and he was not moving as Raff's boot continued to collide with his skull.

There was only one thing to do. Since she presided over this tournament, only she could do it. "Enough!" she screamed, hanging over the banister so that the world would hear her. "Enough." Daryn was unable to surrender himself, so she would do it for him, no matter how much she hated conceding to Raff.

Silence fell, and Raff halted his onslaught. "I pronounce Raff the winner of this match." Her voice wavered. The words were difficult to choke out. The arena master moved out onto the floor and took Raff's arm, lifting it in victory. It was over. Raff had won.

CHAPTER 22

DARYN TAKES HIS LEAVE

THE DAY after Daryn's loss left Lena in a pitiful mood. She lay motionless in bed, gazing out the window to her balcony. She'd done a great deal of thinking in the past few months, first over finding a mate, then over giving up her crown. So much worrying, speculation, anxiety. All she could do now was lay still—numb.

"Won't you take your breakfast, Princess?" Cora peeked into the sleeping chamber.

Her stomach grumbled. "I suppose I must," she said, sighing. With a lack of grace, she rolled out of her bed and stumbled to the table to eat.

A tray of porridge, fruit, bread, and honey waited for her. She dug in, though her appetite was small. After a few bites there was a knock at the door. At first, she thought it might be Daryn, but then she remembered that it couldn't be, and her heart fell. Daryn's heavy injuries had required extensive healing from the Magoi, and he was still recovering under strict bed orders.

Theresa went to the door and came back with a perplexed

expression. Bartlett trailed behind her. "Princess, this…this *boy* is here to see you. I tried to turn him away."

"Oh, it's fine. I wish to speak with him in private. Perhaps the three of you might go down to the market and get me a few shawls. I'd like one to go with my pink gown." Her handmaidens needed no further prompting. They left her apartment.

Bartlett sauntered over and plopped himself upon a chair beside her. Without any invitation, he helped himself to some of her food. She watched him with half-hearted amusement. "Did you enjoy the entertainment yesterday?" she asked.

"Sure did, Princess." He licked his fingers clean after a few bits of fruit, smacking his lips in the process. "I also noticed that the Dragon's Bane wore off too fast." Pouring himself a cup of juice, he drank deeply. "You cannot let that uncivilized *beast* become king."

"Don't I know it," she muttered, her mood darkening once more. "But I am fresh out of ideas. He was *not* supposed to win yesterday."

"I got a fresh order of Dragon's Bane coming in tomorrow morning." He grinned mischievously.

"Absolutely not!" She could not risk another attempt. "Raff is already suspicious."

"Well, that's cos you been missin' from dinner the other night. You let me see to it, Princess. You go to dinner tomorrow night. I know my way 'round the passages well enough." He crossed his arms and leaned back to wait for her permission. "Unless you got another idea? Drengr are impervious to most things, and you ain't got any magic to cast a spell, do you?"

She contemplated the offer. It did not sit well with her. Yet, what other choice did she have? If Raff won the next competition, he'd be ranked in the top two. She couldn't let him get that close to the crown. Even thinking about it left her sick. "Alright." Much to her own unease, she agreed. "You may be good at what you do, but please see to it that you are careful."

"'Pon my honor, Princess. I'll be careful."

Later that day she made her way to the eastern wing of the keep. This portion of the castle overlooked the Bay of Bandu with stunning views of the ships at port. She glanced towards the end of the bay where she knew the *Storm's Maiden* to be. It was there, anchored. Her heart tightened.

She needed to see Daryn, to know that he was okay. She felt responsible for what had happened to him. She couldn't relax without knowing.

A portion of the keep's eastern wing housed the Society. This elite group of Magoi were the best at their craft—each Mage trained from a young age. They were Dragonwall's most advanced magicians. They could cure the sick, conjure objects from thin air, and brew potions capable of killing. Few knew the extent of their true capabilities, not even she.

The Magoi were different from other races. While the Drengr and Sprite races understood what they were from birth, the Magoi rarely did. Signs of magic often waited until late childhood to manifest. And blood often skipped multiple generations before showing itself. To become a Mage was prestigious. Moreover, only the best Magoi came to the Society to train with the Grand Mage and his tutors.

She tapped quietly on the Grand Mage's door and was admitted to his large sitting room. This room held shelves of books, tables lit with ever-glowing candles, and plush couches beside a large fireplace. "What can I do for you today, Princess?" Grand Mage Seda studied her. The glint in his eyes betrayed him. He already knew her purpose in coming.

"I came to inquire about Daryn. Is he healed? May I see him?"

"Ah, he is doing much better. He was in such a weakened state yesterday. His magic was unable to fully heal him in a timely manner. I successfully closed his wounds before they turned deadly."

"That's a relief," she sighed.

"While he is healed, I insisted that he spend the day resting."

"A fitting order. May I see him?"

"Just a moment." Seda shuffled away. The Magoi lived much longer lives than humans. The stronger their magic, the longer they lived. She did not know how old Seda was, but based on her father's hints, she could guess he was somewhere near three hundred years of age. He returned a few minutes later wearing a frown. "Daryn does not wish for *any* visitors."

"But what about me?" She felt her eyebrows pull together. "Did you tell him that it's me?"

Seda pursed his lips. "I did indeed, Princess."

"Oh...Very well." She left the east wing scowling. This time, she did not bother inventing excuses for Daryn and why he avoided her. Anything she might have conjured would have been too painful to bear. Instead, she closed herself in her apartment and did what she could to keep her mind off of him.

The following day, she was a fit of nerves. Aside from her morning archery lesson with Ivrir, she kept herself from sight until dinner. Even her handmaidens were skittish around her, especially after she snapped at Cora for laughing at one of Avra's jokes over Thomas. She had half a mind to skip dinner too, but she remembered Bartlett's mission. She needed to be present to abolish any suspicion of her involvement, should any arise.

Once she was dressed, she proceeded with her ladies

down to the dining hall. As she walked, she tried not to worry too much over Bartlett. Yet, she could only obsess over the consequences should he fail. She had to trust that he knew what he was doing. He would let himself into her apartment, use the secret door behind the wall hanging, and scurry through the passageways. She had taken him on enough missions to know that he had picked up on everything.

"My ladies," a voice stopped her dead in her tracks. Standing before them was Daryn. He bowed deeply before turning his attention directly to her. Health wise, he looked well enough, but there was something in his expression that chilled her blood. "I wonder if I might have a word with Princess Lena?" She stood frozen like a terrified rabbit. Her handmaidens nodded and went on without her.

"You must forgive me, Lena, for not agreeing to see you yesterday. I was too unwell for visitors." His words left her stomach churning. She understood his meaning well enough. If he truly cared for her, he would have wanted to see her no matter his state. She could only panic, for fear of what was sure to come.

"I'm sorry, Daryn." She felt the words rushing from her mouth before she could stop them. "I never should have been cross with you. The match yesterday...I was the one who forced you to promise, to participate. You entered the tournament because of *me*. You could have died!" She swallowed against her dry throat. "This is all my fault."

Daryn frowned. "Hardly, Lena. I made a promise, yes, but it was my own *stupid* pride that endangered me. Even still, I failed." His hands fluttered before reaching into his pocket. "Here, I came to give you this. I will no longer need it." Her emerald necklace dangled from his fingers. She gazed at it without moving. He grabbed her hand and opened her palm, placing the gem in her possession before closing her fingers around it.

There was something in his gaze, something frightening. It took a moment to form her words. "Why…? Why does this feel like goodbye?"

His shoulders sagged. "Because it is. I plan to take my leave after dinner."

"But…you're not supposed to leave yet."

"Says who?"

"All the competitors stay until the end if they wish—to take part in the other events."

"I understand that, Lena. And it's not mandatory. But I—"

"What about the Crowning Ball, Daryn? I had hoped…" She couldn't finish.

What did it matter? If he was going to leave, she was not going to change his mind. Hadn't she already decided it was best to put an end to their relationship? Why was she fighting him?

"My sweet Lena." His face softened. "I have a new mission now, one that requires my immediate attention."

"A new mission?"

"My close encounter with death enlightened me. Daudagher spared me to lead me to my destiny."

"Your destiny?" Her words were little more than a whisper.

"I have struggled to understand many strange feelings recently. Now I understand them clearly, my hesitation towards you, my second thoughts, my misgivings. As I lay in the dirt with blood staining the ground around me, a vision came before me. I was hardly aware of Raff's foot colliding with my skull because I saw her, Lena."

"*Her?*" Lena's hand flew to her stomach. She felt sick.

"Yes, *her*. My mate. I saw her face. She is out there somewhere, waiting for me." He squared his shoulders. "I must find her."

"So…so that's it?" Her voice came out as a mousy squeak. "Everything between us, what we shared? That's…that's it?"

"She's my *mate*, Lena." Daryn spoke as if that was explanation enough. And maybe it was for others, but not for her. "Come now, I hope that we can part as friends."

She shook her head, stepping away from him. "I'm so fed up with this *mate* business," she whispered, eyes filling with tears. "No, Daryn. I do not see how we can part as friends. You misled me."

His mouth went slack. "I cannot take back our kisses, Lena, nor can I change the way you made me feel. I have been lonely for a long time. It was unfair of me to search for love in you. But my mate is waiting for me. I must go and find her."

She shook her head. Her blood burned cold and hot all at once. "If finding your mate is what you care about, Daryn, then go." With that, she fled.

She ran through the keep, furious, upset, sick to her stomach. Tears streamed down her cheeks. At last, she stopped to lean against the wall, gasping at air. What was she supposed to do now?

Her eyes widened. "Dinner!" She could not afford to blow her cover. Quickly wiping her eyes and nose, she lifted her skirts and ran to the dining hall. The hall's patrons were only just taking their seats. She followed suit, doing her best to pretend that nothing had happened.

She refused to look at Daryn sitting with his comrades, trading stories and enjoying his final meal with them. She wanted to curl herself into a ball and sob. To sink away from the public's eye. It took a great deal of strength to keep further tears from falling.

Food tasted like gravel. Her throat was too raw to eat. She

merely pushed the contents of her plate around in circles. Beside her, Briv, Ferand, and Ramar traded stories. She half-heartedly listened to their conversations, just enough to avoid suspicion. Still, they perceived her upset, but when they asked, she denied everything.

Once dinner had finished, her frazzled nerves made her slow to respond. When she stood to leave, most of the hall had already departed, including her handmaidens. She'd given them permission to depart arm in arm with a few of the Drengr competitors for an evening walk through the royal garden. There was no reason her sour mood should ruin their fun. Instead, she turned to Ramar, who stood beside her. "Would you mind escorting me to my apartment?"

"Of course, Princess. It would be my pleasure."

Happy to have his company, they wandered at leisure through the corridors. His patience was a true credit to his character. When she felt calm enough, she told him about Daryn and all that had transpired between them. "It was stupid of me to fall for him," she said when she finished. "Daryn is a Drengr, and I'm just a human. We wouldn't have worked."

"Love makes fools of us all, Lena."

"Even you?"

He smiled a sad, slow smile. "Even me, though that's a story for another time."

She sighed. "I suppose I thought I'd be the lucky one. But I was stupid to—" She faltered. "Do you hear that?" Shouts were traveling down the corridor. Ramar cocked his head to the side. Her heart began to pound as she realized what the noise might mean. "Gods above!" Lifting her skirts high, she took off at a run. Ramar kept pace with her.

As they grew closer, the shouts became louder. She knew at that point with certainty what it meant. They came to a sudden stop beside Raff's chamber door, which stood slightly ajar. She stood just out of sight. Ramar on the other hand, filled the doorway with his large frame.

Raff had Bartlett by the collar, shaking with fury as he screamed threats into the boy's face. Bartlett looked as though death was imminent. His eyes were wide with horror and his face was pale. As Raff shook him, his head bobbled from side to side. "Who put you up to this, you little brat? You weasel?! I'll kill you!" Spittle flew from his mouth as he shouted threats.

In that moment, she truly realized what she had done. The harm she had caused by her meddling. This was all her fault.

"Raff!" Ramar's roar brought a stop to the brutish behavior. Raff stopped shaking Bartlett but did not relinquish his hold on the boy. "What is the meaning of this? Put the boy down!"

Raff rounded on Ramar. "The meaning, you ask? The *meaning*?!" She shrank away further into the shadows, breathing hard. "I found this little pisser poisoning my water! I mean to get to the bottom of it. *Someone* put him up to it and I think I know who."

Ramar sighed. "If that is the case, this matter must go to the king. Come, I will escort both of you."

"Fine, but I want this little shit punished!"

"I can assure you he will be. Come." Ramar took several steps back from the doorway.

Lena's breath hitched. With all the speed she could muster, she took off at a sprint, dodging down a side corridor to beat Raff to the king's tower. Her breathing came in great gasps when she arrived. Little stars popped in and out of her vision. The guards knew better than to question her in a state like this. They let her pass. She raced through the tower and burst into her father's study.

"Gods, Lena! What is the matter?" Her father jumped to his feet, immediately distressed.

She attempted to explain, but her words were coming out slurred and stuttered as she gasped, clutching her side as she doubled over. Her balance teetered. She felt her body heave sideways. Quick hands wrapped around her, putting her back on her feet. "You are unwell," said her father. "I will call for the grand mage at once."

"No! No, Papa." Her vision cleared. Just then, they heard the upset cries from the room above. Raff had entered the king's tower.

"It's my fault, father. Mine! I am to blame. Please!" It was all she could manage before their feet echoed on the stairs to his study. She took several additional deep breaths and composed her face, projecting as much calm as she could.

Her father removed his supporting hands and gazed at her in confusion. "What is your fault, Lena? What are you talking about?"

"You'll see."

The door to her father's study was thrown open. Ramar emerged first, followed by Raff, who still held Bartlett by the collar of his shirt, dragging him across the floor. She tensed. Bartlett, in all his unyielding loyalty, did not so much as look at her. He would die before betraying his princess. She wouldn't have it. Stealing another pleading glance at her father, she used her eyes to tell him everything she needed to.

The king stepped forward. "What is the meaning of this?"

"Your Grace, I found this little shit in my room poisoning my water." Raff had never shown such fury. Storm clouds seemed to follow in his wake. "I was right from the beginning, and you did not believe me about the poison. Do you believe me *now*?" Raff's voice was nearly a growl. His aggression towards her father was clear. King Cornan, in all his infinite wisdom, did not fall to the bait. Kings did not behave the way Raff did. They were above such reckless emotion.

Her father's voice was calm. "This is most unfortunate indeed. And yes, I now believe you." He looked down at Bartlett, studying him. "This is one of our servants, if I am not mistaken. You, boy, what is your name?"

"B—Ba—Bartlett, Your Majesty."

"I see. Explain yourself, Bartlett."

She clenched her fists. Bartlett opened and closed his mouth several times.

"Well, boy? Out with it. Your king doesn't have all day."

Still, Bartlett remained silent.

This further angered Raff. He grabbed hold of Bartlett's collar once more. "Who put you up to this you little shit?! Hm? Was it another competitor? Was it Tristan? Or maybe our princess here? I know all about *her* little tricks."

King Cornan's jaw set. "That is quite unnecessary, Raff. There should be no accusations until we know the truth of the matter."

"No—no one put me up to this, Your Majesty. *Honest.*"

"Then why would you poison my water?" Raff rounded on him again.

"Because you're a *monster* and everyone knows it," Bartlett hissed. Raff slammed his fist into the side of Bartlett's face, sending him halfway across the room. The crunch of bones breaking soured her stomach. She threw a hand over her mouth to keep from crying out. Bartlett crumbled to the floor. The blow was enough to kill the poor boy. She saw his chest slowly rise and fall and breathed a sigh of relief. He was only unconscious.

"That is enough!" Her father's authority ended the matter. "Raff, there is no need for violence. I should hope we are all civilized men here. Ramar, take Bartlett to the dungeons. He will be punished appropriately. Will that be sufficient?" Her father imparted a warning gaze upon Raff, daring him to argue.

Raff clenched and unclenched his fists several times before giving the king a curt nod. He then excused himself. She was left to watch her father and Ramar, as they knelt over Bartlett's unconscious body. Ramar began muttering incants in the the language of magic as he ran his hand over Bartlett's temple. She realized a moment later that he was healing the bones of Bartlett's skull.

"There now, the lad will be alright." Ramar stood, cradling Bartlett in his arms. With that, he left the room.

Her father was livid. She had never seen him red-faced and shaking—not like this. She couldn't bear to look him in the eyes as he turned to her. "Never," he hissed. "Never have I been so disappointed with you. You have put me in a most unfortunate position. While I am certain you have an explanation for your inappropriate meddling, I do not wish to hear it. Leave me—at once." He turned his back upon her without another word. She stifled a sob, covering her mouth with her hand, and fled.

CHAPTER 23

CONFESSIONS OF LOVE

THE QUEEN'S garden was a place for broken hearts. It was a place where tears were freely accepted, where judgement didn't exist, and hurt was made a little easier to bear. The scent of its flowers was balm to the aching mind the way salve was to a gaping wound.

Lena had come to know its sanctuary well, especially after her failure with the Touching Ceremony. She found herself hidden within its refuge again, long after darkness had fallen. Her pride was wounded in more ways than one. Her father's words had cut her deeply, but it was no more than she deserved. And Daryn had discarded her just as easily. She felt her failures like raw chafing after a day of riding.

Sighing, she stood and went to the edge of the garden, gazing out over the tower's parapet wall. The *Storm's Maiden* was nowhere to be seen. The Bay of Bandu was a lonelier place without it. So was her heart. She regretted her parting words with Daryn. They should have parted as friends, just as he had suggested.

Finding his mate was the most important thing for Daryn —for any Drengr. Even though she could hardly understand it, she should have respected his wishes. Instead, she'd shunned him. Now he was long gone, and she could never take back what she'd said.

And then there was the matter of her mistaken interference in the tournament. How stupid she'd been! How careless! Bartlett was sitting somewhere in the dungeons, suffering. Her actions had brought him close to death. Why did she agree to his plan?! He was twelve, hardly old enough to make decisions of merit. But she? She should have known better.

And her father's disappointment? That was something she always feared. She tried so hard to please him, to prove she was worthy of the crown, to prove she was as capable as any male to hold the mantle. Instead, she'd shown otherwise.

Tears of shame slid down her cheeks. Had she the opportunity to do things differently, she would have gone back and changed her actions. Life was never forgiving, and second chances rarely happened. She knew this, so she sat back down against the garden's wall and sobbed anew. Her cries mixed with the crashing waves below and the shrill sounds of the bats overhead, who had come from the sea caves below to feed. This was *her* burden to bear. Her shame. She deserved whatever punishment she had earned.

The sound of a trap door got her attention. No doubt Ramar was coming to keep her company. This time, she didn't want it. She turned to tell him so and her eyes widened. "Tristan?"

"Ramar said I might find you up here." He climbed through and closed the door behind him.

Stopping short of her, he turned to a tangle of bushes and

crouched. His gentle fingers were caressing. "Night flowers," he mused. "I had not expected to see these here." The petals acknowledged his touch and opened a little wider. "In Esterpine, night flowers snake their way up the trees, covering them with vines." His smile was slow, as if he was caught up in his memories. "In the forest, it is forever twilight, so they stay open all the time." He stood and turned to her. "Ramar warned me that you were upset. I was determined to see you anyway."

"You...you were? Why?" Her eyebrows knitted together.

He shrugged. "Hard to say. Just a feeling, I guess. I take it..." He hesitated. "I take it you were close with Daryn?"

Her eyes narrowed. "How much did Ramar tell you?"

"Enough," he said, taking a seat beside her. "Leaving a loved one is never easy. No one knows this better than I."

She gazed back at him, looking for answers in his green eyes. "You were hurt by love too?"

He leaned his head back against the wall and closed his eyes. "I was. Before I came here, I made a difficult decision to leave the one I love. Her name is Evelyn."

"Evelyn? What a pretty name. Is she a Sprite?"

He opened his eyes to gaze back at her. "Yes. And not just *any* Sprite. She is the only daughter of a prominent family, one very close to the queen. Our love is forbidden."

"Oh..." Her chest tightened. She could easily relate to that. "Why did you leave her? If you loved her...?" She bit the skin of her bottom lip. "She didn't love you back?"

He did not answer immediately. "Love is not always clear-cut, Lena. Just because you love someone—*truly* love them—does not mean you can be with them."

"Why not?"

"Because there are boundaries. I love her, yes. Sometimes my love for her hurts. But she is a Sprite and will live for thousands of years longer than me." He ran a hand through his pearlescent hair, smoothing back the choppy locks from his face. She turned away from him to avoid inappropriate staring. "What's worse, her people do not like my race. They tolerate my presence, at best. Besides, when I do find my mate, that pull will be strong and I won't be able to ignore it. What then?"

She schooled her features. "I hope you are not telling me this to diminish my anger towards Daryn for going after his mate."

"Not in the slightest. I suppose I am telling you because I do not like to see you hurt. You are not the only one who is suffering. I am telling you because I do not wish for you to feel alone. I know what it is like to want someone and know that you can't have them."

Appeased, she nodded. "What about Evelyn? What does she say about it?"

"She went along with our secret for a time. And during that time..." His face changed. He smiled and his eyes took on a faraway look. It left her feeling jealous of the love he fostered for Evelyn, though she couldn't understand why. "Well, let us just say the time we *were* together was bliss."

"Wait," she whispered. "Is that why...why you didn't come to the ceremony? Because of Evelyn?"

He exhaled. "The truth comes out at last. Can you fault me for it?"

She shook her head. "No. I suppose I can't."

"As it so happened, when you failed to find your mate, representatives from the Forest Clan came to Esterpine and demanded that I depart for the capital. My competing in this tournament was *their* wish, not mine. With an insider on the throne, they believe they might receive better treatment by the Drengr monarchy. In my opinion, it hardly matters. Their race is dying and nothing I do can stop that. Fewer and fewer eggs hatch every generation. Too many dragons were blessed with humanity by Queen Isabella in her selfishness. Too many to give their race a fighting chance."

"You were forced to come here?" She frowned. "You were forced to compete against your will?"

He rubbed the back of his neck. She was overcome with an intense desire to rub the muscles for him. "I wouldn't say *forced*," he said at last. "The idea was alluring the longer I considered it. At last, I agreed. It was my fight with Evelyn that became the deciding factor."

"Fight?"

"Aye. A serious fight. Her family discovered our relationship around the same time my clan appeared. Words were exchanged. Words I am not proud of." He sighed. "What's done is done."

"I'm sorry, Tristan. I am sorry that you have been kept from the one you love. Truthfully, I don't know if what I felt for Daryn was love—infatuation more like. Still, it was strong enough that his leaving hurt me. Maybe Evelyn feels the same way. Maybe she's forgiven you for what was said?"

"I hope you are right."

They fell silent, sitting side by side, shoulder to shoulder, gazing at the stars. At last, Tristan yawned.

"How selfish of me!" she gasped, jumping to her feet. "You're competing tomorrow! You need your rest. Go! Off to bed with you!" His sheepish smile left her heart unexpectedly warm. He departed, leaving her alone in the garden.

THE FOLLOWING MORNING, another immunity challenge was held. This time it was a spear throwing competition. Raff,

Tristan, and Vigorth, were given a set of five spears each. The competitor to get the largest number on their target's bullseye, would be granted immunity. The two losers would fight.

With Daryn eliminated, Tristan was her only hope. She watched each throw while holding her breath. Vigorth was the worst aim, despite hitting the target each time. Raff was better. Tristan was the best. Much to her delight, he landed all five spears directly on the bullseye. It left her spirits soaring.

Once more, she insisted that he sit beside her in the royal box. The fight that followed was not nearly as brutal as the one between Daryn and Raff. Yet, Raff took the opportunity to display his ruthlessness, something he took pleasure in. There was little surprise when he emerged victorious. When she glanced at Tristan, she saw something she'd never seen before burning brightly in his eyes. He watched Raff parade around the arena, basking in the excited cries of the spectators, and deep in his gaze, a raw hunger clawed to break free.

A smile spread across her lips. Tristan would be the one— he would be the one to beat Raff. He had an appetite for it, and the intensity of his appetite would be enough to earn him victory.

Standing to confront the audience, she lifted her hands. "The time has come," she cried most unenthusiastically, "to congratulate Raff on his win!" She waited for the crowd to quiet themselves once more. "The final match will take place between Raff and Tristan exactly one week from today." The crowd cheered and slowly filed from the arena.

Later that day, just before dinner, she found her father pouring over documents in his study. "I came to apologize," she said, squaring her shoulders as she swallowed her shame. "I should not have interfered with this competition. My actions were dishonorable."

Her father looked up from his work and set his quill

down. "Lena, I hardly know what to make of this matter. While I like Raff as much as you do, which is not at all, your behavior was indeed dishonorable. Can you imagine what the people would say if they knew that this tournament was manipulated?"

She hung her head. The gods were the deciding factors in Dragonwall's fate. As a figurehead of authority, she was wrong to intervene in their matters. Still, she couldn't merely sit back and do nothing. She told her father as much.

"Lena, there will be many times during a monarch's rule when things do not go to plan. I understand your stance on Raff. I am in full agreement with you. No person in the world is less appropriately suited for the crown." He sighed and leaned back in his chair. "Raff's *ill-suited* nature does not give you the right to interfere in matters such as this."

She opened her mouth to protest then thought better of it. Instead, she considered her words wisely, for that was how rulers behaved. At last, her argument was formulated. "Father, remember the uprisings in Celenore, when you discovered the true nature of them? You learned that the lord governor of Celenore had illegally raised the people's taxes, which were already high to begin with. This prevented them from feeding their families. They could not appropriately prepare for the winter months."

Her father nodded. "Aye. I remember."

"Worse still, the lord governor allowed his soldiers to rape their women whenever they wished. They were permitted to pillage the poorer villages."

"It was an appalling matter at best. I recall it as if it were yesterday."

"The farmers were left with nothing. Can you blame them for the uprising? Especially when the lord governor began killing the usurpers rather than bringing matters to your attention. He bypassed your laws."

"Indeed, he did. What is your point?"

"My point is, what did you do with the lord governor?" She had strategically backed her father into a corner.

"I removed him from power."

"Yes, by having him quietly assassinated! Which, mind you, is not how such matters are legally resolved." She scowled at him. Her father lifted his eyebrows but said nothing. "How is what I have done with Raff *any* different? The law is the law. Breaking one is no better than breaking another. Raff cannot become king. I acted with dishonor—I admit to that. But know this, I will die before I let that monster have the crown. He can pry it from my cold, dead, fingers." At this, her father's mouth twitched. "When this is all over, Papa, and Raff returns home, you will release Bartlett from the cells because this was no fault of his. I take full responsibility for him. Until then, I'm taking him food and some books to read. And money—his family needs some money. They will not go hungry while he is jailed."

Her father sighed. "Sometimes, Lena, I forget how wise you are."

She squared her shoulders. "I've been taught by the best."

At this, he cracked a wide grin. "You have presented your argument in a most compelling manner. I have no choice but to release you from your guilt. At any rate, I hope you have learned a valuable lesson here. No more interference with the tournament. Do I have your word?"

"You have my word." She laid her hand over her heart. "After this scare, it will be a long time before you see any further mischief from me."

"Very well, take your friend Bartlett some food and his family some money." He reached into his pocket and removed a pouch of coins, handing it over. "They will be paid handsomely for their son's inconvenience." When she took the pouch and left, she realized that the number of gold dragons would be enough to lift Bartlett's family out of poverty. For that, she smiled. Sometimes, even the worst circumstances had happy endings.

CHAPTER 24
CONFLICTING EMOTIONS

THE FOLLOWING MORNING, she met Ivrir for their archery lessons. Light was spilling onto the practice grounds, driving away the morning mist. With a week of uneventful days ahead, she wasn't sure how she would occupy herself. She would be glad when the tournament was over so that she could resume her emissary duties and begin traveling again.

Ivrir in tow, she marched over to her favorite archery range, attempting to ignore the shirtless group of Drengr exchanging blows with Tristan. Unfortunately, she had a good view of them from where she practiced, which meant her focus would be strained.

Tristan, beloved by all, was sparring with three of her father's Shields, including Briv. What was more, they were clearly enjoying the challenge. *Perfect* Tristan. How easily he bewitched everyone, including her. She rolled her eyes and set her things down, notching the strings on her bow. For some strange reason, she had a sudden intense desire to show off.

"Shall we work on your speed again, Princess Lena?"

"I think so," she agreed. "Though, for once, I would like to hit the bullseye."

"Perhaps we can achieve both." Ivrir sounded hopeful.

Tristan's blade struck a haunting tune, instantly drawing her eyes towards him. How did he do it? How was it that he could successfully fight three of the kingdom's best Drengr and hold his ground? She didn't notice Ivrir's scrutiny upon her until he spoke. "I've never seen anyone fight like him."

Startled, her muscles tensed. She turned to Ivrir, keeping her face calm. "Nor have I. My father's Shields appear to enjoy the competition." Trying her best to ignore Tristan's sparring, she removed an arrow.

"Remember, Princess, keep your motions fluid. Nock, pull, then release."

"All while I manage to aim," she muttered. She was impatient by nature. After many days of practice, she had hoped to have one successful arrow by now.

Once more, just before taking her position, her gaze flicked in Tristan's direction. He was taking a breather. Sensing her regard, their eyes met. Embarrassed, she turned away. With every bit of focus she could muster, knowing that Tristan was watching, she nocked an arrow. She pulled her bowstring tight and released. The pressure of her audience was surprisingly motivating. The arrow whizzed through the air. With a loud thud, it planted itself on the target.

She gasped. "I don't believe it!" The arrowhead was not but a finger's width from the bullseye. Eagerly, she drew another, repeating the same actions. This one landed just as close. With intense determination, she continued releasing arrows, aware that Tristan's eyes were still upon her. It took every bit of self-control to keep from glancing in his direction.

At last, when his blade began to sing, she knew the pressure was off. She sighed and turned to Ivrir. "There, I emptied my entire quiver and look how well I did. But, still no bullseye."

"Indeed. I am impressed. You have improved immensely."

She reclaimed her arrows and began again. By the end of her lesson, only a single arrowhead achieved success, albeit, it merely straddled the white and black border. But for her, that was close enough to warrant celebration.

That afternoon, she gave the details of her success to her father. They had only just set about their task of tedious work. The blazing pride in her father's eyes left her grinning.

She went about organizing the odious documents stacked upon his desk. Nearly all of them were contracts, land exchanges, local tax reports, and the like. She separated them in piles, took note of each on a lengthy ledger, and filed them away in a giant cabinet to the side of the room. She was tucking away the last of them when a gentle knock captured her attention.

"Ah!" her father sighed, pushing his chair back. "That must be Tristan." Her gaze narrowed. "You look skeptical, Lena. I have invited him to join us this afternoon."

While she liked Tristan, she enjoyed the time alone with her father. The king's afternoons belonged to her and she wanted to keep it that way.

Her father invited Tristan to enter. She hid her annoyance and responded to his deep bow with a polite curtsy. "Tristan has come to offer his assistance regarding the recent attacks," said her father by way of explanation. "I thought his fresh mind might aid our strategies."

Her father rarely sought her help in matters of strategy.

He had an entire council for that, not to mention his brilliant group of Shields. Yet, now he was enlisting Tristan's aid? "Since when do we need his help, Father? He hasn't won the crown yet." She felt her cheeks redden the moment the words were out. "I...I'm sorry, Tristan. I did not mean to say that. Forgive me. My father is right. We could use your help." Hadn't they recently become friends? How could she be so petty? So heartless?

Tristan, surprised by her outburst, opened his mouth several times before speaking. "I did not mean to intrude, Princess Lena. Perhaps I ought to go." He took a step back.

She reached out as if to stop him. "No. Please. I spoke out of turn. It was a thoughtless thing to say. I did not mean it. Stay, I beg of you."

Now that she considered it, she *did* want him to stay. But how silly! Just moments before, she had wished for him to leave. It was most confusing.

Only when she noticed her father's smirk over their strange behavior did she realize how ridiculous she was being. Worse still, her father left them to settle the matter. He kept himself quietly tucked in the shadows.

Tristan nodded. "Very well, Princess. I will remain. I do hope to be of some help. I am eager to assist the kingdom in every way that I can, to crush these rotten pirates from pillaging our shores."

Happy to hear it, she gave Tristan a curt nod before turning to her father. Pleased with their reconciliation, he bid them to follow and led them from the room. She knew exactly where they were going. She grew jealous again. Her father rarely took her into his map room. That was mostly reserved for his private meetings with the Lower Council and his Shields. It took years to reach the point where he occasionally enlisted her help with his maps. All of a sudden, Tristan was worthy.

They spent an hour poring over the southern coastline. Her father had already marked all the places suffering from attacks. He also spent a great deal of time explaining the tactics he'd noticed with each attack. "They appear to alternate between Eigaden and Austar," he said, pointing out the order with his finger. "Each raid is at dawn or dusk, never in the middle of the day."

"Perhaps, we might better anticipate them if we send our Drengr patrols out further over the water, expanding our sweeps," said Tristan. "Especially before dawn, the ships are not likely to spot Drengr-Rider pairs in the dark. Perhaps then we might outsmart them more often." Her father liked the idea. She did too, though she said nothing. Instead, she quietly observed their interactions.

It was no wonder her father liked him so much. He was wise for a young Drengr. Moreover, he was patient and his responses were well constructed. She found herself nearly as captivated as the king. Tristan's suggestions were creative. Her jealousy over the matter continued to grow.

Why was it so easy for him to be perfect? He was everything a Drengr ought to be. Gallant, honorable, patient, kind, and direct when he needed to be. She would never forget the way he answered her question the first time she spoke to him. Perhaps it was all a ruse. Maybe Tristan intended to win everyone over so that once he was crowned, he might get his way easier.

Frowning, she shook her head. No, that was not in his nature. If anything, those tactics were inherent to *her* behavior, not his. She bit at her lower lip, watching him converse freely with her father.

Tristan would never judge her the way she was currently

judging him. She was being unfair! The realization made her feel crummy.

A small voice in the back of her mind reminded her of Evelyn, his Sprite lover. Not everything was easy for him, though he made it look that way. No matter how frustrated his perfection left her, no matter how jealous she became, she found herself more and more drawn to his curiosities, almost as if each emotion left her wanting more of him, more of his attention, more of his company. It simply made no sense!

When they were finished, she was relieved. The sooner she got away from his unintentional charms, the sooner she could make sense of the confusing feelings assaulting her mind. Yet, as they walked through the king's tower together, she found herself seeking his company anew. "Tristan, I wonder if you might escort me into the city this afternoon. I know dinner is soon upon us, but I would appreciate a companion for my venture."

His smile left her stomach tumbling. "It would be a privilege, Princess Lena."

Quickly gathering what she needed from her chambers, she bid her handmaidens farewell and set off with Tristan for the Pauper's District. She owed Bartlett's mother a visit. The city was bustling with activity as they made their way through the streets. She couldn't help but be reminded of her walks with Daryn as they neared the dockyard.

Tristan walked with one arm extended to guide her, and the other propped behind him. He smiled often and greeted many of those who passed. His mood was contagious. She soon found herself grinning too.

"Kastali Dun is unlike anything I have ever experienced," he said. "Even the great city of Esterpine is vastly different."

"I would give anything to lay eyes on Esterpine." Her dreamy voice betrayed her deep desire.

"I get the impression you have done little traveling."

"Very little, but that will soon change." She smiled, thinking about all the opportunities ahead of her. "I used to dream of sneaking away and going on my own adventures, hiring a band of robbers to lead on forays into the vast planes of Eigaden, or a troop of nomads to take me along their wandering paths north."

He chuckled. "I have never known a woman with such wanderlust." They rounded a corner, dodging the muddied areas of the street. "I can imagine that you feel cooped up. But it seems that you have made the best of it." The corner of his mouth twitched, as if he were laughing at a secret joke.

"Tell me, Tristan, why are you so determined to help my father with the pirate attacks? I noticed your resolve today. You seem so…so passionate." She glanced up at him. A flash of something crossed his expression. Maybe it was sadness or even longing. It was gone before she could determine its meaning.

"I suppose it might appear surprising to you, my intentions. I assure you they are genuine." Their eyes met before he returned his gaze to the street. "I haven't told anyone, but —" They sidestepped as a carriage blundered past. "I am determined to bring about an end to the pirate attacks because they are responsible for stealing a part of my life that I will never know." She blinked, trying to understand his meaning. "Haven't you, Princess Lena, in all your quizzical ponderings, ever wondered why I was raised by the Forest Clan?"

Her brow furrowed. "Of course I have. Only, I worried that my asking might cause pain."

"Indeed, it is a painful subject."

"You do not have to tell me if it will hurt you to speak of it." She did not want him to hurt for her sake.

"No, I will tell you. You ought to know. I trust that like everything else, you will keep it to yourself." She was happy to guard his secrets. "Fifty years ago, the pirates began raiding the southern coast much like they have recently. My mother and father were very close to the Forest Clan. My father was the fort leader of Fort Lin at the time."

She stopped in her tracks. "No! Truly?! The leaders of Fort Lin died fifty years ago, Tristan, my father told me. They died during a devastating pirate attack. But they never had any children."

He grunted and pulled her along, continuing their walk. "Like most, your father only knows half of the story. It is true that my father fell in battle. But shortly before the attack occurred, he enlisted aid from the Forest Clan. It is a mercy that they came, for I owe my life to them." She listened with wide eyes. "The day the pirates attacked Lincastle, the fort assembled to meet them, aided by some sixty dragons of the Forest Clan. The pirates were using poison on their lances. They targeted my mother and father almost exclusively. At last, my father was struck by two dragonlances. As he and my mother plummeted towards the ocean, towards death, several in the Forest Clan swooped in and successfully caught my mother in their talons, rushing her away from the battle. It is said that my father's body, after falling into the ocean, was never found again." The pain in his voice drew tears to her eyes.

"But…your mother?"

"She was rushed away, taken to the Forest Clan's dwelling where Sincere successfully healed her wounds."

"*Sincere*?"

"Yes, Sincere is my clan's leader."

"Excuse me, but what kind of a name is *Sincere*?"

Tristan chuckled. "Don't you know, Princess? The dragons

are named for traits. It's an interesting form of magic. Sincere is exactly as his name suggests."

"I guess I had forgotten." Indeed, dragons were given names that possessed great magic. Each hatchling was imbued with a name that would define their life's deeds.

"As it was, my mother happened to be with child and not even my father knew at the time. It took her over a month to heal from her wounds. She was so torn with grief at the loss of my father. Sincere wondered if she would heal at all." Tristan shook his head. "Riders never live long without their mates. See, a Drengr's power is tied to his Rider. A human becomes a Rider and takes up the magic that allows them to live a long life. But once a Drengr dies, all those years catch up at an alarming speed, as they did for my mother."

"But…but she had you?"

"Aye, in the quiet of the cave. Just before my birth, she convinced the clan to care for me as one of their own. Perhaps she wanted to keep me from the turmoil of the world, from the attacks that continued along the coast. I cannot say why she chose such a life for me." He shrugged. "I am told that she died minutes after my birth."

Lena faltered, overcome with sadness. "Tristan, I'm…I'm so—"

"It's okay, Princess. I've had many years to accept that which cannot be changed." He patted her hand before turning his attention back to their walk. Now she understood. Tristan had every reason in the world to hate the pirates. It was no wonder he was so eager to help.

They arrived at the home of Bartlett's family. Tristan, eyes full of amusement, watched her greet Bartlett's mother. After the woman recovered from the shock of having Dragonwall's princess grace her doorstep, Lena was able to explain Bartlett's predicament.

At first, Bartlett's mother cursed the gods. "I always be knowin' that boy would land himself in the dungeons some day or other!" She was full of worry, despite her obvious anger. "Gods, it be a good thing the king has him, else I be whippin' him myself."

"Please, mam. This is entirely my doing." She was going to live up to her mistake. "Bartlett is a fine son. It was my meddling that got him locked up. I promise to do everything I can to obtain his release. However, in the meantime, the king wishes for you to have this." She held forward a sack of coins. "Please, I insist. Take it."

"The…the king?" Bartlett's mother was wide-eyed.

"Indeed. This is for your family's inconvenience. And I promise, Bartlett will be returned to you unharmed."

Her eyes had grown so round that her eyebrows disappeared under her cap. She picked through the bag of coins, whispering with shock. "But…I…I can't be takin' this, Princess. We ain't worth this much."

Lena's chest tightened. "Please, mam. Bartlett is worth an immense amount to me. I wish for your family to have it. Use it to buy food, and perhaps a larger house for you and your children."

The woman burst into tears and grabbed Lena's hand, kissing it over and again. Then she turned her praises upon Tristan, as if he too were equally responsible in bringing this about. It was most amusing to see Tristan's reaction as the woman went about kissing his hand. She couldn't help the laughter that escaped her lips as Bartlett's mother fussed over him. "Thank 'e! Oh, thank the gods!" To see someone so happy, so full of gratitude, reminded her that there were cares in this world much larger than her own.

"Please," Bartlett's mother said at last, "won't you join us for dinner? I insist! It would do us great honor, 'specially after all this!"

Tristan looked at her, his eyes gleaming. "Well, Princess? What say you? If you wish to know my thoughts on the matter, I say we should not refuse such a kind offer." With that, the two of them graciously accepted, and stepped over the threshold.

CHAPTER 25
AN UNEXPECTED REQUEST

"Princess Lena! If you do not hold still, I shall poke you with pins." Lena's tailor repositioned her before pinning another section of her gown. This was her final fitting before the Champion's Ball. The event was scheduled to take place shortly following the final match, which was two days away. She admired herself in the mirror while her tailor worked. This gown had a rigid bodice that laced down her back. Its sleeves clung to her skin until they reached her elbows, where they fanned to the floor displaying golden silk stitched to the underside of the emerald material. It reminded her of Tristan's eyes. Her mind turned to thoughts of him.

Less than a week had passed since Daryn's leaving, and already she was thinking of another. She pursed her lips. How crass! The past few days had been that way: confusing emotions vying for acknowledgement between Daryn and Tristan. Whenever she thought of Tristan, she couldn't decide whether to be jealous of him or adore him. In the end, her adoration always won.

Her mind went back to their last moments together, to

dinner at the humble home of Bartlett's family. It had been a grand affair. Memories of the evening had been her constant companion these past few days. She cared little that the bread was stale, or that the table was rather barren. The house itself was immaculate. Bartlett's siblings were captivating, which more than made up for her growling tummy. They told her about their favorite parts of the tournament with excited little voices. She had been especially pleased to hear they enjoyed the acrobatics show.

"Someday when I get big," said his younger sister while pulling on Lena's hand, "I'm going ta be an acrobat just like them ones in the show!" The declaration made her chuckle. Once the children could no longer find things to tell her, they turned their attention to Tristan. They demanded he describe each of his fights in detail. He was more than happy to. As he told his stories, they gasped at all the right moments, listening with wide eyes. He enamored them with every word. She had found herself equally entranced, as he was a wonderful storyteller. It had been a joyous evening.

A knock at her chamber door got her attention, pulling her mind back to the present. Cora came over, her face flushed. "Begging your pardon, Princess. Tristan wishes to speak with you when you are finished here."

"Tristan?" A pleased smile pulled at her lips. She glanced at her tailor, Mistress Falda, who muttered something imperceptible before adding several more pins. She waited, but patience was a true challenge. What did Tristan want?

"There now, Princess, we are finished." Falda collected her things and moved away.

She turned to Cora. "Tell Tristan that I will be along shortly." Cora nodded and left. She got down from her stool, glad to be on solid ground. Even still, it felt as though she were floating on air. Her nerves were all aflutter. Avra and Theresa helped free her of her large gown and dressed her appropriately.

She went to meet Tristan in the corridor. "This is a pleasant surprise." She struggled to stifle her grin as she gave him a graceful curtsy. "To what do I owe the pleasure of your visit?"

"Princess Lena. The pleasure is all mine. I had hoped you might take a walk with me." Tristan bowed before offering his arm.

Her heart fluttered. "Oh? I…of course. I would be delighted." She hooked her hand around his arm, secretly admiring his bicep. Since when did she notice things like that? Her cheeks warmed. She forced her face away, hoping he would not notice.

Allowing him to guide her, they walked for several minutes in silence until they reached the royal garden. Only then did he speak. "I should have called upon you sooner," he admitted. "I have been busier than I anticipated."

"Too much training," she joked. She'd seen him in the practice yard every morning with various members of her father's six. An image of him shirtless swam into her mind's eye. His rigid muscles. His tall form. The sinewy curves of his body. Yet again, she felt her skin warm. Her thoughts were being most unfair!

"Your father's men keep me busy. I need to do my best in the arena."

"Now that you mention it, I was hoping to talk to you about that."

"Were you?"

"I don't want to place unnecessary pressure upon you," she said. They had just rounded the bend in the garden leading towards the large groves of trees. "But, I need you to do everything in your power to beat Raff."

Tristan threw his head back and roared with laughter, causing her to stop in her tracks. She regarded him with confusion. Raff was no laughing matter. "You do realize, Princess, that I have every intention of doing exactly that. Your request is unnecessary. It is no added pressure, none at all." She opened her mouth to speak but nothing came to mind. "Come now, you are not the only one who despises him. He will never be crowned. I will not let it happen."

"How can you be so sure?" She gently pulled against his arm to spur them forward. "Raff is ruthless. He has beaten all his opponents thus far, some more harshly than others."

"Obviously, else he would not be where he is today." Tristan's sarcasm was not lost on her. "See here, Princess Lena, I have spent every fight studying his tactics, memorizing his fighting style. I cannot *wait* to get my hands on him."

"Eagerness does not guarantee a win."

"Ah, and resorting to poison does?" His gaze was all too knowing. Shame seeped into her gut. There was fear too. She couldn't bear for him to think less of her.

"How…how much do you know?"

"Enough." His response left her heart pounding. Afraid to speak, she looked away from him. What if he wanted nothing more to do with her? The same way Daryn had when she interfered.

"You need not fear my judgement, Lena." His voice was soft, drawing her eyes back to his. "I understand perfectly what drove you to do it. While such things are not the way I handle my own business, I understand your side of the story."

"He's a monster," she whispered. "I never thought it possible for a Drengr to be so…so…"

"Tactless and dishonorable?"

"Yes!" She felt immediate relief. "Tristan, you are a

complete opposite to Raff. While I never thought I would find myself saying this, you would make a great king, albeit after some training from my father." The smile he awarded her stilled her heart. "I…" she paused, surprised by her own admissions. "I want you to win the crown. No. I *need* you to win the crown."

He stopped and turned to her. Then he took her hand in his, gazing into her eyes with sincerity. "I promise, Lena, I will win the crown. For you."

Her brow furrowed at the use of his last two words. *For you.* Before she could ask what he meant, he turned and pulled her along, replacing her hand in the crook of his arm.

"Thank you," she said at last. Speaking seemed a challenge at this very moment. "I have seen you fight so many times. Not once have I doubted your abilities. It's just…"

"It is your fear talking, Lena. Only your fear." He scowled. "I can hardly imagine what it must be like…to be you."

"What do you mean?"

He shrugged. "You have every reason to hate me, to hate *us*. The competitors."

"Whatever for? You think I hate you because you have come to claim the crown?"

"Aye. You were born a woman. You do not have the ability to fledge into a dragon, nor the magic that comes with. That alone is a travesty. I cannot begin to comprehend what it must be like for you, growing up believing that you might one day give up your right to rule."

"I had hoped to find a mate. Clearly that did not work out."

Something strange flashed across his features. His jaw flexed and the look was gone. "Perhaps it is not too late for that," he said.

She stopped yet again. They were making very little

progress. "Too late for what?" As soon as the words were out, her eyes widened. She realized what he was insinuating. Each deep breath in her tight corset became exceedingly difficult. "You believe yourself to be my mate?"

"I suppose it is a possibility. I cannot deny the odd inclinations I have towards you. Such strange feelings have plagued me since my arrival."

She shook her head abruptly. "It's probably nothing. I once thought Ivrir was my mate until my mother talked me out of it. She was right, after all." The mere *hope* would bring nothing but disappointment, just as it had done before.

When he saw her expression, his brow furrowed. "You wouldn't even try?"

"I...you...you don't know what it was like for me." A familiar hopelessness resurfaced, bringing back the terrible memory she'd locked away. "You have no idea the courage it took to go out there, the courage it took to relinquish my hold upon the future, the courage it took to place my future in fate's hands. What did fate do? Fate dragged me through the dirt!"

"Perhaps hope is not lost."

"I cannot handle further disappointment."

He didn't understand. Why would he?

"Lena," his voice was soft. "It would only take a moment. I could transform right here, right now."

"Please don't," she whispered, taking several frightened steps backwards.

"You're afraid, aren't you?" He looked incredulous. "You're afraid that I might actually be your mate."

Maybe she was. Maybe after accepting her human life and the new path she was to take, the sudden fear of change was merely too much. There was a chance that he could be correct

—that she was meant to be his mate and had failed because of it.

"It would only take a minute," he whispered, reaching out towards her, beseeching her with his gaze. Her eyes were wide. She shook her head and stepped back a few more paces. He read her expression clearly. "Very well then, Princess. Perhaps now is not the correct time." He stepped forward. "I do not wish for you to fear me. Your look alone is enough to change my mind."

"What look?" she shot back.

"The look of absolute terror upon your face at the mere *suggestion* of a possibility." His shoulders sagged.

Why should he be disappointed? If anything, he should have been relieved. "Tristan, your heart lies with another," she reminded him. "Even if...even if we were mates"—her heart skipped in her chest—"that would not be fair to her, to Evelyn. You love Evelyn, don't you?"

He frowned. "She will never be mine."

"Why does that make me feel like I would come second?"

His jaw dropped. "I would never think of you that way, Lena. You would not be my second. You would come first in everything." His chest deflated as he sighed. "Never mind. I never intended to upset either of us. I respect your declination. I suppose that means you do not wish to be my escort for the ball."

Her breathing hitched. "You...you wish to go to the ball with me?"

"I had hoped, for that was my reason in bringing you out here. To request it."

"Oh..."

"Once I win, we ought to present a united front for the people of Dragonwall."

"That's why you want to take me?" She failed to hide the

dismay in her voice. She should have known, given that his heart was elsewhere, that he would not think of her in *that* way.

"No, Lena. I wish to take you because, well…" He struggled for words. "I suppose it is safe to admit that I like you. I care for you, that is. And I would very much like to dance with you at the ball. Come with me." She had never seen him so tongue-tied.

She felt warm all over. A smile crept to her lips. "Very well, Tristan Forestborn. I shall go with you to the ball. And if you wish it, we may dance together for the entire night." Happily, she took up his arm once more, and they finished their circuit of the garden in silence. Realizing that another pass would not be a good idea, she excused herself from his presence.

"Until next time, Princess." He bowed deeply, keeping his eyes upon her. She returned his gesture with a polite curtsey and strode away. Only when she was out of sight did she allow herself to stop and gasp for breath.

The remainder of the day she was consumed by thoughts of the ball. Sometimes she found it difficult to breathe. Hiding her joyous smile was a struggle. She'd hoped her excitement might die down over the next few days. The last thing she wanted was to betray her growing feelings for Tristan, especially when she couldn't understand why he affected her so. Thus, she decided to avoid him at all costs until the final match of the competition.

HER PLANS TO avoid Tristan were dashed the day before the final round of the tournament. She was preparing for the evening meal when Kenna Margaret rushed into her chambers. The woman was sputtering as she struggled to breathe and speak all at once.

"Come immediately, Lena!" she gasped. Discovering the state of her preparations, Margaret barked commands to her handmaidens. "Quick, ladies. Quick. Get her ready. We must leave at once." Flustered by Kenna Margaret's demands, they rushed to make their princess presentable.

"Whatever is the matter, Kenna?"

"You must…I can hardly…Oh! Just finish your hair so that you can come and see for yourself."

Lena did exactly that, struggling to get her appearance in order. Then they rushed from her chambers.

"Where are we going?" she demanded of her kenna, racing through the keep.

"To the lowest courtyard. We have guests to greet."

"Guests?" They came to a halt in the same shadowy corridor she used before greeting the Drengr hopefuls a few months prior. There was a great deal of activity as occupants lined themselves up in an orderly fashion.

Whenever prominent guests arrived, or when her parents returned from a long journey, it was proper for the keep— servants included—to assemble in greeting. But the royal family was already here, so who was important enough to warrant such a ceremony? She began running through names in her mind, names of lords and lord governors.

Kenna Margaret turned to her, smoothing her skirts and motioning for her to do the same. Her handmaidens rushed forward to put a few locks of her hair back into place. The five of them emerged to stand beside her parents. The king's Shields were already in place, so was Tristan. She tried to keep her eyes from him. It appeared that she was the last to arrive.

When she grew brave enough, she stole several glances at

Tristan. He wore a scowl. Why was he so upset? She pursed her lips together, trying to understand the curious situation. She could produce no answer. Worse still, it seemed that everyone but *she* understood what was happening as they shifted from foot to foot, waiting for their guests.

Out of frustration, she turned to her mother for an answer. Just as she opened her mouth, the portcullis gate opened, drawing her gaze to it. A hush fell upon the gathered crowd. She heard the clip-clop of horses' hooves. Craning her neck, she attempted to see around the bend, but whatever it was, was just out of sight. The sound drew closer and people began to gasp. The approaching visitors came into view. Her jaw dropped. No wonder Tristan was upset. All her questions were answered. Mounted upon the backs of unicorns came six Sprites, and judging by the new look on Tristan's face, one of them was Evelyn.

CHAPTER 26
THE FINAL MATCH

THE FINAL MATCH of the tournament began at midday; clouds in the sky counted as a mercy. The Sprites—honored guests of the capital—were seated beside Lena and her parents in the royal box. They had come to witness history, the crowning of Dragonwall's new prince. She knew there was more to it than that. If Tristan was to become king, the Sprites wanted to be present for it.

After their arrival, she learned which Sprite was Evelyn. Much to her disappointment, the woman was beautiful beyond words, with hair as dark as midnight and ethereal, swirling luminescent marks adorning much of her tan skin. The marks were a sign of their magical strength, and the more glowing marks a Sprite had, the more powerful they were.

Lena was ashamed for wishing Evelyn to be ugly. Worse still, Evelyn displayed an enchanting grace, much like her comrades, while adding a dash of reserve, leaving her mysterious and alluring. It was no wonder Tristan loved her. Yet, behind the polite words they exchanged, she saw how Evelyn's eyes searched her, sizing her up. From their first greeting, Evelyn must have questioned Lena's relationship with Tristan. Jealousy was a difficult emotion to hide, and for all her reserve, the Sprite was forthcoming enough.

When it was time, Lena rose to address the arena. "Welcome to one and all! Lords, ladies, honored Spriten guests,"—she turned to spare a respectful look for the Sprites—"citizens of Dragonwall, Drengr, and dragons alike." A profound hush fell upon the crowd. Today was different than most. Everyone felt the tension. "This day marks the final day of our Tournament for the Crown!" The response from the crowd was mixed. This newfound form of entertainment was coming to an end. "By tonight, Dragonwall will have a crowned prince." As she spoke, racks of weapons were rolled out onto the arena floor. "Today our competitors are allowed their choice of weapons. The match continues until submission or death. Only *one* can be victorious." She swallowed. No one had died yet, not in this tournament, not in the one that took place six thousand years ago when King Eymar had no heir after Princess Irelia's death. "I wish both of our competitors the best of luck! May the gods be with you!" With that, she turned to take her seat.

On cue, Raff and Tristan marched into the arena. The crowd erupted into chaos, chanting their names. For every time Tristan's name was called, there was an equal number of Raff supporters. Didn't they know what a monster he was?

They positioned themselves in the center of the arena. Tristan reached forward to take Raff's forearm in a mutual show of respect. The gesture was forced on both accounts. She kept her eyes on Tristan, watching as he got into position. It was difficult to read his expression, but if she wasn't mistaken, he glanced in her direction. Her stomach jolted with excitement until she realized he was probably looking for Evelyn. She glanced beside her. Evelyn's fierce regard was locked upon her lover.

The arena master came forth and silence fell. He mentioned something to both competitors. She strained her ears, but his voice was too low. Then in a fluid motion, he lifted his right arm and brought it down shouting, "Begin!"

Dragons roared overhead. Tristan's two dragon companions were back to witness the final match. The crowd issued its own battle cry as their anticipation split the arena asunder. Simultaneously, Tristan fell into an easy stance, legs bent to afford him dexterity. She held her breath as he circled Raff, staying just out of reach. Neither bothered to take weapons from the racks, not yet.

Tristan circled Raff for what seemed like an eternity. She grew lightheaded from repeatedly holding her breath. Tristan had his Sprite blade in position, waiting for Raff to make the first move. As Tristan moved, Raff shuffled to keep him in sight. She could make out Raff's scowl. Tristan was patient where Raff was not.

Raff leapt forward, Sverak raised to deliver a devastating blow. Tristan crouched low before stepping aside, swinging his arm up to meet the blade with his own. The pure note rang through the air. She glanced over at Evelyn whose smile had filled her face with beautiful radiance. The blade was singing the song of her people.

She frowned before returning her attention to the spectacle. Tristan moved his sword in a blur, aptly blocking each of Raff's attempts to hack at him. Their blades were nearly impossible to follow as her eyes darted back and forth. Music from Tristan's weapon created a backdrop of eerie noise that gave her goose flesh.

Tristan played defensively, allowing Raff to bombard him. It would take a long time to tire either Drengr out, but that was not his intention. She'd seen him fight enough to know he was patient, like a trained hunter. He was waiting for the perfect moment. There! Just as she thought it, Tristan's sword blocked a blow before slashing downwards from Raff's chest to navel. She heard the rip of fabric just as Raff cried out in frustration. Injured, he jumped back to place himself out of reach. The crowd cried out with glee. She exhaled.

Tristan dived forward, moving with cat-like ease, exhibiting all the efficiency she knew him to possess. His blade stabbed at Raff, forcing the Drengr back further as he waited to heal. Raff attempted a careless downward blow to distract Tristan. The Sprite blade blocked Raff's Sverak just as Tristan's foot kicked Raff in the stomach. Raff flew backwards. Her heart nearly leapt from her chest.

Seizing the moment, Tristan, vaulted over to the nearby weapons rack. With his free hand, he grabbed a spear and sent it sailing towards Raff. Raff easily dodged it, but the act was enough to catch him off guard.

Tristan temporarily sheathed his sword and collected a handful of knives, storing some in his belt while sending others flying. Raff, who attempted to move towards the racks was thwarted, forced to dodge the sailing knives, which kept him back just far enough. Moving along the rack, Tristan reached for an ax and sent that at Raff. One by one he acquired weapons, lobbing them so quickly that Raff scarcely had time to dodge.

The arena floor grew littered with the means of dealing death. It took some time for Raff to realize he could merely pick one up from the ground, but this was Tristan's plan all along. Not only were the they strategically placed throughout the sand for Tristan's usage, they offered a distraction to Raff, who began looking around for his weapon of choice.

Keeping Tristan in his sights, Raff bent to retrieve a shield, which had been flung in an attempt to slice his head from his shoulders. Raff did not see the blade that Tristan produced from his belt. The knife flashed through the air and with a sickening thud, embedding itself into Raff's arm. Blood leaked down his tunic.

The crowd shrieked with excitement. Raff however, growled in anger, baring his teeth to Tristan. Raff had a choice to make. He could remove the knife to allow his arm to heal or grab the shield, which he had failed to do initially. He chose the shield.

Just as Raff stood, Tristan gained ground and snatched up a spear in the sand. He sent it soaring through the air, giving it a wide arc. Raff allowed his eyes to glance upward briefly. Too late. Tristan produced another knife and sent it into Raff's midriff. The Drengr hunched over, screaming more out of fury than pain.

Jumping through the air, Tristan drew his Sprite blade and brought it down upon Raff's shield. Raff reclaimed his own blade, which had been sheathed. It was a poor decision. Just as his fingers wrapped about the grip of his Sverak, Tristan sliced him deeply across his thigh. The pleased song of the Spriten blade sent the crowd wild. Blood sprayed from the gash. Tristan sliced again and again, at his side, his arm, his hip, creating music, forcing Raff to stumble backwards.

Her chest pounded. Tristan was winning! He was doing exactly as she had hoped!

Just as Tristan forced Raff to his knees, she opened her mouth to scream with the crowd but refrained. The Sprites held their composure, watching in silence. She couldn't risk looking childish, not in front of Evelyn. So she pursed her lips and watched with pride as Tristan dealt Raff everything he deserved and more.

At last, Tristan got Raff flat on his back, dealing blow after blow. He was not ruthless in his attempts, not like Raff. Rather, he did what he needed to do to keep his victim on the ground, just enough. Stubbornly, Raff *refused* to submit. If he did not surrender and she failed to step in, Tristan would be forced to kill his opponent to claim victory. Did Raff deserve death? Perhaps. But Tristan did not deserve a burdened conscience.

Tristan continued his onslaught. Still, Raff refused to give up, lying bloodied in the dirt, doing just enough to fight back. She glanced at her father, whose face was hard, but satisfied. "Father?" She wanted his approval before she resorted to interference. At last, without looking at her, her father afforded a small nod. She stood and went to the edge of the box.

"Enough!" she cried, lifting her hands. "Raff is not fit to surrender so I must do it for him." At that moment, Tristan turned his face to her. Under his gaze, her heart skipped a beat. Just then, in the single blink of an eye, everything fell apart.

Raff, privy to Tristan's distraction, rolled over and thrust his uninjured leg forward. Tristan was swept from his feet. He fell to the ground just as Raff threw himself over, Sverak raised to deal a death blow. She gasped. Raff intended to kill Tristan. Hadn't he heard her call an end to the fight? Tristan, understanding the threat, reacted instinctively. Quicker than a heartbeat, he lifted his Sprite blade. Raff came down upon him, sinking into the blade. A sickening bone against metal noise met her ears followed by the blade as it sang its pleasures, drinking the blood of its enemy. It entered just above Raff's collar bone and came out the back of his neck. Raff went limp; it was over.

Tristan scrambled to his feet with jerky, uncoordinated movements and pushed Raff away, removing his blade.

Surely the blow wasn't fatal? Still, in his weakened state, there was a chance Raff might heal. Those of the Drengr race could heal from nearly anything, unless they were too weak. Raff lay unmoving on the ground.

Stunned by the turn of events, Tristan stumbled backwards looking from his blade to Raff's body as an immense amount of blood poured out of Raff's neck, nearly cleaved in two. She glanced beside her and noticed the looks of triumph upon the Sprites' faces. They hated the Drengr. What did they care if one lay dying in the dirt?

Turning to her father, she managed to choke, "Father… is…is he…*dead*?" As she said it, guards rushed from beneath the arena to ferry Raff's body away to the Magoi healers. Somehow, her heart already knew the answer. Blood rushed to her ears as her heart pounded. She hardly noticed the crowd's jubilation. To them, this was prime entertainment. She felt sick to her stomach.

Raff was carried from the arena. There was no way to tell if he lived. Perhaps if the guards got him to Grand Mage Seda in time, he might survive. She glanced at Tristan. His face was crestfallen. No amount of hate warranted death. That was not Tristan's way.

Her hands were white as they gripped the banister railing. Swallowing several times, she turned back to the crowd. Her first attempt to speak was drowned out by their voices. After she cleared her throat, she managed to croak, "Tristan is victorious! Let us cheer for our new crowned prince!" It was all she could muster. She stumbled back to her chair and sank into it.

The world around her blurred. She hardly noticed the shapes moving by. She was vaguely aware as the king's Shields rushed away, some going down into the arena to collect Tristan, others to check on Raff. The Sprites muttered among themselves. Moments later, they too followed the stairs down to the arena floor. Meanwhile, she could only sit and blink. The rest of her body remained motionless. It wasn't until her handmaidens ushered her back to the keep that her senses returned. Once she reached her room, she burst into tears.

It took a long time for Cora to calm her down. Kenna Margaret was there too, insisting she take a long, hot bath. After several protests, she did, allowing the water to relieve her tense muscles. When her kenna returned, the woman brought bad news. "The Grand Mage did all he could for Raff. I am afraid the Drengr did not survive the fatal blow."

A sob escaped her chest. "It was not supposed to happen this way," she gasped. Her stomach twisted and she clutched at it.

"There now, Princess. Deep breaths." Kenna Margaret ran her fingers through her hair, rubbing her neck to soothe her.

"I never liked him," she gasped. "I *hated* him. But...he wasn't...this wasn't..." She was overcome with horror. The tournament was *her* responsibility. No one was supposed to die.

"Lena, it was hardly your fault, nor Tristan's. There is always a measure of risk in tournaments like this. The competitors knew this going in."

"I can hardly think!" She began shaking her head. All she wanted was to be alone—for everyone to leave her alone.

Kenna Margaret pursed her lips. "No thinking is necessary, child. There is no time to wallow in your shock and emotions."

"But we must mourn!" She tried to stifle her sobs. Ignoring the death made her feel like a terrible person.

"We may mourn soon enough. The feast and the ball are to continue as planned."

"What?" She felt the blood drain from her face as she rounded on her kenna. "I'm supposed to present my face as if nothing happened?" She stood in her bath robe and went to the mirror. A pale reflection of herself gazed back with unseeing, blank eyes. It was the face of someone who had seen death.

"Look as grim as you wish, Princess Lena. Your father has given his orders. Tristan has earned the crown. That is a thing of merit, a thing to celebrate. He deserves our praise today and his crowning tomorrow, just as Raff deserves our mourning in the days following."

Three days was the customary mourning period for the dead. She supposed that it would not be fair to make Tristan and his guests of honor wait three days to receive that which was fairly won.

"Very well," she said at last. "Prepare me for the evening."

CHAPTER 27
GALLANT REVEALED

LENA GAZED AT HER REFLECTION. Her handmaidens were finishing up their final touches on her hair. She looked other-worldly in her gown of emerald and gold. Its folds of fabric fanned out at her waist, sweeping down over the floor like a silken waterfall. With each movement, the rustling gently tickled her ears. Her hair was done in elegant twists and braids, pinned up against her scalp.

"Are you sure you wish to wear the Sprite crown, Princess?" Kenna Margaret eyed her suspiciously. "There are other more *opulent* options."

"Kenna Margaret! I did not take you for a vain woman!" She imparted a stern look upon her for showing such vanity. It was not in her tutor's nature to say such things. Her voice came out more harshly than she intended. Raff's death left her patience thin, and she grew upset over the simplest things. She sighed, begging the tension to flee her shoulders. "This crown will do fine. I have beauty enough in my gown. Besides, I am no longer the Crowned Princess. I am just…"

"Just a princess, but a princess nonetheless."

She nodded, agreeing with her kenna. At that same moment, a loud knock captured their attention. "That will be Tristan." Her stomach fluttered. Despite Evelyn's appearance in the capital, Tristan still insisted he escort her to the ball.

Finished with their work, her entourage left her alone to greet him. She took several deep breaths, smoothing her gown, adjusting her tiara, and gathering her composure. Then she stepped from her private chamber, shutting the door behind her before entering the living area. The moment she looked up, she found Tristan's gaze intent upon her.

His face flushed. "You...you look incredible, Lena." Warmth pooled in the pit of her abdomen. He watched her for the length of several breaths, which felt like an eternity, before smoothing his expression and stepping forward to offer his arm. She tried to read him. Only his eyes spoke of the emotional blow he'd been dealt.

"Tristan," she whispered. "I..."

Pain flashed across his face. He shook his head, clearing away the expression. "Say nothing of it, Princess. Not tonight."

She nodded, allowing him to escort her away. Her hand-maidens hurried out behind them, dressed in their finest gowns. In the hall, they gathered with her parents and their entourage before the group proceeded through the castle to the lower floors.

When they reached the sweeping staircase that led down into the entry hall of the keep, her father halted. On the marble floor below, hundreds of guests were gathered to celebrate. It was a sea of silks and lace, of vibrant colors and lavish riches, of jewels and precious metals. She and Tristan stood beside the king and queen as her father made his announcements, congratulating the crowned prince. He also thanked the competitors for their participation in the tournament. He did not mention a word regarding Raff's death. This night belonged to Tristan.

As she traced her eyes over the audience below, she found the Sprites gathered together with their smug expressions. They may have hated the Drengr and dragons alike, but somehow this victory pleased them. She had a feeling it was because Tristan used their fighting tactics to win. They probably felt as if some of the credit belonged to them.

Her eyes settled on Evelyn. She was regal in her gown of pure silken silver. It was plain compared to her own emerald dress, yet, the subtilty of the fabric only increased Evelyn's inherent beauty. She noticed Evelyn's gaze raking over her. The scrutiny left her uneasy. She was beginning to feel faint. She turned away to watch her father instead.

As he spoke, her father's voice sounded like a distant hum in her ears. It vaguely floated over her. The evening was turning dreamlike. Overwhelmed with emotion, her mind struggled to process the constant stimuli feeding it. She needed peace and quiet after Raff's death, not lavish festivities. Breathing became difficult. She wanted to pull on her corset, loosen the ties, but hundreds gazed upon her. So she stood still, using only Tristan's arm for support. He must have felt her increased unease, for his arm tightened with strength when she leaned against it.

When the time came, she was hardly aware of him guiding her down the stairs until they reached the floor. The royal family was expected to lead the ball. Her mother and father took their place upon the floor as the musicians gathered upon the landing above. They struck a tune and the dance began. After a few measures, she and Tristan were supposed to join them.

The world was spinning around her. How would she manage? "Follow my lead," Tristan whispered, sensing her unrest. His voice soothed her. A small piece of reality returned as he guided her out onto the floor, taking her right hand in his left, and placing his arm firmly about her back. Relying on him, she allowed the music to sweep her away.

For the last two days, eager anticipation consumed her. Now she struggled to enjoy the moment she'd so desperately looked forward to. She never expected to be here under such unanticipated circumstances. Raff's death settled over her like a poisonous cloud. And despite her efforts to forget the afternoon, her mind was fraught with emotional distress.

Evelyn's presence did not make matters easier. She couldn't bear to look into the crowd, for fear of laying eyes on the woman Tristan should have been dancing with. It was a relief Tristan's arms offered so much comfort, else she might have crumbled to the floor. She allowed his calm reassurance to wash over her as the music progressed. Without realizing it, she pushed herself closer to him. When the last notes faded away, she found herself nestled flush against him. Their proximity was hardly appropriate. She tensed as she realized what she'd done. Mumbling an apology, she pulled away from him, angry at herself for being so careless.

What would Evelyn think upon seeing their closeness? Tristan showed no disapproval for her behavior. The crowd's applause rang in her ears like the blood drumming against her senses.

Moments later, the music began again; this time numerous couples rushed out onto the floor. "You look pale, Princess." Tristan studied her, concern etched into the frown on his face. "Shall we get you something to eat and drink? We can wait to have our next dance."

Perhaps that was best. Nodding, she allowed him to guide her away from the floor. Pushing their way through the many bodies, they made their way to the dining hall where refreshments waited.

Both the entry and dining hall were so packed with bodies that the rising heat was stifling. It was difficult to proceed; every person they passed wished to greet them. Most wanted to congratulate Tristan. In the act of bowing and curtsying, they became separated, but as they were headed for the same place, she moved there promptly. She filled a plate with small delicacies and gathered a goblet of wine. When Tristan *still* didn't appear, she took a seat at the head table and allowed herself several moments of quiet. With a bite to eat, she felt a measure of strength return. But her attempt at peace was in vain. Guests insisted upon coming up to the table to wish her well.

A few times she thought she saw Tristan's head in the crowd, his gleaming pearlescent hair. It was not his fault everyone insisted on stopping him. She drained her goblet of wine and tried not to let her frustration get the better of her. It set her insides aflame with boldness. She felt better than she had all evening.

With new resolve, she set out to find Tristan. Proceeding through the crowd in search of him, she instead found her parents, and pulled her mother aside. "I cannot find Tristan," she explained, trying to suppress her emotion. "Have you seen him?"

Her mother's lips pursed into a thin line. Hardly a good sign. "I believe I saw him speaking with the Sprites several minutes ago. He did not look happy. Can you think of why he might be upset?"

She frowned. Her mind immediately went to Evelyn. "I cannot say. Do you know where I might find him *now*?"

Her mother's hesitance remained. "I believe I saw him sneak away with one of them—Evelyn." There was so much accusation in her mother's gaze that she knew what the queen thought of Tristan's actions, especially when it was her daughter Tristan was supposed to be dancing with for the night. "The two of them went into the corridor leading to the south wing. But Lena—" Her mother hesitated. "Proceed with caution. I have warned you before about getting your heart tangled up inappropriately."

Her insides turn to ice. "I know, Mama. Thank you." With that, she shrank away. Her feet had a mind of their own, taking her to the corridor her mother spoke of. It was lit with an orange glow from the sconces lining the walls. She found its entryway empty, so she crept along in silence, moving farther from the sounds of the ball.

What did she expect to find? Part of her urged retreat, that this was a bad idea. The other part of her was infuriated. Tristan was supposed to be *her* date for the evening. He was the one who had asked her to accompany him. The separation brought on by the crowd was understandable. But his failure to find her, and his audacity to sneak away, irked her. At last she heard raised voices. Tristan and Evelyn were arguing.

She should have turned back. Whatever they spoke of was their business. Like a moth to candlelight, she couldn't pull herself away. She crept closer. They stood halfway up a staircase under the bright light of a torch. She placed herself in the shadows beneath, looking up to them with an unimpeded view.

"I thought you loved me, Gallant." Evelyn's voice was filled with accusation. Her face was not composed as it usually was. Instead, she looked close to tears.

"I do. You know I do." Tristan's words were hushed.

"Then why are you doing this? When you fled Esterpine, you left me without so much as a goodbye. Now...now you're to become *king* someday? Am I to be cast away? Nothing more than a memory?"

"You know why I left you, Evelyn. I had no choice."

"But you have a choice now, Gallant. Choose me." Her gaze was fierce. Her eyes sparkled like stars in the darkness. The luminescent markings upon her skin glowed like the night flowers in the queen's garden. Why did she keep calling him *Gallant*?

"You wish for me to renounce the crown? Is that it? You wish for me to give up my title?"

"Your title?!" Evelyn cried. "Your crowning is not until tomorrow. You can still turn away from this path."

"And turn where, Evelyn? To you? You made it perfectly clear last we spoke that a Sprite could *never* be with a Drengr."

"I was not in my right mind. I was upset! You know my parents. You know what they said to me."

"Then what now?!" Tristan threw up his hands, frustration getting the better of him. "You would be with me only to have me be shunned by your family? Or have you finally agreed to run away? You balked at the idea last I gave it. Have you changed your mind?" She knew Tristan well enough to read his tone of voice. His request was only half-hearted.

"I have! I have changed. I would run away with you, Gallant. I would! Renounce the crown. Come away with me. We can leave tonight."

There was a long pause. She held her breath waiting for Tristan's answer, too stunned to move. "No," Tristan said at last. "You are a Sprite. Sprites belong in the forest. I am a Drengr. My place is here now."

Evelyn looked as though she'd been doused with ice water. "It's because of *her*, isn't it? The princess! You have fallen in love with her. I see it on your face every time you look at her. You look at her the way you used to look at me." Anguish was rolling off her in waves, and the glow of her markings dimmed to a shade dull blue.

"That isn't true, Evelyn." His voice did not mirror the sentiments of his words. "I am not doing this for anyone but myself, myself and the kingdom of Dragonwall."

"Then you are doing it for everyone but *me!*" With that, Evelyn fled down the staircase and rushed away, none the wiser that Lena stood in the shadows.

Tristan gave a defeated sigh and sank down onto the stairs. She watched him in silence for the length of several heartbeats before he spoke. "You can come out of the shadows, Lena." Her face burned.

She slowly stepped around the staircase, climbing the stairs to sit down beside him. "I'm sorry," she whispered, gazing at the wall instead of him. She couldn't bear to look at him for embarrassment. "I shouldn't have listened. That was a private matter. Forgive me." Ashamed, she rose to leave. He captured her hand and pulled her back down.

"Do not leave me now. Please."

She nodded and sank back down. They sat together in silence for a long while. It took time to work up the courage to speak. At last she said, "Why did Evelyn call you *Gallant?*"

"Because that is my name."

Her brow furrowed. She turned to him at last, noticing the pain in his face. "Truly? Then the name Tristan…is that made up?"

He shook his head. "Tristan is the name my mother wished for me to have. I was raised by dragons, Lena. Dragons name their offspring for the traits they wish them to possess. I was named Gallant in the hopes that I would be exactly that. There is magic in the name. I cannot be hard-hearted. I cannot be mean or ruthless like Raff. I cannot be judgmental like so many, not even if I wanted to be."

Understanding dawned upon her. She remembered all the times she witnessed his behavior, all the times she wondered if it was just for show. "I sometimes wondered if you were merely acting. I thought perhaps you were trying to win us over. I couldn't understand how someone could be so perfect, so…so…"

"Gallant?"

She nodded. The word perfectly encompassed everything that he was.

"I do not *appreciate* the name. I am a Drengr, not a dragon. But that was the deal made between my mother and the clan that raised me. I did not take up the name of Tristan until I left the forest to come here. That is why Evelyn calls me Gallant."

"Prince Gallant," she whispered, gazing into the darkness, letting the words roll off her tongue. "It has a nice ring to it."

He grunted but otherwise fell silent.

"I'm sorry about Evelyn, Tristan." And she was. The hurt of Daryn's departure was still a fresh memory. Though it was nothing compared to what Tristan must have felt for Evelyn. "I know you love her. I thought…" She hesitated briefly, her own emotions getting the better of her. "I thought I loved Daryn. I knew him for such a short time, nothing compared to how long you and Evelyn have known each other." She shook her head, ashamed with herself for her behavior. "I never meant to intrude on such a private moment between the both of you. And while it is not my place to say, I admire that you have chosen duty over love." After saying this, she rose. "I should get back. Perhaps the best thing for you tonight is to sneak away to your chamber. You probably want to be alone. I can go out and display a brave face for both of us."

Tristan stood. "No, Lena. That will not be necessary. I asked you to the ball to spend time with you. I asked you so that we might dance together. I have hardly lived up to my intentions with one single dance." He held out his arm to her. She eyed it with hesitance before accepting. He then led her back to the ball and they did exactly what they'd set out to do, as if nothing had ever transpired in the darkness of the corridor.

CHAPTER 28
HANDING OVER THE CROWN

THE MORNING FOLLOWING THE BALL, Lena found herself at the archery range. The sun was not yet up, but its glow on the horizon was adequate. The sea fog lay heavy upon the grass, snaking about her ankles and bathing everything in misty droplets that sparkled like glitter.

Tristan's crowning ceremony was scheduled later that afternoon, creating a swell of new emotions for her. She was eager to take advantage of the morning's quiet to gather her thoughts and calm her mind. Firing arrow after arrow, she allowed herself to meander over the events that had transpired, tripping and stumbling over the finer details. Raff's death was a heavy blow, and not just for her; Tristan would suffer from guilt. But ultimately it was the argument between Tristan and Evelyn that continued to replay in her mind.

She was jealous of Tristan's love for Evelyn. Was she mean for deriving happiness from his choice of the crown over love? It meant he would remain in the capital close to her. Evelyn would depart, and Tristan's attention would be hers once more. Her thoughts felt selfish but she couldn't stop herself.

Ivrir joined her as the sun broke free of the horizon. "You look as though you haven't slept."

"Little surprise there. I haven't." She glanced at him, offering a small smile before returning her gaze to the target. Sleep had been impossible after the ball. Nocking another arrow, she pulled her bow string tight and released, watching it soar to the target. It landed firmly in the center of the black dot. She had come a long way—and not just where her archery skills were concerned.

"If you would like to be alone, I can leave you." Ivrir was always thoughtful, always respectful. He could read her emotions easier than most. It was hard to believe she once hoped they were mates, for she greatly valued his friendship now.

"I never mind your presence, Ivrir. It calms me. Stay and practice." At her invitation, he remained, and perceptive as he was, afforded her silence. They stood side by side, emptying their quivers. Each time they finished, they walked to the targets together to retrieve their arrows.

The practice grounds were slow to fill. Everyone slept in, exhausted from the festivities. Once the sun was shining brightly overhead, several soldiers found themselves sparring, filling the air with the sound of metal. Her mind flashed back to the day before, to Tristan's fight with Raff, and its outcome. "I think I've had enough for today," she said.

He agreed and they put their things away. On their way from the range, she spotted Tristan at the edge of the grounds sparring with one of the visiting Sprites. In passing, their eyes met briefly and her heart tightened with longing.

"Are you ready for this afternoon?" Ivrir asked, forcing

her attention away. They approached the portcullis on the second level leading into the main portion of the keep.

"As ready as I'll ever be," she admitted. "I'm eager to put an end to this debacle and get on with my life. I'm ready to travel. To be of some use."

He nodded. "Understandable, even admirable. You're brave, Lena. I admire your ability to display such fortitude during this time. It is no small thing to hand over a piece of your life you believed would always be yours."

She considered his words at length. "I have come to understand and even accept that we cannot always get exactly what we want in life."

"A hard-learned truth, I think."

"Indeed. Very hard-learned." She nodded toward two guards in passing. "No matter how much I feel I deserve the crown, no matter how much I kick and scream that it ought to be mine, no matter how unfair it is, things are the way they are. I can either accept that or fight it. If I fight it, I will be unhappy forever. I have a new path now—one I never expected but am glad for nonetheless. What is life if not the pursuit of happiness?"

Ivrir's eyes gleamed. "You have come a long way, Princess, from the woman I met some months ago to the woman you are now. You've earned my respect and adoration in more ways than one, and I am honored to count you among my friends."

His words brought a certain warmth that spread through her body. "Thank you, Ivrir. I'm lucky to have you too. Good friends can be hard to find."

He chuckled. "Yes, they are. I will always be here for you, whenever you have need of me."

THE CROWNING CEREMONY was held in the throne room, with full pomp and circumstance. The kingdom's throne room was the most magnificent hall in all of Dragonwall. Vaulted ceilings, finely carved wooden pillars, and stained-glass windows displayed the richness of the Drengr monarchy. No architecture paralleled it in all the kingdom.

The room was packed with spectators such that there was scarcely room to breathe. The only empty space was the narrow aisle down the middle—the path down which Tristan proceeded. His approach to the throne was so profound, Lena thought she could hear imaginary trumpets bugling, crying their praise.

Tristan wore a royal-blue tunic of velvet and black trousers. His black boots were knee-high and polished to perfection. About his waist, a bejeweled belt held his Sprite blade. He looked every bit the prince he was about to become. And if that wasn't enough, the Drengr monarchy's sigil was embroidered in silver just above his left breast. He displayed it proudly.

She allowed her eyes to wander up and down his appearance, admiring every bit of him. His pearlescent white hair contrasted richly with the dark color of his clothing. She took the time to study his face, realizing that he was far more handsome than she had previously considered. Her skin flushed.

Forcing her eyes from Tristan's approaching figure, she turned them upon Evelyn. Evelyn stood beside the other Sprites, just below the dais. Her face was ashen.

Had Lena failed to overhear their argument, she might have believed someone close to Evelyn had died. In a metaphorical sense, that was true. Knowing where Tristan's allegiance stood—with the crown and not Evelyn—greatly increased her admiration of him.

She adjusted her hold upon the wooden box in her grasp, allowing herself to glance down at it. Sitting within was Tristan's crown. This was the second crown ever gifted by the Sprites to the Drengr monarchy. It was wrought of silver, woven together with meticulous detail. There were no jewels —it didn't need them. When he became king, Prince Gallant would trade in his silver crown and receive a golden one. It pained her to think she would never see that day come.

The king and queen stood beside Lena. She couldn't help but notice how proud her father looked. Could she blame him? No. Not now. She was no longer upset by his happiness. Tristan was the best heir Dragonwall could hope for. He was the best *she* could hope for. Ivrir had been correct. She had changed a great deal in the past few months.

Tristan reached the base of the dais and stopped. The steward came forward bearing a large scroll from which he read. As his voice droned on, she found Tristan's gaze over and again. Each time their eyes met, he afforded her a small smile, and with each smile, her heart soared a little higher. Then it was her turn to present the crown. She moved to the base of the dais with her father.

Holding the box forward, she said, "I, Selena Ironborn, have failed to find a mate by the age of eighteen. I have upheld the law. With the conferral of this crown, I renounce my hold upon my title. He who should wear it will be afforded the right to rule in my stead, and should he take a mate, she will become his queen."

Her father reached into the box and removed the crown. He bowed his head in acknowledgement of her abdication, allowing his gaze to linger. She saw within his eyes everything she wished he would say aloud. She had already accepted her failure and her future. Her father had not. A heavy weight pushed upon her chest. King Cornan appeared to be crying inside. Knowing that his only child would lead a human life hurt him. No parent should have to watch their child die, but he would outlive her. This ceremony merely made it real. Her eyes filled with tears. Swallowing, she turned her gaze away from him.

King Cornan cleared his throat and turned to Tristan. "With this crown, I acknowledge Gallant Forestborn as my heir, to learn from me, and abide by me, until my death elevates him to kingship. From this day forth, he will be a part of the royal family. His rule shall mark the *seventh* generation of the Drengr monarchy." She was surprised that her father knew Tristan's true name. "All hail Prince Gallant."

"Hail, Prince Gallant!" As a wave, the entire room fell to one knee. Only those higher in position remained standing. As she was no longer the *Crowned* Princess, she too lowered herself to the ground, bowing her head and averting her eyes. In that moment, ready as she was, she couldn't hide the tears that dripped onto the skirts of her gown. It was over—done.

Before standing, she blinked away the remaining moisture from her eyes. She stood tall. She was still Lena Ironborn. And now her future was certain. She needn't fight it any longer. She would never be queen.

CHAPTER 29
TRISTAN GOES AWAY

IN THE DAYS following Tristan's crowning, things went back to normal. The Sprites departed for their forest, the competitors went back to their forts, and the guests housed within the keep dispersed. Ivrir was obliged to bid Lena farewell. Her archery skills had surpassed his benefit of teaching. She knew enough tricks that practice was all she needed henceforth. She was heartbroken to see him go, but he promised to visit on occasion. It would have been selfish to request he stay longer.

Only those belonging to the royal court remained: council members and nobles who lived in permanent residence within the keep. With the number of people reduced, Lena could breathe again. But adjusting was still difficult.

Three days of mourning were allotted to Raff, though no funeral was held. At the request of his father, Lord Azrith, his body was returned to Fort Edge where a proper funeral could be observed. It was Tristan who struggled the most, suffocated by guilt. He hid it well from everyone but her. Keeping busy was the best thing for them both. In that time, she had already started a chain of correspondence with all the lord governors of Dragonwall, scheduling her next visits into the kingdom.

Six days following the crowning, Whitesholes, a town at the far side of Eryas, suffered a heavy attack from the pirates. Fort Kastali and Fort Lin were mobilized to meet the attack, but having arrived late, only saved half of the lives they might have. Meetings were called, strategies discussed, plans arranged. Lena was not invited to assist with these, though her father still called upon her in the afternoon to assist with his mundane affairs, which she happily accepted.

She could feel her time in the capital coming to an end as the desire to travel grew deeper. Yet, something held her back, making it difficult to take the final leap into her new life. Perhaps it was knowledge of the increasing pirate attacks. Or perhaps it was something else entirely.

She and Tristan had taken to spending increasing amounts of time together. He made it a point to walk with her after dinner each evening. She cherished his attention, especially since his time was valuable.

Two nights following the attack on Whitesholes, they were meandering through the royal garden when he announced his orders to depart. "Your father wishes for me to travel to Whitesholes. I leave in the morning." She felt a pang of disappointment. "I am to assist with the repairs and shall be gone for a week, hopefully no longer."

"Can no one else oversee such a task?" The news was unwelcome, but perhaps it was the push she needed to begin her own work. Her hand, which was hooked around Tristan's arm, received a reassuring squeeze.

"No, Selena, it must be me." He'd taken to using her full name at every opportunity. He no longer called her Princess, or Lena, though everyone else still did. When she tried to argue the matter, he refused, claiming to enjoy Selena more, so she gave up on it.

"Anyway," said Tristan, "your father is adamant that I go. It is a good opportunity to acquaint myself with the people of Dragonwall. I must show them that their welfare is my chief concern. Your father told me about the funds you have allocated for survivors, and I will see to it that all who need assistance are properly cared for."

"My father is correct. And they will be grateful for the help." She did not want him to know how much she disliked the idea of losing his company, but it was difficult to hide. "I suppose I must find a new way to occupy my evenings."

He chuckled. "You sound as though you will miss me."

Her mouth broadened into a smile. "Yes. I think I shall. Sometimes I feel as if you understand me better than others. With Ramar so busy these days, and Ivrir gone, you are all I have for company."

"What of your ladies?"

She sighed. "I spend my whole day with them already. Besides, I enjoy my time with you."

"As do I," he affirmed. "I depart before sunrise, so I do not expect to see you in the morning. I suppose this is good-bye, for now." They had reached the garden's entrance. More often than not, she found herself wishing their visits were longer. "I bid you farewell until I return." Taking her hand, he kissed the back, leaving tingles to spread up her arm. Then he bowed deeply. As the Crowned Prince, he was now her superior. Yet he still treated her as if she outranked him. It was sweet. She liked him all the more for it. Straightening up, he turned and strode away, leaving her to stand alone in the dark. Instead of going in, she went and sat upon a bench to pine after him.

Her mother found her in the same spot nearly an hour

later. "Come inside with me, my sweet thing. Let's have a drink together." Together they went to her mother's parlor and sat before the fire. "I see your feelings plainly. You ought to guard them, daughter. Do not forget the hurt Daryn caused."

"I have not forgotten, Mama." She reached for her goblet and drank deeply. In the past few months, she'd taken to wine. It no longer held the bitter taste it once did.

"Love is a hard thing, dear girl. However, I do not judge you, no matter where you wish to place your heart."

"I once wished to place it with Daryn." She sighed. "It is unfortunate that he did not guard it better. Worse still, I have nearly overcome the hurt. My sights have changed to Tristan. To think, I first disliked him." Having never told her mother about their first words together on the arena floor, she shared the story. "I was certain he cared nothing for my future."

"He ought to have come when he was summoned," said her mother. "Sometimes I wonder..." She shook her head. "Well, never mind that now, darling."

"Never mind what?"

"Oh...nothing."

She eyed her mother a moment longer. "I think this time, I will be more careful. I will not place my heart out in the open as I did with Daryn."

Queen Amara nodded. "Your heart is not delicate, Lena. But love can break even the hardest of hearts."

THE DAYS FOLLOWING Tristan's departure felt the longest of her life. His leaving was harder to bear than she anticipated. It felt almost as if she could feel the distance between them, like they were attached by invisible strands that were now pulled tight, and if they stretched any further, she worried her heart might rip from her chest.

She promised herself that she would depart upon her first mission north, but only *after* he returned. She longed to visit the Scattered Islands, and the lord governor of Redport had extended a generous invitation. But she couldn't leave on such a long trip without saying goodbye, so she lingered…waiting.

Not a day went by that she wasn't scolding herself to control her emotions, to forget Tristan, to renounce her feelings for him. That alone was difficult, especially when her strange dreams resurfaced. Tristan floated in and out of her sleep. Ships came in vast numbers. They filled the bay and fired giant projectiles upon the city. Dragons and Drengr alike tried to battle them.

Each night she awoke drenched in sweat, running out to her balcony to ensure the bay was empty before collapsing back into bed. She rarely slept following each episode. By the end of the week, she was desperate for Tristan's return. More than once she considered telling her mother, but always thought better of it.

On the ninth day of Tristan's absence, she finally felt the winds of change. That morning, her heart did not feel as pained. The pressure had lessened gradually as the day progressed. She couldn't explain how, but she knew Tristan was on his way back to her. She was in her room that afternoon when Cora came to her breathless. "The keep is assembling in the lower courtyard, Princess Lena. We must go now."

"Is it Tristan? Has he come back?" Her heart raced and her face flushed.

"Indeed. He is not long off. Minutes away."

Lena jumped to her feet, running to the mirror to adjust

her gown and smooth back her hair. "Why does no one tell me these things in advance?! Must everyone know before I?"

They rushed from her apartment to the lower levels. She arrived at the same moment as her parents and placed herself beside them. Blood rushed through her ears. She had to wipe her sweaty palms upon the skirt of her gown.

Excited cries broke the calm as people began pointing skyward. A group of Drengr appeared above them, descending in lazy circles. She picked out Tristan's pearlescent white form among the others. Her eyes fixed upon him. He was so majestic. Just as the group neared the ground, they transformed midair and landed on human feet. Tristan was there, offering the gathered spectators his famous lopsided grin. Why was her corset so tight? She could scarcely breathe.

Beside Tristan, Aki, Briv, and Ramar landed just as gracefully. The four of them strode forward to greet their king, grasping forearms in turn before giving their respects to the queen. When Tristan caught her eye, he winked, sending a wave of heat over her skin. She took a deep breath, attempting to regain her composure.

"Selena," said he, bowing to her deeply. He hadn't given the same greeting to her father nor mother. Embarrassed by the singular show of respect, she glanced to her father and noticed his smug expression. Did he know something she didn't?

Aki, Briv, and Ramar greeted her warmly with a hug, as big brothers would. She laughed when Ramar lifted her from the ground and twirled her in a circle. "I certainly hope you have behaved yourself whilst we were away, Princess. I know what kind of trouble you are capable of."

She laughed. "My days of trouble making have been put on hold, remember?" She did not need to remind him about Bartlett's misfortune. He'd only just been released that week and permitted to return to his mother. She and Tristan exchanged another knowing glance before the lot of them retreated into the keep discussing business.

She trailed behind with her mother, allowing the men to discuss Whitesholes and the progress they had made. "He fancies you, does he not?" Her mother walked with her hands clasped behind her back. Even her mother's knowing glances could not take away from her heart's pleasure.

She grabbed her mother's left arm and leaned into her. "Now, now, Mama. He is a wise prince. We must trust that he knows what he is doing."

Queen Amara smirked but said no more. At that moment, Tristan chose to fall behind. "If I may, my queen, I wish to request your daughter's company for a walk." At Tristan's invitation, she turned to her mother and grinned. The queen was resigned to sigh and nod before increasing her pace to join the others.

Before anyone noticed, Tristan grabbed her hand, something he'd never done before, and rushed her away. They continued down a side corridor, and then another, until they found themselves in their usual place, the royal garden.

"Did you miss me, Princess?"

She barked a laugh. "I should have known that would be the first question from your mouth."

He chuckled. "I missed you, if you wish to know. Very much so."

"Truly?" Her heart dared to hope. "You were not so busy that you had no time for it?" They walked through the flowerbeds. The garden was entirely empty, everyone was still making their way back into the keep from the lower level courtyard.

"I had plenty of time to miss you. And plenty of time to get you a gift too."

She faltered. "You...you got me something?" Seeing her shock pleased him. He smiled wide and reached into the leather pouch attached to his belt, procuring a small package wrapped in brown paper.

"It isn't much, but the moment I saw it, I knew I had to have it for you." He handed it over. She quickly untied the little string and unfolded the paper. A beautiful hair comb with emeralds and tiny diamonds tumbled into her palm.

She squealed with delight, pretenses forgotten. "It's perfect!"

"You like it?" The hesitance in his voice moved her.

"I love it! Thank you!" Without thinking, she threw her arms around his neck and hugged him. He froze in place. She realized what she had done. Entirely embarrassed, she went to pull away, but his arms reacted more quickly than she, tightening around her back, pulling her flush against him. Heat erupted and pooled in her abdomen as every curve of her body met his.

He inhaled deeply, his mouth against her hair. "I meant what I said, Selena. I missed you. Our separation...it was difficult for me." Releasing her at last, he stepped back several paces. "I constantly found myself thinking of things I wanted say to you, silly things too, my thoughts throughout the day, things you might like to see." He shook his head. "I suppose it is wrong for me to wish our minds were connected." His brow furrowed. "I suppose...well...I think I know what your answer would be." Then, before she could express her confusion, he reclaimed her arm and began walking again. She was left to wonder...to hope.

CHAPTER 30

KASTALI DUN MAKES
PREPARATIONS

LENA ENTERED her father's study the day following Tristan's return and noticed his absence. Since his crowning, the three of them often worked together. "Ah," her father said when he noticed her searching gaze. "I have asked Gallant to join us a little later than usual. I hoped to have some time alone with you."

She smiled sweetly at the unexpected gesture. "I'm flattered, Papa. Just like the old days, huh?" She went to his cabinet and removed the stack of documents she'd been combing through for weeks.

"Come and sit here at my desk, dear girl." Her father pointed to the chair across from him.

She arched an eyebrow. "This alone time isn't what I think it is, is it?"

After years of working together, he was too easy to read, even for a Drengr. "I wanted to talk to you about Gallant."

Her face flushed. "Let me guess, you are going to lecture me. You're going to tell me that it is dangerous to open my heart to a Drengr, especially an unmated one who will drop me the instant he finds his life partner." She was ready for this argument. She'd already had it with herself multiple times, first with Daryn and now with Tristan.

Her father chuckled and his eyes danced, confusing her. "No, dear girl. It is not my intention to scold you."

"It isn't?" The tension in her shoulders increased.

"I am curious, Lena, why did you refuse Gallant's offer to touch his scales?"

The color drained from her face. "What? What are you talking about?"

"It is not a loaded statement, darling daughter. Prince Gallant offered you the opportunity to touch his scales, to see if you were mates, and you refused." She opened her mouth, but nothing came out. "Gods, girl! Can't you see it?"

Her heartbeat quickened. "He...he told you? That was between us. Besides, it happened before he won the tournament." She trusted Tristan to guard the things they discussed. This betrayal unnerved her.

"Don't hate him for it. Gallant is upset. It doesn't take a king to see that. I insisted he come clean on the matter. He would not dare lie to his king."

"But...why would Tristan be upset? He never seems bothered around me?" She scowled. What he said made no sense. If anything, her relationship with Tristan was stronger than ever.

"Can you not see his affliction, Lena? The signs are there. He suffers the same way I did when your mother refused me."

She crossed her arms. "That's different and you know it. You and mother were mates."

"So are you and Gallant."

His words were slow to sink in. "What? No...we can't be."

"You heard me, dear girl. Put him out of his misery and agree to his request."

She began shaking her head repeatedly. "How can you be so sure? It's...it's impossible." She slumped back in her chair. "Tristan's request was a mere whim, an offer to reconcile past behavior. He wanted to put my mind at ease. That's why he offered, to prove that his lapse in behavior wouldn't have changed my future."

"Gods above!" Her father pushed his chair out and stood. He placed his palms on the desk and leaned towards her. His eyes blazed with determination. "If you think Gallant's request was merely to make amends, then you've got your head in the clouds. Gallant knows what he feels, the same as I knew with your mother."

"Yeah, and you forced Mama to do something she didn't want to. You transformed and captured her. You gave her no choice."

He stood erect and studied her a long while. The silence that followed was deafening. "I thought you wanted to be queen," he said at last, his voice low. "I thought you wanted to find your mate. Your work as an emissary will be a great alternative, but surely it doesn't trump your initial dream." He shook his head. "Help me to understand, Lena. Is it your disbelief or your fear talking?"

She was at a loss for words. Didn't he see? Even if they *were* mates, she'd renounced that path. Besides, how could he know with certainty? And how could Tristan? The only way to be positive was for skin to touch scale. There wouldn't be a song about it if it were otherwise.

She shook her head, keeping her eyes fixed on the dark wood of his desk. "I know what's going to happen, Papa. I'm going to allow myself to hope. I'm going to work myself up the same way I did before, and when I touch Tristan's scales, nothing is going to happen. It will devastate me. Can't you see that? Don't…please don't make me go through that again."

Her father sank back into his chair. "Then I have my answer. It is your fear talking. Do not be a coward, Lena. Put the poor man out of his misery. He's no good to me pining after you all day."

"Tristan doesn't *pine*. And he doesn't love me, he loves Evelyn."

"You are mistaken, Lena. He loves you because you are his mate. The bond does not allow him to love another."

Her frown deepened. Surely Tristan loved Evelyn. She saw it on his face when Evelyn left him in the stairwell after their argument. She saw his pain.

Her father's gaze was unwavering. "Lena, a Drengr can only truly love one."

She was about to protest when the door bust open. Tristan, followed by the king's Shields, rushed into the room. Their faces were pale with shock. They were breathing like they'd just run a race.

"Your Grace." Pedrus stepped forward. He was the highest ranking of the six. "We have a problem. A *serious* problem."

Worried, she glanced at Tristan. He avoided her gaze. Why? Did he know what they'd been discussing? Her skin flushed.

Pedrus glanced at Lena, remaining silent. Her father spoke, "It's okay, Pedrus. Lena can stay. What's so urgent?"

"We are under attack."

"What?" Her father jumped to his feet, looking in turn at each of them. "What do you mean?"

"The information we received regarding the attack on

Westerloach was incorrect—a diversion to separate our forces."

King Cornan shook his head, not quite following. "I still don't understand. We sent half the fort's forces there just this morning. They are supposed to arrive in time to assist Fort Lin with the attack."

"But the enemy isn't on its way to Westerloach," Ramar cut in. "It's on its way here!"

"Here?! But…" The king hesitated. "How…how can they hope for success against a city of this size? This is our capital, our most heavily defended fortress. It would take hundreds of ships to bring us to our knees. A pirate fleet of near fifty does not stand a chance."

She followed the exchange, her gaze darting back and forth to each speaker as her eyes grew wider. An attack on Kastali Dun? It was madness. Even with half the forces of Fort Kastali away, how could a fleet fifty strong hope to bring down a city well-guarded with a fleet of its own, not to mention ten thousand standing foot soldiers and horsemen?

"It is not merely a pirate fleet that sails for the Ports of Kastali, Your Grace. These ships are Oshean. The pirates have joined with them. Given this intel, I believe Oshea was behind the pirate raids all this time. I believe they have been manipulating the pirates to attack our various ports to distract us from the fleet that has been sailing our way for some weeks."

"Oshea?" Her father looked as though he'd walked through ice water. "What does Oshea want with us? They have never traveled this far."

"Their purpose seems clear enough to me. The report came in from our sweep teams not but ten minutes ago. A fleet, three hundred strong, a mix of Oshean ships and pirate ships, is sailing directly for us."

Her body turned cold. She watched her father sink into his chair, deflated. "How long have we got, Pedrus?"

"At the most? A day and a half." Those words knocked the air from her chest.

They had the same effect on her father. He sat silent for several moments. Blinking, he turned to her. "Lena?"

"Yes, Father." She lifted her hands from the armrests and placed them in her lap. Her fingers trembled, but she laced them together tightly to hide her fear.

"Go and find Captain Marda. He is to attend to me immediately. Then go and help your mother. There is much to be done…much to do…" His gaze took on a faraway look. He was sending out the silent call to the Drengr within hearing range. The capital was under attack.

No sooner had Lena followed her father's orders then the klaxon sounded. Every bell in the city rang from afternoon until night and then until morning. There was little sleep to be had, nor any time for it. The city prepared for the coming attack and the keep prepared to take its citizens should the attackers breach city walls.

Lower levels of the keep were cleared, valuables locked away in the keep's vaults, food stores inventoried, weapons carted from their storehouses, and all posts manned. People rushed to and fro wearing looks of desperation while soldiers raced through the corridors adding a constant clank of armor to the prevailing noise. Kastali Dun had never been attacked.

During this chaos, Lena managed to sneak into the city under the disguise of a cloak. She needed to ensure Bartlett's family took proper precautions. It was fortunate they now resided in better circumstances because if the armies came ashore, the lower levels near the dockyard would be the first to fall. The entire Pauper's District would go up in flames.

Bartlett's mother was fearful, but she hid it well, overseeing her children's efforts to board up the windows and doors of their home. There was little else the citizens could do, other than stay out of the way of the soldiers. Lena warned Bartlett to stay out of trouble, though she feared her warning would go unheeded.

When she returned to the keep, dinner of bread and cheese was passed around for all. No one assembled to eat— there was no time for that. She could hardly stomach food but scarfed down what little she could. Then she set out in search of Tristan. She desperately needed to see him. Everything her father had told her replayed in her mind and she wanted to talk to him about it.

After two hours of fruitless inquiry she was no closer to locating him. Night had already fallen when she ran into her mother. "Stay out of the way tonight, dear heart." Queen Amara glanced over her shoulder and called out a few orders before turning back to Lena. "Best you take cover."

"But Mama, I want to help." Having no purpose made her useless.

"We have all the help we need. The noblewomen are terrified. I have sent them to the dining hall. Your father's minstrels have been called to entertain. Their husbands are assisting elsewhere. Tend to them. You are not to leave the south wing until the battle finishes. Gods help us. Let us pray we make it out alive." Her mother turned to assist several passersby, momentarily distracted.

"That's hardly fair, Mama! I want to fight. I have my bow!" She had every intention of using it too, especially if enemies scaled the walls of the keep.

"No, Lena. I want you safe. Now go! That's an order." Her mother rushed off.

She had no choice but to present herself before the noblewomen gathered in the dining hall. They huddled together in little clusters scattered about the large tables. Their looks of disbelief mirrored her own. Signaling the musicians for momentary silence, she spoke. "My ladies, you need not fear. This city is designed to withstand an attack. Your husbands will be safe. You will be safe. The enemy will never reach the keep. This I promise." It was reckless reassurance. Their safety was no more certain than victory. But they were heartened.

After that, the musicians began again. The melodies were calming. She circulated the hall with her handmaidens, stopping to speak words of encouragement to each of the women. Refreshment was presented. They ate and continued their vigil throughout the night. She was happy the music helped to drown out the sounds of chaos outside their refuge.

At dawn she slipped away, leaving Kenna Margaret in charge. A last effort was made to locate Tristan. As before, he was nowhere to be found. Disheartened, she fled to the King's Tower and discovered it deserted.

The sun was just shedding its first rays upon the world when she entered her mother's massive wardrobe. Her mother was a tidy woman, but not today. Things were tossed around haphazardly and her mother's favorite set of flying gear was gone. Confident that her mother would not miss it, she gathered a spare set of gear: a belted tunic, full length pants, black leather boots, and light armor. All Riders wore light armor into battle, and her mother's would be sized perfectly to fit her.

When she reached her apartment she quickly changed, tossing her gown upon her bed. Her hair she pulled back into a single braid, managing all right without her handmaidens. She went to the shelves near her fireplace and took the gift box from Ivrir. Removing the lid, she pulled out her bow and quiver of arrows, taking another moment to admire them as she always did. In front of the mirror, she gasped. Staring back at her was Queen Amara herself, or a very close likeness. In riding gear, she looked almost identical to her mother, as if she were meant for it.

Her stomach flipped over as she thought of Tristan, of the potential bond they shared. Dare she hope for it? Could she afford the disappointment if her father was wrong? Shaking her head, she pushed the thought from her mind and proceeded to the balcony. The sun was up now somewhere out of view. Stretched before her was the sea. At its horizon she saw them coming—more ships than she could count. They were still small, barely discernible, but they were moving rapidly and would be upon them by midday. Her blood turned cold.

Oshea was a country far west, somewhere over the Dragonfire Sea. Those brave enough to venture there were merchant ships, eager for trading beyond Dragonwall's coasts. Some said it was a magic-heavy place, that the first sorcerers in Dragonwall came from Oshea in search of power long before dragons ever stalked the land. But Dragonwall's sorcerers were mostly gone, leaving behind only lesser magic. What of the magic of Oshea?

It didn't take long before the scene before her grew more detailed. She blinked, trying to rub the fatigue from her eyes, focusing on what was before her. As the ships neared, she began to make out their sails, their flags, their subtle differences. Her stomach sank as recognition washed over her. This was a familiar image, one she'd seen before. Memories pooled up in her mind. But they were only dreams! With them came Tristan's face; she had seen this coming since he arrived. There was always Tristan, followed by the appearance of ships. Was it an omen? Was he to die today in battle?

The ships were close enough to count now. The tightly

packed fleet plowed through the waves, creating white foam in the water as it churned about their prows. The wind blew them closer to Kastali Dun. It was the same breeze she felt against her cheek. Such a wind spoke of death, whispering its intentions as it swept around her.

A roar split the air. Her eyes widened. Fort Kastali's Drengr flew out into the open. They were near enough to see the Riders upon their backs, bearing bows. Pride flared up within her. How could the enemy stand against the might of the Drengr?

Each V-formation was tightly packed and twenty strong showing a plethora of colors. They streaked past the ships circling just out of reach. As a warning, they spewed red-orange flames. This was their way of saying, *turn back now or suffer the consequences.* The flames would do little against the magically protected ships. Yet, the sight left her heart soaring.

She searched for Tristan's white body. Her frantic eyes flicked from formation to formation. He was nowhere to be seen. Had he fled? No. That would be unlike him. Tristan wanted more than anything to destroy those responsible for killing his parents.

When she spotted her father, she breathed a sigh of relief. Her mother was upon his turquoise back, bow armed at the ready. Flanking her father were his Shields, three on the left and three on the right. This small formation was known as the King's Wing. Her gaze lingered over Ramar's fiery red scales. If anything happened to *any* of them, she would be heartbroken.

The Drengr circled three times, but it was evident that the ships had no intention of stopping. Her stomach plummeted—there would be no surrender. The Drengr fell back. Her eyes dropped to the ships. She noticed the large ballistae upon their decks. Each was armed with dragonlances, taller in length than any human, with lethal arrow-heads larger than her hand. The weapons were meant to kill dragons. Fear took her, knowing they would be imbued with poison.

A still silence had fallen all around her. The wind had ceased to blow. There was no longer a muffled chanting to ride its currents. It was as if the world had taken a deep breath. She too held hers, watching. A roar sounded—the roar of a Drengr king—giving her goose flesh. Her father's signal. In the blink of an eye, the world went from motionless order to blurred chaos. Nearly four hundred Drengr flew into action.

She watched, frozen in place, as the V-formations began attacking the ships. Each group split up and spread out, diving and dodging. When a formation got too close, they changed direction, increasing altitude to keep away from the spears. The repeated fly-bys allowed for their Riders to release arrows.

At first, nothing beyond that happened. She watched with fascination, admiring the Drengr's tactics. They were doing their best to shoot down soldiers upon the ship decks. Perhaps if they kept the ships busy, they might never make it into the bay.

A pained cry met her ears. The hairs of her arm stood on end. She watched with wide eyes as a Drengr-Rider pair fell from the sky. A spear protruded from the Drengr's glistening blue scales. Several in the pair's wing rushed to their aid, disturbing the formation as they assisted in the spear's removal.

It was too late. The distraction was enough. A net shot into the air, fanning out before wrapping around the injured pair. "No!" A gasp escaped her lips. The net tightened so that the injured Drengr could no longer flap its wings. Trapped, the pair plummeted into the sea, sending up a wave of water before popping up like a buoy.

Her stomach flipped over. Another pained cry split the air. She saw the same thing happen again moments later. Horrified, she covered her mouth, stifling a cry. The Drengr were being wounded and netted so that they could not free themselves.

She could only watch wide-eyed and helpless as the scene unfolded before her. Didn't the Riders have magic? Why couldn't they break free? A concerning realization came to her. "The nets are woven with magic," she whispered. Oshea's sorcerers ensured that the magic was not broken.

The Drengr's efforts to keep the ships from moving forward failed. Those who fell, bobbed in the water, only to be attacked close at hand by the ships that surrounded them. Still, the fleet moved onward. The capital's own fleet would do little to hinder them. If the enemy reached land they would disembark, wreaking havoc upon the city.

She panicked as she searched the sky for Tristan's body. There wasn't a flash of white to be seen. Not anywhere! Where was he? Why was he absent when they needed him the most?! She panicked.

A new sound split the world apart, rattling the walls around her. It was deeper, rawer, more guttural. The roar of a dragon! Her heart raced. More roars followed, announcing the arrival of reinforcements.

She gazed directly upward as newcomers emerged. Some fifty wild dragons soared out over the keep joining the fight in the bay. At their lead was Tristan. She cried out in jubilation, throwing her fist into the air. He was here! He was safe!

She watched, her eyes fixed upon his figure as he led the dragons into battle, but just as soon as he arrived, he circled around and disappeared behind the vast battlements of the keep. Her forehead furrowed. Where had he gone?

She hadn't long to wait. Five minutes later there was a loud crash behind her. She whirled around and fled the balcony. Tristan himself stormed into her room, his chest heaving. He tossed something at her feet. She glanced down. A Rider's harness. There was a crazed look in his eyes. He looked between her and the leather straps. "There is no turning back, Selena. Not now. It's time."

CHAPTER 31
DEFEATING OSHEA

Lena's first instinct was to throw her arms around Tristan's neck. Seeing him alive lifted an indescribable weight from her chest. She could breathe again. Remembering her father's words however, she refrained. If the king was correct, Tristan was suffering behind his façade, hiding what he really felt. "What's that for?" She glanced at the harness even though she already knew.

"It's for me—for us." A long silence stretched out before them. Her heart was jumping in her chest.

"I've only been using a bow for a few months. I can hardly hit a moving target. You cannot be serious…" Her voice died on her lips as fear twisted her stomach into knots. She shook her head back and forth. "I've…I've never flown on the back of a dragon. For gods' sake!"

"Never mind that now." His brow furrowed as if he'd not yet considered her vast inexperience. "I will keep you safe."

She wanted to trust him but…

"Would you rather hide away and do nothing?" He

glanced at her attire. "Besides, you're dressed for the occasion."

She opened her mouth but nothing came out. He was right. Being useless was the last thing she wanted. "I..."

He held out his hand. "We must do this, Selena. We must. I cannot do it without you." The image of his outstretched arm flashed through her mind. He'd said something similar in her dream. She remembered it now.

Fear lurked in Tristan's eyes like dancing flames. He was doing everything he could to contain the burn. When pirates attacked Fort Lin's coast, his father fell in battle, leaving his mother pregnant and alone to die in childbirth. All that pain left him a prisoner to his emotions. He needed her. She needed to do this for him.

"Okay," she said at last, her voice little more than a frightened whisper. He gave her a single nod, snatched up the harness, grabbed her hand, and pulled her from the room. His fingers felt good in hers—too good.

They raced down the hall and entered the king's tower. Pulling her across the room, they took the staircase that lead to the top, then climbed the ladder to the queen's garden. Blinding sunlight left her eyes watering as they emerged through the trapdoor. The highest point in the Great Keep offered an unobstructed view of the battle. Soldiers were already disembarking from their ships into rowboats, heading to the docks. The king's own foot soldiers were there on the walls, firing arrows while they waited for the breach.

She froze, searching for her parents. She found her father as he dived at a ship, his six guards in tight formation around him. Her mother was firing arrows into the crew below. Sighing with relief, she turned to Tristan.

He handed her the harness. It wasn't anything like a horse's saddle. The leather straps were meant to wrap around a dragon's neck. These would hold her in place during flight. Tristan could roll over in the air and she would not fall from his back.

After quick instructions about how to fasten herself in, Tristan transformed. His body expanded outward so quickly, she could hardly tell when his skin morphed into scales. After blinking twice, a pearlescent white dragon stood before her. He immediately made himself smaller by plopping down upon his belly. She exhaled in wonder, gazing at him, taking in the sight as if this was her first time seeing something so beautiful.

Tristan's scales glistened, reflecting hues of color, from light blue to lavender to pink. She loved the way he changed with each of his movements. It was mesmerizing. His giant head swung around to regard her. Only then did she realize she'd been avoiding the inevitable.

Gripping the leather straps more tightly than necessary in one hand, she stepped up to him and lifted the other. She could have simply climbed atop his back, fastened the harness, and taken flight, but this special moment was too profound to rush.

Just before she touched him, the memories from her experience in the arena forced her to hesitate. She recalled the twenty-seven scaly hides she'd touched, and the feeling of disappointment that came along.

She could allow her fear of failure to hold her back, or she could draw strength from Tristan in the same way he was about to do with her. A distant roar from the battle left her no other choice. Taking a deep breath, she brought her hand down upon his scales.

Warmth seeped into her skin, then everything stopped. For an instant in time, the world no longer existed. There were no ships. There was no battle. Fear and death weren't real. Instead, she felt an instant connection to the depths of the unfamiliar. She struggled to comprehend what she was experiencing. This was Tristan's mind. If her mind was a room filled with places to store everything that made her who she was, his was a vast canyon with numerous ledges where his memories and thoughts lived, everything that made him who he was. She stood at the edge, gazing out over the seemingly infinite distance. There was nothing left to do but step forward and fall in.

Emotion slammed into her. At first there was only joy. She was overcome. Tears pooled in her eyes. Tristan was the piece she'd been missing. In him she had found something that she never thought she needed.

His mind rejoiced too. He had been so desperate to show her what he had known for weeks. He was her mate all along.

The deeper she went, the more she saw, until she found his fear lurking at the lowest part of the canyon. He couldn't fly out to meet the Oshean ships—not without her. Seeing how much she was needed aligned something within her. It was his duty to defeat the Osheans and she would be with him every step of the way.

"I cannot do this without you, Selena."

His voice was music. She gasped. *"Is this what it feels like to speak between minds?"* It was different than she'd imagined, effortless, natural.

"It is." Tristan's happiness was powerful, but his worry was urgent. *"We must go!"*

She was hesitant to sever the contact, but she had to pull her hand away to place the harness around his neck. The connection disappeared. As quickly as her trembling fingers could move, she fastened the hooks on the straps. Each time her skin brushed his scales, their minds reconnected with powerful waves of emotion.

Climbing upon his back was difficult. She sat at the base of his neck and could feel his powerful shoulder blades as he rose from his belly. *"Are you safely secured?"*

"Yes." As he positioned himself at the edge of the garden, careful not to trample any of the queen's prized flowers, her skin tingled with excitement. The desire to fly had never been so strong. All her life she had missed the sky without ever knowing she needed it. It took Tristan to make that clear. Everything she believed she wanted and needed was suddenly different but still the same.

She read his intentions a moment before he sprang into the air. Connected minds laid everything bare. She could predict his movements, for they were hers too. Yet, it did not prepare her for the sensations she felt.

The tower fell away from them. A heavy weight pushed her down into the dip of Tristan's neck. She gripped the leather harness, forgetting to breathe. Higher and higher they went as his spring carried them skyward. His wings extended, leathery and white, stretching tightly to catch the air currents. As soon as they met the first stream of air, his body was sent speeding away.

She studied everything from her new vantage point, too stunned to do much else. She was seeing the world—finally seeing it—for the first time. The city of Kastali Dun stretched beneath her like a map upon unrolled parchment. The lines of the buildings, the winding paths of the streets, the people moving about like ants—it was all there below her. Tristan took them toward the docks. She narrowed her gaze. The rowboats had reached land and Oshean soldiers disembarked in droves. They moved toward the walls, hoping to scale them.

"Look ahead," Tristan warned, turning on his wing tip as they swept around. She was forced to look down at the ships.

A catapult upon the deck of the nearest ship groaned. Its lever arm swung up and around, releasing a massive boulder. It pelted past them, smashing into the city's wall. Her stomach plummeted as she watched. Rock and mortar smashed apart, sending dust and debris everywhere. Screams followed.

"The city won't stand a chance!" she cried as more projectiles were released.

"They can't have many rocks aboard each ship," said Tristan. *"Too heavy."* He circled around, affording them a good view of the damage. No one in the sky had noticed her yet. *"I must open my mind now, Selena. Otherwise I cannot communicate with the Drengr wings and dragons. Prepare yourself. It is a shock at first."* To spare her the initial effects of numerous voices during the heat of battle, Tristan had temporarily sealed his mind. Now he reopened it and a cacophony of voices and images began to flood his consciousness. She could see each one flashing past. *"You do not need to decipher or separate them,"* he added. *"My mind is built for it. Yours is not. Relax and focus on the task at hand."*

What was her task supposed to be?

"Your bow," he answered.

Her eyes widened, only just remembering that it was slung over her shoulder. Reaching for it, she brought it forward and nocked an arrow, just as Ivrir had taught her. Tristan was circling by the breached city wall. Taking aim, she let an arrow loose. It sped through the air and struck an enemy soldier.

"Well done! Your aim is true." Tristan turned on his wing tip and brought them around once more.

A thrill rippled through her. This was what she had trained for. Countless hours spent practicing and she could finally use what she had learned. Another arrow was released. Then another. She began firing them off with all the precision she could muster. Tristan kept them close to the city wall at the dockyard, flying steady to afford her clear shots.

His senses were impeccable. Each time a projectile came towards them, he swerved to avoid it. The wall was not so lucky. Neither was the Pauper's District. The giant boulders destroyed everything they struck.

In a panic, she glanced out into the bay. Nearly half the remaining Drengr stayed with the ships while the other half aided the city walls. As they circled around again, she watched the ships. Together in groups, the Drengr had managed to lift some of the vessels from the water, breaking them apart with sheer force. But it wasn't good enough! Worse still, it required them to get too close, putting them in danger.

Their numbers were falling. Many injured pairs, tangled in nets, bobbed in the bay's waters. If they didn't free those injured and remove the spearheads from their bodies, the poison would weaken them enough to kill them. *We need a better strategy, Tristan!*

Memories of a conversation with her father came to the forefront of her mind. It was impossible to tell if Tristan had conjured them or if they merely appeared unaided. Her heart beat a little faster as she analyzed the possibility and measure of success.

"It's worth a try," said Tristan. He saw her plan as clearly as she did. *"But I cannot lift the boulders alone. We need a sling of some sort."*

An idea came to her. *"Take us over the city to Bartlett's!"*

Tristan did as instructed, staying one step ahead of her commands. When they reached Bartlett's home, he tucked his wings allowing them to land safely in the street. The roads here were not as narrow as elsewhere. "Bartlett! Bartlett, come out!" She called and called for her accomplice until he ran from his house to meet her.

"Princess Lena!" His face was lit with amazement. "Wow! A dragon?!" His wide eyes studied Tristan.

"I've got a job for you," she called from Tristan's back. In rushed sentences, she explained what she intended. He was to round up everyone he knew in the Pauper's District, gather nets from the market and shipping yards, dodge the enemies, and get the boulders rolled into the nets so that the Drengr could lift them. Bartlett bobbed with glee.

They hadn't a minute to spare. To speed up Bartlett's task, Tristan scooped him up within his forearms, grasping him gently, and leapt from the ground with his mighty hind legs. She marveled at his strength. When they cleared the rooftops, Tristan spread his wings wide and took them to the Pauper's District. Bartlett was whooping with excitement the entire way. "You'll have a great story for all your friends when this is over," she called to him.

Setting Bartlett on a low rooftop, Tristan was up and away. They circled around the city walls and she went back to firing arrows at the enemy. Her aim wasn't fantastic. She'd had little practice with moving targets, but since there were so many and they were so tightly packed, more often than not her shafts struck true. She fired until there were none left.

"The lad should be ready for us now," Tristan announced. He turned sharply, putting her sideways in the air. She saw the ground beneath her but did not fear. The harness held her tightly against Tristan's scaly hide. They swept away to the Pauper's District. It was time to change tactics.

When they arrived, enemy soldiers had successfully gotten through the first ring of the city walls. They were on the streets fighting with soldiers and civilians alike. She spotted Bartlett and his crew. Bartlett signaled to them, pumping his fist in the air. The large boulders from the enemy catapults lay scattered. Several had already been rolled into nets.

Tristan swooped low and gathered up the first net in his claws. Beating his wings in downward sweeps, he rose into the sky. Before disappearing into the white mist above, she could hear Bartlett's crew cheering them on.

"I will take us behind the clouds, so they do not see us coming." Damp mist surrounded her, soaking her. The intense heat through Tristan's scales was welcome warmth. Minutes later they descended. *"We are above a ship now. It will do more damage from this height, but I would like to go a little lower to ensure my aim is true."*

They descended beneath the clouds. She leaned over to see the ships below. Her stomach lurched. At that same moment, Tristan opened his claws. Both net and boulder plummeted downward. The giant rock crashed upon the ship's deck below falling clean through. For a moment, it looked as though the damage had no effect. Then she heard groans of protest from the wood. The front and back ends of the ship pointed upward while the middle took on water, effectively folding the vessel in half. The crew bailed. The pieces began to sink. *"It worked!"* She could hardly believe it.

Overcome with success, Tristan began relaying the message to the other Drengr. *"Gather more boulders from the city and drop them on the ships!"* There were so many replies in his mind, she was forced to turn her attention elsewhere, ignoring them. Groups of Drengr turned on their wingtips in perfect formation, heading in the direction of the city.

Tristan followed. A moment later, she heard her father's voice in his head. *"Is that my daughter upon your back, Gallant Forestborn?"* There was a measure of pride in King Cornan's words, but there was also fear.

"Oh no…" She half expected her father to send them back to the keep for disobeying her mother's instructions.

Tristan had no intention of complying with such an order. *"It is, my king. She fights well and is well protected."*

"I ought to ground the both of you! She is untrained. Keep her away from the dragonlances."

"Yes, Your Grace." Tristan's words left her grinning.

The sun crept across the sky unnoticed. The battle raged on. Smoke could be seen rising from the lower levels of the city. It was the enemy's doing.

Her boulder idea was a turning point. With each wrecked ship, fewer dragons were harpooned. And fewer men made it to shore. After a time, the rowboats stopped coming entirely. All that was left were those in the city streets.

At that point she and Tristan were forced to retreat and collect arrows from Fort Kastali's weapon stores. The sun was setting when she jumped from his body onto solid ground. Her legs ached, her muscles cramped, but she ignored the discomfort.

Away from Tristan, there was no mental contact. After hours in his mind, she felt empty. She rushed about to gather the arrows needed from the weapons master, refilling her quiver. Then she bounded back to Tristan, vaulting onto his back in a very sloppy and untrained manner. Once more they were skyborne. She sighed with relief, happy to be back together with him.

By full dark, she'd fired well over three hundred arrows, making multiple trips to Fort Kastali for refills. The few ships that remained intact had already started their retreat. The enemy had done what they could to save their drowning comrades. Likewise, the Drengr had done well to fish out theirs, nets and all, from the bay's waters.

Not long after, her father ordered Tristan back to the keep.

She heard the king's command as he gave instructions to various fighting wings. His Shields were to oversee the remaining efforts. Some of their forces would track the retreating ships to ensure they departed. Others would assist within the city to kill any remaining enemies who did not submit. Those injured were to return to the fort for healing, while those too weak to do so were carried by their wing-mates. Her heart constricted when she realized that not every Drengr-Rider pair had made it out alive.

Tristan followed her father's orders without question. She was a little more reluctant. *"Can't we stay until the fighting is over?"*

"It nearly is, Selena. I must get you to safety so that you can rest. You are my chief concern now." He said this with a great deal of love and pride. She was overcome and could say nothing more.

He took them in lazy circles about the keep as they slowly descended toward its lowest courtyard. Away from the foray, she realized how truly exhausted she was. Her shoulders sagged under their own weight, and her breathing felt heavy. It was a mercy the harness held her against him, else she would have simply tumbled from his back.

He landed in the courtyard.

Her father's turquoise form came to the ground beside them. She hadn't yet freed both legs from her harness before her mother was upon them, pulling her from the leather straps and ferrying her to the ground. There she gathered Lena in loving arms to kiss her face, weeping with joy and exhaustion all at once. "Gods Lena! I ought to be so angry with you. But all I can do is weep with gladness. You have your mate. Thank the gods!"

In this time, both the king and Tristan had transformed. Her father took her into his arms next. Tristan waited patiently for her parents to release her. At last, they stepped away. Her father looked at Tristan, fierce pride blazing in his eyes. "You may have some time with her, Gallant, but please bring her up to the tower at your earliest convenience." He said no more as he took her mother's hand and strode away, leaving them alone.

She turned to Tristan, uncertain of what to say. When their minds were together, she knew exactly what he was thinking. Now she could only read his face, but there was enough there.

Without wasting another moment, she rushed to him and threw her arms about his neck, burying her head against him. He held her tightly because she was the only thing that mattered to him. After all this, all the doubt, all the disappointment she'd faced, all the heartbreak, she'd finally found her other half.

CHAPTER 32
MAKING HER DECISION

Lena and Tristan saw little of each other in the days following the attack. They were resigned to the occasional glimpses during dinner. Shortly after his crowning, a chair had been added to the head table beside her father's. If she wanted to speak to him, she was forced to lean around both her mother and father. Moreover, their usual evening walks were temporarily canceled because her father wished to include Tristan in his evening meetings.

She knew better than to protest. Her father kept Tristan busy cleaning up after the fallout, utilizing the opportunity to train him. However, the crowned prince wasn't alone. They all had new responsibilities, even she.

Her tasks never aligned with Tristan's, which meant they often found themselves on separate sides of the city. Had their bond been sealed, things would have been easier. She could have used their shared minds to bridge the gap. She was left to her own thoughts.

Seeds of doubt began to grow. Was Tristan really over Evelyn? Or was she to become a way to fill the gaping hole left behind in the Sprite's wake? She tried not to think about it during her day-to-day duties, but her mundane work made it easy.

Numerous structures along the city's wall were damaged, burned, or both. Soldiers lay wounded in healer houses. It was a mercy she wasn't enlisted to move the dead bodies from the streets. The enemy's dead were set outside the city and burned in a heap. A stench settled over Kastali Dun and took days to dissipate. Their own dead were returned to their families for proper burials.

Most heart-wrenching were the Drengr-Rider deaths. Forty-three pairs lost their lives out of the near four hundred that flew into battle. The loss brought devastation, for their numbers were already falling. Those weren't the only losses, either. The wild dragons did not escape unscathed. Of the fifty that came, six died. That made their survival more imperative.

She well understood the reasons why the Forest Clan pressured Tristan to compete in the tournament. With so few wild dragons left, their race was all but gone. They needed someone of power to fight for them. Tristan was their hope. "That's why they named me *Gallant*," he had said.

She had not yet grown used to calling him by his true name, though she did take the opportunity when she was cross with him, or when she teased him. In her heart, he was still Tristan. He always would be.

A week following the attack, she found herself in the Pauper's District overseeing the reconstruction of a poor-house when Tristan appeared. She did not notice him at first lurking in the shadows. She was busy helping a mother and child move their belongings off the street. When she looked up, she spotted him leaning against the wall opposite her. She ushered the woman inside before slipping away.

"How long have you been watching me?" she asked, rushing to him. Her hands were balled into fists, gripping her skirts with uncertainty.

Without answering, Tristan took her into his arms and held her tightly. At first, she tensed up. She'd had a full week to doubt their bond, to doubt Tristan's feelings for her, to doubt her own for him. After hating the idea of mates for so long, was she allowing the excitement of their first flight to persuade her into something she'd sworn against?

Tristan sensed her hesitance and held her all the longer until she sighed and melted into his embrace. "Something is bothering you," he whispered before releasing her. He didn't fully let go. Rather, he grasped her shoulders and held her at arm's length. There he studied her. "You are upset with me for not making more time."

She shook her head. "I…"

"I wanted to get away sooner, Selena. I promise you that. This is the first opportunity I have had to sneak away. Believe me, it took a measure of cunning on my part. I am all yours now."

Her heart quickened. She liked the sound of that better than she willingly admitted. But there was still doubt. Where did they stand? She chewed on the skin of her bottom lip nervously.

"Come, Selena. Let's walk." At his prompting, she gave the poor house a backward glance. "They will be fine without you for a short while."

Nodding, she slipped her arm through his as he led her away. They were silent for some time before Tristan said, "I have spoken with your father. As soon as the battle's aftermath dies down, we may begin planning our ceremony."

"Ceremony?"

Tristan stopped and turned to her, his brow furrowed.

"Yes, our bonding ceremony. You aren't having second thoughts, are you?"

More rapidly than necessary, she shook her head back and forth, lying outright. "It's just that, I was supposed to travel to Redport. The lord governor there is expecting me. And... I've made a lot of other travel arrangements too. I shouldn't keep them waiting or cancel."

"Why not have us go together?" he asked. "I can get you there much faster if I fly you."

A thrill shot through her. "I suppose I hadn't thought of that. But you're right." A smile pulled at her lips. "Plus, you need to see our people as much as I do. Most will be eager to meet their new Crowned Prince."

"Exactly! Then it's settled." They took up their walk once more. "Listen, I know life is chaotic now, but there will be plenty of time for us once things die down."

"You...you still want me even though you love Evelyn?"

Again he stopped, turning to her. "*That's* why you're behaving strangely? I had wondered. Of course I want you, Selena. How could you doubt that after seeing my heart? I laid myself bare to you in the sky."

Her cheeks burned. "I merely thought—"

"You thought because I loved Evelyn, I couldn't possibly love you? Selena..." He brushed a lock of hair from her face. "What I once felt for her is nothing compared to what I feel for you."

She sighed. "That's just our bond talking."

"No. It is my heart talking." He must have sensed her continued uncertainty. "Selena, listen to me. When I came here, Evelyn was still in my heart. I believed that I loved her. Yet the moment I saw you, everything changed. My feelings shifted rapidly. My heart knew you and rejoiced. At the same time, I battled my anger and shame. How could I allow my heart to wander? To stray? I chastised this heart of mine, rebuking my weakness. I questioned my love for Evelyn, even then." He hardly stopped to draw a breath. She listened without blinking.

"I soon realized what was happening. In hindsight, I knew shortly before I asked you to the ball. I so desperately wanted you to accept my offer that day in the garden. Remember? When I asked you to touch my scales? I wanted to transform then and there. I needed to be certain that I wasn't merely imagining my love. But I also needed to reassure myself that falling out of love with Evelyn was okay because I was quickly falling in love with you."

"But…"

"But what?"

"I saw your face when Evelyn left. I saw the way it hurt you."

He sighed. "Whatever hurt I displayed was not from losing her. It was driven by my guilt. I could not be what she needed." He shook his head. "It wasn't easy letting her go, seeing the way it ripped her apart. I want her to be happy. She deserves love, but that kind of love is not something I can give her."

Her mouth opened and closed several times in an attempt to speak. She had been wrong all along. "I…I misjudged you, Tristan. I'm sorry."

They had made a full lap around the block of buildings. Tristan came to a stop before the poorhouse and turned to her. He took her face in his hands and gazed into her eyes. Her skin warmed beneath his touch. "Selena, I do not wish you to believe me a slave to our bond. Could I love you the same without it?" He shrugged. "Who can say? But I rejoice knowing it exists. I may have come to Kastali Dun to win the crown. And win it, I did. But to love you, to love you and have you—*that* is my prize."

His words poured through her like sweet honey, leaving her warm all over. "You...you mean that?"

"I do." His eyes beseeched her. "I must ask you now for a truthful answer. You once told me that you hated the idea of mates—of binding yourself to another for life. I cannot help but think these sentiments have changed. Tell me truly, will you agree to fulfill our bond? And do not say yes simply because it is inescapable. I want this consent to come from your heart...only your heart."

His face was so close to hers that she could hardly think, but his question did not require thinking. "My heart wants you, Tristan, only you." She hesitated before smiling. "Yes. Let's fulfill our bond."

His smile was slow, as if he thought she might have declined. Without another word, he pulled her face to his and brought his lips to hers, sealing her acceptance with a kiss. Together they were whole-hearted. She needed him to become queen, and he needed her to rule by his side.

As his mouth moved over hers, gentle but insistent, she understood something. Everything she had ever needed, her life's purpose, the crown, a desire to do good, was standing right before her.

CHAPTER 33
JUST LIKE FLYING

"Come and fly with me, Selena." Tristan stood in her room the evening before their bonding ceremony, arm outstretched as he waited to take her hand. She gladly went to him, eager to escape the confines of the castle.

Weeks had raced by after Tristan's declaration of love. When they weren't adhering to their duties, they were flying. That time was special. It allowed them to link their minds together and be whole. Not a minute passed without her longing for his mental touch, for the warm comfort it brought when their consciousness joined. It was the only time she felt complete.

Some, like Kenna Margaret, advised her to enjoy her independence while it lasted. Perhaps the old Lena would have agreed. But she never heard that kind of advice from Riders and their Drengr. Mated pairs rejoiced in their connection. Without it they would have felt exactly as she did: incomplete. But that fragmented existence wasn't forever. Once they were mated the bond would be sealed, connecting their minds permanently.

Taking Tristan's hand, the two of them slipped away to a quiet courtyard where he transformed. Tristan was always careful when he flew with her, careful not to turn too sharply, or dive too deeply. She never felt unsafe or endangered. If anything, the sky was safer.

As she climbed atop his back, using his neck ridges to hoist herself up, she felt their instant connection. Soon after their bonding, they would begin training with Fort Kastali, learning to become a true pair. Until then, they enjoyed the lack of structure to their knowledge.

Their moments in the sky together were intimate. She loved searching his mind for memories, watching them like stories while the ground sailed by beneath them. Sometimes they glided over the plains of Eigaden. Other times they flew out over the bay. When they had more time, they visited Irelia Island to bask on its sandy shores.

Her father had given them permission to continue her emissary duties in the midst of their upcoming training schedule. Her first trip to Redport had been postponed until after their bonding ceremony. She and Tristan were treating it as their first getaway together—their first real adventure.

"You're nervous for tomorrow," said Tristan. It wasn't a question, merely an observation plucked from her mind. He loved delving into the places she'd walled up, places she isolated to avoid vulnerability. He enjoyed breaking down her barriers. The rights to her mind now belonged to him and she offered herself freely.

The sea sparkled beneath them. She felt her cheeks burn as she considered the root cause of her nervousness. Tristan was correct, she was nervous. There was only one way to seal their bond. While his kisses were always enough, they were both eager to go further. She wanted him, all of him, and he

wanted her. That was what made her fluttery and anxious—
the ultimate unknown.

When they said their goodbyes later that evening, he held
her longer than before. "Tonight will be our last night alone,"
he said. "After we mate, I will always be with you, and you
with me." She knew what he meant. She would never feel
useless or lonely. She would always be needed. They kissed
goodnight and then he was gone.

She did not sleep when he left. Instead, she sat with her
mother, Kenna Margaret, and her handmaidens. The vigil had
begun. They would stay with her the entire night, helping to
keep her calm, offering their warm reassurances. It was tradition for the night before the bonding ceremony. She was glad
to have their company.

The morning however, was anything but calm. It began
in a chaotic rush. Someone had lost her crown. She couldn't
seem to remember her lines. Each time she recited them,
they came out wrong. Her gown pulled too tightly in
certain areas. The tailor was summoned to make adjust-
ments. When she was finally dressed and ready, it was a
relief.

It was customary for a Rider to wear the colors of her
Drengr. Tristan was difficult to match so her gown was white,
but every measure of it was covered in tulle and tiny pearls.
When she moved, the fabric shimmered with white pearles-
cence to mimic Tristan's scales.

Her long hair was woven into a single multi-stranded
braid down her back. Tiny white flowers and ribbon had been
laced into each of the strands. Atop her head rested a stunning silver crown of diamonds and white opals.

The queen and her ladies all wore gowns of golden silk.
They stepped back to admire her. "She's marvelous!" Cora
was breathless. Her mother was too stunned for words, but

her eyes were filled with tears. Kenna Margaret insisted upon giving her a kiss on each cheek in admiration.

She was not permitted to lay eyes on Tristan until the ceremony. When the time came, they proceeded to the throne room escorted by a group of the keep's guards. The halls were empty until they neared the lower levels. Servants lined the corridors, each eager to catch a glimpse of the princess on her bonding day.

When they arrived, the doors to the throne room were closed. She was glad of it. "I need a moment to breathe," she whispered. Her entourage stopped beside her.

Her gown was so heavy that it took a great deal of effort for the simple journey. Its bodice was pulled tight, squeezing the air from her lungs. Its skirts hugged her waist and flowed outward, fanning out around her like a foamy waterfall, trailing far behind. The weight of it was crushing but she held her head high and her back straight nonetheless. Today she was bonding to Prince Gallant Forestborn and she'd never worn a grander work of art.

At last she sighed. She was ready to proceed. One of the guards rapped his spear against the doors and they swept open. She gasped, losing her breath all over again. Then a smile, spurred on by the splendor before her, anchored itself to her face. The entire hall was bending beneath the weight of massive floral garlands strung about the rafters. Little glow lights twinkled within them. Layers of tulle were wrapped about the pillars lining the hall. And the floor before her was covered in white petals, like snow.

A sweet scent met her nose and she inhaled, closing her eyes in delight. "Whenever you are ready, Princess." She heard Kenna Margaret's voice like a distant whisper. She opened her eyes. Hundreds of elegantly dressed guests gazed upon her in awe. This was her moment, but in just a few more, her life would change forever. She was ready for it. Lifting her chin, she took her first step, and then another, making her way to the king's dais.

When Tristan came into view, she began to tremble with emotion. He gazed upon her with intense green eyes, watching her progress. Her father was there too, smiling and radiant as she'd never seen him before. A more perfect dream could not be crafted. Yet, it wasn't a dream.

She stopped before the dais. Tristan came beside her and took her hand. His warm touch steadied her. "You take my breath away, Selena." His whisper was for her ears alone. Together, they climbed the steps to stand just beneath her father.

When they were settled, the King spoke, lifting his voice to permeate the hall. "Lords and ladies, today we gather to celebrate the bonding of my daughter, Princess Lena, to the crowned prince, Prince Gallant. Such a blessed day has never been seen—a princess of Dragonwall who believed all was lost, has found everything she needed in her mate." Her father's loving gaze met hers before continuing. Tristan squeezed her hand. "These are unusual times in which we live. Our race is new, our traditions in their infancy, and history still in the making. And today, we make a *new* history." Her father finished his introduction and the room fell silent. She took a deep breath, stealing a glance at Tristan. He stood proudly beside her, his skin flushed.

Her father offered a brief nod to his six and Ramar came forward holding a bow and quiver of arrows. Tristan released her hand to take the gift. Her father spoke, "Prince Gallant will now present his mate with her bow. Let her fly with him and protect him in her own way."

Tristan held the bow forward and she took it. Every Drengr presented his Rider with her own bow as a symbol of her new status, that of a Rider. This one was decorated much like her mother's, except that there were tiny pearls embedded into the wood rather than turquoise and diamonds. The quiver was much the same, with white goose feather fletching. After she examined it she turned to Tristan, smiling proudly. "I thank thee for such a fine gift and token of your love."

In turn, Avra was signaled to come forward and take it away to free Lena's hands. Then her father nodded to her mother. The queen handed her a smooth pearl that filled the palm of her hand. She could barely clamp her fist around it. This gem would fill the empty place upon the pommel of Tristan's Sverak, which her father had gifted him only recently. It was tradition for a Rider to present her mate with the stone that would complete his sword. Since Tristan never knew his father, hers had done the honor.

"Princess Lena will now present her mate with a pommel stone, so that the foundation of his Sverak may be complete, so that he may protect her in his own way."

Tristan took the stone from her. "I thank thee for such a fine gift and token of your love." He handed both the gem and Sverak to her father. Her father put it into place and declared, "*Asamat.*" Beneath his hand she saw a radiant blue glow as the king's magic permanently bonded the pearl to the metal above the grip. Then he handed it back to Tristan. Tristan sheathed it.

Her father spoke again. "Prince Gallant, Princess Lena, take each other's hands." This was the part she'd been nervous about—reciting the Drengr-Rider words of magic. She and Tristan faced each other. His hands were comfort to hers. His eyes were her encouragement. They opened their mouths in unison and recited the words every Drengr and

Rider must, their voices weaving the magic of the bond that was soon to come to pass:

> *Rejoice!*
> *A bond is discovered —*
> *a lifetime destined by fate.*
> *A commitment unbreakable,*
> *until Daudagher takes us.*
> *A Tender comfort to ease the hardship*
> *the other's labor has brought.*
> *A love that takes root,*
> *encouraged by caring hands and gentle kisses.*
> *A promise is made;*
> *a promise is sealed.*
> *A single mind from two combined:*
> *a Drengr and his Rider.*

When the words died, she felt tingles pass through their clasped hands, traveling up her arms through her body, all the way down to her toes. They both smiled, gazing into each other's eyes.

"And so it is said. So it shall be!" cried the king.

The audience erupted into cheers, clapping and shouting, "Congratulations!" She exhaled and together they turned to face the onlookers. As was customary, they proceeded from the hall first, followed by the king and queen, and their entourage. The crowd filed out last.

"We did it!" she cried, looking at him with tears in her eyes.

He squeezed her hand. "We did!"

The dining hall was nearly as splendid as the throne room. Everyone took their seats and the celebration began. It was the greatest she had ever witnessed, but perhaps that was because she was overflowing with happiness.

So many friends had come, including Ivrir. When she saw Daryn hand in hand with his new mate, a woman with red hair and a radiant smile, she was filled with joy rather than jealousy. "Lena, I would like you to meet Maia." Daryn introduced them at the first opportunity. She congratulated them, knowing that Daryn would be as happy as she. He kindly did the same, his eyes sparkling as he took her hand in his, adding, "I could not be happier for you, Princess Lena. All my best to both of you." Then he clapped Tristan on the shoulder in hearty congratulations. "A perfect match, my friend! May the gods smile down upon you."

Tristan held fast to her hand the entire evening, as if he was afraid to let her go before sealing their bond. They both knew what was coming. They were both eager for it. At last, that time did come.

Guests sent them from the hall with whoops of excitement and bawdy innuendos. "Take her home!" some called. "Give her a night she'll never forget!" cried others. The king and queen followed, but no one else. They were escorted to a new set of chambers prepared just for them. From this day forth, they would dwell together.

Her mother hugged her and kissed her, then hugged and kissed her again, with tears of joy streaming down her face. Then it was her father's turn. They both paid that same attention to Tristan, too, for he was their son now.

And then they found themselves alone…

Tristan led her by the hand into the bed chamber. She was nervous until he said, "Don't fret, Selena. It will be just like flying," and pulled her into his arms.

Together they soared into the clouds, relishing in the ecstasy that each turn of Tristan's wings offered. His caresses were like those of the wind, gentle and playful against her skin. Together they climbed higher and higher into the sky until only the stars were before them. When the stars burst into millions of glittering fragments, their minds connected, twisting into a single being, until she could no longer understand where he began and she ended. There in the night, they floated down with the drifting sparks into the depths of their consciousness, into the crevasses of their shared soul. Together with bodies entwined and minds as one, they sealed their bond in the only way a Drengr and Rider could.

ACKNOWLEDGMENTS

I would like to thank my husband, Matthew Mitchell, for his love and support throughout the writing, editing, and publication process of For the Crown (back when it was titled Prince Gallant). Behind every successful wife is an incredibly supportive husband. I couldn't have taken this journey without him. This is the first full book I wrote after moving to Atlanta, Georgia. The transition was a huge change for both of us. Things were still very new and starting a project like this was a big undertaking. I'm so thankful for all the ways he helped me, allowing me copious time to write when I could have been cooking or doing chores.

I have a huge support network that I would also like to thank. Everyone who helped me with beta reads, edits, feedback, etc. Specifically, Tresha Shelton (my mom), Bernice Demaree (my grandma), Madeleine Randall (one of my biggest fans), Jeanine Croft (my bardic sister) and Jordyn Brinkley (my ideas gal).

I must also thank the incredible Wattpad community, a group of amazing readers and aspiring writers who first read this story in its infancy, not knowing quite what to expect. You guys are amazing. Thank you!

Finally, to you the reader, thank you for giving this book a chance, knowing it would be different than my main Dragonwall Series. Your support means the world to me.

ABOUT THE AUTHOR

Melissa Mitchell is a physics Ph.D. by day, and fantasy writer by night. She is a California transplant, who moved to Georgia with her husband and three dogs to chase her engineering career in illumination design. Aside from her love of tea, wine, desserts, and writing, she loves reading, playing piano, baking, and bullet journaling (in no particular order).

Visit her at <authormelissamitchell.com>

facebook.com/MelissaMitchellAuthor

instagram.com/melissa.nicole.mitchell

amazon.com/author/mitchellmelissa